CANELANDS

CANELANDS

a novel

GERRY HARLAN BROWN

WordCrafts Press

"Jesus Loves the Little Children" by Clare Herbert Woolston, music by George F. Root, circa late 1800s. Public Domain.

"I Come to the Garden Alone" by C. Austin Miles, circa 1913. Public Domain.

"Blest Be the Tie That Binds" by John Fawcett, 1782. Public Domain.

"The Good Old Way" attributed to George H. Allen, circa 1867. Public Domain.

"Just As I Am" by Charlottee Elliot, 1835. Public Domain.

"Shall We Gather At The River" by Robert Lowry, 1864. Public Domain.

Published by WordCrafts Press
Cody, Wyoming 82414
www.wordcrafts.net

For Cathy
and
The Least of These

. . . and the greatest of these is love.

Chapter 1

"Watch your floater, Sarah."

"It's moving! It's moving, Poppy!" she yelled as the red and white plastic float cut sideways in the creek, sending ripples across the surface. Sarah hopped to her feet and grabbed her fishing pole. She raised the tip to take the slack out of the line like her Poppy had taught her.

"Wait till it goes all the way under," Paul cautioned his four-year-old daughter.

"I know," she answered, her eyes locked on the floater.

It suddenly disappeared with an audible *plop*. Sarah jerked the pole, and the floater shot up out of the water. Beneath it, a tiny sun perch flipped wildly on the hook.

"I got it!" she shouted, swinging the fish over toward her dad.

"Easy," Paul warned. "Don't slap me in the face."

In a moment he had the hook out and was holding the fish by its bottom lip. He extended it toward her. Sarah reached out tentatively, her index finger no longer than the fish, and touched it.

"Oooh! Icky!" she exclaimed, using her favorite new word. "Put it back, Poppy."

"Okay." He laughed. "It does look kind of small."

"He's a lit-tle baby," Sarah replied, dropping to her hands and knees at the stream's edge. She watched intently as her daddy gently lowered the fish back in the water. It disappeared in a flash. "Come back when you grow up," Sarah said, waving bye.

"Yes, when you grow up," Paul echoed, rinsing his hands. Standing, he wiped his fingers dry on his pants legs, then reached for her cane pole. "Now, let me bait your hook so you can go after his big brother."

"I'm tired of fishing," Sarah announced, taking a step up the bank and plopping down in her spot at the foot of a big sycamore.

1

"Well, if you're done, I'm done," Paul said. He spun the pole in his hands until the line was wrapped tightly around it. Then he threaded the hook through one of the turns and leaned the pole against the far side of her tree. He quickly repeated the process with his. "Fish are not biting for me, anyway," he said, settling back against the sycamore's stout trunk beside his daughter.

"That's because you're a fisher of men," Sarah said matter-of-factly.

Out of the mouths of babes. He had to laugh. "I think you may be onto something there," he said as she laid her head against his shoulder.

They sat quietly, the warmth of his daughter's face warming him. Sarah was the first to speak.

"You got my fishing pole over there," she said, pointing to a modest stand of cane just upstream.

"Yes, I did," he answered. "Beside our path back home. Same place my daddy cut mine way back in the old days, when I wasn't any bigger than you." *Wow*, Paul thought, shaking his head, *that was twenty-five years ago.*

"Tell me about the old days, Poppy. 'Bout when there were fishing poles everywhere."

"That story again?"

"Please."

"Okie doke." Paul chuckled. "Just this once," he tacked on, knowing he would tell it a thousand times if that was what his daughter wanted.

"Well now, the way I heard it told, when ole Dan'l Boone came wandering into Kentucky, there were huge patches of cane growing everywhere. Each patch was like its own enchanted forest of skinny trees. All kinds of animals made paths down through the skinny trees to wherever there was water, so they could get a drink when they were thirsty. No telling what you might see on one of those paths. There were cute little deer, and big elk with huge antlers, and furry rabbits hopping and dancing around with raccoons wearing sunglasses, and fat cuddly bears, and mean-old wolves and panthers. If you were real, real quiet and didn't move a single itty-bitty muscle, a great shaggy buffalo might come wandering along. And if you held your mouth just right, maybe even a monkey," he added, his hand shooting across to tickle her belly.

"Don't, Poppy!" she squealed, rolling up into a giggle ball against him.

He waited until she was settled in her nest again before continuing.

"And sometimes a little Indian girl would come down our path through the caneland with her poppy, until they reached this same pool of still water. Her poppy would cut her pole from that little patch over there, just like I did for you and my daddy did for me. Then they would go fishing, too."

"I wish she was here," Sarah said, clapping her hands. "We would run and play on the path and catch a fat red rabbit and name him Brutus, and I wouldn't be scared or nothing."

"Brutus?" He asked with a laugh, taking advantage of her pause to catch a breath.

"Yes," she answered, looking up at him as if to say, *Why not?*

"If you say so," he agreed, still smiling at the idea. Then it hit him that she had also said something about being scared. "Is there something on the path that frightens you, hon?"

"I don't like it when the skinny trees get really close and touch my arms and it gets dark all around. I'm afraid I'll get lost," she said, her voice suddenly small. "But when we hold hands it's okay."

Paul thought awhile before he said anything. Being a man of *the Word*, there was something of import to be mentioned here, if he could but draw it out. Finally, he spoke.

"You should not be afraid, Sarah. The cane is a place of refuge." He stopped. She was gazing up at him again, her expression a knot of confusion.

"Refuge means a safe place, somewhere to shelter from the storm. Understand?"

Paul was relieved when she nodded.

"Imagine when the cane touches your skin that it is God reaching out His hand to guide you. Okay?"

After a moment, she nodded once more.

"Find the straightest path and you will never be lost. He will hold your hand every step of the way until you get to the still waters."

Sarah nestled in closer. A long, quiet period began, punctuated only by the soothing sounds of a distant babbling flow and the scattered, sweet songs of the birds. She spoke at last.

"Is heaven like this, Poppy?"

Paul did not answer immediately. Then he noticed the warmth of her face against his arm.

"Yes, it must be."

Chapter 2

"Do unto others as you would have them do unto you," Preacher Paul—still called Brother Lockhart by some—said in closing his sermon. "It is that simple, isn't it? The Bible tells us in so many ways, in verse after beautiful verse, how we should live our lives. Yet it all comes back to that one sentence, that one simple instruction, doesn't it? Do to others as you would have them do to you. This is God's law. If we follow these words, this golden rule given to us by the Son of God, we shall act as Christians."

Preacher Paul ceased speaking and allowed his gaze to roam slowly across the small sanctuary. Today's attendance was better than most Sundays—about seventy-five he would guess. In some faces he saw agreement in a subdued nod, a faint smile. A few people fidgeted a bit in their seats, probably ready to get home for Sunday dinner. His eyes lingered a moment on his wife, Jennie. She flashed a wink, their signal that he had done a good job delivering his message. Beside her sat their little girl, Sarah, staring up at him with the rapt adoration one can only find in one's child. He could not help but smile his love back to her.

Lifting his sight once more, he looked toward the rear of the sanctuary. On the back pew, Thomas Ivy Cole—Tick to one and all—sat off to himself, rocking on the edge of his seat. The young man's face was clearly troubled. *Could it be today?* Paul asked himself the question for the umpteenth time. *Please, Lord,* he prayed. *Help him find the strength to open his heart to You.* Then the preacher spoke aloud.

"Before we bring our service to a close with the invitational, I ask that you please join me in a moment of silent prayer."

Sarah waited a minute before she bowed her head. She was studying her Poppy's hands as they clutched the outer edges of the pulpit, as if he feared he would fall if he let go. Sarah reached forward with her tiny hands and grasped the slat of thin wood on the back of the pew before her, where the hymnals were nested. She squeezed, locking her fingers down tight, like her Poppy. Then she bowed her head so far forward her chin dug into her chest.

Thirty seconds passed, stretched into a full minute, without a sound rising from the group of worshippers. At a minute and a half, Paul opened his eyes and lifted his head. "Amen."

"Amen," the members answered as one.

"For our invitational this morning we will sing "Just as I Am." Let us rise."

In just about any other small Baptist church on the planet the minister would lead the congregation in song. That's because in just about any other small Baptist church the minister could actually sing. In Caney Creek Baptist Church this was most decidedly not the case. The sounds that came from Paul's mouth when he tried to carry a tune had been compared to many things: tom cats fighting; chalk screeching across a blackboard; a lovesick Billy goat. Yet never had the *joyful* noise he emitted been called anything close to singing. Preacher Paul had a wonderful speaking voice, all agreed. The consensus among the members, however, was that was where he should stop. That was why when he opened his mouth to sing this day, as on any Sunday, every member of the congregation was off and running, each one raising their voice to the Lord before the preacher could get the first word out. It was a matter of self-defense.

"Just as I am, without one plea, but that thy blood was shed for me," the members of the congregation sang.

As usual, Paul smiled to himself in amused resignation. There was nothing to fight here. The truth was the truth. How many other churches, though, could boast such enthusiastic participation when it came to singing hymns? He simply moved his lips to the words without trying to join in, feeling the lullaby-like rhythm of the song. His eyes swept from face to face along the pews. All were standing and singing now—all except one. Tick Cole was rocking faster in his seat. Suddenly he was on his feet, but he didn't join in the hymn. He took a nervous step into the aisle, then froze in place. His eyes cast down at the worn floorboards. The seconds crawled by as he simply stood there.

"Oh Lamb of God I come, I come."

A few noticed the preacher's eyes were turned to the rear of the sanctuary and glanced back to see what had his attention. Seeing the first ones turn, others followed suit. Soon practically the entire gathering was staring at Tick, including little Sarah, who was standing up on her pew facing backwards, her fingers grasping the rounded edge along the back. Like Paul's words minutes before, other simple prayers were being lifted in silence by many.

Please, Lord.

The sense of expectation was palpable in the air, as if electricity had somehow assumed a form that settled like a crackling fog across the pews.

Tick slowly raised his head, his gaze at first unfocused. Then he seemed to notice something in the far distance. Suddenly he spun about and returned to his seat. He sat down to an audible groan rising from the gathering, apparently unaware of the attention directed toward him, of all the prayers that this day, at last, he would come forward and be saved. Everyone who had been watching turned away—all but Sarah. Jennie finally noticed her daughter standing on the pew and gave the hem of her dress a sharp pull. It took a second, sharper tug a few seconds later to get her to turn around and sit down. As the hymn came to its close, the muted sounds of crying drifted up from the same pew where Tick was seated. A handful of people twisted about once more to see, then quickly turned back. Most didn't bother to look. They knew whose heart was broken. It was not the first time they had heard Marian Cole weeping for her wayward son.

Paul stood at the rear door of the sanctuary, shaking hands and exchanging a few words with individual members as they passed outside. Sarah stood on the concrete walk a few feet beyond the short reach of limestone steps. She, too, was shaking hands with people. Over the last couple of months, she had been doing this after services. When Sarah first started, Paul and Jennie were taken aback, even a tiny bit embarrassed. They gently tried to dissuade her. Then they realized what joy people got out of it. Indeed, each person would smile, usually say a few words, as they shook hands with the precocious child. Since there was no harm, Paul and Jennie relented and allowed Sarah to carry on.

"Bless you," Marian Cole said to Paul, giving his hand a hard squeeze. Her red eyes were the only sign that moments before she had lost her composure. Tick came next.

"Preacher," the young man greeted the minister with a firm grip. Unlike his mother, Tick did not exhibit any sign that he had just passed through an emotional battle.

As usual, eighty-one-year-old Deacon Henry Jackson was the last to leave the sanctuary.

"Saw you walking down the road by my milk barn the other day," the deacon began.

"Yes, I walked that way last Thursday, I believe it was," Paul replied, choosing not to remind his aged friend that on that morning the two of them had a short conversation over the fence by that very barn.

"I've got to ask you," the deacon went on, a pained expression on his face. "Were you singing when you went by?"

Paul honestly didn't remember. He very much doubted he was singing as he walked that day, however. Even if he was out on a country road by himself, his singing was anything but pleasant to his own ear. Nevertheless, he wasn't about to mess up the joke he knew was coming.

"Why yes, I believe I was," Paul answered.

"Thought so," Deacon Henry said after a moment, as if the memory had aroused a subject he was reluctant to discuss. "My cows quit giving milk right after you passed, and they didn't start back till yesterday morning." Then he cut loose with a loud cackle, grabbing Paul's hand and shaking it vigorously.

"You're a good man, Preacher."

"So are you, Deacon," Paul laughed. "So are you."

They were silent for a moment as the people in the line slowly made their way past Sarah.

"Almost," the deacon spoke first, nodding toward Tick, who was next up to shake hands with the child.

"Almost," the preacher agreed.

"In God's good time," the deacon said, reaching up to squeeze Paul by the shoulder.

"In God's good time," Paul nodded.

The line eased forward a pace. The two friends started down the steps side by side. They had to stop almost immediately. The holdup was with Sarah. Tick offered his large hand for her to shake, yet Sarah lifted both her tiny hands toward him, beckoning for him to bend over. Instead of bending down, Tick squatted before the child. Her arms instantly encircled his neck. Then she spoke, her words carrying clearly to her father on the steps above.

"It's okay, Tick. God still loves you."

Chapter 3

"Brutus is scared."

Paul looked up from his laptop to see Sarah standing in the bedroom doorway. She held the red rabbit pressed tight to her chest with both arms. He had not seen one without the other since bringing the stuffed toy home to her a few days ago.

"You just bring him over here," Paul said. "Let's see what's the matter."

Instead of coming around to his side, Sarah went to the footboard and shoved the rabbit—which was half her size—up on the bed between Paul and Jennie. Climbing up after, she pushed Brutus over on her father's legs. Then she snuggled her back up against her mother. Jennie's arm automatically moved to encircle her daughter's shoulders.

"He was crying," Sarah explained in her most pitiful little-girl voice. "He saw a boogey man."

"A boogey man?" Paul asked, setting the rabbit on his stomach. "I thought I ran all them off the other day."

"One came back, Poppy."

"Then I'll just jerk a knot in him right now. Right, Brutus?" Paul asked, pulling the rabbit's mouth close to his ear. "You got it," Paul nodded after a moment. To his wife and daughter, he said, "I'll be right back. Y'all hold the fort down."

Before he slid off the bed, he handed Brutus back to Sarah. Then he headed down the hallway toward his daughter's room, his bare feet making sticky sounds on the hardwood.

"My Poppy will chase him away." Sarah twisted her head around to look up at Jennie. "Won't he, Mommy?"

"Yes, he will, hon. He'll chase every mean thing away, so we will always be safe."

They both jolted upright when the shouting started.

"Get out here you nasty old boogey! I know you're in that closet! I can smell you!"

Sarah looked at her mother, eyes filled with wonder. "Poppy can smell him?"

"Yes, he can." Jennie nodded. "Your Poppy's like an old bloodhound. Nothing can hide from him."

"'Bout time you showed yourself," Paul said, his voice not quite so loud. "You ought to be ashamed, scaring my friend, Brutus, and making him cry. You've got my baby girl upset, too. Now you get on out that door, and don't you dare come back. You hear me? See you around again, I'll kick your stinky butt right over the roof."

A distant door slammed, but neither Jennie nor Sarah reacted to the sound. They were still staring goggle-eyed at one another, their mouths frozen open in surprise. Sarah was the first to speak.

"Ohhhh! Poppy said *stinky butt.*"

"I know," Jennie replied in a stage whisper, the shock in her voice matching her daughter's.

Paul came back into the room before they could say anything more.

"That ought to take care of things," he said to the rabbit, sitting down on the bed and reaching over to rub behind its ear. "I let that old boogey man have it with both barrels. Bet he's still running."

"Thank you, Poppy," Sarah said as she crawled over to give her father a kiss on the cheek. "Give Poppy a kiss too, Brutus," she added, pressing the rabbit's face against Paul's.

Jennie smiled at the scene for a few moments before shifting into mother mode. "Alright, you two," she started. "It's time to go beddy-bye."

"Okay, Mommy," Sarah answered, yet she didn't offer to move. After a few seconds she turned again to look up at her mother. "Can we sleep in here for a little while? Brutus said he's still kinda scared."

Jennie looked past her daughter and the stuffed rabbit to her grinning husband, who was stretching out on the bed once more.

"You had to know," he said.

"Of course," Jennie answered, shaking her head. Then she turned her attention to Sarah and her precious stuffed animal. "Just this once," Jennie agreed, using the same stern tone she always used when the need arose for their daughter to sleep with them. She wagged a finger first at Brutus, then at Sarah. "And don't you all be kicking like you were the other night. I couldn't sleep a wink."

"We won't, Mommy," Sarah replied, her face screwed up in a frown. Then she pulled Brutus close to her and commenced wiggling until she was at last settled in her nest between her parents. The child was asleep in seconds.

Paul leaned on his elbow toward Jennie as Jennie leaned on her elbow toward him. They met over their precious baby and briefly kissed each other on the lips.

"I love you," they spoke at the same instant. As Jennie settled back on her pillow, Paul reached out to the side and turned off the lamp.

Chapter 4

I *cannot say I am in a hurry to graduate. College has been challenging, rewarding, and more fun than I could have imagined when I first stepped onto the hill. Of course, I am getting the cart ahead of the horse. My final semester does not start until Monday. Still, I find myself thinking more and more of what lies for me beyond the halls of WKU. That is a little scary, going out into the world on my own, being a responsible adult. I guess it is time. My driver's license says I am old enough. I turned twenty-three last week. Twenty-three! Time to grow up.*

Camilla, Cami to her friends, clicked the *publish* button and released her blog into the ether. She enjoyed putting her thoughts down and sharing them with others. It was a good thing, for as a journalism major, she would be doing that a lot this last semester. What she would do with her education once she graduated, however, was something she was still trying to figure out. She was certain of only one goal: she wanted to tell people's stories.

Her phone whistled *bob white*, like the quail, the ringtone a reminder of her country roots. She answered the call immediately.

"Hello."

"Hey there, Cami," a familiar voice sang. It was her best friend, Emmy.

"What's up, girl? I was just thinking about calling you."

"Tonight's up, that's what."

"And what's that supposed to mean?" Cami teased.

"It means I've been back on campus forty-eight hours—most of it in this same dull cell on the sixth floor of Perkins Hall—and I am bored out of my red-headed skull. It means we are young and reasonably good looking, and we should go out on the town this evening so the young and reasonably good-looking members of the opposite sex might feast their eyes upon us and be so enamored they will ask us to dance. What do you say, Miss Camilla? Want to go to the Blarney Stone and shatter a few post-pubescent hearts?"

"Hmmm," Cami mused. "I don't know. Did you say we get to shatter hearts?"

"Most assuredly. What young, virile man of the bluegrass can resist our wit, our charms, our sterling intellects honed by countless hours of higher education? Is not the pleasure of our company a prize to be sought by brave knights sworn to defend our honor against knaves and fools? We'll have them lined up out the door on their knees begging for our hands in holy matrimony, or at least asking for our phone numbers."

"Begging, huh?" Cami giggled.

"Sure," Emmy answered. "That's where the heart breaking comes in. When they ask you just say, 'No thanks, Jack. This chickadee ain't ready to build a nest.' We'll leave them crying like babies."

"You are cray—zee!" Cami laughed.

"Why yeah!" Emmy laughed in return. "What do you say, woman? I need to bust a move. Coming or not?"

"Sure. I can't turn you loose on your own at the *Stone*. You'll set off a riot."

"That's my exact intention," Emmy stated flatly.

"Calling the M&Ms?" Cami asked, referring to two of their friends, Maura and Melanie, who roomed together two floors down. The four of them had been tight all through college.

"Of course. Lobby at eight?"

"Then."

"Then," Emmy affirmed, hanging up.

Long and narrow, the Blarney Stone was one of those just-off-campus dives common to college towns. It was wrapped on the outside by lapboard siding. Here and there, a few splotches of faded green paint—or mold—still clung stubbornly to its surfaces. Inside, the décor was best described as hard used. What paint or varnish that once protected the closely crowded tables and chairs had been mostly worn away. Over the years enough beer had been spilled on the floor to give the boards the patina of an ancient brewery, and the smell. The walls were covered in graffiti—everything from poetry, to numbers to call for a good time, to an extensive list of tortures to be inflicted upon old Professor Adolph Hatler for grading like a Nazi. A patron could cast a ballot for his or her preference by placing an X, or a swastika, in the appropriate column. Choices involving wire pliers and cattle prods appeared to be the top vote getters.

Even with all those things going for it, the primary attractions of the Blarney Stone were location, cheap beer, and live music. It also had a dance floor the size of a postage stamp. As Cami, Emmy, and the M&Ms entered that Friday evening, they miraculously spotted an empty table just across the dance floor from the three-piece band. They rushed as one to grab it. Before they were seated, Emmy ordered a round of drafts from a waitress who was pivoting back and forth through the packed room as if skiing the gates of a slalom course.

Emmy was right—at least partly so. The four young women suffered no lack of attention from the young males. Fifteen minutes from the time they stepped through the door, Cami took her seat after dancing with her fourth partner. She looked up and thanked him. He smiled and nodded, then disappeared into the crowd. So much for the bended knee stuff. Thirsty, she took a sip of her beer. Setting the mug back on the table, she glanced up and noticed a familiar face. Tick Cole was making his way through the crowd, more or less moving in their direction. As big a man as he was, the cramped space gave him a bull in the china shop appearance. A couple of seconds later they made eye contact. She motioned him over.

Chapter 5

Tick tried to stretch, once he was sitting up straight on the edge of his bed, reaching for the ceiling with both hands. He didn't make it far. A catch in the small of his back just below his right kidney, where the second guy had kicked him last night, decided to sink its teeth in at that moment. The memory made Tick grit his own teeth. Kicking him was downright sorry, no matter how you looked at it. *Never kick a man when he's down*, he thought, *even if he is down on the floor, sitting on top of your cousin's chest and beating on his head like it was a set of bongos.* Tick twisted and turned, working the muscles back and forth in slowly lengthening increments, until the knots began to loosen up.

He heard his mother making her way down the hallway, the old, warped floor creaking and squeaking with each step. As she had on every morning he could remember, she was no doubt headed to the kitchen to get breakfast started. Preparations for a workday got going early on the Cole place. The sun's first light was just now making its presence known, he sensed. Tick could not see things well enough to tell much more than that. Everything was blurry, as if he were in a cave, and up ahead at some indefinable distance was the cave's mouth with a spot of gray twilight peeking in.

That spot of gray was growing no larger, however, so he finally pushed up from the bed and slipped out into the hallway. Keeping one hand sliding along the wall so he knew his place, he went shuffling along like a man four times his twenty-one years. He wasn't the least surprised he couldn't see much of anything. The way his eyes felt they must be nearly shut. The dull scrape of an iron skillet being shoved into place atop a burner came back down the hallway as he eased into the bathroom and closed the door behind him.

The bathroom light was like a starburst when he at last found the switch and flicked it on. Tick squeezed his eyes closed tighter in response, or at least he tried. He might have gained half a millimeter. One can only draw a blind so far. Reaching a hand forward until it was flat against the glass, he leaned in toward the mirror. With the index finger and thumb of his right hand, he pried against the upper and lower lids of the same eye. The action made him flinch in quick pain. The sight in the mirror made him flinch a second time.

Whew! What a mess. His eyes were fat sausages with tiny little slits in their centers where the bruised and puffed-up lids almost met. All around them the skin was purple and blue and black, with streaks of yellowish green radiating outward from the deeper shades. *Boy, mama's gonna have a cow,* he thought. He didn't let the worry occupy his mind more than a few seconds. All that mattered was he could still see, at least some, at least with one eye. Well, that, and the fact he had been the only one standing when the fists quit flying.

He stayed in the bathroom a long time, splashing water on his face. The water helped some. It seemed to drain a bit of the soreness away. He eventually managed to pry his left eyelid up a fraction. Like the right, it wouldn't stay open on its own. The view from that eye was not any better, so he quickly let the lid fall back. Then, for a full minute, he left the faucet flowing while he stuck his whole head under the cold stream. Now that felt good. It helped rinse some of the cobwebs and frayed edges away. Finally, he stood up and turned the water off. For the first time, he thought there was a chance he might get his full vision back, though he could still only see little slivers of things. It remained easier to get about by feel and memory. He was fumbling around with a hand inside the linen closet, trying to find a towel, when his mother called out that breakfast was ready.

"Be there in a minute," he answered, though not too loud. Between the whisky hangover and all the licks to his head the night before, a section gang was dropping rails and driving spikes at a mad run inside his brain. Even the cold water hadn't helped dull that racket much. Raising his voice seemed likely to make it worse. He took his time, gently rubbing his hair with the towel. The racket didn't seem quite so loud, the pain just a little less, when he moved slower. More like being whacked with a rubber mallet instead of a spike hammer.

Tick didn't allow his mind to reach out and embrace her until he dropped the damp towel in the hamper. Camilla Lynn Whitley. He had known that girl just about his entire life, he supposed. They were from the same wide spot in the road, went to the same school until she graduated—she was a couple of grades ahead—attended the same church. Even with all that, until last night they hadn't said two words between them in years. He didn't know why exactly. Maybe because she was older? Maybe because she had been away at college for the last several years? Of course, he had spent his time chasing girls in his class, mostly, while he was still in school, and afterward…well, afterward, he was just chasing.

Then last night at the club there was Cami, seated at a table with some other girls. She motioned him over. Even through this morning's fog, he remembered everything. He had swaggered up close enough to speak, and Cami spoke back, telling him to have a seat. He pulled up a chair, spun it halfway around, and plopped down. Then, with studied nonchalance, he initiated one of his proven moves and pushed the bill of his cap up, so that a lock of dark hair spilled out in a loose curl across his forehead. Girls seemed to like his curls. Resting his folded arms across the curve of the chair's back, he leaned forward a few degrees, as if he were seated in a saddle. His feet tilted up on tiptoes automatically. Finally situated, he looked straight across at her with her strawberry blond hair pulled back in a ponytail, and her green eyes, and those freckles, just a pinch of them dusted across her cheekbones on each side of her nose. Then she smiled, revealing tiny dimples. That's when the lightning bolt struck him right between his eyes and knocked him, as he was to forevermore describe it, plumb stupid.

Rainbows. Tick found himself thinking of rainbows again, like last night. Living on a farm and being outside much of any day, rainbows had been something he had always known. He had wondered about them, but not been particularly filled with wonder. That changed late one summer afternoon. He was six or seven—he couldn't remember exactly, and it didn't matter. He and his father were walking across a corner of damp pasture, having waited out a passing shower huddled in the hay barn, when his father suddenly pulled up still and straight. Tick glanced up at him, then turned to follow his gaze. Hanging in the eastern sky, framing their home, was a double rainbow. The ends of each arc were rooted in the earth on either side.

"The last time I saw something that beautiful," his father spoke softly, "was the first time I laid eyes on your mother."

His father washed away in swirls of vivid colors. Last night, as Tick found himself staring across the little table at Cami, the words came out of his mouth on their own.

"You're as pretty as a rainbow."

For a moment it seemed all sound had ceased, even from the band. Then the other girls began to giggle. It didn't bother him. Tick was barely aware they were even there. Cami blushed and glanced down at her drink. Still, he kept staring at her. No problem there. He didn't care to see anybody else. At last, she looked up at him and smiled an easy, knowing half smile that radiated warmth and interest.

At that instant, Tick felt himself melting into streams which poured off his chair. Then Jeff Edgewater stuck his fat drunk head in between them and tried to get her to dance. Jeff shouldn't have called her what he did when she said no. His words brought the red bull out. One second Tick was pawing and slinging dirt behind him and the next he was throwing Jeff around the room like he was an empty sack.

Now, despite his many pains, Tick grinned to himself, satisfied with life for a change. He had fought over girls any number of times, but last night's festivities were different. It was the first time he had fought *for* a girl.

Tick reached for the doorknob. He missed it on the first try, but instantly recognized the old-fashioned door hook his hand brushed against instead. Readjusting his aim down a couple of inches, he caught the knob and swung the door open. There was a gasp for air, his mother's voice.

"Jesus God! What have they done to my baby now!"

Chapter 6

"Push me, Poppy! Push me!"

"Okay, Sarah girl. Let's make sure you're sitting right first. Hand Brutus to me. I'll set him over here by the tree for now."

Paul took the big stuffed rabbit and sat it down against the tree trunk. Then he stepped back behind his daughter. He placed his hands under Sarah's armpits and lifted her just enough to scoot her forward inside the tire swing.

"Can you touch the ground with your feet?" he asked. "You have to be able to stop okay if you need to."

Sarah leaned forward and stretched her legs out until she was able to touch the ground with her tippy toes. "I can touch, Poppy," she answered, looking up at him with a wide smile. "Now push me, please."

"Just a second, baby," Paul said. "You've got to hold onto the rope with both hands, okay? Squeeze it real tight."

"Yes, Poppy. Push me. Push me," Sarah insisted.

"Alright, here you go," Paul answered, placing a hand against the small of her back. "One, two, three," he counted, giving her a gentle push on *three*. Sarah swung a few feet away from him. When she came drifting back, he gave her another shove, a bit harder this time. In seconds she had the swing going on her own, kicking her little legs together at the start of each arc. "Look at you," Paul laughed. "Flying like a bird."

"Not too high." His wife's voice came from close behind. Jennie stepped up beside him and rested a hand on his shoulder. "Another milestone," she said.

"Yeah," Paul nodded. "Coming too fast to keep up with. Sometimes I almost wish she would just hold still for a day. Don't you?"

"Absolutely," Jennie replied with a laugh, "so I could catch up. Of course, you can't blame anyone but yourself for this one."

Paul hesitated a moment before speaking. "Yeah. Guess I did have a hand, didn't I?"

"You had no choice," Jennie said, giving his arm a squeeze. "Your baby girl wanted a swing, so Poppy had to make her a swing."

"Hey, what can I say? I'm putty in the hands of the women around here."

"Careful, Sarah," Jennie cautioned in what Paul called her *listen-to-me* voice. She leaned forward so she could see around him better. "Slow down a little. You're going too high."

"But it's fun, Mommy."

"It's fun, Mommy," Paul mimicked, turning to smile at his wife. He got a look in return which made him turn back and speak to his daughter. "Not so high, Sarah, like Mommy said. Okay?"

"Okay," Sarah answered over her shoulder, disappointment in her voice. She didn't kick as strong at the start of her next arc, however.

"Good girl," Paul approved.

The happy parents watched her swinging for a few minutes, neither speaking, simply enjoying the act of seeing their daughter master something new. Jennie finally ended the silence.

"Well, Poppy, think you can take a break from swing building long enough to work up a little spot of dirt for me? Mrs. Falin gave me some yellow iris bulbs. I want to set them out over here by the front porch."

"Your wish is my command, my love," Paul said, sweeping his arm in a wide flourish as he bent at the waist to bow toward her. "Just let me fetch my shovel." As he started toward the shed, he took a quick look toward his daughter. "Way to go, Sarah. You're doing fine."

"I love my swing, Poppy," she yelled back instantly.

It didn't take long for Paul to work up a little patch of ground for Jennie. They kneeled to spread dirt around the flower slips, just barely covering the roots as Mrs. Falin had instructed. Both checked frequently on their daughter, sometimes warning her not to go so high and to hold on tight, or just as often giving her words of encouragement. Jennie gave the soil one last pat with the palm of her hand and pushed to her feet.

"That's everybody," she said.

"Huh?" Paul looked up at her, confused.

"Now we have something in our yard from every lady in the church. I'm so proud. It's kind of like having our own temple of flowers, don't you see? Of course, Mrs. Falin gave us these irises, and the forsythia is from Mrs. Bartley," she added, pointing to a green bush down where their drive met the county road. "See forsythia blooming and you know spring is here. Our little snowball over at the corner came from Mrs. Noel. It's really starting to take off. Elsie gave us the buttercups. Remember how you bragged on them?"

Paul was laughing softly, watching Jennie turn and point to first one thing then another, hardly pausing to take a breath in between. Here was the woman he had fallen in love with, the woman who saw God's beauty wherever she turned and who rejoiced in the seeing.

"Angela came over and set out our tulips herself. Wouldn't anything please her but to do it. And Pat," she nodded toward a bush in the center of the yard, "gave me the purple crepe myrtle for my birthday. It's the prettiest shade ever, I believe. Marian's roses of Sharon have really drawn the hummingbirds this—"

"What are you doing, hon?" Paul cut Jennie off, raising his voice to Sarah. He had glanced over to see her struggling to get back inside her tire swing. She held Brutus in one hand.

"Brutus wants to swing, too," was Sarah's answer as she twisted about, settling into place again inside the tire.

"I don't think that's a good idea," Paul said, rising to his feet and dusting off his knees. "You need both hands to hold on."

"I know, Poppy. Brutus can hold on, too, see?" Sarah answered, moving a forefoot of the rabbit up to touch the rope. She let go of the stuffed animal then, as if she knew it had a strong grip. Brutus fell instantly, bouncing off her lap and landing on the grass a bit behind her. Sarah reached down with her left hand to pick the rabbit up. She couldn't quite reach it, though.

"I'll get him, hon," Paul said, taking his first stride toward the swing. He was only 20 feet away.

"No, Sarah!" Jennie's voice blew past his shoulder, a mother's intuition ripping the air.

22

Paul's feet seemed made of lead. Each step was more labored than the one before, as if everything was shifting into slow motion— everything but what Sarah was doing. Each separate movement of hers flashed clear and distinct. He saw her let loose of the rope with her remaining hand, saw her lean further back, twisting toward Brutus, saw her flip upside down with the sudden shift of her center of gravity, saw her falling free…

Chapter 7

Marian looked out the side window of her kitchen, checking on Tick. It was a habit of hers going back to when she and Tick's father had first moved to the farm. She had worried so when her husband was out working alone. Practically all farm work was hard. Much of it was dangerous. People got hurt. Keeping an eye out for those laboring in the fields might just keep a modest injury from turning into a true emergency and an emergency from becoming a disaster. How often had she sought out her husband on some far point of the farm, and subsequently Tick himself, with a glass of lemonade or tea, some home-baked cookies, or a fried pie in hand, not because she thought they might be thirsty or hungry, as she claimed, but because her imagination was getting the better of her and she wanted to make sure they were okay?

Tick was like his father, for he was not afraid of physical work. Her husband had always proudly said as much, and no one could disagree. If anything, since his father had died when Tick was fifteen, her son was even more of a worker now. Every day he was early to take after whatever needed doing, and he generally didn't come in of an evening until it was done.

Without a strong male model to guide him when he was away from the farm, however, Tick had become a wild buck, drinking and fighting almost every weekend. She had tried to slow him down, to tame some of the meanness and mischief out of him, without any luck. Oh, he would nod and seem to go along with whatever advice or fussing she sent his way. He never smarted back, never said a single cross or disagreeing word to her. Yet he was twenty-one now and of legal age to buy a drink. It seemed to her it was what he needed to prove he was an adult, for if anything, her son was a stubborn mule, determined to do what suited him. He would go straight out after one of her warning sessions on a Friday or Saturday night and prove he was as hardheaded and independent as any Cole man to ever walk the earth. The way his eyes looked Sunday morning a week ago was proof certain.

Still Marian remained a God-loving person. She had been one since she made her proclamation of faith at the Caney Creek Church when she was but a skinny stick of a teenager. Prayer was a frequent companion, nearly a constant state of life for her, for she sent word up at the first thought of a need. She was not one to pray much for herself. Family, friends, and neighbors found their way onto her list daily, though, as well as any stranger, near or far, who she heard was in need. And her son. Especially her son. Not just daily. Sometimes hourly. Sometimes by the minute. *Lord, this boy will wear my knees to the bone,* she would say to herself after he staggered in drunk or beaten to a pulp. Then, once more, she would kneel and speak through her tears to the Lord.

Things were not hopeless, however. Once, back in the middle of summer, Marian had talked Tick into going over to the next farm with her to visit the Lockharts. Tick and the preacher had gone off in the yard by themselves and huddled together for a time, at least until little Sarah spotted where they were and raced across the grass to intervene. The girl was crazy about her son, and he was crazy about her. The rest of the visit he carried her about on his shoulders or swung her in circles as she laughed and screamed with the pure, unrestrained joy of a child.

Though nothing major, religious-wise, came of the visit right away, it was still a start. At least now he made an effort to get up on a Sunday morning, no matter how late he came dragging in, and go to church with her. The last few Sundays had been especially promising. She sensed each service he was close to professing his belief in the Lord. Then yesterday, when they sang the invitational and he stepped out into the aisle, she had thought the time had come at last. She hadn't meant to cry when he sat back down on the pew. The tears had just come.

Marian leaned against the windowsill and looked down the slope to the far corner of the pasture field where Tick was working in the late afternoon sun. He was replacing some fenceposts. Her son was a big man, like his father, only bigger. He stood an easy six foot four and weighed in at something over 200. If there was a drop of fat on him, it was well hidden. As her granddaddy would have said, he was solid as a chunk of lead.

When Tick told her at lunch he would be replacing fenceposts this afternoon, she asked if he needed help hooking up the auger on the tractor. He laughed and said he didn't need that ole thing for a job so small. She hadn't been surprised when she glanced out the window half an hour back and saw him walking down the fencerow by the road with several cedar posts thrown over one shoulder. A set of posthole diggers dangled from his other hand. Now she watched, partly in awe, partly with pride, as he rifled the long-handled diggers deep into a hole with one hand, as if he were doing nothing more than throwing darts.

The hole apparently dug and ready, Tick picked up one of the new posts. Marian was just about to turn away when Tick suddenly flung the post aside. Something down the road toward the preacher's place had his attention. He was faced that direction, locked up as still and straight as a bird dog on point. All at once he was running, his strong legs sending him flying down the road. Something must be bad wrong. Marian did not hesitate. She snatched her car keys off the hook on the wall by the back door. Less than a minute passed before she pulled out on the county road, heading the direction her son had gone.

Moments later Marian turned into the preacher's drive, guided by the screams penetrating the closed space of her car. "Oh, dear God! Oh, dear God!" she kept saying over and over as she threw the door open. Near a tire swing in the front yard Preacher Paul sat on the grass. Jennie also sat, her head pressed against Paul's chest, her legs drawn up beneath her. They were cradling Sarah between them, the child's head lolling at an odd angle within the basket made of their arms. Tick knelt behind the family, one great arm draped around the shoulders of each distraught parent.

Chapter 8

Deacon Henry looked out across Paul and Jennie's front yard. It's the way he thought of them today, not as his minister and the minister's spouse—as a practical matter, roles of equal importance in their church—but as two close friends he was happy to call by their given names.

Happy? Deacon Henry shook his head, half in wonder, half in anger at himself for even thinking of the word now, here. It did not fit, maybe it would never again fit in this place. This was a place of profound sorrow. This was a place one simply could not imagine to ever again know anything approaching happiness, for a child, a lovely gift from God child, had been tragically, inexplicably, called home from this spot only a short while ago.

He allowed his gaze to sweep over the assembly gathered on the lawn. It looked as if the entire Caney Creek membership was there, as well as every other resident of the community. Deacon Henry thought back to words of his mother he had first heard as a child. "You never have to go looking for bad news. It will always find you." And today it had. He had just stepped inside the back door to his house, coming in from milking, when the phone rang.

"Get that, Henry, will you?" Elsie said. "I've got flour all over me."

He grunted in reply and stepped around her at the kitchen counter, where she was kneading a ball of dough. Taking the phone from its wall receptacle, he brought it to his ear.

"Elsie."

He recognized Marian Cole's voice, though it was flat, detached, unlike her usual pleasant tone.

"No, this is Henry. Just a sec—"

"Need y'all down at the preacher's," Marian cut him off. "Baby Sarah's been killed in an accident."

"We're on the way," he said, barely noticing Marian had ended the call. He dropped the phone on its hook and glanced over at Elsie. Having heard only his side of the conversation, she was already turning knobs on the stove. Done, she jerked her apron off, used it to give her hands a quick rub to wipe away the worst of the flour, and dropped it across the back of the nearest kitchen chair. Giving her hair a quick brush back from her eyes, she finally glanced up at her husband and spoke.

"What is it?"

"Little Sarah's dead," Deacon Henry replied, dropping his gaze.

Elsie's hand flew to her throat. She already knew the news was bad. His last words on the phone said as much. But the death of a child, that child! Merciful father! Her hand reached toward her mate. He stepped forward half a step and caught it in his calloused fingers. For the briefest moment they squeezed, allowing, accepting the strength each needed to flow between them, something they had done many times over the years to help get through a tragedy. Then they released their clasp and moved with purpose toward the door, Elsie in the lead.

How long ago had it been? the deacon asked himself. *What does it matter?* came his immediate retort. Long enough for the coroner to arrive. Long enough for Elsie and Marian to gently persuade Jennie to release her daughter. Long enough for Tick and him to do the same with the preacher. Long enough for the members of the shocked and silent gathering to bow their heads in prayer as Paul and Jennie slowly made their way inside the house, Marian and Elsie supporting Jennie's arms, Tick practically carrying Paul.

Now, feeling every one of his eighty-one years, the deacon made his way over close to the swing. With some difficulty, he slowly bent down and picked up the stuffed rabbit, Brutus. He allowed himself a quick flicker of a smile at the name. Paul had repeated himself twice, explaining what he wanted the deacon to get before the older man understood. He carried the rabbit back to the house through the loose crowd, the subdued voices from groups of two or three or four falling quiet at his approach, at the realization of what he carried. Inside he made his way over to where Paul sat gazing at a framed picture on a small side table. In the photo Sarah stood between Paul and Jennie, each of her tiny hands hidden in the hand of a parent. The church filled the background. All three were in their Sunday best. They were smiling broadly. *Probably laughing at something Sarah said,* the deacon thought absentmindedly as he placed his free hand on Paul's shoulder.

"Here's her rabbit," he said.

"Thank you," Paul answered, taking the stuffed animal and laying it in the crook of his arm as he had seen Sarah hold it.

The deacon left his hand on Paul's shoulder. It seemed the right thing to do. After a few seconds Paul reached up and laid his own hand to rest atop the deacon's.

"You are a good friend, Henry." The words made the deacon choke up a bit. "Jennie and I are so blessed to have our many friends here to help us get—" Paul didn't finish the thought, didn't say anything for a minute. When he started to speak again, he sounded tired beyond going. "I do hope, though, no one else says to me God needed another angel."

For the first time since Marian's awful call, the deacon allowed tears to spill from his eyes.

Chapter 9

Paul still labored hard on their farm every day save Sunday. Jennie continued with her job in town at an accounting firm, although she switched to full-time, like she had worked before Sarah was born. When a church member was sick, whether at home or in the hospital, the couple would come of an evening to visit and pray, as they always had. At church, Paul remained the same Preacher Paul, his sermons filled with Christian understanding and insight. When services ended came the most remarkable time, for Paul continued to take his place at the head of the church steps, shaking hands and exchanging a few words with the members as they left. Jennie still stood several feet out on the walk, where she engaged the young mothers in conversation about whatever new was going on in their babies' lives. Neither Paul nor Jennie ever mentioned how Sarah had once occupied a spot between them, doing her own special version of visiting.

Paul and Jennie were not the same, however. Some of their differences were subtle. Jennie didn't smile like she once had—openly and genuinely. Now her face appeared tense and tight, any hint of a smile worn like a mask. On the rare instances when she laughed, it was broken, cryptic, as if she were not certain it was something she should do. Paul, always one for conversation regardless of subject, might simply look away in the middle of a sentence, his train of thought derailed by what the other party generally assumed was a memory of Sarah. The other party was always correct with that assumption. The most obvious thing about the young couple was how very tired they looked, and how much older. It was something all their friends remarked on among themselves, yet no one questioned. How could they not look that way? That was their only question.

Early in the second month signs began to appear that instead of time being the healer, things might be getting worse. At a shower for a soon-to-be mother, one woman remarked that Jennie hadn't asked about her children after church the previous Sunday. Another noted that the same thing had happened with her. A third pointed out that Jennie was not here at the shower, something she would have never missed before. Comparing notes, the mothers soon realized that it had been several weeks since Jennie said a word about anyone's children. The mothers did not take offense. Instead, they shared a moment of quiet prayer for their shattered friend.

Paul's most significant change in behavior was not noticed by anyone at first. Weather permitting, he always took a morning walk of a mile—maybe a mile and a half when work on the farm wasn't pressing—along the country lanes that crisscrossed that corner of the county. Oftentimes, before the accident, he would also take a leisurely stroll in the evening, usually with Jennie and Sarah joining him. This was especially true in warmer weather. It was no secret that the morning walks were when the preacher developed his sermons, and the afternoons were when he and his family worked at catching up with what was happening with their neighbors. This included whatever gossip might currently be in circulation. He had said as much from the pulpit any number of times, always laughing about the gossip part, calling it the holy nosary.

Deacon Henry was the first to realize Preacher Paul's walks were different now. After the morning milking on a Friday, he made the short trip to the hardware store in the Grove. He needed a few nuts and bolts to repair a gate. On the way he passed Paul on the road. Coming back home he passed him again. Each time they met he honked the horn on his old pickup, and Paul waved back. Seeing Paul twice in such a brief span wasn't unusual. It wasn't far to the Grove and for once he hadn't hung around gabbing and whittling with the loafers on the liars' bench outside the hardware.

Thirty minutes after getting home, Deacon Henry was traveling again, yet headed in the opposite direction from his last trip. This time he was on the way to Merry Oaks to check on what would be for sale at a farm auction there the next week. He could use a new cultivator. His old one was about past fixing. If there was one going up for sale, he aimed to check it out ahead of time. On the way, he passed the preacher a third time. He honked, and Paul waved, same as before.

There was only one cultivator at the auction site and the deacon found it to be in such pitiful shape it made his old one look almost new. Disappointed, he headed home. A hundred yards outside the village he met the preacher again. He simply waved this time and the preacher waved back. Paul was headed in the direction of Merry Oaks. This instance, like the last, he would have walked right past the lane to his own place on the way to where they crossed paths.

That's when the wheels really started turning in the deacon's head. By the time he swung into the drive at his house he thought he had it figured out. The preacher wasn't walking any mile or mile and a half this morning. He was walking a six-mile circuit. And if that was so, according to the places where he had passed him, Paul probably wasn't covering just six miles, he could be well on the way to walking twelve. The deacon did one more quick set of calculations in his head. If he was right, as the preacher neared the end of a second circuit, he would come by the entrance to the deacon's drive from the direction of the Grove in about an hour and a half. Deacon Henry planned on being there to meet him.

✝✝✝

It was pushing 10:00 when the deacon let down the tailgate to his old pickup truck. He was parked at the entrance of his drive, the rear of the truck facing the county road. Back at the house minutes earlier, Elsie had raised an eyebrow when he filled two mason jars with iced tea.

"Preacher's out on a long walk," he explained. "I thought I'd flag him down when he came by. Let him cool off and talk a spell. It's been awhile."

"Okay," Elsie replied, suppressing her smile. She was quietly proud she'd married a man who recognized when there was a need to help. "It'll do you both good."

"Uh-huh," the deacon grunted as he pushed the screen door open with an elbow and stepped outside with the tea, a jar in each hand.

Now, having carried the jars from the cab, he set them on the tailgate. Then he carefully scooted up to sit on one corner of the gate so he could rest an arm on the side of the truck bed as he watched for the preacher. It wasn't hot, but the promise was there that the heat wasn't long in coming. Rays of sunlight found their way through the overhanging branches to strike the pavement of the county road, forming bright, irregular pools that shifted with every leaf-waggling breeze. The deacon liked these late-summer days with their cooler mornings. *A man could get a lot of work done on a morning like this without melting down,* he thought, *or take an extra-long walk to help ease his mind.* He glanced up the road about a hundred yards toward the Grove and saw the preacher come fast stepping around a bend.

"Have a seat and cool your heels," Deacon Henry called out as Preacher Paul came within speaking distance. "Got a jar of Elsie's sweet tea here for you."

"Morning, Henry," Paul said as he stopped before the older man. He eyed the jar suspiciously for a moment, then reached for it. Nearly half the contents disappeared before he lowered his arm. "Ummm, that hit the spot. Thank you." As he moved over against the truck, he added, "Don't mind me asking, what're you up to? Operating a rest area for wayward souls?"

The deacon waited for the preacher to take a seat on the opposite corner of the tailgate before speaking.

"Well, I guess you could call it that. Depends on if you're wayward or not." He laughed. "No, I just saw you walking everywhere I went this morning, and I imagined you could use a drink when you came back by. Twelve miles is a right smart pull."

"Twelve miles?" Paul asked. He sounded genuinely puzzled.

"Yeah, that's what I figured. You went toward Merry Oaks to begin with, right?"

"I did."

"Then you took the state road around English Knob to the Grove."

"Yes," Paul replied, turning to stare at the deacon.

"Then you came back on the Grove road past your house and started over," the deacon spoke as if there were no arguing. "It's a six-mile circuit. Two laps make twelve. Sound about right?"

Paul looked at the deacon for several more seconds. He finally looked away and took another strong draw of tea, almost emptying the jar. Wiping his lips first with the side of his hand, he glanced back toward the older man.

"Okay there, Mr. Detective," the preacher began. "I don't know if you've been following me or not. I'll admit I got to wondering when I saw you up there at Merry Oaks. The fact is, you're right about my route. Now the distance, I don't know. Seems high."

"I knew it!" Deacon Henry slapped his knee. "Couldn't have been but one other way. Walking straight up the road to the Grove, then turning around and walking back the same way to Merry Oaks. I suspicioned that was unlikely. Don't know why. Time of day, maybe. You're usually out walking a lot earlier, so I had an idea you'd been at it for a while already."

"True on all counts," Paul had to laugh.

"Now the distance," the deacon took off again. "I've got that down to the yard. It's a mile and a quarter to the Grove, a mile and eight-tenths to Merry Oaks, and two skips and a jump short of three miles taking the state road back around to the Grove. Six miles."

"I'm impressed," Paul smiled. "I had no clue it was that far."

"Know my ciphering," Deacon Henry said. "And how far it is from here to there for about anywhere you can pick in these parts. Ought to. Lived here long enough. Moved in right after we kicked the Kaiser's butt. Ha!" he ended with a shout. Paul shared in the laughter.

"So, you got it all measured and calculated out," Paul said once they quieted down. "Then you came down here to bring me some cold tea. Like I said, I'm impressed, and grateful."

"About messed up and let you slip by," the deacon admitted. "I had you down for covering two and a half miles an hour—which is a fair enough pace—then here you came around the bend thirty seconds after I plopped down on the tail gate. You were really stepping. Pushing three miles an hour, I imagine. That's picking 'em up and putting 'em down pretty good."

"If you say so," Paul shrugged.

"I do," the deacon replied, his tone serious. Then he laughed out loud. Paul joined in with him again. Like Elsie had said, it did them both good.

Neither man spoke for some time once they quieted down, simply enjoying one another's company, enjoying being outside on such a fine morning. Deacon Henry eventually broke the silence.

"Rough, isn't it?"

"Very," came Paul's immediate answer.

"I've been around a long time," the deacon said. "Seen my share and then some, I reckon, and I still don't know what to say."

"If I were in your shoes," Paul replied, "I don't know what I'd say, either. Pretty sorry when a preacher gets tongue-tied. Giving words of comfort are right up there at the top on my job description."

"No cause to be hard on yourself. Sometimes the hurt is bigger than any words can ease."

"Makes me wonder, Henry, about all the times I've said things meant to help someone through something awful. They must have thought it was all just b. s."

"No, they didn't," the deacon was quick to answer. "I don't want to hurt your feelings, but there's a fair chance a lot of them didn't remember a word you said. The fact you were there was what mattered. People expect to see their representative."

"Excuse me?"

"You're the middleman. You help bring them to God, but more important, you bring God to them. You show up, people figure God knows about their troubles. They need that more than anything you can tell them."

Paul didn't say anything in return. The deacon remained quiet, also. A minute passed before Paul cleared his throat.

"I've been at this preaching business five years, and you have to remind me of what it means."

Deacon Henry gave a little chuckle. "You seminary boys ain't got nothing on me. I've got a fifty-year head start studying *the Book*. Makes you feel any better, I don't know near half what I let on."

Paul turned at that and smiled broadly. He reached out a hand

and patted the older man's shoulder. "Any way you look at it, you know twice as much as me."

Now it was the deacon who sprouted a wide smile. They fell quiet again for a few moments. The deacon finally spoke.

"How's Jennie doing?"

The time stretched out until it became uncomfortable for both men before Paul replied.

"I can't really say. We haven't spoken in three days."

Stunned, the deacon simply stared at the preacher. Another long, uncomfortable stretch went by before he said, "I don't know that it's a sin, Paul, but turning your back when your loved one needs you can't be what God expects of marriage."

Chapter 10

Paul sat on the top step of their front porch. He was hot and tired from cutting hay. It was late afternoon now, and he had been at it since leaving the deacon that morning. Normally, he would have worked out whatever issue might be weighing on him while he did his farm work. It was a proven method of his. The solitude and physical labor helped create the space he needed to think. Yet this once it had not worked. He remained troubled, out of sorts.

None of his routines seemed to fit him today. His walk had been much longer than usual, taking up half the morning. He had skipped lunch, not feeling the least bit hungry. When he came in from the field, he hadn't gone straight to the shower, either, like he usually did, and not having bathed, he certainly hadn't put on fresh clothes. He felt clammy with sweat and dirty. A layer of leaves and dust and slivers of stems from the hay were stuck to his skin, causing him to itch, and he did not care. He didn't even bother to scratch. The only thing he had managed to do since making his way to the house was step inside the kitchen long enough to get himself a big mug of ice water. The mug sat beside him on the step now, half empty. Occasionally, he would pick it up and take a swallow to cut at the coat of grime clinging to the back of his throat.

There were much more comfortable places on the porch to sit. He could have taken one of the two rockers, their seats and backs softly padded with the cushions Jennie had stitched together herself. That's what he usually did when he found himself out here alone, especially those times when an aggravation was grating crossways at the rough edges of his mind, like today. A rocker was a great place to sit and relax, and to think. Or he could have sat on the glider, found ease in the gentle back and forth swaying, in the little squeaks and metallic pops of the hinges, and maybe have also found peace. That's where he usually sat with Jennie and…and…Sarah.

Paul was suddenly angry with himself. How could he have hesitated to say his child's name? He felt his face burning with shame. What kind of father, what kind of man would ever do such a thing? He dropped his head and wept. The tears were never far these days. He didn't bother to brush them away now. They had been right at the brim since he spoke with the deacon this morning. He needed to feel them coursing down his face, cutting gullies through the dust of the field.

After a time, the tears ceased. Paul said a simple prayer asking for strength, then he raised his head and looked out over the lawn. His gaze quickly fell on the tree branch that had supported her swing. "Sarah," he whispered. Then he straightened his back and cleared his throat. Forcing himself to keep looking straight at the tree, he spoke again. "Sarah," he said, his voice strong and certain. "I love you, my darling."

Seconds later he heard the crunch of gravel at the end of the lane and was reminded of why he had decided to sit here on the step to begin with. The spot afforded him a view of the full length of their drive. In a moment Jennie came rolling up in her car. She braked to a halt just outside the garage.

He could see her plainly through the door glass, looking over at him. Long seconds dragged by before she at last swung the door open and stepped out. She took a deep breath, her chest rising and falling, then she slowly, reluctantly began walking toward him. At the steps she hesitated a wordless minute before she turned and dropped down to sit beside him. He noticed—a pain arcing across his chest—that she sat just far enough away that their bodies did not touch. Her head lifted, following his gaze.

Neither spoke or even so much as glanced toward the other. Their eyes stayed locked upon the tree. After a spell, Paul picked up his water and took a sip. He placed the mug back on the step between his feet, then coughed a small, nervous cough to clear his throat before speaking.

"Busy day?" he asked, still not looking her way.

"Not bad," she answered, not turning to face him, either. "Rather be busy."

"Yeah," he replied.

Jennie waited a while before noting, "I see you got the hay cut." A hint of sarcasm was unmistakable in her tone. She almost added, "finally," catching herself at the last instant.

"Yeah. Got it all done."

"Good. I know you're glad to have that out of the way," she said, then fell silent.

"I'm always glad of that." He waited a few seconds before continuing. "We should get one more cutting, but dry as it's been—"

"It has been dry," Jennie agreed. She also let a few seconds go by before asking, "Did you have a good walk this morning?"

"I guess you could say so. Deacon Henry said I covered twelve miles."

"Hmmm," Jennie said, her eyebrows rising. "I'd say that qualifies." Once more she allowed a while to slide by before speaking further. "Strange that you talked to Henry. I spoke with Elsie for a bit this morning. She was putting something in her mailbox and flagged me down."

"Oh really?"

"She's so easy to talk to. I hope I'm half that wise by the time I reach her age. She says what you need to hear without making it sound like advice."

"Way Henry is, too," Paul said, shaking his head in agreement. "Lucky to know them."

They fell silent then, as if this, the their longest conversation in days, had drained them both of words. One minute of silence dragged into two, then two into three. Still, they both stared at the big maple, at Sarah's tree, where her swing had hung from that first stout limb extending toward where they now sat.

"I'm sorry!" they both suddenly said in unison, each surprised by the other's exclamation.

Then they were in each other's arms, neither knowing how it had happened, nor caring. All that was important to either was that they were being embraced by the one they loved. For a long while they stayed that way. At last, they both leaned back a bit, as if by some pre-agreed arrangement, though each kept their hands touching the other. Suddenly the words were flying between them.

"If I hadn't hung that swing—"

"I wanted those stupid flowers planted."

"I know you blame me."

"No! It's my fault," Jennie sobbed, burying her face in Paul's chest.

Paul held her as she cried out all the same pent-up, horrible pain that he had cried out minutes before. He cried, too, yet not in the same, uncontrollable torrents. Such a flood was not left in him. His grief was softer, sadder, for he understood that Jennie had secreted away the same guilt he felt for what happened. When her sobs at last began to wane, Paul whispered in her ear.

"No one is to blame, hon. If we are guilty of anything, it is of loving to hear our baby's laughter too much."

"Yes," Jennie whispered back. "I think so, too." Several minutes passed quietly. When Jennie spoke again, her voice was nearly normal. "I'm glad Tick stopped you from cutting that tree down. It's the prettiest one around when it turns in the fall."

"It is, isn't it? Yellow as a gourd."

Jennie allowed a moment to drift by before answering. "Would have taken you half a day anyway," she giggled a little.

"No doubt," Paul laughed. "Did you see him? Snatched the ax right out of my hands. Held it up in the air with one fist and me up with the other. Like my Uncle Lester used to say, 'That boy ain't natural.' Of course, he was already mad because I took the swing down."

"I don't know about him being upset with you," Jennie smiled. "He could have been, I guess. I just remember that right before you came marching out of the garage with that ax, he said to me, 'Every time I come by here, I see your little Sarah playing beneath that tree. I expect I always will.'"

"Wow," Paul said, the brief spell of laughter knocked out of him. "I didn't know."

"Sorry I didn't tell you," Jennie replied, their eyes meeting. "That was so sweet. All I could think to say was, 'I pray you always do.'"

Paul had to look away, afraid the tears would come again. He didn't want that, not now when they were just starting to find reasons to smile and laugh a little. He turned his focus back to the big maple. Jennie put both hands on his arm and pulled herself in closer, until their heads rested against each other. She, too, found herself staring again at their daughter's tree. After a couple of minutes, she said, "It just doesn't look right, does it?"

"No," he agreed. "Seems empty."

Suddenly Paul was on his feet. Striking off at a fast walk, he felt Jennie beside him.

"I'll meet you there with it," she said, ducking inside the garage.

"Okay," he answered as he disappeared around the corner of the building.

Less than five minutes later Jennie cautioned him from the ground, "Watch that last step. I don't want you to fall."

"Right, I don't either," Paul said, hesitating for her to move aside from where she was holding the foot of the ladder steady. Once he had both feet on the ground, he leaned the ladder back slightly and walked it down, hand over hand, until he could step out and lay it flat on the grass.

"That looks better," Jennie said as she came over to stand beside him. She wrapped an arm around his waist.

"Yes," Paul agreed, draping his arm across her shoulders in turn. Together they looked at the tire swing hanging from its previous spot on the first limb on the maple.

"Our baby will always play beneath her tree," Jennie said softly, "and now she can swing away to her heart's content."

Chapter 11

Paul and Jennie had hardly stepped inside the house before the swing was noticed. The word spread like wildfire. Consensus was quickly reached among the neighbors; this could be nothing other than bad news. The young couple had obviously lost their minds. Why else would they have done such a thing? Why else would they wish to confront their tragedy every time they looked out on their yard? What could they possibly hope to gain? It made no sense.

Talk about Paul and Jennie continued to flow like water down through the Caney Creek community all day, every day, and washed over into each night. This was hardly idle gossip. Insanity, even the suspicion of insanity, cannot be ignored. It must be explained. It must be understood. Folks worried aloud, in hushed tones in public, in long winded, one-to-one sessions over the phone, trying to do just that, to understand what was going on in the minds of a couple they all held dear. Strangely, not a soul did the most obvious thing—simply ask the preacher and his wife why they hung the swing back up. Some feared upsetting them further. A few worried about getting too close to whatever might be going on in their minds, as if thoughts were germs and insanity might be catching. Some did their best to act as if nothing had happened, hoping it would all clear up on its own.

Lingering at the kitchen table after their evening meal, Miss Elsie and Deacon Henry were only two of many who had Paul and Jennie on their minds. Though the Indian Summer heat still held, the days were now noticeably shorter. Outside the light was already fading. "Before you know it," Elsie said in a low voice, half speaking to herself as she glanced through the screen door, "we'll be eating supper after dark."

"Yeah," Henry nodded without enthusiasm.

Rising, Elsie gathered a handful of dirty dishes, then carried them to the sink. She returned with the coffee pot. Henry filled their cups as she moved over to the pie pan on the counter. Working a serving knife, she lifted a slice from the pan, and with her free hand hovering alongside as a just-in-case guide, slid it onto a saucer. On plating a second slice, she set one before Henry, the other by her coffee. Taking her seat, she scooped out a spoonful of sugar and stirred it in her cup. Henry waited patiently until Elsie lifted the cup to her lips.

This was their after-supper ritual. They always had coffee and something sweet. The cups were on saucers. Pieces of pie, or cake, or cobbler, were set on their own dishes. Tonight, as usual, they ate with the small dessert forks passed down from Elsie's mother.

"Good, hon," Henry said, nudging a second bite off with the edge of his fork.

"I'm glad you like it," Elsie replied. "Haven't made a sweet-potato pie in a while. I just had a hankering for one today."

"I love your hankerings," Henry said. "Always have. I'm a lucky man. Got a pretty wife who's also a great cook."

"You're a good man, Henry, and I love you, but sometimes, I swear, you act like you're a little touched in the head. I'll allow I can cook—managed to keep you fed all these years, and you never complained once, thank you—but pretty? If I ever was, I don't remember. Now days I look in the mirror, and I see a scarecrow staring back."

"Then it's time you got a new prescription for your glasses," Henry said with a grin. "When I look across this table, I still see that same darling girl, pretty as the first flower of spring, who kissed me that first time we went walking together. You remember. We were under that big sweet gum tree back of the church. You acted like you'd stepped on one of those spiked balls and fell right over in my arms. I hadn't even got up the nerve yet to ask if I could hold your hand, then before I knew it, you'd done smooched me right on the lips."

"Oh, eat your pie," Elsie ordered, blushing, though the hint of a smile played at the corners of her mouth.

For a few moments they ate in silence. Henry finished first, pressing his fork into the last few crumbs of crust then dragging it across his lips. "That was delicious, hon," he said, rubbing his stomach. "Believe that's the best you ever made."

"I don't know about the best," Elsie replied, laying her fork on her empty saucer. "It was tasty, though."

They allowed a minute to pass quietly, each sipping their coffee.

"I've been worrying about our lovebirds down the road," Henry said at last. "Of course, so's everybody else."

"I know it," Elsie nodded. "I get five or six calls a day." She picked up her cup, took a tiny sip, and set it down again.

"Most folks I talk to think they've gone crazy," Henry said. "I don't believe that's the case, but Paul does concern me some. He hasn't backed off on all his walking, that I can tell. I've got to where I see him almost every time I get in my truck."

"People talking about that, too," Elsie said. "First one runs into him in the Grove, then another in Rocky Hill, and the next over past the knob. I asked Jennie about it after church Sunday, kind of joking-like, you know. She just said that it helps him to figure things out. She didn't seem tore up about it, so I didn't push."

"It a puzzler," Henry replied after a moment. "She didn't offer anything about the swing, I suppose?"

"Lord no," Elsie answered with an emphatic shake of her head.

"That stumps me more than the walking," Henry admitted, reaching for the toothpick holder at the center of the table. "You know he had me bring the stuffed rabbit to him that same afternoon. I could see that. It was Sarah's favorite plaything. The swing, though? Why put it back up? Surely it hurts them to see it hanging there empty."

"You'd think." Elsie shook her head. She waited a few moments before going on. "But I don't believe it hurts them as much as you might suppose. It surely doesn't hurt them as much as what they're afraid of."

Henry didn't say anything in return for several seconds. His face screwed up in confusion, he finally leaned forward over the table and rested on his elbows.

"What do you think has got them scared?" he asked.

"Forgetting," Elsie answered, her gaze seemingly cast somewhere off in the far distance. "They're afraid of forgetting their baby girl."

Henry leaned back into his chair until he felt his spine press against the slats. Memories came flooding in: the breath-stealing sight of a baby's rattle left atop a small tombstone; stopping to help an old gentleman he thought was broken down on the roadside, only to discover the man was putting up a new cross where his son died years before in a car crash; his own mother keeping his daddy's work hat on her nightstand after he passed, where it would be the first thing she saw in the morning and the last thing she saw at night. *Yes*, Henry mused. A person kept those kinds of things in sight to remind, to remember, and if seeing them sometimes knocked the scab off, well, that was no bother. The pain of loss ran deeper than that.

"I think you're right, hon." Henry nodded toward Elsie. "There's nothing crazy about either one of them."

Had the deacon been able to see the preacher and his wife at that moment he might have reconsidered.

Chapter 12

Cami swung out of her car and started across the front of the Double Dip's concrete patio. She had just reached the order window when the door to the seating area came flying open with a bang. Spinning that direction, she saw the beast, Tick Cole, come lumbering out. He pulled up short when he spotted her. For a moment he simply stood there staring, holding a Styrofoam drink cup high in one hand, the sipping end of its straw in his mouth. That's the way the straw stayed when he raised his head, the top end still pressed between his lips. The bottom end, however, popped out of the cup's top like a section of broken well pipe. Strawberry shake immediately began dribbling from the rupture. In an instant he had a fast-growing pink smudge down the front of his tee shirt.

"Most people do it the other way," she said.

Tick's eyebrows shot up in confusion.

"They leave the straw in the cup."

"Huh?" Tick grunted, then glanced down, causing the straw's free end to drag across his chest. A chunk of strawberry plopped out and stuck to his shirt. "Oh crap," he said, tilting his head far back and noisily sucking out whatever was left in the tube. Then he took the straw from his mouth and jammed it back through the cup's plastic lid. Finally, he flicked the chunk of strawberry off his shirt with a fingertip. It just missed Cami's face, splatting against something behind her. She managed not to duck.

"Do you eat like that at home?" Cami asked, pulling a wad of paper napkins from the holder near the window and extending them his way.

"Not when Mama's watching," Tick replied with a crooked grin as he took the napkins. While he brushed at the stubborn streaks down his shirt he said, "What do you want? Milkshake? Ice-cream cone? Chili dog? My treat."

"Hmmm," Cami mused, placing her hands on her hips. "If I let you buy me something, then I'll feel obligated to sit with you while I eat."

"That's my intention," Tick nodded emphatically, still grinning.

"Well," Cami began, "I don't know if that's a good idea. Are you planning to hit anyone today?"

"It hadn't crossed my mind," Tick assured her, not adding that he seldom knew what was coming more than a second or two before he swung a fist.

"Let's hope it doesn't," Cami said, a quick smile gracing her lips. At the sound of the order window's sash lifting, she turned to see a hand holding a wash rag extend out to scrub at something red stuck on the frame. Looked like strawberry. "Hi, Joyce," Cami spoke to the lady's face that replaced the hand. "I'd like a small hot-fudge sundae, please, and could I also have a bibb for the gorilla?"

"We usually just rinse him off with the hose out back," Joyce deadpanned. "I'll get you a sheet of plastic to cover up with, though, so he doesn't sling stuff all over your clothes."

✝✝✝

As he stood waiting for Cami's sundae at the inside counter, Tick took the time to look her over. She had on sandals, cut-off-jeans shorts, a simple green shirt, untucked, and a matching ball cap. Her ponytail was pulled through the back of the cap. To Tick it seemed she might as well have been sporting a Derby outfit. *Some girls can make whatever they wore look good,* he thought, *and she is sure one of them.* As he stared, she removed her sunglasses and placed them on the table off to one side with her billfold. Then she looked up at him and flashed a tight smile. He suddenly realized her eyes were the same color as her shirt and cap, except her eyes were sparkling. His words from the Blarney Stone came back to him. She was absolutely as pretty as a rainbow.

"You're drooling," Cami said.

Tick's hand shot up to his bottom lip, found nothing. He inspected his fingers to make certain, before glancing back at her. Though the joke was hers, Cami's cheeks were flushed red. She cast

47

her eyes downward and fiddled for a moment with rearranging her billfold and sunglasses on the tabletop.

"Here you go," Joyce spoke from behind Tick. He turned to face her as she continued, "Try not to stick your thumb in it or drop it on her lap. Okay?" Leaning to one side so she could see around Tick, Joyce added, "Good to see you, Cami. Your folks doing all right?"

"Good to see you, too," Cami answered. "Dad's still having trouble with the bursitis in his shoulder, but otherwise they're both getting along as fine as can be expected. Appreciate you asking."

Joyce gave a quick nod, then added, "You need to get up here more often."

"I know," Cami agreed. The thought that she might just do that—now that she possibly had a good reason—rolled through her mind. She had her eyes on Tick, the possible reason, as she added, "School really keeps me busy."

"I'm sure. Hang in there, hon. We're proud of you," Joyce said, turning away from the counter.

"Thank you," Cami replied, touched by the words because she knew Joyce was sincere. People were always saying things like that to her when she came back home. "Oh, thank you," she said again, this time to Tick, as he placed her sundae on the table. He was as careful as if it were made of eggshells, gently moving the short cup sideways a few inches with both hands until it was centered before her. Then he tore the wrapping off her plastic spoon and placed it on a napkin beside her dish. Returning to the counter, he grabbed a couple of extra napkins and brought them back to her. "Thanks," she said a third time, a bit taken aback by his attentiveness. "Ummm, this looks yummy."

"You know it is," Tick agreed, plopping down into a chair across from her. "Best ice cream in the Grove."

"You're right, even if this is the *only* ice cream place in town." She nodded, scooping out a spoonful.

As she ate, Tick slurped away at his milkshake. It didn't take him long to down what remained, finishing it off with a wet, gurgling racket. Cami imagined a vacuum machine sucking a mud puddle dry. She looked up from her sundae and shook her head.

"Sorry," Tick said, acknowledging her admonishing glance. "I had a strawberry stuck."

Cami rolled her eyes as she took another bite of ice cream. Tick continued to stare at her as she ate, his face seemingly frozen into a permanent grin. A minute passed before she spoke again, dabbing at her mouth with a napkin first.

"It's impolite to stare," she said, though she had to admit to herself that she really did not mind him looking.

"I can't help myself," Tick replied, his grin growing a bit wider. "It's just that you're pretty as a rainbow."

"You've already used that line on me once," she noted, swirling her spoon around in the cup to get a mix of ice cream and fudge in her next bite.

"It's not a line if it's the truth," Tick said, his tone suddenly serious. "And that's the truth if I ever told it."

Cami didn't reply right away, seemingly electing to concentrate on her ice cream. In reality, she was trying to make the blush leave her cheeks, for she could feel them burning once more. At last, she turned her eyes toward him and spoke.

"You're kinda cute, yourself, for a simian."

"Ha!" Tick's sharp laugh was loud and genuine. "I'll take that as a compliment and do my best not to scratch under my arms when I'm around you."

"I would appreciate that," Cami smiled back at him. *What's got into me?* she asked herself. It was very unlike her to flirt so with a guy. But there was something about *this* guy.

"So, tell me," Tick began. "What brings you back to the Grove late on a Friday afternoon? I'm like Joyce. I don't see you around very much."

"Well, I was going to come up Sunday, anyway. Mother talked me into going to the potluck at church. Since I didn't have but one class this morning, I thought I'd take a long weekend at home." Scraping the spoon around the bottom of the cup, she gathered what remained of the now mostly melted ice cream, then took the last bite. She dabbed at her mouth again with the napkin. "That was delicious. Thank you very much, Tick."

49

"Sure." Tick flashed a smile. "I'm tickled you're going to the dinner," he said, switching rows back. "We're going, too. Mom's fixing her green-bean casserole. I could eat a truckload of that stuff."

"Oh, I know it," Cami nodded. "All that good food. Mother didn't have to do that much arm twisting to get me to come."

"And Miss Elsie's pecan pies," Tick exclaimed, not even trying to curb his enthusiasm. "Yes sir! I might just eat a whole one, myself."

"Not if I beat you to it." Cami vowed.

Suddenly they were out of words. Neither minded. Being in one another's company was enough. A full minute passed before Cami spoke. It was her turn to change the subject.

"My folks told me you were the first one there after...after the accident. How you comforted them." She reached across the small table and laid her hand atop his, a simple gesture she intended to show nothing more than recognition of his decency. The spark of electricity she felt unsettled her so much she struggled a long moment to regain her voice. Finally, she could say, "I'm proud of you, Tick. That was so kind, so sweet."

Tick felt the spark, also. He didn't reply, however. He was trying too hard not to break down for him to say anything.

Chapter 13

Friday night was pizza night. Jennie had picked up the large pie—loaded with everything, the way they liked it—when she got off work, along with a small cheesecake. The cheesecake was part of their tradition, too.

"That's enough for me," Jennie announced as she got up from the kitchen table. "It's time for dessert."

Opening the refrigerator, she reached inside and removed the plastic box.

"Want me to cut you a piece?" Jennie asked, opening the silverware drawer and pulling out a knife.

"Yeah," Paul replied, picking up the pizza slice from his plate again. He took a huge bite. "Might as well," he mumbled around the mouthful.

Paul sounded distracted. His head was turned toward the television on the far wall of the combination den and kitchen. Before the accident, they never watched television while they were eating. It had been a time for family conversation. Now—well now, they both welcomed the noise. The anchorman on the national news was speaking.

"We warn our viewers this next story is disturbing. Let us go to Adriana LaFluer, our reporter on the scene in Brownsville, Texas. She is following the immigrant situation at our southern border. Adriana."

Paul reached past the pizza box and grasped the remote. He adjusted the sound upward a couple of clicks.

"Stephen," the reporter began, standing before a stretch of the border wall, "the family separation issue is the most controversial element of the administration's policy on immigration. Thousands of children have been taken from their parents and held in separate facilities; some are infants, many are preschoolers. A significant percentage have still not been reunited with their parents, although officials assure us progress is being made. We have made numerous requests to speak to these children, or to at least see inside the buildings where they are being held.

"In addition, complicating this sad and chaotic situation, many unaccompanied children continue to arrive daily at the border. It is difficult to imagine how dire the situation must be to send one's child, alone, to another country."

Jennie picked up the paper plates with their slices of cheesecake and brought them over to the table. She sat them down, but instead of taking her seat, she hesitated beside her husband. Her eyes were turned toward the TV, too.

"To date, all our requests to speak with a child have been denied. We have only been given a few perfunctory tours of empty play and exercise areas. Recently, however, we received a short video from inside a children's detention center in this community."

The shot changed from the reporter to a little barefoot girl in a torn, dirty dress. She was standing on the other side of a section of chain-link fencing inside what appeared to be a warehouse-like building. The child was saying something in Spanish, her wide, brown eyes glistening wet. Suddenly, she burst into tears. Jennie's hand reached out, found Paul's shoulder. He lifted a hand to cover hers.

"Serena is four. She came here from Guatemala with her mother, walking nearly 1,300 miles. They were separated at the border. It is difficult to describe where she is being kept as anything other than a cage. The floors, the benches, are made of concrete. There is no bed, or cot, or even a thin mattress for her to rest on. Her blanket is a sheet of aluminum foil."

"Jesus Lord," Jennie said. "She could be—"

"Yes," Paul managed to reply, his chest so tight it hurt.

"The full video runs for two minutes and thirty-five seconds," Adriana continued. "Throughout its length, Serena repeats the same words over and over. 'I am scared. I am scared,' until near the end."

The child looked directly into the camera. She was bawling, her tiny shoulders rising and falling with each new sob. "Mom-ma, Mom-ma." The girl spoke a few more words in Spanish.

"Where are you, mother?" she asks.

Jennie was crying softly now. Paul's hand squeezed down tight on hers.

The reporter appeared before the camera once more. "Earlier today, I showed this recording to a ranking official of Customs and Border Patrol. He refused to comment. Stephen."

"Adriana," the anchorman replied, then hesitated for a long breath. "A child—" he finally said. That was as far as he got. For the next five seconds, an age in the business, he said nothing. Then, "We will be back in a moment."

For an instant the only sound was Jennie's weeping.

"Goddammit!" Paul exploded from his chair. "What kind of worthless piece of—of—Heartless bastards! God damn them all!"

His hands clenched into fists, he spun about, wild eyed and crazy, looking for something. Spying the TV remote beside the pizza box, he snatched it up and sent it flying toward the television. He missed high. The remote shattered against the wall.

"How in God's name can you do a baby like that? I hope they all burn in hell!"

He went storming back and forth as he cursed. Suddenly he stopped before the end table next to his recliner. He looked down at the family picture on its polished surface. For a moment Paul simply stood there shaking. Without warning, he snatched the picture up in his fist, raised it above his head—"

"No!"

Jennie was suddenly clawing at his arm, grabbing for the picture, screaming hysterically as he held it just out of her reach.

"Paul, stop it! Stop it! Please God, make him stop! Oh, please God," she begged, at last melting down onto her knees. She reached out, wrapped her arms around Paul's legs.

A long minute passed. Paul continued standing over her, his face red with rage, holding the picture above his head. Slowly, his fit of madness began to wane. At last, he lowered his arm, took a long look at the photo of the three of them, softly touched a fingertip to Sarah's image. Gently taking Jennie's right hand, he peeled it away from his legs, then pressed the picture frame against her palm. She instantly grasped it with both hands. Cradling the picture tight against her heart, she collapsed onto her side, her back turned to him.

"Oh God, please," she moaned.

Paul dropped to his knees beside her. He reached out to stroke her hair. Jennie responded by drawing up into a fetal position. For several minutes he remained on his knees, waiting for his wife's moans to cease. They eventually came further apart, until at long last they stopped. He paused a moment longer to make certain. Then he began to work his way to his feet. Grasping the chair arm beside him, he pulled, struggling to stand upright. All the fire was gone out of him. In its place, the only thing left was the horrid chill of shame.

"I am sorry," he said, his voice low, hollow. "I am so sorry."

Then Paul looked about, seeming to view the room for the first time. After a moment, he stepped out the door. Head hanging, he crept down the porch steps, made his agonizing way across the grass.

In an opulent bedroom many miles to the southeast, a TV remote control protruded from a dead screen.

"Whaa, whaa, whaa. Damn stupid press just won't let it go."

The thinner man still stared at the TV, his face twisted into an ugly snarl. "You tried to tell them," he said. Then, under his breath he added, "They'll learn to listen."

Chapter 14

J ennie stood a few feet out from the porch steps and moved the flashlight's beam slowly around the fringe of the yard. Nothing. She swung the beam along their drive, starting near the garage and sweeping out to the county road. Again nothing. Hardly an hour before, Paul had exploded in rage over the scene on the evening news. And the picture—She had never been so frightened in her life. From the floor she had become vaguely aware of shuffling sounds as he eased out the door. Now the last light brushed a lavender streak along the wooded crest of English Knob, and Paul had still not returned.

"Paul!" Jennie yelled. "Please come in."

She moved toward the road, the fear touching her mind that he had gone off on one of his long walks again. People flew up and down this country lane. It was hard enough to see any distance in broad daylight, with all the tree-lined fencerows walling in the road's shoulders and hiding what was just ahead in any curve. At this hour, seeing someone on foot in time to swerve was literally a hit and miss proposition. Jennie could not help but wonder. Had something happened? Was he hurt?

"Paul! Paul! Come to the house"

Only the crickets answered. Jennie slowly made her way around the border of the yard, her light sending ghostly shadows Druid dancing among the trees, wandering among the tall rows of the cornfield. A breeze, the day's final exhalation, rolled through the dry stalks and leaves, setting them to rattling and scratching against their neighbors—such lonely, lost sounds.

"Paul! Where are you?"

At last Jennie came to the edge of the canebrake. The beam caught the narrow opening where the path to the creek began.

She moved toward it, hesitated a moment, then stepped into the labyrinth. Every few feet she called out for him, but all she heard in return was her own small steps crunching the detritus carpeting the path and the soft rustling of the cane's leaves as she brushed against them. It was a stifling, smothering place, practically a tunnel with the cane arching close overhead and her light tripping through the jumbled stalks. She stopped a minute in, working to keep her breathing under control, and almost turned around. Then in the back of her mind a memory flashed, something Paul had told her he once said to Sarah about the cane being a place of refuge. She moved forward again.

Without warning, a voice! Jennie suddenly emerged into a clearing by the creek. Her light bounced off the water, then settled on a mass. There, at the water's edge, Paul knelt on the damp ground.

"Why, Lord?" he implored, his voice a hoarse moan.

Jennie held back. Paul did not respond to her light, even when she rested the beam on his face. She tried to pray, also, yet her mind could not form a coherent plea. A minute passed, then two, and Paul still knelt, still implored the Lord for an answer. A third minute came and went before Jennie was at last able to whisper.

"Heavenly Father, please lead my husband out of his terrible wilderness."

Chapter 15

J ennie tried to place the remote on the kitchen table. All the wrappings of tape made it so sticky the thing wouldn't let go. It clung to the skin of her slender fingers until it at last slowly dropped one end, then the other, as if reluctant to part ways. Sometime earlier—she couldn't have said exactly when—she had crawled over the floor on her hands and knees, gathering the shattered pieces of the device. For an age she had painstakingly taped it back together. She felt no sense of amazement when it worked, as anyone else might. Her mind was too numb for that. Memories of the awful night continued to swirl across her vision, tightening her stomach until it cramped. The most painful sight of all, Paul still kneeling at the water's edge as she left him.

After a while, she started flipping channels again. She stopped punching the buttons when she came to the Weather Channel. She had seen the forecast enough times by now to have it memorized, yet she couldn't have answered a thing about high temperature or low, rain or sun or wind. The pictures, the charts, the muted voices of the forecasters were simply company, comforting, like a pet dog softly snoring at her feet. Jennie leaned forward and rested her head on her folded arms on the tabletop, closed her eyes and slept.

Paul had been on his feet for a few minutes. The sun was up high enough to send narrow fans of light sweeping low through gaps in the cane. He felt stiff and sore, as if he had tumbled down a rocky slope. The discomfort was greatest in his knees. Almost as troublesome was the way his skin felt. It seemed there was not a single square inch that didn't demand to be scratched. Raising the flat of his hand to a cheek, he felt the bumps and whelps of bites too numerous to count.

57

He squatted on the creekbank and scooped up a double handful of water, splashed it on his face. The coolness gave a tiny touch of relief.

Such was the state of his physical being. More important was the newfound state of his emotional being. A short while ago, in that moment when the faintest wash of pink touched the rim of the eastern sky and the deep blue just above it subtly shifted to a lighter shade, he had heard the voice. There was no mistaking it, no mistaking what was expected. For the first time since Sarah's death, he knew with certainty the path before him. The knowledge brought peace to the long, wrenching evening. It was time to return to the house and share the news with Jennie. First, however, he must seek her forgiveness.

† † †

Jennie pushed up from the chair, trying to rub the sleep from her eyes, and ambled out onto the porch. She would wait here for Paul. Turning, she eased over to the glider and took a seat. The entrance to the path through the cane was in plain sight there. Soon, her lids drooped again in response to the birds' early morning songs, sweet as any lullaby.

Her eyes flew open at the sound of a creaking board. For a moment she was confused. Then she saw Paul standing there, a few steps away.

"I am so sorry," he said, his voice hoarse.

Jennie did not want to look him in the eye. She simply turned her head and stared out across the yard for a long moment before answering.

"You ought to be." She allowed seconds to tick by before adding. "You scared me to death."

"I lost my mind."

"Yes, you did."

"Jennie, if I could only take it back, you know I—" he cut short his apology. She had raised her hand in a signal for him to stop.

"We both lost our minds because we saw the same thing. We saw our Sarah there in the face of that beautiful child and went crazy. In our place, who wouldn't?"

Paul could only nod. They remained quiet for a short spell; their pain too sharp to allow anything else. Jennie finally spoke.

"I took you for better or worse, Paul, and I will stand by my word until the day I die, but I will tell you one thing. I did not expect my promise to include some of the language that came out of your mouth last night. Though you said things I agree with, God help me, I ask you to remember you are a minister. Please step outside, very far outside, if you ever again feel the urge to let loose with such vile." She paused a few seconds. "I will not have you scorching the finish off our furniture."

It took a moment for her final words to register. Then Paul stepped forward to stand close before her, the beginnings of a smile lifting the corners of his mouth. Jennie turned her head fully toward him for the first time.

"My goodness, Paul! What happened to your face? You look awful."

Paul hesitated. "Critters found me. I think the mosquitoes were calling in relatives from the next county. I look pretty rough, huh?"

"I don't know how to describe it. It's like you caught measles from a porcupine."

"Hmmm. I look bad enough to run you off?"

"Not a chance."

Jennie rose from the glider. They didn't kiss. It was not a time for kissing. It was a time to embrace and embrace they did, as if either were to let go both would surely drown. At last, each pulled back a little, so that their hands held on at the other's elbows. Leaning their heads forward, they finally shared a quick kiss, a *good morning I love you kiss*; the kind that always started their day.

Finally, Jennie released her hold and started to move away.

"Wait a minute, hon," Paul said, his fingers tightening around her arms. "I need to tell you something."

"Yes?"

"Let's sit down first."

On the glider, each half turned toward the other, Paul took one of her hands in his. Without any preamble, he simply launched into what he had to say.

"The Lord spoke to me last night."

"Okay," she answered after a few seconds' pause. Her expression was attentive, serious. It was not the first time he had said something like that to her.

"He called me to do something."

Jennie took a breath in slowly. This was more than hearing the voice of the Lord offering words of comfort or forgiving one's sins. In their faith, being called by God to do something was expected. It was not an everyday thing, and certainly not a small thing, for it meant God had issued an instruction to do His bidding in a specific way. They had still been dating when Paul was called to preach. She well remembered that time, how he looked when he explained it to her. The same look of certainty, of peace, about what he must do was in his eyes now.

"What?" she whispered.

For the next few minutes, he spoke. Jennie listened in rapt attention, not interrupting.

"It explains so much, don't you see?" Paul said, winding down.

"Yes—yes, I think so." She wanted to say more, though she felt too tired to fully grasp his words, yet she knew she had heard him quite plainly. She wanted to say that perhaps, somehow, he had misunderstood, even exaggerated the call, but she knew it was not the case. Paul was too certain. She wanted to say surely another could do this, yet she felt from deep inside her soul Paul was the one chosen. The idea frightened her, for Paul, for herself. It would be a tremendous test of love and faith for them both.

"You are with me on this, aren't you?"

"Of course," she answered immediately, shoving her doubts and worries down so hard she thought she might choke on them. Neither said anything for a minute, the weight, the import of what they had discussed stifling any further words. At last, Jennie spoke again. "When are you going to tell the church?"

"I'll call a business meeting after services tomorrow; tell them then."

"We have a potluck dinner set for after church. Remember?"

"Yes, of course. I won't keep them but a minute or two. It shouldn't take longer."

"So, this will start soon?"

"A week perhaps. No more. The seasons will not wait."

"We have much to do."

"Yes," Paul nodded.

Jennie quietly thought for a few moments. She tried to imagine the solitude, the loneliness, for them both; the seeming physical impossibility of the task before him. Her fatigue was such, however, she could not fully wrap her mind around her thoughts. The time for those worries would come soon enough, she reasoned. Now was the time to accept and believe, to gather the strength to act. When she spoke once more her tone was the opposite of what it had been.

"First things first," she commanded. "You are filthy dirty, you smell like roadkill, and you've got a million bug bites. Get in there and take a hot shower, then I'll paint the worst spots with calamine lotion. After that, I'll get my bath—feel like I've been wallowing in mud, myself—and both of us will get some sleep. When we get up, we'll start working on whatever we need to do."

Paul simply smiled in response.

"Hop to it," she ordered.

"I love you," he said, leaning forward to kiss her.

"I love you, too," she replied after their lips touched briefly, grasping his arm and working to lever him upright. "And scrub under those fingernails. Enough dirt there to plant corn."

Paul laughed softly to himself as he made his way to the door. Jennie watched him impatiently, wishing he would hurry up. As soon as the door snapped to behind him, she bowed her head. Sometimes she just couldn't wait to pray.

Chapter 16

Jennie awoke to the sound of Paul's voice. She was groggy, though, and unable to make out what he was saying. She stretched as far as she could stretch, her forearms grating across the headboard, toes digging at the sheet. That perked her up a little, though she still couldn't understand Paul's words. *Why can't I get going this morning?* she thought. *It's late. The sun's up. Sarah! Better check on her.* She had no more than swung her legs off the bed when reality hit. *My baby's gone!*

It took her a moment to get to her feet, weighed down as she suddenly was by the awful knowledge. She turned to glance at the alarm clock on Paul's side of the bed. The LED display read 3:00. How could that be? Then the memory of their early morning conversation came rushing back. Now it was 3:00 in the afternoon! At last, she made her way into the bathroom. Once she had a chance to freshen up, there was work to be done, and questions, no doubt, she had not yet even imagined to be answered.

A few minutes later she came walking into the kitchen.

"Heard you talking," Jennie said.

"Did I wake you?" Paul asked, rising from his seat at the table to meet her. "Sorry. I was trying to hold it down."

"It's okay," she said, leaning in to touch lips in a quick kiss. "I just can't seem to get going."

"Let me fix you a cup of coffee," Paul offered.

"No. You never get it right; it's either too sweet or not enough cream or something. I'll get my own. Thanks for offering, though," she added, softening her complaints with a quick smile.

She stepped to the counter. Her cup was already by the coffee pot. After a minute she had it filled, the contents doctored with creamer and Sweet'n Low to suit her. She lifted the cup and took a sip, then turned back to face him, cradling the cup in her hands.

"Did you clean up in here?" she asked, looking about the room. "I thought we left some of that pizza on the table."

Paul nodded. "We left the cheesecake out, too. No problem. I took care of everything. It didn't take but a minute. I was starving, so I ate what was left of the pizza—not but a couple of pieces—and then I had dessert. Best cheesecake I ever tasted."

"Oh, you did not."

"Did so. Surely you don't think I'd lie."

"Well, if you ate it, we better run to the E. R. and get your stomach pumped. And if you are lying, you should get right with the Lord in a hurry, before He slings a bolt of lightning straight through that halo on your head."

"Hmmm. Think you've got me," he admitted, stepping around her to the coffee pot. "Truth is, I threw everything in the garbage. Hogs wouldn't touch that smelly pizza. Now the cheesecake, I almost tried it, but then I chickened out. Never had any with green-fuzz icing."

"Oooh!" she said, managing to giggle a little. "Thank you for telling the truth, I think."

After refilling his cup, he turned back to face her.

"Want to go out on the porch? Sit in the glider? There's a good air stirring."

"Sure."

Moments later they were in their usual spots. It was warm, though the breeze made it comfortable. For a few minutes they were content to rock back and forth while they sipped at their coffee, the dry rattle of leaves in the cornfield and the birds' songs making a comforting background. At last, Jennie took her final little swallow. She placed the empty cup on the end table beside her, then spoke.

"You never did say who you were talking to. Not a secret, I hope."

"Lord, no," Paul shook his head. "I was on the phone with Bruce MacDonald."

"Oh, yes. The Scotsman."

"I don't know about that. He is from Glasgow, but it's Glasgow, Kentucky, not Scotland."

"With all that red hair and those ruddy cheeks, all he needs is a kilt." Jennie smiled. "So, what did you and your old seminary buddy have to talk about? Bet I can guess."

"Bet you can, too. As luck would have it—" Paul hesitated. "Maybe it's not luck at all," he said, his voice suddenly dropping. Then, speaking at his normal volume, he continued, "Bruce's been filling in over at Carters Chapel for a spell while their minister recovered from surgery. Now their minister is back on his feet, so Bruce is available. Said he'd be glad to fill in for me."

"Wonderful. Everyone already knows him since he led the revival. I'm certain he will be welcome."

"Me, too," Paul agreed. "That's a big worry lifted. He's coming over tomorrow, just to talk things over."

"Good."

Neither said anything more as Jennie examined her empty coffee cup. Both were thinking about the coming conversation. Jennie went back inside the kitchen after a few minutes and made herself a fresh cup. Returning, she took her seat on the glider once more. She glanced toward Paul, her eyebrows rising in question.

"You want something to eat before we start trying to figure everything out?" Paul asked.

"No. My stomach's a little queasy. I'll fix some toast or whatever in a bit."

"Sure?"

"Yes. Let's get started. I see you've been making a few notes." She flashed a smile, nodding at the legal pad on his lap. The page was covered with scribblings.

"Yeah, I have." He grinned. "Okay then. Well, I guess the first thing—"

"Just a second, Paul," Jennie said, reaching to cover his hand with hers. Paul looked into her eyes, waiting. "I'm sorry. There's something I need to get out of the way before we start on the details."

Paul waited patiently while she bit her lip, obviously working to arrange her thoughts. At last she spoke again.

"I know this is going to be challenging in ways we cannot imagine. It will test our faith at times, I'm sure."

"Undoubtedly." Paul nodded, encouraging her to go on.

"It will also test our marriage."

Her eyes locked on his. He was surprised to see them brimming with moisture, the tears threatening to spill. He was more surprised by her words. They left him ashamed. She was right. Terrific stresses on their relationship were bound to arise, and he had scarcely given the idea a thought.

"Yes, it will be hard on us," he finally managed to say. "Our faith will carry us through, however."

"I know." Jennie flashed a smile. "And I know that is what you, the preacher, *should* say. Well, this is what I, the preacher's wife, have to say. My faith is unshakeable. So is my belief in you. Sometimes, though, it doesn't hurt to have a few ground rules. This is one of those times."

"Okay," Paul said, wondering where she was headed.

Leaning toward him, Jennie reached across with her free hand and took his, so that their hands formed a loose knot between them. "I will do my best to visit whenever I can, no matter where you are, and I expect us to stay in touch every day."

"I would certainly hope so on both counts," Paul answered emphatically.

Jennie straightened her back. "I'm not finished. *Hope* won't get it. If the best you can do during the day is text or message me, that's okay. We will both be busy. Before I lay my head on the pillow at night, though, I expect to hear your voice. I don't care how you do it, whether you have to climb a telephone pole and tap the wires or throw a lasso around a satellite. Whatever. Each and every day I want—I need—to hear you say, *I love you.*"

Paul hesitated too long.

"Is that too much to ask?" Jennie said, canting her head slightly to one side.

"No. No, it absolutely is not," he rushed his reply. "You have my word. I need to hear you say the same thing."

"And you will," Jennie stated, her expression blooming into her first genuine smile of the day. "Over and over and over again."

They leaned forward and kissed, sealing their agreement. Then each settled back in their spot and allowed their hands to slide apart.

Jennie took a sip of her coffee, then spoke. "Alright. Now that we have that straight, what's at the top of your list?"

"Let's talk about you and things around here first. Okay?"

"Suits me."

"I've already checked the weather for the week. It's supposed to be dry throughout, so I should be able to get the corn in, if nothing breaks down. Ought to have done it already."

"You've had other things on your mind," Jennie said, her tone soft, understanding, as she thought of their daughter.

"And I'll at least get the hay rolled. Won't take more than a day. Henry was aiming to buy it all. He can come get it out of the field, himself, if I don't get it over to his place in time. That should hold things on the farm for a spell. Glad we sold the cattle off. You've got our nest egg from that, if you need it."

"Yes," Jennie nodded. "I almost forgot. We had to let them go, of course. The price was up, and Sarah had already given each one a name. Then when she heard people ate them… Oh my."

"Still feel bad about telling her we were sending them to a special home."

"It's alright," Jennie said, laying her hand on his arm. "It was a white lie told to keep from breaking her heart."

Several moments passed quietly, both remembering, before Paul spoke.

"Anyway, you've got that money to fall back on if you need it."

"I'm not worried about me, Paul. We're caught up on everything, and between the money from the cattle and my salary, I can cover the monthly expenses. You will need some money, though."

"Not much. The Lord will provide."

Jennie simply stared at him for a moment. Suddenly, she pushed to her feet. "Come in here," she said, striding through the doorway.

Paul followed seconds later. In her hands, Jennie held the big cookie jar she kept on top of the refrigerator. She placed it on the kitchen table and removed the lid. She reached a hand in and came out with a fistful of coupons.

"Surely you don't expect me to use those?"

"Don't be silly. Sit down, please," she commanded.

Paul took a seat at the table as he was told. Jennie kept digging out handfuls of coupons, building a small mountain of paper next to the cookie jar. All at once she stopped. Her hand remained hidden in the jar.

"Well there, Dan'l Boone, has it even crossed your mind what you might eat, or where you might sleep?"

"It doesn't take much to feed me. I'm kind of on the skinny side as it is. And as to where I might sleep, I've still got my old sleeping bag out in the garage somewhere. I'll take it."

"For heaven's sakes. You eat like a horse, and for a man that checks the weather every day, I can't believe you don't know sleeping on the ground when its pouring rain is hazardous to your health. Here."

She dropped a small, fat envelope on the table in front of him. It was one of those used for offerings at the church. Confused, he just sat there looking at it.

"Go on. Open it," Jennie said.

Tentatively, Paul slid a hand forward, picked the envelope up and turned the flap back. Then he shook the contents out. A wad of bills and coins spilled onto the table.

"Count it if you want," Jennie said, "but I can promise you there's three hundred and four dollars and eighty-seven cents. I've been saving since last Christmas, a dollar here, a quarter there. I intended to buy you a new suit this year, and some nice ties. You've been wearing that same suit since your first sermon. Looks like a flour sack. And your ties… I wouldn't use those raveled-out things to hang a polecat. Anyway, there's a more important use for this now."

Paul continued to stare at the money for half a minute more, touched by her efforts to save, knowing she wasn't exaggerating much about his preaching clothes. Finally, he looked up to meet Jennie's gaze.

"I don't know what to say."

"Then I will tell you." Jennie smiled. "You will promise me that you will not sleep in the mud every time it rains, and when you are hungry you will eat. I don't care if it's a bologna sandwich and a MoonPie."

Paul got to his feet and stepped toward her. Taking her in his arms he said, "I promise. Thank you."

For a long while they held each other. As they broke apart at last, Jennie happened to glance at the legal pad on the table where Paul had dropped it. She reached over, picked it up, and read the handwritten numbers aloud.

"*1,285 – 1,285.*" Looking at Paul, she asked, "What's this?"

"Oh, just out of curiosity I checked on how many miles it is from here to Brownsville, and then from Brownsville on down to Guatemala City. Same distance either way. Kind of hard to believe that's a coincidence."

After a moment, Jennie nodded in agreement. For the first time since Paul had told her of the calling, Jennie knew with certainty the Divine Hand was guiding him. Here was confirmation.

Chapter 17

T he service closed with "The Old Rugged Cross."

No one came forward this morning during the invitational. Preacher Paul cut the hymn short after only one verse.

"In concluding our message today, I remind you of the words of Jesus: *Suffer little children, to come unto me.* Now, let us join in a moment of silent prayer."

Preacher Paul bowed his head, and the members of the con- gregation bowed theirs. Thirty seconds into the stillness Preacher Paul began speaking aloud.

"Heavenly Father, we thank You for the blessing of children. We thank You for the joy their laughter brings, for the purity of heart revealed in their innocence, for the privilege of being able to watch them grow and learn. Most of all, Father, we thank You for the unconditional love they so readily give, for in this it is they who become the teachers, showing us what we should feel for You, what we should feel for one another. We ask that You forever keep this knowledge in the forefront of our minds so we, in turn, may always show that same unconditional love to our children, to all children, for in this way we shall multiply Your blessings a thousand-fold. In Your name, Father. Amen."

"Amen," the members echoed.

A few hands immediately dug into purses for tissues or pockets for a handkerchief. All had no doubt that Preacher Paul's words, both in his prayer and his sermon, had come out of pain from the loss of his daughter. It was the most he had revealed to them of his feelings since Sarah's funeral.

Paul looked at Jennie. She gave him a dry-eyed wink, for she was determined to control her emotions on this day. He smiled back. Her strength gave him the strength he needed to hold it together. Still, he waited a moment for those who had dabbed at damp eyes to regain their composure. He risked only glances at these individuals until he saw the handkerchiefs and tissues begin to disappear. At last he spoke.

"As I said earlier, we need to convene a business meeting. I promise it will be short. I am acutely aware there is a ton of food ready to be served at our pot-luck dinner. Fortunately for all, my growling stomach will not let me ramble on for long."

He moved half a step forward, so his mid-section pressed against the back edge of the pulpit. Then he leaned over the top, his hands clutching the pulpit's sides. He needed the support, especially to get through the first part of what he had to say. It would be the hardest.

"My dear friends," he began, allowing his gaze to slowly sweep across the assembly, "as you can tell from my words this morning, I have been thinking much about children. Of course, Sarah is never far from our minds. Jennie and I shall forever mourn our loss."

He looked straight at Jennie. Her facial expression was determined, almost stern. Her gaze meeting his, she nodded once.

"Throughout this time of trial, there has not been a moment when we did not feel your prayers. Indeed, I know I can speak for her when I say, we feel them this very instant. We thank you and ask God's blessings upon you.

"We know how fortunate we are to live here, to be surrounded by such wonderful friends. It is evident to us that you, too, have shared in our suffering, for Sarah loved all and was loved by all in return. It is more than a father's pride—it is my steadfast belief—when I say she helped lead us to understand we are all but one family."

Jennie nodded emphatically a couple of times as he paused. The moment of quiet stretched out until several members began to glance about at others in the congregation, wondering if the preacher was done. Suddenly he looked up toward the ceiling. The symbolism was inescapable as he continued to stare at the rafters: he was looking to God for inspiration, or strength. At last, he brought his eyes down to sweep out over the pews.

"Friday night is pizza night in our house. This past Friday evening Jennie and I were at our kitchen table having pizza, as usual. The national news was on the TV. Jennie got up to get the cheesecake for dessert—yes, cheesecake. And yes, we know our Friday suppers may not be the healthiest of meals, but they sure are good," the preacher said, smiling.

Many of the members smiled back in agreement, glad for the break in the tension.

"Anyway, this reporter was down at the southern border, in Brownsville, Texas, talking about a little girl from Guatemala. The child's name was Serena. She was barefoot. Her dress was dirty. She was standing on a bare concrete floor behind a chain-link fence. The enclosure reminded me of the pens where many of you men here keep your hunting dogs."

The preacher waited a moment, allowing his words to sink in.

"Now, I must tell you, Jennie and I looked at that child, and we saw our Sarah. We saw her standing there alone and afraid. You see, Serena has been separated from her parents—deliberately separated, per *our* government's policy—since her family came across the border. All Serena could say, over and over, was, 'I am scared. I am scared.' When she started crying for her mother, I lost it. I lost my mind."

Once more, the preacher paused a moment. Once more, he looked to Jennie to steady himself.

"I was angry beyond measure; angrier than I have ever been in my life. Instead of asking the Lord to remove the scales from the eyes of those responsible, to show them the error of their ways, I begged Him to damn them all. I screamed at Him to burn them in hell.

"I cursed. I ranted and raved. I broke things. The greatest thing I broke was Jennie's heart—a heart that has scarcely had a chance to heal."

The preacher looked toward his wife. She could not meet his gaze and for a moment bowed her head. When she looked up again, her expression was even more determined than before. She mouthed, "It's okay."

A single hot tear suddenly broke from the corner of the preacher's right eye, challenging his ability to keep his composure. He pulled a handkerchief from the inside pocket of his jacket and dabbed the tear away. Then he looked out across the congregation once more, ready to proceed. Seeing that handkerchiefs and tissues were once more out in force with the members, he paused a few moments before speaking. When he started, his words came softly in a matter-of-fact recitation.

"I spent Friday night wandering in the wilderness, I guess you could say, stumbling through the patch of cane down from our house, slipping and sliding and sometimes falling along the banks of the creek. The Lord did not let me go unpunished for my transgressions. He sent about a million mosquitoes and who knows what other kinds of creatures to poke holes in my flesh," he explained with a quick smile. "When the first rays of dawn cut through, I was on my knees there at the creekbank, worn out and burnt out. I tried to pray, but I'll be honest, it was a poor effort. The words would not come. Finally, I said, 'I am Yours, Father. Use me.'

"In that very instant I heard a voice. It took me a moment to realize that the voice was not speaking into my ears, but through my heart, as it had when I was called to preach. My friends, the Lord has called me again. I am to go to Brownsville, Texas, to pray for the children. He has given me only one other requirement for this journey. As Serena walked from Guatemala to Texas, I am to walk all the way from here in Kentucky. I will be leaving in about a week."

Stunned. That was the only way to describe the looks on the faces of the individual members. After a moment, murmurs began to rise from the pews. The preacher decided to push on before control was lost.

"Okay. I've said all that to lay out the reason for our business meeting. Now, let us get to the actual business portion. I will be gone for several months, which leaves you without a minister. To address that issue, I spoke to our good friend here, Reverend Bruce MacDonald, to see if he could fill in. You know him. He has preached here several times when I was absent for one reason or another, even led our revival a couple of years ago. Now, this kind of situation is all new to me, but I guess we should have a vote or something to approve his taking the reins."

The quiet was suddenly so deep, so pervasive, the preacher hesitated to say more. In that interlude, the sharp sounds of knees popping came to fill the space as Deacon Henry Jackson rose to his feet.

"If you're about to cast a *no* vote, Henry, let me ask Brother Bruce to step outside," the preacher grinned. "I don't want to hurt his feelings."

Deacon Henry stared back at the preacher so long Elsie finally spoke up, her voice crackling across the room. "Well, get on with it, old man. We're all getting hungry."

"Oh, all right," Henry said, shaking his head at Elsie, but grateful for the ripple of laughter rolling through the congregation. "Far as I'm concerned, I reckon he'll do. Anybody got a problem with this MacDonald fella, time to speak up."

A chorus of *he's a good one* and *glad to have him* rose from the group. Most of those who remained silent at least nodded their approval.

"Very well then, Brother Bruce," the deacon grinned. "Sounds like you've got the job. Proud to welcome you, and I'm especially proud to have a man up front there who can sing."

The congregation burst into laughter this time, loud and prolonged, the members glad for the chance. Laughing loudest were Jennie and Paul. As everyone quieted down, Henry began speaking once more.

"Good. That issue is settled; but that's not why I got up. I didn't aim to call for a vote. Now preacher," he said, focusing on Paul, "don't get me wrong when you hear what I've got to say next. I've been fortunate enough to have the Lord speak to me—several times. I'm not questioning your receiving the word. I would never question that of a single soul, but I've got to ask—and I think most of us may feel sort of the same—walking all the way to Texas? Have you lost your mind?"

A loud *pop* echoed across the sanctuary, followed by an even louder wave of laughter. Elsie had smacked Henry on his butt. Now he was glaring down at her as he rubbed his wounded cheek. Preacher Paul was laughing, too. He waited for the commotion to completely die down before answering.

"Henry, I am not at all certain about my sanity, but the walking was not my idea."

The older man stared at the preacher for a long while before nodding his head. "There's nothing to argue over then, I reckon. Therefore, I move we declare this meeting adjourned. Time to eat."

"Amen," most of the members responded.

†††

Amid the bustle and chatter as people made their way to the front of the sanctuary to take Paul and Jennie by their hands, no one noticed that Tick Cole remained seated rigidly upright on his pew. The church was all but empty when he at last nodded sharply once, as if in agreement. Then he pushed to his feet and made his way toward the door.

Across the space, Cami stared straight ahead. She had remained seated when her parents made their way into the aisle. Now the hint of a smile played at the corners of her mouth as her first transfixing spark began to swell into an idea.

Chapter 18

Paul thought his talk would be enough to answer most of the members' questions. He was wrong. Questions were all he heard after stepping out to the picnic area behind the church. One person after another had approached him. That began thirty minutes ago. The interruptions were such that he was still working on his first plate of food. Now he stood at the end of a row of tables, his plate in one hand and a fried chicken leg in the other, listening to Miss Lucille Kirby. At ninety-six, she was the oldest member of the church. She was seated on the end of the bench to his left. Jennie and Miss Elsie sat facing her.

"Brother Paul, I've been paying attention to what people been saying," Miss Lucille said. "I do not think you'll end up in a feud in Tennessee, nor be eaten alive by fire ants in Mississippi. Bunch of foolishness, ask me. Strikes me there's more important things to worry over, like the way you're going. You can pick up the Natchez Trace at Nashville, you know; follow it all the way to Louisiana. That'd be my choice—less traffic. If my eyes were not acting up, I would drive the Trace again. Did it when I was eighty-nine. Beautiful. Simply beautiful."

The preacher smiled, but inside he cringed. Miss Lucille still raced along these country roads like a bear was after her, often forcing another driver to choose between the ditch and a head-on collision. He had a quick vision of her massive 70s-something Olds roaring through the South, clouds of dust boiling behind, with dogs and chickens and people scrambling for cover.

"Sounds like a good way," he said, skirting the edge of a white lie. He and Jennie, pouring over his atlas the evening before, chose the Trace as the second leg south.

"Went that way to visit my niece in Corpus Christi. Over a

thousand miles. You'll still have a good stretch left, time you get there."

"Yes, ma'am," the preacher nodded, the great distance he must travel giving him reason to pause.

"Anyway, I wouldn't be concerned about a gator dragging me off in Louisiana, long as you don't sleep in a swamp. Eat some of that good Cajun food every chance you get. That'll keep you high stepping. And there's no reason to fret over gunslingers or wild Indians, once you get to Texas, no matter what Cleave Pearson thinks. All you need to do is what it says in Proverbs about trusting in the Lord with all your heart. Do that and He shall direct your path."

"Yes, ma'am, I shall," he nodded, glad of the Biblical reminder. Then Miss Lucille took off on Cleave Pearson.

"Sometimes, I swan, that old man just acts a fool."

The preacher managed to hold back a smile as he took a bite of deviled egg. Mr. Cleave was ninety-five. He had been Miss Lucille's on-again, off-again suitor since they were teenagers, according to Deacon Henry. Apparently, they were off again.

"Last Friday," Miss Lucille continued. "I saw that little darling on the TV, like y'all did. I thought the whole mess was about the craziest thing ever. It's unchristian. How can a little child, a baby, be an illegal anything? What that empty-headed Cleave called her: illegal.

"I will be praying for you the whole way," Miss Lucille added, turning on a dime. Her hand reached out to grasp the preacher's forearm. "We all will; every soul in Caney Creek."

"Absolutely," Elsie joined in. "You are a good man from a good place. The Lord knew what He was doing. The right man got the call."

"Thank you." Preacher Paul smiled. "I feel very humbled."

"And don't you worry about your sweet wife," Miss Elsie added, wrapping an arm around Jennie's shoulders. "We'll take good care of her."

Miss Lucille let go of his arm and reached to take Jennie by the hand. "Yes, we will."

"I'm in good hands," Jennie said, smiling up at him.

"Yes, literally," he answered, smiling back.

The ladies switched abruptly and began discussing the different dishes at the potluck.

"Did you get any of Marian's green-bean casserole?" Elsie asked.

"Oh, that's the best stuff." Miss Lucille rolled her eyes.

The preacher nodded his agreement. He'd managed only a spoonful because of all the questioning. The only food left on his plate now was a serving of Jennie's scalloped potatoes. Poor girl completely forgot and had to go flying around the kitchen to get the dish ready before church. He hesitated to eat his last bite until Jennie glanced up at him. *Delicious*, he mouthed, making certain she saw what was on his fork.

"Excuse me, ladies," the preacher said, "I believe I hear dessert calling."

"All my pecan pie's done gone," Elsie said.

Preacher Paul didn't try to hide his regret, frowning and shaking his head.

"But," she added, lifting a paper napkin from a plate, "I saved you a piece."

"Bless you," he said as Miss Elsie handed him the pie. "I would've been sick if I didn't get some of this."

"And get some of my banana-walnut Jell-O," Miss Lucille said as he turned toward the food tables.

"Oh, I can't forget your Jell-O," the preacher answered, thinking *I wish I could.* To put it kindly, the concoction, which Miss Lucille always fixed, was not highly sought after. *One of the hazards of the job*, Paul mused. He couldn't slight anyone.

As he worked his way along the rows of food, he took a spoonful from each offering he had not yet sampled. His obligation met, he wound up with his plate heaped high. *Well*, he thought as he took a couple of steps to the side, *Grandma always said, 'Do first what you dread the most.'* He managed to nudge a bite of Jell-O off with the edge of his fork. The banana slices were green and hard, the walnuts were somehow mushy, and the Jell-O? *Make truck tires out of this*, he said to himself, trying to chew. He glanced up to see several ladies watching him. They were all doing their best to avoid laughing it seemed, for their smiles were tight-lipped and half hidden by raised hands. *Oops. Must have made a face.*

Paul turned away, his gaze coming to rest on the men. They were formed into a tight group over by the edge of the woods, each with his head bowed. Brother Bruce appeared to be leading them in prayer.

Wonder what that's about? Paul thought. He quickly finished off the heap of samplings, then shoveled the pecan pie in his mouth, one quick bite after another. Moving over beside the rusty trash barrel at last, he tossed the sodden paper plate and empty paper cup.

For a few moments he simply stood there bloating. He briefly considered getting more tea, but he knew there was no room for it. *Lord, I could make it all the way to Texas on that meal,* he thought.

Glancing at the group of men once more, he noticed Henry was waving him over.

The other men moved in to circle him as Paul walked up.

"Preacher, we've been talking about your little stroll, and we figured you might be needing a few things along the way."

"The Lord will provide," Paul answered with certainty.

"Yeah, yeah," Henry acknowledged, holding up his hand for quiet.

"Now," Henry started up again, "we figured you're going to go through maybe two dozen pairs of shoes—not to mention socks and underwear and britches—so we took up a little offering to make sure you're always dressed decent. Can't have you representing us in rags. Here." He extended his hand. There was a wad of cash in it.

"You all don't need to do this." The preacher hesitated, shaking his head. He could see a few $20s mixed in, even the corner of a $50. "I know how hard a dollar comes around here. I've got a little nest egg, and like I said, I truly believe the Lord will provide whatever I need."

Henry leaned forward and grabbed the preacher's wrist. Pressing the cash into the younger man's palm, he said, "Just take the money, Paul. Who do you think told us to give it in the first place?"

When Tick spotted Cami getting something to drink, he wandered over beside her, doing his best to act casual. Though he had seen her in the sanctuary, this was the first time they had been close enough to speak.

"Get enough to eat?" he asked, reaching past her for some iced tea.

"Lord, did I! Feel like I swallowed a basketball."

"Yeah, me too. I'll be glad when I get to where I can breathe."

"Yes," Cami exhaled. "Potlucks and smorgasbords are both dangerous—eat a ton at either—but potlucks are worse. Everything is sooo good. Where do you stop?"

Tick grinned. "I don't have the slightest idea."

They fell quiet, each waiting for the other to make the first move. Tick couldn't hold himself back but half a minute.

"Strange day at church," he managed to say.

"Very much so. The strangest I've ever seen," she added, then paused a moment. "It gave me a lot to think about."

"Sure enough," Tick agreed.

They fell silent again, each a little surprised at feeling so awkward. Then again, they were at a church gathering, so restraint was in order.

"Are you heading back to Western tomorrow?" he finally asked.

"Yes." She frowned. "It's time to put my nose to the grindstone again."

"Too bad. I was hoping, well, like maybe, you know, we could see each other later in the week, before…"

"Before what?" she asked, thinking this suddenly bashful man was actually adorable.

"Before—well—What are you doing Friday night?" he suddenly spat out.

"Oh, I don't know. It depends, I guess."

"Depends on what?" he demanded.

She smiled at him coyly, the sight of her dimples reeling him in like a hooked fish. "On whether you ask me out or not."

The condition, welcome as it was, left him speechless for a moment. He rebounded nicely, though.

"I'm not going to have to get down on my knee, am I?"

"Please don't," she quickly replied, more than a little afraid he might do just that.

"Good." He smiled, having won the point. "I'm still so full, I don't know if I could get back up. Okay then, here goes. Ms. Camilla, would you, uh, anoint me with the pleasure of your company this coming Friday night, say around seven? We could get a burger or a bologna sandwich or something. Maybe catch a movie."

"Anoint?" she smiled back, giggling.

"I don't know where that came from." He chuckled in return. "You know what I mean. Want to go out?"

"Why thank you, kind sir. I would be delighted."

Chapter 19

Marian Cole raised the footrest on her recliner and settled back. The casserole dishes were washed and put away. There was nothing else to do. After such a feast, a nap couldn't be far off, especially with the soft breeze coming through the screen beside her. She turned her head to look out the window. Tick was ambling across the pasture.

Her son had been unusually quiet after they got home, even for him. He had not said a word as he uncharacteristically dried the dishes for her and stowed them in the cabinet. Only then did he speak.

"Think I'll walk some of that food off."

"Okay, hon. I'll be in my chair. Probably be asleep in two seconds."

At the screen door he hesitated, then turned back to face her. She was untying her apron. He waited until she hung it on a wall hook.

"They were all bragging on your casserole. It made me proud."

For a moment Marian didn't say anything. Compliments were not the norm for her son.

"I'm tickled," she finally answered.

"I could have eaten it all myself, but I didn't want to start a fuss over not leaving anything for everybody else."

With that he spun around and went out the door, leaving her happily perplexed. Now she snuggled deeper into the cushioned chair. The breeze felt so good. Marian closed her eyes.

"You know I'll make it up to y'all."

Tick's voice interrupted her slumber, but where was he, and who was he talking to?

"I really appreciate it, brother."

The snap of a dry stick made her realize she had overheard

her son as he walked past the window. Seconds later came the familiar muffled bang of the screen door in the kitchen. Footsteps approached.

"Mama, you awake?"

Marian turned her head to see Tick standing before the sofa. He sat down on the front edge.

"What is it, hon?"

Clasping his hands together, he leaned forward and rested his elbows on his knees. Though his posture signaled he was troubled, anxious, his expression was—peaceful? At ease? She levered the footrest down and twisted around to face him.

"I want to talk about the preacher, you know, going to the border and all."

"Okay," Marian nodded, at a loss as to where this might lead. "What's on your mind?"

"I'm going with him."

Marian thought she might faint. After a few seconds, her mind came back around enough to prompt a reply. All she managed was, "Good."

"You okay, Mama?"

Marian tried to say more. She finally got out, "Oh my." After a brief pause, she added, "You really caught me off guard."

"Yeah, I was afraid of that, but I didn't know how to do anything other than just tell it. You're not upset, are you?"

"No. No, I'm not upset," Marian answered, brushing a stray strand of hair from her forehead. She could feel a swelling in her chest, a sense of pride, of relief, for her son.

"Don't worry about me being gone. I just got off the phone with 'em ole boys. They'll take care of the farm."

She smiled broadly at his name for his older cousins in Merry Oaks. When he was little, Tick had trouble saying the town's name. It would come out as Wherry Oats. Eventually, he shortened it to "M. O." The three older cousins soon became, "'em ole boys." They still called him, "little brother," never mind that he was the largest member of the group.

"One of them will stop by to check on you every day."

"It won't be necessary. I'll get along just fine."

"Done settled," Tick cut her off. "Like Silas said, they wouldn't have it any other way. They think of you as their own mother."

Marian could only smile again, knowing that was how her nephews felt, thinking of how proud her late sister would have been.

After a moment she switched topics. "That's a long way to walk." It surprised her how easily she had accepted Tick's intent. "Half the country. We'll have to get you some hiking—"

"We don't have to get me anything, Mama. I'm driving. I figured on taking Daddy's old van. It still runs okay. Change the oil and it's good to go. The way I see it, I'll scout ahead, find places to eat and stay. When the weather gets bad, Preacher will have a place to take cover."

"Silas said they'd chip in on gas," Tick continued. "They're calling it their tithe. And I've still got some of Daddy's insurance money. I was aiming to buy some calves, but this seems more important."

Marian nodded her head slowly in agreement. After a moment she said, "Sounds like between the preacher and your cousins, y'all have everything figured out."

"Preacher Paul doesn't know yet."

Marian's smile vanished.

"I thought I would tell him this evening," he explained. "You want to go with me?"

"Sure. I imagine there's plenty to talk over."

Silence settled over them as each sought questions yet unasked and answers yet unimagined. After a couple of minutes, Marian spoke again.

"I'll miss you, son, but like you said, this is important. Your daddy would be proud of you."

Tick looked uncomfortable. Half a minute passed before he spoke.

"I haven't done anything to be proud of, Mama. I was just sitting there listening to the preacher when all these questions started popping into my head. The answers would come half a second later. Kind of spooky. Then I got this feeling that me going was, well, right. It wasn't something I asked to do. It was like I didn't have a choice. Like I was being sent."

Marian's features froze in surprised wonder. After a moment her smile returned. Tears began to trickle down her cheeks, joyful tears, as she thought about how often she had prayed for the day when the Lord would touch her son.

Monday, 5:16 p.m.

Cami walked out of the office of the last professor on her list and turned left, her footsteps echoing loudly in the empty hallway. She turned again at the stairs. At the first landing she stopped and leaned back against the wall. She could finally exhale.

Cami had been on campus since 7:00 a.m. when she made her first stop at her advisor's office. She knew Ms. Graham always came in early. Cami caught her at the door. The advisor grabbed a cup of coffee first, then listened patiently to her explanation of why she needed to withdraw. She quickly saw the student had a unique opportunity, one that would greatly enhance her education. Ms. Graham promised her enthusiastic support. Then she quickly laid out the best way to approach each of Cami's four professors, predicting rightly, that old Dr. Harmon would be the most reluctant to allow her to withdraw without impacting her grade.

Journalism professor Cal Wetherton was Cami's next stop. He instantly saw the potential, even the need, for what she intended to do. He promised to arrange for her to get credit, calling it a self-designed study. She began to wonder if he was ready to go himself as his suggestions started to pour out: talk to the editor of the school paper; visit every newspaper office, television and radio station on the way; never go more than two days without blogging; advertise where they would be and when, then interview those who showed up.

Cami had been on the paper's staff her junior year. Her blogs still ran often in it as columns. Local media outlets were something she had not thought much about, however. As the professor explained, one of the best ways to become a good interviewer was to be interviewed oneself. She should also be there when anyone else related to the story was being interviewed, especially *the man*. And finally, he suggested asking people if they believed in what the preacher was doing? Unearthing the *why* was the real story.

The next two instructors were not nearly as enthusiastic, though both saw enough merit in her plan to promise her GPA was safe. Then she went to see Dr. Grantlee Harmon.

He made her wait an hour before wordlessly ushering her in with a curt wave. Dr. Harmon had enjoyed tenure since Babe Ruth was a baby, it was claimed on campus. Looking at his gruff expression, Cami wondered if the white haired, old man was yet capable of smiling, providing, of course, he had once been capable. For ten minutes his expression never changed as Cami explained her intentions. Then she came to the point of the meeting. Could she withdraw without harming her grades?

Dr. Harmon offered no sign of interest as he sat stone-faced, staring at her. At last, he spoke in that great gravelly voice of his, the precise words coming slowly.

"I expect you to re-enroll in this class immediately upon your return."

"That's my intention," Cami nodded. "I've come too far not to complete my education."

"Your GPA shall not suffer," Dr. Harmon said.

"Thank you, Doctor," Cami replied. "I sincerely appreciate it." Proffering her hand, she rose to leave. He made no move to reciprocate, however. After an awkward moment, she turned toward the door. The creaking of knees long worn out, made her glance back. The doctor was on his feet.

"I am envious," he said, extending his hand. "Godspeed, Camilla."

"Oh my," Cami said, gently shoving the large bowl to the side. "That was delicious."

"Ready for dessert?" Tick asked.

"Are you kidding? I can't touch another bite."

Tick was not kidding. His prime rib was gone. So was his baked potato and house salad. Two slabs of Texas toast had also disappeared. Now if someone would just bring him a piece of pie with ice cream he could get where he needed to be. Something told him it would not be wise to devour any of that, though, while Cami sat without a crumb before her. *This acting like a gentleman stuff sucks,* he thought, his eye landing on a couple of bites of grilled chicken left atop her rabbit food. With an effort he looked up to meet her gaze. Seeing those sparkling green eyes made him forget food. Then she smiled.

It took him several seconds to formulate something to say. Finally, he managed, "Uh, Friday night's always crowded at the movies." Then he glanced at his watch. "I guess we've still got plenty of time, though." Meeting her eyes again, he momentarily forgot what he had said seconds before. Cami bailed him out.

"Why don't we just sit here and talk for a few minutes?"

His mind barked, *Talk? About what?* He was suddenly nervous.

"There's something I need to tell you," she continued, leaning toward him a bit.

"Oh, okay then," he replied, remembering. "I have something to tell you, too."

"You first," she smiled.

"No, you."

"Alright," she said, reaching for her glass, her fingers brushing lightly against his hand. She took a quick sip and began. "I'm so excited."

Tick concentrated on his breathing. Her touch, that spark, thinned the air to nothing. She was saying something.

"Huh?" he grunted.

"I'll be sending out a blog every few days, and interviewing all sorts of people, and maybe even being on TV sometimes, just like a real reporter. Imagine, following along with Preacher Paul all the way to the Mexican border."

That got through, especially the part about following the preacher. Tick sat there slack jawed, not saying a word, knowing his life had just become incredibly complicated.

"Tick? Tick, did you not hear what I said? I'm going to Texas with the preacher."

He stared straight into her eyes for several seconds before nodding. "Yeah. I heard you plain enough. I'm going, too."

Chapter 20

There was barely enough light to see as Paul slowly traced the letters on the stone's face with his fingertips: S-A-R-A-H. Once he finished, Paul and Jennie each reached out a hand, found the other, bowed their heads.

That had been half an hour ago. Now Paul stood on the bench seat of a picnic table on the grounds where a week earlier the members had held their potluck dinner. It was Sunday again, minutes before 7:00 in the morning. In a short while he would start his journey. A thick fog lay low across the bottomland of Caney Creek, enveloping the adults so that only their heads and shoulders were clearly visible, as if they were living hatpins stuck in an enormous layering of fresh cotton. Parents held smaller children on their hips or shoulders so the little ones could see. A handful of older kids stood atop the trunk of a great oak felled in a late summer storm.

It was that time of year for morning fogs to fill the creek bottoms and sinks, to guard gaps in the woods and drape the shoulders of the knobs with feathery capes. This morning, though the hour was early, the damp, heavy air held surprising heat. Paul felt it on his skin. There was something unique about the feeling, something to share with those gathered, though the words to define it eluded him at that moment. He knew to be patient. The words would come, as they always did, when his heart and mind joined fully.

Paul was humbled by the number present. He had anticipated some of his church members would show up once the word got out what time he was leaving. It appeared, however, that every single one was there, even the two oldest, Miss Lucille and Mr. Cleave. What was even more humbling was the number of others from the community. Indeed, he could not think of a single resident who was absent.

Turning to his right, he saw a group of local ministers standing at the foot of the church steps. Brother Bruce was among them. Paul counted each one a friend, white and black, male and female. He knew they represented every denomination in the area. They came from the Grove and Oakland, Hays and Rocky Hill, Merry Oaks and Bon Ayr, and tidy spots of ground cut from corners of the fields and woods where little churches like Caney Creek stood in solitude, their modest steeples pointed toward heaven. Seeing his fellow ministers moved him deeply. He had to look down to compose himself.

When he looked up again, he began to speak in a voice strong and certain.

"My friends, there can be no doubt that God is here among us this fine morning."

A chorus of "Amens" answered.

"A moment ago," he continued, the words seeming to come of their own volition, "as I looked out across this wonderful gathering, seeing all of you standing here in this dense fog, the thought came to me that this is not fog at all. It is but the sleeves of God's pure-white robe. He is holding us in His arms."

Again "Amens" rose from the congregation. Paul turned to the group of ministers.

"My sisters and brothers, how your presence humbles me. It also gives me strength, for I know you are not here representing any one branch of faith. You are here because you represent the only denomination that is truly of consequence to God—that of the believer."

The group of ministers replied with a mix of nods and smiles and "Amens" softly voiced. Paul turned to look out over the congregation once more.

"When I start on my journey a few minutes from now, I know in my heart with absolute certainty that God will walk with me. He will take me by the hand, as always, and show me the way. I also know that I will go with your prayers. For those, I thank you.

"Yet others will need your prayers, for God in His wisdom has provided me with companions for my journey. As some of you know, Tick Cole will drive along beside me, handling the support side of things."

Voices rose from the crowd:

"Go with God, Tick."

"Proud of you, son."

Paul waited a moment for the crowd to grow still once more.

"What most of you probably don't know, is that Cami Whitley will also join us. I only found this out Thursday when she and her parents came to visit. Cami is a journalism student at WKU. She and her professors have decided it would be worthwhile to document this journey as part of her degree work."

Comments arose from the gathering, similar to those just directed at Tick, replacing his name with Cami's.

"Please keep these wonderful young people—as well as their families—in your prayers," Paul continued. "Theirs is no small sacrifice.

"Finally, I ask that you pray for my wife, Jennie. She is my soulmate, my steady rock in a world of shifting sand, my life. Being away from her is my only regret. Though she is a strong person, knowing you will always be there for her does more than I can say to ease my mind."

The preacher looked down to see Henry and Elsie, Marian Cole and Miss Lucille, standing close at his feet, nodding in assurance. Jennie stood in their midst; her dry eyes turned upward to meet his.

"Now, as John Wayne would have said, 'We're burning daylight.' It is time I was on my way. I would ask that each of you take the hand of the person next to you. Then we will join in a moment of silent prayer for the children."

Preacher Paul waited a few moments as people made connections. He used the time to steal a glance toward his fellow ministers. They knelt in a circle, their hands clasping the hands of their neighbors, their heads bowed. He took Jennie's uplifted hand in his left, Henry's in his right, and bowed his head.

Moments later dozens of "Amens" answered his. Paul stepped down from the table. He bent to lift his backpack. Slinging it over a shoulder, he began to slowly make his way through the throng toward the county road. There were a hundred handshakes and a hundred hands laid on his shoulders, with as many blessings softly uttered. The crowd at last began to thin. By the time he reached the end of the gravel drive only Jennie was beside him. He paused to work his arms through the pack's shoulder straps, then bent forward to shift it into balance and snugged everything tight. As he stood upright again, Jennie reached toward his chest with both hands and worked her fingertips beneath the edges of the straps. Holding tight, she pulled the two of them close as his arms reached to embrace her. Their kiss was brief. There were no words between them as each allowed the other to take half a step back. They had said it all last evening, said it again this morning in the cemetery, over and over. Paul hesitated but a moment before turning on his heel. His feet found the pavement and propelled him forward. He did not look back as he disappeared into the fog.

Chapter 21

It was only 8:00 a.m. when the congregation began spilling from the rear doors of the church. The outside preachers and non-members had departed shortly after Paul took his first steps down the road. When Brother Bruce met with the men at the potluck, he asked that a sunrise service be held this day to pray for Preacher Paul. His sermon had been brief, yet moving, holding up Paul as a man of God doing His bidding. During the invitational, two young men came forward to be saved, one twelve, the other eleven. In their emotional pleas, both professed a desire to follow Paul's example. Afterward, Deacon Henry lingered a moment on the steps to tell Brother Bruce he couldn't remember two people coming forward at the same service since a particularly intense hellfire and brimstone revival twenty some years before. It had to be a good sign.

Tick and Cami had stayed to worship. There was no need for them to rush onto the road. Paul's first day of walking would cover familiar ground. It was slated to end eighteen miles away in Bowling Green at the home of a minister friend. Tick would spend the night in town with a buddy, then meet Paul early in the morning to sketch out the day's route. Cami planned to write her first blog that afternoon. It would center on the gathering in the fog here at Caney Creek. She would stay the evening on campus with Emmy, then see the preacher off in the morning.

Now, Tick and Cami stood in the tattered remnants of fog lingering about the gravel parking lot, Tick beside his father's old van with his mother, Cami with her parents near her small sedan—a high-mileage hand-me-down—once the family car. A steady stream of well-wishers had stopped to speak with first one, then the other, before heading home to what promised to be an out-of-sorts day, given the service's early hour and the sense of disrupted normality felt by many following the departure of their spiritual leader.

"Yes, Mama," Tick was saying. "I'll be real careful, and I'll call you every chance I get. Don't you worry 'bout me. You just tell 'em ole boys whatever you need, and they'll take care of it. Okay?"

"I'll be fine," Marian answered, her hands coming together behind the neck of her much taller son. Between standing on tiptoes and pulling him down toward her a bit, she managed to reach high enough to give Tick a brief kiss on the cheek. He hugged her tight and kissed her on the forehead in return. As their embrace came to a quick end, Marian took a step back. Instead of turning to leave, however, she continued to face him. Both hands grasping the strap of her purse before her, she squared her shoulders and began to speak.

"Remember what your daddy said when he gave you your nickname?"

Tick hesitated a moment. He hadn't thought of that in a long time.

"Yes, ma'am," he finally answered. "Whenever somebody needed me, I was to stick right to them, just like a tick."

Now it was Marian's turn to remain silent for a moment. She suddenly nodded, just once, as if she agreed with some unseen speaker.

"I can feel it in my heart, son, plain as anything. I don't know where and I don't know when, but there'll come a time when the preacher will need you. Do like your daddy told you, and everything will work out."

Afraid the tears would come pouring out at any second, she spun on her heel and walked away without saying another word, leaving her puzzled son to stare after her.

"I'm so excited for you!"

"Oh, I know, Mother," Cami said, beaming, as she grasped the middle-aged woman's hands. "I've got butterflies like crazy."

"Me, too," Rachel Whitley nodded. "The places you will see, the people you will meet, and you'll be spreading the word all along the way about what the preacher is doing. It's the trip of a lifetime."

"Yes, Mother. And like I promised, I'll call every day and let you know what's going on."

"Please. I want to hear everything."

"Got your debit card?" The man's voice came from the front of her car. Cami turned toward the wiry, leather-faced man leaning against the fender.

"Yes, Papa," she answered. "It's in my purse."

"And your credit card?" he asked, levering himself upright with a sun-browned arm.

"Yes, sir."

"Emergency cash?"

"Stuffed up under the seat springs, like you told me."

"Lots of meanness out there," her father said, stepping slowly toward her. "You be careful. And stay away from the boys. They'll be chasing after you all the way to Mexico."

"Oh, Frank," Rachel waved her hand, as if to fan his words away. "She's a grown woman. She can handle herself."

"I know," he answered, lifting his arms to invite Cami forward. "Just doing my job, worrying about my little girl," he said as Cami stepped into his embrace.

"Don't worry, Papa," Cami assured him, kissing his cheek. "I'll be fine."

"Of course, you will," he agreed, hugging her like he was afraid to let go. After a long moment he pushed back and held her at arms' length. "But sometimes things happen. If you need me, call. I'll be there in a flash."

"I know, Papa," Cami said, stepping in and kissing him again. "I know."

Her father released her after a moment and moved back. "Proud of you, girl." He suddenly twisted around, fighting against the lump rising in his throat. "Where's that Tick?" he asked no one in particular. "I guess I ought to wish him a safe trip."

Tick was inspecting a wiper blade—something he meant to check earlier in the week—when he felt a hand on his shoulder. He turned quickly, ready for trouble, and was surprised to see Cami's father standing there.

"Just wanted to wish you luck," Mr. Whitley said, extending his hand. "Going to be quite an adventure, I'd say."

"Thank you, sir," Tick replied, a bit taken aback at the strength of the smaller man's grip. "I imagine it will be."

"You call me if there's anything you need, anything at all. Okay?"

"I appreciate that. Thank you."

The men ended their handshake. Cami's father took a step back. He didn't turn and walk away, however, as Tick expected he might. The older man just stood there staring at him. Several seconds passed in silence. Tick began to feel there was more than simple staring going on. It felt like . . . like maybe Mr. Whitley was looking down a rifle barrel at him.

"Understand you and my gal had a date Friday night."

"Yes, sir. We went out to eat and then to a movie. Cami's very nice, and smart, too," Tick added, thinking he needed to head something off, though he wasn't certain exactly what.

"That she is." Mr. Whitley paused a moment, nodding. When he spoke again, he changed tack. "You've got quite a reputation, son. Folks say you run wild as a deer, fast and loose."

Tick didn't reply. He was afraid of digging the sudden hole deeper.

"You wouldn't be thinking of maybe taking advantage of the situation, would you, with just you and a pretty girl a long way from home and nobody to watch over your shoulder?"

"Oh, no—I mean," Tick stuttered. "I like your daughter—and—I don't know—this is a serious trip—a very serious trip. I respect Cami. I wouldn't do nothing—anything—out of the way. Honest, I wouldn't," he finally swore, feeling as if he had just run a wind sprint.

Mr. Whitley allowed several seconds to crawl by as his eyes bored a hole into a spot between the young man's brows. "Good," he finally said, smiling wide. The smile flipped to a block of cold stone an instant later. "I'd hate to have to kill you."

Chapter 22

Jennie shut the car door, took one step, and stopped short. She had attended the sunrise church service—sat in her usual seat, surreal as it was without Paul at the pulpit—and sought out Cami and Tick in the parking lot afterward to thank them again and wish them a safe journey. Then she drove straight home. Now she stood rooted to the concrete floor of the garage, completely at a loss as to what to do next. There was no child to laugh with, to urge to change out of her church clothes. There was no husband beside her to hug simply because she felt like hugging him, to tell that their Sunday dinner would be ready in just a few minutes.

The emptiness was everywhere, inside her and out, as if she had somehow been transported to a place which looked like her home but was only a one-dimensional rendering, devoid of love and care or any other warm emotion. Alone. That was the great emptiness threatening to suffocate her. For a moment she considered driving along Paul's route until she caught up to him. If she could only hug him close one more time—

They had already discussed this the night before, however. One goodbye was enough, itself almost too much to bear. She forced herself to take a deep breath and exhale slowly, just to feel she had some control over something.

The breath helped. Simple as the act was, it brought her back to her usual state, to a place where self-pity was not allowed. There were things to be done. She strode out of the garage, intent on going into the house and preparing something to eat. At the edge of the front walk she stopped again. *First things first*, she told herself. Without conscious thought, her eyes moved to the entrance into the canebrake. A couple of minutes later she found herself standing beside the creek, standing in the very spot where she had

found Paul on his knees that terrible night. She knelt, clasped her
hands and bowed her head.

"Father, I come to Thee—"

For several minutes she prayed aloud, her voice barely above a
whisper. Hearing herself in her family's sacred place added something special, somehow. She asked for God's constant guidance
along His great path for Paul. She asked for strength for herself;
strength that she might withstand the loneliness and face the emptiness in her heart with courage. She asked for Paul to find strength
in the knowledge of her love when his feet became weary, when his
heart grew heavier over their loss of Sarah. Most of all she prayed
that Paul's prayers for the children be heard and repeated by others,
all in furtherance of His plan.

Then Jennie thanked God for sending Cami and Tick to aid
her husband. She asked His blessings on them both. She went a
step further with Tick, asking that he fully surrender himself to
the Lord. She and Marian had discussed how he came to his deci-
sion to go with Paul. Maybe he had already found God that day,
given himself over. All that was lacking was his coming forward
to publicly proclaim it.

Her prayer finished, Jennie continued to kneel for a few moments
more, allowing—welcoming—the Presence. Comforted, she rose
at last. Turning onto the path, she heard a car door close. Hurrying
along she quickly came to the end, expecting to see a vehicle pulled
up before her house. She froze in place when she found no one
there. Searching, she swept her eyes back along the drive until she
was forced to lean to one side to see around a stand of cane. An old
van was pulled off on the shoulder of the road a few yards short of
their drive. Tick stood beside it, staring at the house.

Jennie almost stepped out to yell and wave. She hesitated, however, and leaned back a bit, watching instead through slender gaps
in the cane stalks. Without understanding why, it seemed important she did nothing to disturb Tick. For a minute, then two, he
continued to stare toward the house. Suddenly Jennie realized he
had bowed his head. He didn't keep it down more than a handful
of seconds, but it was long enough for Jennie to raise a hand to

her throat. Done, he spun about and disappeared around the front of the vehicle. A door creaked, then closed with a metallic crunch. The van pulled away seconds later.

Oh my, Jennie thought, stepping out into the open. *Thank you, Lord.* She stood there a while, savoring the sweetness of the moment. At last, she began to stroll across the yard. A breeze came up and held steady, warm air gently caressing her face as she casually moved from one spot to another, inspecting her flowers and plants. Most of them had passed their blooming phase, though the zinnias in front still waved a mix of colors. She could see butterflies weaving from one flower to another. The hibiscus and crepe myrtles bore a handful of late blossoms. Out by the county road some wildflowers flashed yellow in the breeze.

She soon found herself at the beginning of their drive. Glancing down, she could plainly make out where the dry grass had been crushed flat when Tick pulled over. Jennie took a few wandering steps before she came to the spot where he had been standing. Looking in the same direction he had looked, to her surprise, she could see very little of the house. The big maple almost completely blocked it. It was not difficult to understand what had held Tick's attention, however. Hanging from a limb in plain sight was Sarah's swing.

Chapter 23

Paul came to a halt at the top of the rise. The air was heating up now that the fog had burned off. He pulled a water bottle out and took a couple of swallows. The old gateposts were in sight. He glanced at his phone to check the time. Just over an hour ago he had kissed Jennie goodbye. Having walked this way many times, he knew the posts were at the four-mile mark. Paul didn't expect to hold this pace. Nervous energy had propelled him so far.

Still, as he started down the far side, he gave into the feeling the walk would not be particularly difficult. He could do this. His legs felt strong. All he had to do was stay hydrated and take care of his feet. He hit bottom and started up the next rise, crossing a shoulder of Little Knob. Halfway up, the soles of both feet seemed to catch fire. At last, he came to the crest and stopped.

Okay, Lord, I get it. I am not invincible.

Paul gingerly made his way over to one of the gateposts and took a seat, leaning back against the stones. The burning pains began to ease almost immediately. He slithered free of the backpack's straps and dug out a mandarin orange. Popping the sections into his mouth one at a time, Paul sucked the juice out before chewing.

This was a good shady spot. The stones were cool against his back. His elevated seat provided a clear view of the way ahead. The road stretched off before him, crossing open farmland to meet the U. S. highway somewhere in the distance. Paul had deliberately chosen this route to avoid traffic. It had worked. He'd only seen one car since passing through the Grove.

The fields were covered in frazzled brown cornstalks. When the breeze stirred, the leaves rubbed against each other and crackled like strips of dried parchment. Along the outer rows, mats of violet-eyed morning glories clung to the stalks. Scattered throughout were occasional splotches of deep green where stands of trees camouflaged a sinkhole. Fencerows ran on like ragged hedges, staking boundaries. To his right, the wooded face of a bluff rose vertically in a high wall. Vultures drifted in fat, lazy loops above—sentinels holding watch over the respiratory status of everything within a glide and a hop.

In the distance he spied a vehicle sailing silently on the U. S. highway. It was hardly quiet here, however, thanks to the bugs. Legions of crickets chirped loudly in the corn. In the woods behind him, work gangs of cicadas fired up rusty chain saws and old motors with burnt bearings until something broke or locked up and the racket momentarily collapsed.

He imagined Jennie's fingers working to sooth the aches where grooves had been cut by the pack's straps. Paul twisted and turned, dug into the taut mass across the small of his back, felt the tenseness abating as the strings of drawn bows slowly eased to rest. He rubbed his thighs, squeezing out the kinks. Leaning forward, he worked down to his ankles. It all helped. Paul realized he was setting a pattern. He needed to rest every hour and loosen his muscles.

A sudden pang of guilt stabbed at his heart. Jennie! For a moment he considered calling her to join him for one last hug, one last face to face *I love you* before the distance between them became too great. He quickly dropped the idea, though if felt as if he were deserting her. The break had been painful enough.

Paul bowed his head and whispered, "Lord, I am grateful for Jennie's understanding. I thank You for giving us the ability to love each other. In moments of trial, especially when the pain of Sarah's absence seems unbearable, I ask that You help Jennie know my love yet exists, as strong and certain as the love of our daughter. In that knowledge, may we both find comfort. Amen."

He opened his eyes. It was time to move, yet he wanted to linger a few moments more. Paul swept his gaze across the plain, along the seemingly infinite ridgeline to his right, following it to—

The epiphany arrived quietly. All at once it was just there. Paul nodded in understanding. He pushed to his feet and shouldered the pack. Moving his left hand out a few inches from his side, he felt it suddenly full.

"Leaving home now, we'll follow along close to the ridge," he began, "till we get to Bowling Green. The ridge is an escarpment, the Dripping Springs Escarpment. Crazy name, huh? Fancy way of saying a long cliff or bluff."

He gently squeezed his left hand, felt pressure in return as he took a step toward the road.

"The old timers called that high ground the Shawnee Hills. I always loved the name. I think it's beautiful, don't you, Sarah darling?"

Chapter 24

Cami's Blog

For the next several months I will chronicle the journey of my minister, Preacher Paul Lockhart, as he walks from the rural community of Caney Creek, Kentucky, to the southern border at Brownsville, Texas. His journey is inspired by a news report of a little Guatemalan girl being deliberately separated from her mother when they entered the United States. Distressed by the report, the minister sought answers from the Lord. During this communion God called upon Preacher Paul to go to Brownsville and pray for the children. Furthermore, God specifically instructed him to walk the entire way. The preacher reports it stunned him when he discovered the distance from his church to the border was the same number of miles the little girl walked from her home in Guatemala City to Brownsville.

The great trek started this morning minutes after dawn at the Caney Creek Baptist Church in northeastern Warren County. It was a surreal setting, the bottomland along the creek blanketed in low fog so thick only the heads and shoulders of those in attendance could be seen. Preacher Paul described it as, "being held in God's arms, for the fog was but the sleeves of His pure white robe." After brief remarks and a prayer with the members of the community and pastors from area churches, the minister kissed his wife goodbye and stepped onto the Grove Road, destined for Texas.

This afternoon, having covered eighteen miles on day one, Preacher Paul arrived in Bowling Green where he planned to spend the night with friends. Tomorrow, with only 1,266 miles to go, he will head south.

†††

"Thank you," Paul said to Reverend Huston and her husband, Willie, on their front porch. "The blueberry cobbler last night was fabulous, Megan, and Willie, I'm excited about what you're doing with the farm."

The reverend gave Paul a hug, saying, "Be praying for you every step."

"Take care, my friend," Willie said, shaking Paul's hand.

As the Hustons turned to go inside, Paul pivoted to face Cami and Tick on the sidewalk.

"Okay gang, we ready?"

"Yes sir," the pair answered.

"Please drop the sir stuff," Paul grinned.

They grinned back. Then Tick spoke, "Well, Preacher," he said, his eyebrows rising in question. "What's the game plan?"

"Heading to Franklin. Straight down 31W."

"Alright," Tick replied. "I'll find us a place to camp."

"No need," Paul waved him off. "I've got a minister friend there. We will be guests of the Presbyterians this evening."

"Good," Tick nodded. "Have you got enough groceries in your pack to make it to lunch?"

"I have a Gatorade and a water, some mandarins and a pack of peanut butter and crackers, plus, three sausage and biscuits I liberated from the Huston kitchen. Surely that'll do."

"If you say so." Tick shrugged. "I'll find you around noon. Holler if you need anything sooner. The ladies back home really loaded us up. We've even got one of Ms. Elsie's pecan pies," he added as he turned toward his van. Cami stayed with Paul.

"Do you mind if I walk with you a bit?" she asked. "I left my car over on the Bypass."

"I'm glad to have your company," Paul answered, shrugging into his pack. "At least we're starting out downhill." He cinched the straps and rolled his shoulders to get the load situated. Then they moved off. "Of course, yesterday I wasn't certain I was going to make it to the top. I told Megan I didn't know why they live on a hill. She had the perfect reply. They're getting a head start on climbing to heaven."

"I like that," Cami giggled. A moment later she asked, "How do you feel this morning?"

"My feet and legs are sore. It'll take me a few days to get worked into long-haul shape."

They paused at a corner for traffic, then hurried across.

"It'll take a while to get our routines down, too," Paul continued. "Some things will really slow us up, like walking through the city here. Umpteen streets to cross. It adds up."

"Yes," Cami agreed. "I'm dreading Nashville."

"No kidding," Paul nodded emphatically. "I can't find my way around there with my GPS, let alone walking. Who knows, I might wind up at the Opry. I'll have Tick get me a map."

"I'll remind him," Cami said, smiling. She hesitated a moment. "Okay if I run a few questions by you—for my blog?"

"Sure. Go ahead."

"Great." Cami dug a small recorder out of her jeans pocket. She spoke into it, noting the date, time, location, and who was present. "Alright. How does it feel to be underway on this great trek?"

"Trek?" Paul raised his eyebrows.

"Means an arduous journey," Cami explained.

Paul grinned. "I like the word. Well, it feels good, except I already miss Jennie something crazy. I don't expect that to get better. Otherwise, I imagine I feel about like anyone starting on a long trip, which means I'm hoping I didn't forget anything. Most of all, I guess, I feel relieved. Since the call, it has seemed like I was keeping God waiting. I don't believe that's a good thing."

Cami glanced at Paul and saw the hint of a smile bending the corners of his mouth. Also smiling, she spoke again.

"Every so often, I'll ask what you've learned. It could be anything. This sounds presumptuous, but it seems to me you will have extended opportunities to simply think, since you will be alone so much."

They came to a halt at an intersection to allow a car to pass. Paul turned and stared at her. He continued to stare for some seconds after the car was gone.

"You are going to make a great reporter," he said. Then he turned toward the intersection and started across. "Very perceptive on your part."

"I just thought," she said, stepping onto the sidewalk. "I know it's too soon."

"It's not too soon. Actually, the learning is already underway." Cami glanced his way in surprise. "Last night at dinner, Megan pointed out what an opportunity this is to have an in-depth conversation with God. That had not occurred to me before, partly I think, because I speak to God daily in my ministerial work. This—this *trek*—is different, however. First, the time I'll have to talk with God is much greater. And like you said, I will have long periods alone when I can simply think. I look forward to both, but especially to hearing His voice.

"There's one other thing. I had not contemplated the conversations I'll have with others I hold very dear. I'm especially looking forward to those."

Cami was a bit taken aback. *What others?* She thought. Then it occurred to her the preacher was likely talking about her and Tick. She was partially right.

"Well, Ms. Press Officer, got anything lined up for today?"

"Yes," Cami answered. "A local radio guy, Denny Dell, said he would join you at Lost River. He'll do an interview while he walks with you. It'll play this afternoon on WBGK at 3:00."

"Okay. I don't mind sitting down with a reporter at night, but I don't want to interrupt the trek."

"Understand," Cami nodded. "And I'll do a TV interview on Channel 17's noon show."

"Great," Paul replied enthusiastically. "Nervous?"

"Not yet," Cami giggled. "I'll probably be once the camera starts rolling. It's my first time."

"You'll do fine. Just act like you're talking to friends." A moment later he added, "Do your folks know to watch?"

"Yes," she smiled. "Mom's all set to record."

Paul gave a quick laugh. Cami had something more to ask, but she hesitated, knowing it would probably be touchy. Finally, after hurrying across another intersection, she spoke.

"I hate to bring this up, but have you thought about what you will say when they ask about Sarah? They will, you know?"

Paul walked half a block before answering, his voice so low Cami had to strain to hear.

"I know they will ask. Anyone would. All I am certain of is God did not take Sarah so I would open my eyes. It's not the way He works. What the Lord will do—and I believe He has done so here—is help us see a way we can bring something good out of something tragic. If I can do that—"

Paul left his answer hanging as he increased his pace. Cami managed to keep up. She almost wished she had not posed the question. Facing the inevitable had caused him to feel the sadness of loss again. Finally, she said, "I had to ask."

"Of course, you did," he replied, turning to offer a faint smile. "It's okay."

She smiled back, her angst easing slightly. They walked another block before Paul suddenly spun around.

"Wasn't that your car we just passed?"

She glanced back.

"Oh—oh yes, it is! Well, I'll see you down the road then."

Moments later, before she turned the key, the thought came to her this journey was something more than an adventure. There might be excitement for her, with many opportunities to hone her craft, but there would certainly be pain for the preacher. She could only hope her question had helped prepare him for the next time, for all the next times, he would hear it.

Chapter 25

Paul left Franklin at daybreak. The morning was cool, the way sheltered by a thin fog. He marched forward with fresh purpose on rested legs. At 8:00 a.m. he crossed the line into Tennessee. Strangely, this simple act, a single step carrying him from one state into another, felt momentous, as if it placed him beyond a point-of-no-return. He hesitated a moment, almost looked back, then resumed walking.

Tick met him at noon. They ate from the stash provided by the Caney Creek ladies. Now, it was 2:30 and hot—much hotter than the first couple of days. Sweat and humidity clung to his skin like a damp sheet. He was moving through farm country. The land had been flat for the first few miles. Now it tended toward gently rolling. It was still good walking. Houses were scattered widely, with most set well back from the road. Traffic was light, but he was on 31W, a U. S. highway. Cars moved at speed. He worked to stay alert, facing oncoming vehicles and moving a step to the side when one approached, ready to hop further if need be.

He had soaked through his shirt, which wasn't a big problem. It helped cool him when the breeze got up. Unfortunately, it didn't get up very often. He drank water or Gatorade frequently to stay hydrated. His feet were burning enough to make him think they might get bad soon. The pavement was blistering, with the sun sliding into the hottest part of the day, so he stayed on the grassy shoulder as much as he could. The late summer doldrums were here, leaving everything looking tired and smothered. Even the weeds were sagging. The bugs had fallen quiet, as if they had retreated to their holes for an afternoon siesta.

Down the highway, trees crowded close to the pavement on both sides. He decided to take a break in the shade there. As he neared the spot, he noticed a small brown house on the far side of the road. An elderly man wearing a John Deere cap was sitting in a lawn chair, shaded by a large sugar maple. Another lawn chair sat a few feet to the side, empty. Between the chairs the necks of four or five bottles protruded from a galvanized bucket. The man raised a hand.

"Come over and give your puppies a break," he said, his voice barely loud enough to cross the highway.

"Thanks. I believe I will," Paul answered, checking for traffic before he stepped toward him.

"Got one sitting there idling," John Deere said, hooking a thumb toward the empty seat. Paul quickly shucked his pack. As Paul sat, the man asked, "You want a beer?"

"Appreciate it, but I'll pass."

"Good. I don't have any." The man grinned. "I've got a root beer and a couple of Dr Peppers. That green one's some kind of mineral water," he pointed a bony finger. "I don't care for it myself, but the woman said you might."

"I'll try a Pepper," Paul said, extending his hand. "I'm Paul."

"I figured you was you," the man said, grinning wider as they shook hands. "You were Paul, I mean. You're the preacher man. I'm Raymond."

"Well yes, Raymond. I'm a preacher. How'd you know, if you don't mind me asking?" Paul said, reaching for a Dr Pepper. Ice cubes clinked and grated as he pulled the bottle free.

"The word's out. We heard you were up in Franklin last night. I imagined you'd be along this way about now and might be thirsty."

"You are right on both counts, and I'm glad." Paul smiled, twisting the cap off. He took a long pull from the bottle, paused to breathe, then took a second swallow.

"Baptist, aren't you?" Raymond asked.

"Yes," Paul replied, raising his eyebrows.

"You know how I knew?" The elderly man didn't wait for an answer. "You drink like you're trying to dunk something," he said, laughing aloud.

"You got it." Paul laughed in turn. "Trying to dunk this thirst. What denomination are you, if I'm not being too nosy?"

"I don't mind telling," Raymond replied. "I'm a hammer-headed atheist and a slew-footed agnostic, reformed branch."

Paul didn't know what to say, so he simply stared. At last, he spoke, "Well, I believe you are the first person I've met of that particular affiliation."

"To tell the truth, me and the woman go to a little church, Sawyer's Bluff, just over on the ridge a piece. We're a denomination all to ourselves. Report straight to the Lord. We kind of figure it's all that matters."

Paul nodded. "I agree. It's all that matters."

"The other stuff, that's what I used to be before I got reformed. Korea slapped my doubts clean out. If you want to get close to the Lord, let somebody shoot at you."

"I would imagine," Paul replied, shaking his head.

The two men fell quiet for a spell. Paul sipped his drink until the bottle was finally empty. He looked at Raymond.

"Set her there by the bucket," he said. As Paul leaned down, Raymond spoke. "Where's your walking stick?"

"I'm afraid I don't have one."

"You mean to say you've done come over fifty miles emptyhanded? Can't be doing that. You've got to have something to keep the dogs poked away."

"I never thought of it," Paul replied, shrugging.

"Take a look behind the tree there, back of us."

Paul rose to his feet and stepped behind the maple. A thick staff of hickory, roughly four and a half feet long and stripped of bark, rested against the trunk. The wood had a couple of gentle turns where there were knotholes. Irregular grooves rambled down its length where worms had cut. Near the top a hole had been drilled. A rawhide string passed through the hole, with its ends tied together to form a loop. Paul picked it up and ran a hand down the varnished wood, admiring the handiwork. He stepped back to his chair but did not sit down. He looked over at Raymond and spoke.

"It's beautiful. Your work, I take it?"

"Finished it a couple of weeks ago," Raymond nodded. "I've got to be straight with you, though. It's not for walking. That's what you call a *leaning* stick."

"Huh. I never heard of such," Paul said, looking over the wood again, tracing the worm grooves with a fingertip.

"Try it out," Raymond said.

"What do you mean?"

"Hold it in front of you standing straight up." Paul did as he was told. "Put one hand flat on top of the end up there. Now put your other hand on top of the first one. Un-huh. Now lean on it."

"Okay," Paul said, feeling the wood take part of his weight. Suddenly, there didn't seem to be so much pressure on his feet. "I see what you're talking about. Yeah."

"It looks about the right length for you. Hard to measure exact, but I had some help. Comfortable?"

"Very." Paul nodded. "Leans good," he added with a smile.

"It's yours."

"But—I can't just take this."

"Of course, you can. It's a gift, so it's not like you have a choice. Besides, a man can't walk all the way to the Rio Grande without something to help hold him up. People be talking, thinking you're not all there."

"I don't know what to say. Thank you." Paul fell silent as he looked over the stick again, studying Raymond's craftsmanship. Finally, he said, "A leaning stick. I like the name."

"It's really a *Jesus* stick, if you go by the proper nomenclature."

"How's that?" Paul frowned.

"Lean on Jesus, and He will hold you up, sort of like that stick will when you get weary, only Jesus does it a lot better."

For a moment Paul didn't speak. When he did, he was smiling toward Raymond.

"I love the name. I appreciate this more than I can say."

"You are more than welcome."

After a moment Paul set the gift aside and picked up his pack.

"I hate to, but I guess I better get going. Need to put a few more miles behind me. Thank you for this," he said, picking the piece of hickory up and balancing it in his hand, "and for the Dr Pepper."

"No problem, preacher. Proud to meet you."

"It's been a pleasure," Paul replied, shaking hands.

He stepped toward the road. At the edge of the blacktop, he stopped and turned back toward Raymond.

"I was going to ask what you meant about measuring this," he said, holding the stick up. "You said something about having help getting the length just right?"

"Yeah, somebody told me where to cut before I put the finish on."

"But that was two weeks ago, didn't you say?" Paul asked, counting the days to himself since the Lord's call. Eleven. No one, not even him, knew about the walk then. "I mean, it fits me perfectly, but how did anyone know the right length?"

Raymond smiled his widest smile yet.

"Let me put it this way, preacher. When I hear a voice in my head telling me to do something, I just do it. I gave up a long time ago trying to figure out the mysterious ways."

Chapter 26

Paul was a couple of miles south of White House by the end of the third day. It was where the chain of nights at the homes of ministers ended. The minister in Franklin had made arrangements with a pastor near the town. At midday, the second pastor called to apologize. Unexpected company had filled his home to flood stage. He offered his church, instead. After raiding their food stash, and after Paul had called Jennie, he and Tick unrolled their sleeping bags in the church's vestibule.

The men were awake before dawn. They took advantage of the outdoor privy, then shared water from one of the plastic jugs in the van to wash up. Breakfast took the last of the fried chicken, as well as what was left of Elsie's pecan pie.

"I've got to say," Paul began, dropping his scraps into a trash bag, "that was a meal fit for kings."

"Yep," Tick nodded, tossing his scraps in after Paul's. "I hate to see it go. Especially the pie. We've still got almost a whole ham and I don't know what else, but it won't keep forever. It'd be a shame to throw anything away."

He tied the top of the trash bag in a loose knot and tossed it in the van. Turning back, he said, "You've got an hour and a half, maybe two, before you hit Nashville. Millersville's first, then Goodlettsville. You know what you're in for."

"Yeah," Paul nodded. "Big city. I'll just put my head down and keep plowing. Thanks for the map," he said, patting his back pocket.

Tick nodded. "It'll be hot again today. Make sure you've got plenty to drink and enough munchies."

"Yes sir," Paul gave a half salute, then started shoving bottles and snack packages into his backpack. It didn't take long to fill it. He leaned forward a bit and slung the pack in place. Grabbing his Jesus stick, he said, "See you in Nashville."

"Alright. At least your first few miles will be downhill."

Paul hadn't gone ten steps before Tick's cellphone went off. A mooing cow!

"It's Cami!" Tick barked, holding the phone out.

"Tell her hi for me," Paul said over his shoulder.

"She's going to be on TV, morning show in Nashville."

"Great!" Paul replied, far enough away by then he had to yell to be heard. Suddenly, he turned and started fast walking back. "Don't hang up! I've got something to tell y'all."

"What's up?" Tick asked as Paul came alongside.

"Put it on speaker," the preacher replied. "I'll tell you both at once."

A minute later Paul ceased explaining what he wanted.

"You sure about this?" Tick asked.

"You're the one who said it'd be a shame. Right?" Paul grinned.

Tick smiled as he answered. "I'm in if you're in."

"Me, too," Cami's voice came over the speaker. "I'll let you know as soon as I find out."

✝✝✝

"Welcome back to *Morning! Music City*," the show's hostess smiled from behind the glass studio desk. "So glad you're starting your day with us. I'm Barb Jordan, here with my co-host, Jase Humphries."

Jase picked up the narrative. "We are talking with Cami Whitley, a journalism student at Western Kentucky University, just up the road in Bowling Green. She is here to tell us the extraordinary story of her minister. He is walking from tiny Caney Creek, Kentucky, to the Mexican border, a distance of nearly 1,300 miles."

"Extraordinary, indeed," Barb agreed. "Cami, what led your minister to undertake such a journey?"

Cami reflexively reached for the earpiece and pushed it in tighter. Instead of inside the studio, she was seated on a high terrace of the station's downtown building. Behind her, Titans Stadium formed a backdrop. She drew in a shallow breath and began to speak.

"Preacher Paul became upset over a TV report about a young Guatemalan girl. She had been separated—deliberately separated—from her mother at the border."

"Excuse me, Cami," Jase cut in. "I believe we have a clip from the network."

The screen filled with the picture of the child crying for her mother. The clip ran for ten seconds.

"That was very hard to watch," Barb said softly after it ended. "I couldn't help but think of my nieces." Then, "Cami, this led to the preacher deciding to go to the border in protest, I suppose?"

"Not directly, and not in protest, either. He spent an entire night wandering in the wilderness, as he called it, in a patch of cane near his home. As the sun started to come up, he quit raging and surrendered to God's will. That's when he received the call to go to the border and pray for the children."

"By *the call*, you mean like someone is called by God to be a minister? Jase asked.

"Yes."

"Just pray for the children?" he pressed. "That's all?"

"Yes," Cami nodded.

"And the walking?"

"The preacher said it was part of God's directive."

"Not sure I see the connection," Jase frowned.

"The day before we left," Cami began, "Preacher Paul told us he had discovered it is the same distance from Guatemala City, where the little girl came from, walking all the way, to the border at Brownsville, Texas, as it is from Caney Creek to Brownsville."

"Oh, really?" Jase's eyebrows went up. "What an odd coincidence."

"Some might call that confirmation," Barb said in an aside. "Oh my," she returned to her normal tone. "Well, Cami, what a story you have to follow. Now the minister, Preacher Paul, will arrive in Nashville today?"

"Yes. He's coming down 31W. He should be reaching the northern side of town shortly."

After the hosts thanked Cami, a third voice said, "And, we are gone to commercial."

✝✝✝

Realizing they were about to lose contact, Cami shouted, "Barb?"

Barb's perky voice came back. "Yes, Cami?"

She briefly explained the preacher's question.

"They're going to cut your mic any second," Barb warned. "We'll be done in about, oh—eight minutes. Meet me in the lobby."

When they met, Barb led her to a window. "See those patches of color across the river?"

Cami stared a moment. "What are those?"

"Tents. It's what you're looking for. He's on 31W. It runs straight by there."

As the two parted, Barb keyed the news director's number on her cell phone. She might be riding herd on a morning show, but she was still a reporter with a scoop. Finished with the news director, she punched in a second number. It belonged to an old friend—a special friend—who used to work with her.

Chapter 27

"**I** thought I would hear from you sooner. It's dark already." The Big Guy—his chosen code name—sounded irritated.

"I was tied up watching something you might want to keep an eye on," the thin man replied, holding the phone out as he scratched his shaved head.

"Whatever." The Big Guy was definitely irritated. "What about the boys? They still on board?"

"They spouted off some stuff about pulling them out of the fire if things go south. I blew it off. They're putty in your hands."

"Silly putty." The Big Guy laughed. "I'll call them when the time comes. They'll be useful, as always. Just need to pet 'em every now and then, make them think they're something special. The *Pat Henrys!* Ha!"

"Liberty or death," the thin man chuckled.

"Yeah. My kind of people." The Big Guy's voice trailed off, sounding bored. "Okay," he said after a moment. "What's this thing I need to keep an eye on? Got aliens flying around down there?"

"Worse. We've got a preacher."

"And that's worrying you?" The Big Guy sounded upset again. "You found a preacher? Just one? They're thicker in that town than crap between a hillbilly's toes. It's Tennessee. What'd you expect?"

"This preacher is different. People here are starting to pay attention to him."

"Give me a break! Yokels following a preacher in Nashville. You have anything else?"

"You need to hear me out. He's walking from Kentucky to the southern border. He says he's going to pray for the children."

"Well, ain't that sweet?"

"Remember the little Hispanic kid crying for her mama in

Brownsville?" The thin man ignored the sarcasm. "She was on the national news a couple of weeks ago. That's what set the preacher off. They've had that same clip on the local news here at least three times today."

"I don't remember it," the Big Guy said dismissively. "So, what's the big deal? You've got a redneck preacher from Kentucky says he's walking to the border. He'll never make it."

"Maybe not. But if he does, he could stir up a mess. It might make people start giving the policy a second thought."

"Bullshit! That's locked up tight. All I have to do is yell, 'They're attacking us!' People start grabbing their guns and nailing their doors shut."

"I'm trying to give you a head's up."

"Sure, sure. We'll deal with that loony tune if we have to, the hard way."

It was dark as Tick drove the van back into Nashville. Cami sat in the passenger seat. She had accepted his invitation to ride along as he checked out the route for the next day. Tick would drop her off in a few minutes at a friend's apartment close to Vandy. The pair were in pensive moods as they watched the lights along Harding Pike blink past.

"I'm sorry," Tick said, glancing over at Cami.

She turned toward him. "There's nothing to be sorry about. All I said was we need to be careful."

"I should have stopped at holding your hand."

"Tick, please. It's not like you did anything crazy."

"I kind of goofed up our evening. I shouldn't have."

"Find a place to pull over," she commanded. "Right now."

Tick found an open slot in front of a coffee house. He was going too fast and misjudged the distance. The front tires bumped the curbstone, bringing them to a rocking halt. "Oops! My bad," he said, gritting his teeth in a *Joker* smile as he turned to face her.

He was surprised to see her finger pointed in his direction.

"Thomas Ivy Cole, don't you dare."

"Dare what?" Tick asked. "I didn't mean to hit it."

"Not that, *Mr. Whaa Whaa, I shouldn't have.* Obviously, you did not understand what I said. I mean we have to be careful to keep our feelings in check. This is not the time."

"Huh?" Tick asked, his expression revealing how truly lost he was. "But—What I heard—"

"Will you please shut up and listen. Can you do that?"

Cami's words were harsh, though her tone was gentle, almost pleading. She paused a few seconds, looking away to gather herself. "I will not have our moment ruined," she whispered, barely loud enough for him to hear. Another second and she turned toward him.

"What a beautiful spot you took us to. Even the name was beautiful. Birdsong Hollow. I will never forget the name. And I will never forget standing there on that high bridge, holding hands, watching the sun go down behind the hills. It was perfect, just perfect. But the most perfect thing of all was when the last thin line of the sun melted away. The sky caught fire that instant! A hundred shades of orange and red. My goodness! I have never seen anything like it. A mad sea of flames washed over us. I could feel the glow on my skin." Cami leaned halfway across the distance between them. "That's when you pulled me close, you big ape, and kissed me. And you know what? I wanted you to."

Without warning she caught him by the collar with both hands and jerked him toward her. Then she kissed him full on the mouth. It was no light peck, but a long joining, filled with yearning. As suddenly as she had grabbed, she pushed him away.

"There," she said, flashing a tight smile. "That will have to hold you a few months."

Chapter 28

"Do you miss me?" Paul asked.

"Like a hole in the head," Jennie answered. "Do you miss me?"

"Like stepping on a rusty nail."

"Yow! That'd be rough," she replied. "Um, I miss you like a toothache."

"I'd rather have a nail in my foot," Paul said. "I miss you like—like when you get a little piece of skin torn on the side of your fingernail, so it sticks up, and you hang it every time you brush your hand against something, and it hurts like the dickens and won't heal for days."

"Oh, those will bring tears," Jennie groaned.

Whenever they had been apart, Paul remembered, from the day after their first date, they had bantered back and forth like this over the phone. It could go on for a while, and neither cared. It was their reverse way of saying *I love you.* The turn would always come, however, and the truth would spill out. This evening, Paul quickly steered the conversation that way. His heart did not allow him a choice. He simply missed her too much.

"Have I told you today how much I love you?" he asked.

"No, and I've been waiting hours and hours to hear you say it."

"I love you with all my heart, with all my soul. If my arms could reach around the world, they still couldn't hold a drop in the ocean of the love I feel for you."

"You're doing good," Jennie whispered.

"A second with you is a sunburst of pure joy. A second away is as if the stars had all blinked out, the moon suddenly burned to a black cinder. I stumble about in the dark, weeping."

"I miss your touch," she began. "The way your fingers feel against my back when you hold me close, the warmth of your shoulder against my face. I feel so safe then, so certain of everything, most of all our love."

"Would you marry me again, Jennie girl?"

"Ask me each day, ask me three times every day for the rest of our lives and you'll hear only one answer. Yes! Yes, Paul, I would."

"Can you feel me holding you now?"

She purred in response.

For a while there was silence. At last, as if they were truly standing together, embracing, each felt the other pull back a half step. It was simply too sweet, too painful, to continue.

"Tell me about your day," he said.

"A skunk walked across the road right in front of me." She laughed. "Don't know how I missed it."

"I'm glad you did." He laughed in return. "No wonder the goofy things get run over. They just come bouncing out without looking, like they don't have a care in the world."

"I don't think they do," Jennie agreed. "Well, work was pretty quiet. Same old same old. I stopped by to see Henry and Elsie on the way home. They're fine. They said to tell you hi. And Marian Cole phoned a while ago. She said Tick hadn't called her but once since you left. You better get on him."

"I will," Paul chuckled. "Can't miss calling your mama. And when you see Elsie again, tell her Tick and I finished off her pecan pie for breakfast."

"I'm so glad you're eating healthy." Jennie giggled. "That's about it for me. Oh! The last two nights there has been a big owl in the poplar out back. He calls, 'Who, Who,' and I sing, 'You, You,' back to him. He doesn't fly off when I sing. It's like he's there to watch over me."

"I like that. A wise owl protecting my love."

"It's a sweet idea," Jennie agreed. "So, tell me about your day. I know you were on TV. Everyone saw you feeding homeless people and talking about praying for the children. I heard Cami was on this morning, but I missed her."

"I heard she did good," Paul said. "I really didn't expect reporters at the camp. It brought some needed attention, I suppose. Here's what happened—now don't spread this around because I don't want anyone getting upset—our ladies loaded Tick's van up with so much food we couldn't possibly eat it all before it ruined, so we decided to give it to those most in need."

"That was a great idea," Jennie agreed. "It's awful for people to go hungry."

"Exactly." He paused a few seconds. "Did you see the little boy?"

"Yes, sitting on your knee. He's so cute."

"Rascal ate two whole ham sandwiches. I'm ashamed because I thought it was funny at first. Then, when he started on that second sandwich, I realized he was starving. His parents lost their jobs awhile back, then their home. They live in a tent now. It's heartbreaking."

"Oh my," Jennie said, her tone sad. "I will pray for them."

"That was this afternoon. But the strange stuff started happening this morning."

"What do you mean?" Jennie asked.

"Well, first—this was right after I walked down a long hill near Goodlettsville—was a little black lady. She was sitting on a rusty metal lawn chair, close to the road. Bless her, she had on this huge, wide-brimmed straw hat, like people used to wear when they were working outside. Remember those?"

"Yes," Jennie answered. "Aunt Bertha never went to the garden without hers, even if it was just to pick tomatoes for supper."

"Aunt Lula was the same way," Paul added. "Anyway, when I started getting closer, I realized this lady was old, very old, and just tee tiny. I bet she didn't weigh seventy-five pounds, and her without a speck of shade except her hat."

"That is strange," Jennie said. "Surely, she could have found a spot out of the sun. Any idea why she was out there?"

"She was waiting on me."

"Really?"

"When I wasn't but three or four steps away, she jumped up like she was a teenager and shouted, 'You that Preacher Paul fella?'

"Of course, I stopped and said, 'Yes ma'am.' All at once she grabbed my arm—she was strong as could be—and pulled me down toward her and kissed me on the cheek."

Paul could hear Jennie giggling again.

"You haven't been gone a week and already you've got women grabbing and kissing on you!"

"She's pushing ninety-five, hon, so don't be getting too jealous."

"I'm not." Jennie laughed out loud. "What an extraordinary thing."

"That's not all. When she let go of my arm, she took my hand in one of hers and started patting it on top with her other hand. You know how some older people do that?"

"Sure. Ms. Lucille does me that way all the time."

"Yep," Paul agreed. "And then this little lady tells me, 'I'm praying for you, preacher. When you get to that old border, you listen for me, 'cause you and I'll be praying for those babies together.'"

"Oh my," Jennie whispered. "That gives me cold chills."

"It did me, too," Paul sighed, grateful to share the moment. Jennie had been so right to insist they talk every night.

And the rest of today? He'd met others alongside the road. Some held a small child by the hand. A few held babies, doing their best to shield their faces from the sun. A number offered encouragement. Some men stepped up to shake his hand or pat him on the back. He continued telling Jennie about them as their conversation became more introspective.

"The little lady threw me for a loop. The others—I guess they must have seen Cami on TV. She mentioned the road I was on. I didn't quite know what to make of it then, and I can't claim to understand it any better now that I've had time to mull it over. It sounds awful, but sometimes I felt like I was the circus coming to town."

Jennie thought a moment before answering. "There is no way to determine any one person's motivation, short of asking. I don't think you should question too much. This journey has just started, Paul." She paused a few seconds. "I believe more people will come to meet you. I'm not certain why, either. I have an inkling, though. It seems something about your walk has struck a chord in people's hearts. Perhaps you should be careful about coming to expect the attention—after all, this is not about you—but you should be just as careful about wondering why."

"You are right, of course. I should simply take it at face value."

"Yes," Jennie agreed, a bit of excitement in her voice. "I believe so. You were called to do this, but you should not think God has sent you out alone. It makes sense He would provide you with support and encouragement. Right?"

Paul shook his head, exasperated with himself. Jennie was saying the obvious.

"I am lucky I have you to explain what anyone but me can see," he said to her. "This has already happened, others coming to my support. Look at Tick and Cami. For some reason, they felt compelled to come forward. And yesterday it was Raymond with the leaning stick. Could it be that God had a hand in guiding all of them?"

Jennie laughed. "You're the preacher, and you're asking me? Why, of course, He has a hand in guiding others. She paused a moment. "Think back. This has been happening since the start. What did Henry tell you at the potluck about the men's offering? Remember? You fussed and said you couldn't take it."

Paul didn't hesitate. "He said, 'Who do you think told us to give it in the first place?'"

"Exactly."

Paul waited a moment. "We can go back even further. You never hesitated when I first told you."

"Well," Jennie answered. "I'm not certain that was so much about the calling. What I do know is God placed belief in you in my heart the instant we met. It alone is enough."

Chapter 29

Paul awoke to the sounds of people stirring in the homeless camp. Yawning, he rubbed at his eyes for a moment, then stretched his arms above his head. There was enough light to make things out.

"Tick," Paul whispered.

"What?" Tick bolted upright, his head turning side to side, scanning for trouble.

"Relax." Paul smiled. "Time to get moving, that's all."

"Oh yeah, sure," came the answer.

Routine took over. They quickly rolled up their sleeping bags and stowed them in the van. Tick set out a fresh jug of water. They shared it to brush their teeth, wash their faces, and scrub up a little.

"You first," Tick said, waving Paul inside to change clothes. The preacher was back out in minutes, dressed in clean cargo shorts and a tee shirt. He sat on the back bumper to put on fresh socks and his hiking boots while Tick climbed inside. When he emerged several minutes later, he had a bag of bagels he had bought last night and two bottles of tea. Both men dug out a bagel and were about to uncap their teas, when a tall older gentleman called out to them.

"Y'all want a cup of coffee?" the man asked. He was heading their way with a paper cup in each hand.

"Sounds good," Paul answered.

As he neared, they saw his clothes were nothing more than filthy rags. His face and hands were just as dirty. He was so skinny it looked as if he didn't so much wear the rags as carry them draped over his bones, like a living clothes rack.

"I've got an old Coleman stove. Can't swear the coffee's any good, but it's hot. I'm Pap," he added as he handed one cup to Paul, the other to Tick.

"I'm Paul." The preacher shook Pap's hand. "And this is Tick," he added, canting his head toward the younger man. Tick, following suit, didn't hesitate to shake Pap's hand.

"You care for a bottle of tea?" Tick asked.

"Well, I don't know. I'm not much of a tea drinker."

"You can have mine, too," Paul told him. "Even if you don't drink it, you can trade for something else."

"Yeah, I guess I could," Pap nodded. He shoved the bottles in his back pockets.

"Want a bagel?" Tick offered the bag.

"I doubt I could chew that. 'Bout half my teeth are gone."

"Try one," Tick insisted. "They're soft. I got them fresh last night."

"I guess it won't hurt none to try," Pap answered.

"Take the bag," Tick said, pushing it into the man's hands.

Pap hesitated a moment, then nodded. He dug a bagel out and tried a bite.

"That's not bad," he said. "Believe I can gum it okay. Obliged."

"We're obliged for the coffee," Paul answered. "Good," he added, managing to swallow a sip. Tick didn't do as well, scrunching his face up. Fortunately, Pap was busy chewing and didn't notice.

"So, you're that preacher fella," Pap said, his Adam's apple bobbing as he swallowed.

"I am," Paul nodded, "and Tick is our chief navigator and supply officer."

"It's been a long time since I talked to a preacher. I haven't seen the inside of a church in ages."

"You still pray, I hope," Paul said.

Pap turned his head and stared toward the big buildings downtown. "Well, I'm ashamed to say it, but no. I reckon I've about forgot how."

After a moment's pause, Paul began. "Praying's a pretty straightforward process. You just talk to God about whatever you want to. Most people thank Him for the good in their lives or ask for help with their problems."

To Paul's surprise, Tick cut in. "What would you pray for, Pap?"

"My babies," Pap replied immediately. "I've got a slew of grandbabies and even some great-grandbabies. I'd pray I could hug everyone and tell them they're in my heart."

Seconds drifted by in quiet, all three men visualizing Pap surrounded by a crowd of children, hugging each one in turn and being hugged back. Paul broke the silence.

"We've got to get going in a minute, Pap. Before we hit the road each morning, we say a silent prayer to get us started off on the right foot. Care to join us?"

"I'd be proud," Pap nodded.

For a minute the three men stood quietly in a small circle, eyes closed, heads bowed, as the sounds of traffic drifted around them. At last, Paul said, "Amen." Raising his head, he looked at Pap and said, "My prayer is that your prayer be answered."

"It's mine, too," Tick joined in.

"I'm obliged," Pap replied. "After I said some words for my babies, I prayed for y'all, too." He paused a moment. "I can't claim I understand all what's happening at the border, but I prayed y'all get there safe and fix whatever needs fixing."

Chapter 30

Looking in the rearview mirror, Tick saw Paul turn around. He eased to the curb and watched as the preacher lifted the little boy they'd met the evening before. He didn't drive away until they finished hugging and Paul set the child down.

Now that he was alone, Tick felt a jumble of emotions mixing up his insides. The first few days had been no big deal—like going on a camping trip—kind of fun and interesting. He hadn't figured on anything confusing him, like that twinge in his chest when he saw the preacher and the little boy hugging, or the kiss Cami planted on him last night. This was all too much.

He turned right and rolled onto the Woodland Street Bridge. Glancing over the railing, he caught a glimpse of a tugboat pushing a couple of barges up the Cumberland. At the other end of the bridge, he noticed a group gathered on the sidewalk. They were all facing his way. Past this momentary distraction, his mind flipped back to his confusions.

What was it about Cami? Tick had chased and caught plenty of girls, though serious feelings had never been part of the equation. Last night, however, right after her kiss, he almost said, *I love you.* The words were suddenly on the tip of his tongue. Close! No wonder he had tossed and turned all night.

And now? Now his stomach didn't feel right. It wasn't the plain bagel or Pap's coffee, either. He'd swallowed a worse combination without complaint. It was a weird feeling, a new feeling, and though he couldn't explain it, he knew exactly what was causing it, or rather, who. Camilla Lynn Whitley, of course! He sensed danger. This woman was doing something to his equilibrium! Last night she'd left him so swimmy headed he didn't know how he'd made it back to the camp.

If he could see her for a few minutes, maybe he could settle down. His brain locked on the idea. He found himself scanning the sidewalks. If he spotted her, he would swoop over, snatch her up, and take off.

A moment of clarity gave him second thoughts. Why Cami might be walking along this street at this early hour didn't make sense. Even if he found her, she probably wouldn't care to be snatched up.

Beep! Beep!

"Watch it fella! I'll stick that horn—

Wait! Tick exclaimed to himself. *How did I get over here by the Parthenon?*

Walking again, Paul soon found himself halfway across the bridge over the Cumberland. Downtown, with its gaggle of tall buildings, began at the far bank. He paused a minute to watch the river flowing by below. The interlude was interrupted by the ringing of his cell phone.

The call was from Cami, their conversation short. A group of ministers were waiting to meet him near the bridge. Also, the local press was gathering at the nearby state capitol for a brief press conference with him. Would he talk with the reporters?

"Of course," he replied. "For a few minutes."

Hanging up, he was not surprised to see a group of about two dozen people gathered at the bridge's far end. When Paul was only a few paces away, a man stepped forward.

"Hello," he said as Paul neared, extending a hand. "I'm Reverend Jim Hardesty, Nashville Third Christian, Disciples of Christ."

"Paul Lockhart. Caney Creek Baptist," the preacher replied, taking the fellow minister's hand.

"We know of your mission, sir," Reverend Jim said, "and we wholeheartedly support it. Ours is a mixed group, representing a number of faiths. Our bond is a desire to help those in need. On occasion, we have been known to stir things up a little. Why we call ourselves, *The Disorderly Order.*

Paul smiled broadly, his gaze moving from face to face as he said, "I am very pleased to meet you. With such a name, I feel certain I am in good company."

He was answered with laughter.

"We do not wish to delay you," Reverend Hardesty said. "Just the same, we were hoping you could spare a couple of minutes to pray with us at the Capitol. I understand you are heading to the Natchez Trace. Correct?"

"Yes," Paul replied. "I'm going out Broadway, to start."

"Good. This won't cost you but a handful of extra steps."

"I'll be glad to join you," Paul said.

"We probably should introduce ourselves first, sir."

"Just a moment. Please drop the *sir*. I'm Paul."

"And I'm Jim." Reverend Hardesty smiled.

Smiling in return, Paul said, "I'll do my best to remember your names. If I'm successful, we can be assured Divine intervention has taken place."

That brought light-hearted laughter from the group. A moment of shuffling by the *Order's* members ensued as they formed into a receiving line. Each member, male or female, black, white, or otherwise, included their faith and house of worship as they took Paul's hand. With each new introduction Paul felt something inside himself grow stronger.

Reverend Jim led the group off at a fast pace into the heart of downtown. In a few minutes, they were at the front steps of the Tennessee State Capitol. The *Order* quickly formed into three succeeding lines along the front steps, as if they were posing for a graduation photo.

"Paul," Reverend Jim began, "we felt it important to come to this spot. Our state laws, of course, are written here in our Capitol. They are argued in the Supreme Court building to your left. Since so much of what effects our lives is decided only a few strides from where we stand, we thought it an appropriate place to say a few words, if you wish, and to lead us in prayer."

With that, the reverend moved to join the other members on the steps.

Paul glanced over at the Supreme Court building, then at the massive Greek columns of the Capitol serving as the backdrop for the group. He allowed his gaze to rest on each individual member a second or two. Then he looked down at his feet for a moment. When he looked up again, he began to speak.

"Last Sunday, when the members of my community came to see me off, all the area ministers came, too. Those leaders, like you, were united in support, not for me, but for the mission God has called me to perform.

"I am heartened to see so many of you here, from so many faiths, some of which have found themselves in opposition at one time or another. That opposition, my friends, is distant history. This morning we stand as one, in recognition of God's calling. I ask His blessings upon each one of you and your particular faith. In meeting you, God has already blessed me.

"Will you please join me now in a moment of silent prayer, for the children."

All bowed their heads, the traffic swirling through the city raising the only sounds. After a minute Paul said, "Amen." The Disciples replied "Amen" as a group. Paul and the members stepped toward each other and quickly touched hands. Then he turned about, ready to step off again on the great trek. Only then did he notice the television cameras set up off to the side. Halfway between Paul and the two groups, Cami was hurrying toward him.

Chapter 31

"Speak," the thin man said into his phone.

"He's heading down Seventh Avenue toward Broadway," Mr. Smith said. "Prayed with a truckload of ministers, then talked to a bunch of reporters."

"I saw it. All the local stations there?" the thin man asked.

"I think. There was a big pile, for sure."

"Okay. Lay into him hard, like we said last night."

"I'll get a rise," Smith answered."

The thin man hung up and laid his phone on the bedside table. Picking up the TV remote, he began scrolling through the local stations. He left the sound turned down. There was no need for it. All the morning shows were airing the same thing: Preacher Paul—how quickly that name had stuck—praying with a group of Nashville ministers on the steps of the Capitol. He settled on one station and turned the sound up. A familiar small face appeared on the screen.

"This young child has been separated from her mother at the southern—"

He clicked the set off. The Big Guy might think there was no need to get excited, but he knew better. It was always best to nip things in the bud. He sensed this country preacher deal could blow up into something major, in fact, it might already be well on the way. Things could get messy. Maybe, just maybe, aliases Smith and Jones would pull it off. Between them they couldn't ring up a double-digit IQ, but they sure as hell were an aggravating pair. He had little choice but to give them a try. They were all he had available in town.

The thin man suddenly reached for his phone again. He punched a number.

"I need you to check on somebody. It's a preacher, Paul Lockhart, from Southern Kentucky. See what you can dig up."

Paul was heading south from Capitol Hill. The impromptu news conference had gone as well as could be expected, he guessed, considering he had never been through one before. The question about Sarah had been asked, as Cami had predicted. Somehow, he had slogged his way through the answer, saying much the same as he said to Cami days before. The reporters let it go at that, perhaps sensing further digging would do nothing other than pile more dirt around a hole the preacher had no hope of ever climbing out of.

The buildings had height along this street. This was nothing like back home, where a person couldn't sneeze without rattling the neighbors' windows. He felt claustrophobic. As quickly as the feeling arrived, it left, driven away by the sight before him. A few blocks down the hill, perfectly framed by the buildings along 7th Avenue, a tall steeple rose from a red-brick church. *Confirmation,* Paul thought with a sudden smile.

A small green car came creeping by, but Paul did not notice it or the two men inside, even as it gushed coal-colored smoke from the tailpipe when it finally went buzzing away. His gaze remained locked on the tall steeple.

Drew P. McNaughton had grown up without much of anything. Born in the not-so-wide place in the road of Tilly, Arkansas, a flat rock's skip from the headwaters of both the South and Middle Forks of the Little Red River, he remembered little more about living there than joining with his angel-voiced mother to sing in church and her holding him on her lap as she showed him where to put his fingers on her guitar's strings. When he was five and a half, a year after his mother died, his daddy moved Drew, his two brothers, and baby sister further west across the Ozarks to a hog farm outside of Brashears. There he started to grow like crazy. In the middle of his freshman football season, his daddy got a job with Walmart up in Bentonville and moved his brood again. The football coach in Brashears promised everything he could think of to Drew's daddy, including his firstborn, if he would leave the six foot three, 245 pounds *boy* with him. His daddy said, "No." Four years later Drew was a buff six-six and 280 when he ran out on the field at Razorback Stadium in Fayetteville. It was the opening game of his freshman year at the University of Arkansas. Another four years passed and Drew P. *Droopy* McNaughton left the university with second-team All-American honors, a hip injury that ruled out a career in the NFL, a degree in business management, and a satchel full of songs he had written.

Droopy turned the TV off when the segment about the walking preacher ended. He swung his feet to the floor and pushed himself upright. The hip told him to hold on a minute, like it usually did, before he tried to walk. He glanced at his fancy wristwatch—the most obvious emblem of his success—while he waited for the sore joint to get enough blood flowing through it to warm up. There were still three hours before his meeting on Music Row. He had rather be at home in the hills outside Fayetteville, but this was part of the business, five gold records or not.

The hip finally signaled it was loose enough to move, and Droopy made his way over to the window. He pulled the curtains open and looked out on a sunny morning in downtown Nashville. Stretching and twisting in his red sweatpants for a moment first, he moved up closer to the glass and looked down on 7th Avenue. A number of people were hustling along the sidewalks. One looked strangely familiar: a slender man in a white tee-shirt, cargo shorts, and a blue ball cap. It took a minute for it to dawn on Droopy that the man was the preacher he had just seen on TV. As he watched the minister make his way down the hill, he thought of the little girl crying for her mother at the end of the morning show. Then he remembered a little boy in a tiny Arkansas town standing before a plain casket and crying for his mother. Quick tears blurred his vision. When he wiped them away, he caught a last glimpse of the preacher as the man swung right onto Broadway.

Turning from the window, Droopy made his way over to the bed.

He fluffed the pillows up against the headboard, then climbed atop the covers and leaned back. As always, his leather binder was on the nightstand. Grasping the binder, he flipped it open and bent the scribbled-on pages over the top until he came to a clean one. Then he pulled the pen from its sleeve and began writing.

Walking down this endless road,
Burdened by my heavy load.

Chapter 32

"Who you think you are, asshole?" Smith barked, stepping to block Paul's way as he came past the Union Station Hotel. Down the street twenty yards, elbows propped on a blue mailbox, Jones zoomed his video camera in for a close-up of the preacher's face.

"Excuse me?" Paul calmly replied, thinking this was another one of the poor, confused people one met on big city streets. Jones checked the audio from Smith's mic as Paul spoke. Loud and clear. They would, of course, edit Smith's comments later.

"I'm talking to you," Smith kept on, getting louder with each word. "You're the one," he shouted, poking a finger into Paul's chest, "wants to let them filthy-ass Mexicans in."

"I have not said that." Paul shook his head.

"Don't bullshit me! You're the son-of-a-bitch!" Smith screamed, jabbing Paul in the chest again.

"You are mistaken."

"We don't have any jobs now!" Smith yelled. "Immigrants took 'em all. And you're going down to Texas to let more thieves in."

"I'm going to pray for the children," Paul answered, shaking his head.

"No shit, Sherlock? Come up with that by yourself?"

Paul drew a deep breath. "I've been called to go."

"Well now," Smith grinned, sensing he was close to paydirt. "Just who in God's name would give you a call like that?"

"God."

Smith was suddenly at a loss for words. Paul took the opportunity to step around him and start walking again. Then Smith found his voice. "Heard about your little girl," he said to Paul's back. "Bitch died of shame, having you for her daddy."

Paul froze. For several seconds he didn't move. Finally, he spun around and walked back toward Smith. There was that instant when he didn't know what he would have done had Smith been within reach. He wasn't accustomed to thoughts of violence, but they were suddenly there, primed and ready. A change came over him, however, in the few steps it took to cover the space. The rush of hot blood cooled. With their faces only a foot apart, he said, "I will pray for you." Then he turned and walked away.

It took a moment for Smith to answer. "Hey," he called, hustling after Paul, but Paul did not stop. When Smith reached the spot where Jones stood filming, he pulled up short and yelled again. "Hey, I'm talking to you!" Paul kept walking. Before Smith could yell a third time, he suddenly noticed a shadow moving across his path.

Actually, it was two shadows, each cast by something of serious bulk. A pair of men in dark suits, each the size of a pro-football tackle, now stood in front of him and Jones. Smith leaned his head back enough to read *Union Station Security* stitched in gold above the left breast pocket of the giant directly in front of him. Then he allowed his gaze to wander over to the right breast pocket and the gold name plate. *Guiterrez.*

"You are disturbing the peace," Guiterrez said, looking down into Smith's eyes. "You should quieten down."

"Just who the hell do you—"

Smith stopped speaking because he couldn't anymore. It felt like his head was caving in, like everything inside was being squeezed through his pursed lips.

"That was not a suggestion," Guiterrez said in the same controlled voice as before, his hand spread across Smith's face like a huge spider. Jones glanced over at his partner and let out a little squeal.

"I'll take that."

Jones looked toward the beast speaking to him and saw a hand the size of a dinner plate extended his way, palm up. He stole another look at Smith. Something in his partner's head was making crackling sounds, like a weight slowly settling through a pile of corn flakes. In a flash, Jones dropped his camera on the dinner plate.

Exhibiting amazing dexterity, the second security guard had the camera open, and the card removed in seconds. The card went in his pocket. The camera fell onto the sidewalk. His foot came up, stomped down, his heel twisting and grinding the device into ever smaller pieces.

Smith nearly passed out at these new sounds, thinking it was his facial bones giving way. Suddenly, the pressure was gone.

"You boys move along now," Guiterrez said, his voice still soft, controlled. Smith and Jones didn't wait to be told twice.

From his room in the Union Station Hotel, the thin man watched the whole pitiful exercise. "Morons," he said aloud as he pulled the drapes closed.

Chapter 33

Late afternoon found them on the Natchez Trace. Tick came driving toward Paul and eased to a stop beside him.

"Do you have a spot picked out for the night?" Paul asked.

"Yep. There's a bridge over a pretty valley. It's got a place to park." Tick paused to glance at the odometer. "I'd say it's about four miles. How you holding up?"

"My feet aren't happy, but I'll make it, I reckon."

Paul sat straight up at the sound. Tick followed a split second later. Both instantly realized what had awakened them was the drumming of raindrops. In the faint light of dawn, they could see them splattering on the windshield, meandering down in thin streams.

"It doesn't look bad," Paul mused. "Maybe it'll let up soon."

"Let's see," Tick replied, thumbing up the weather radar. Their spot was in a sea of light green. In fact, everything all the way to the Mississippi was the same weak shade. "Crap."

"Is big stuff coming?"

"No," Tick answered, sliding the projection bar. "Nothing heavy, but we'll have this all morning. Sorry, I forgot to check last night."

"There's nothing to be sorry about," Paul assured him. "We can't change the weather. I'm walking, regardless."

They ate a cold breakfast of beanie weenies and crackers, washed down with Gatorade and topped with a banana. The preacher fished his raincoat and floppy hat from the backpack, then loaded it with drinks and snacks for the morning stretch. At the rear door, he turned to Tick.

"Hand me a jug of water, please. I think I'll do a quick rinse."

"There's a park on the other side of the bridge," Tick replied. "It's got restrooms. I can run you over there."

Paul hesitated a minute before asking, "Is it close to the road?"

"Yeah."

"Hot water?"

"I think so."

"That'll work. I'll walk, though," Paul said. "Give my beanie weenies time to settle."

"I hear you," Tick laughed, rubbing his stomach.

†††

The rain had slowed to a mist by the time Paul reached the bridge's midpoint, giving the view a surreal cast, like looking in a mirror lightly fogged. He stopped and rested his hands on the wet guardrail as his mind took snapshots. Heights made him queasy. Focusing on the hills in the distance helped. Had he looked back before he started walking again, he would have seen Tick standing at another spot on the bridge—a place he had stood before.

As Paul stepped off onto paved earth once more, Tick came driving past. He was waiting outside the van when the preacher reached the park entrance, apparently unfazed by the raindrops gathering on his curly hair.

"I apologize, Preacher. Everything's locked up. Too early, I guess."

"It's no big deal," Paul replied, dropping a white lie. In truth, he had been looking forward to scrubbing and a fresh change of clothes. "I might not smell pretty, but I'm depending on you to tell me when I start smelling ugly.

Compared to Nashville and its countless intersections, Paul found walking the Trace easy, even soothing. The road rolled through a series of gentle turns, with frequent short hills, none of which were steep enough to hamper his pace. The shoulders were wide and mown. If a car approached, he could quickly step to the side and safety.

Half a mile into the day, he encountered his first surprise: three deer, all does, standing on the opposite shoulder. They paid him scant attention, glancing his way a few seconds before returning to their grazing. Once he was past, he glanced back to see two were already gone and the third was gliding silently over the split-rail fence.

The next curve revealed a conga line of wild turkeys. Half of them immediately flew over the fence. The rest paraded up and down in an uncoordinated mob, apparently discussing the incursive nature of Paul's sudden appearance in excited gobbles. By the time he drew even, the rear guard had flapped a retreat over the fence and disappeared into the woods.

It became quiet, with only an occasional brief interruption from a passing car. Yesterday came to mind—that horrible man and his disgusting words, particularly about Sarah. How would he have responded a month ago, before the call? Paul remembered his flash of anger, white hot and reason blind. Perhaps the encounter had not been as far from his rage as he would have liked to believe. But as he turned toward the incensed man, a new feeling came, a calming sense. He could only describe it as *grace*.

No doubt, he would meet others along the way who would misinterpret his mission, or even reject the idea that children at the border should be prayed for. Paul said a prayer that when those moments occurred, he would be able to find the same state of grace as had enveloped him yesterday.

He had just finished his prayer when another thought—even more disturbing because it involved a failure to understand on his part—entered his mind.

Chapter 34

Cami's Blog

 his morning I met with Preacher Paul at the Water Valley Overlook on the Natchez Trace. I had a radio interview in Columbia
scheduled for 10:00 a.m. and wanted to get an update. The preacher
was in excellent spirits, though he looked a little worse for wear.
The most uncharacteristic thing was his several days growth of
beard. He volunteered that he had not shaved since his last night
in Kentucky. He promised to do better and asked that I not tell
his wife. Oops! Hope you're not reading this, Jennie! His clothes
were clean yet wrinkled. He sheepishly explained he had washed
up at the Garrison Creek facilities yesterday and had not changed
clothes since. Last evening, he rested in his sleeping bag beneath
the trees on a stretch of the historic Trace route, thus his slightly
rumpled condition.

We stood for a while, looking out over the beautiful valley below.
Then we took our seats on the grass. Preacher Paul immediately
launched into a fuller explanation of his appearance.

"I had an epiphany yesterday," he began. "I realized I had been
pampering myself, sleeping in the van or at the home of a minister—even in a church. I believe Serena must have spent most
nights under the stars as she walked from Guatemala. There may
be stormy times when I am driven to seek shelter, but for the most
part, from here on I intend to mimic her experience. I feel this is
in the spirit of my calling."

After hearing that, he didn't look shabby at all.

†††

"Let me think on this. I'll get back to you before the day's out,"

Chief Ranger Langston Herbert said, hanging up his office phone in Parkway Headquarters a few miles outside Tupelo, Mississippi. The caller was a supervisor in Middle Tennessee, responsible for the first section of the Trace south of Nashville. A combination of a ranger's sudden illness and a moratorium on overtime as the fiscal year wound down had resulted in a thirty-mile stretch not being patrolled the last two evenings.

This, in itself, was not a big problem. The supervisor reported there had been no accidents, no assaults or thefts, nothing that would raise a headline. Yet he had discovered something had taken place, something that had the prospect of being repeated over and over, unless staff intervened. Then he had taken the unprecedented position that, in this case, the standard procedures should be ignored. To follow that recommendation raised a new set of concerns for Chief Herbert.

The chief was not upset over the call. In fact, he appreciated it, for the supervisor had exhibited a keen political awareness of how any action, or lack thereof, could become a hot potato. It seemed a hiker from Kentucky was walking the full length of the Parkway on his way to the border with Mexico. No problem. At any time, there were hikers on the Trace, some going the full route through. Like this individual, many camped along the way, which was nothing to worry about unless one set the woods ablaze by not properly attending a campfire. His rangers worked to keep campers in designated areas to lessen such dangers. The problem here was a vehicle, a van, had stayed overnight in a location where overnight stays were not permitted. His man in Tennessee had gathered from locals that the van was a support vehicle for the through hiker. In other circumstances, a ranger would simply advise the van driver that overnight parking was not permitted, then likely direct him or her to a designated site or even to a community outside Parkway boundaries where they might find accommodations. The problem here was twofold. The hiker was a preacher, *and* he had garnered significant positive publicity as he passed through Nashville. Any actions on the part of his rangers that could be construed as interfering with the preacher's mission, such as instructing him to pack up and move along, had the potential for creating a backlash with politicians and the public alike.

The first thing Chief Herbert wanted to determine was if the hiker was legitimate. He called an old friend, his counterpart at Mammoth Cave National Park in Kentucky. Within minutes he had confirmation. The Kentucky ranger had seen local televised reports on this Preacher Paul, as he was called, when he passed through Bowling Green. His friend related how the minister was from a tiny rural community only a few miles outside the boundaries of his park, and he had been *called* to walk to the border.

After hanging up, the chief immediately called his subordinate in Tennessee.

"Charlie, I need a little more information. I know the minister is called Preacher Paul. I'm looking for his last name, and—"

"Lockhart," Charlie interrupted. "I remember because it's my mother-in-law's maiden name."

"No relation, I hope," the chief replied, smiling at the bit of unnecessary information as he wrote *Paul Lockhart* on a pad.

"Not to my knowledge, sir."

"Okay. I also need the name of the van's driver, as well as the vehicle's model and license number. You know. All the usual."

"Yes, sir. I'll get right on it."

The chief ranger hung up and rocked back in his chair. He tried to imagine what it would be like to hike all that great distance. Hiking was something he had loved to do all his life. It was one of the things that attracted him to the Park Service. He liked the physical challenge certainly, but the sights of Nature's beauty were something he never tired of. That was something he couldn't find on the south side of the windy city.

Who was this Preacher Paul? What would prompt such a calling? Though the chief didn't parade around showing it, he was a man of faith, himself. Well, one thing for certain, Preacher Paul Lockhart would be needing some assistance along the way. Come Sunday, he would address the congregation about it at his little church outside Mantachie. His mother had attended there as a child, before the family moved to Chicago. She never knew he had joined her old church, but it still felt good knowing he'd closed that circle.

Stepping outside, the chief pulled a Swisher Sweet from his shirt pocket. He spun the wheel on his lighter and held the flame to the cigar's tip until it was glowing. A good smoke was one of his few vices, a way of celebrating. Though he didn't understand exactly why, it felt like it was time for that.

He hadn't smoked half the cigar when his administrative assistant stuck her head out the door. "Charlie Utley's on the line."

Five minutes later the chief had what he needed and began writing his memo to staff.

He smiled to himself as the words came. Knowing how to explain to people what you wanted without actually spelling it out was something he was good at.

A Baptist minister, the Reverend Paul Lockhart, is currently hiking the length of the Parkway as one leg of an extended mission trip. He is being accompanied by Thomas Cole, the driver of the minister's supply van (information listed below). As you are aware, distances between restrooms/camping sites are irregularly spaced. This may result in one or both men staying at a particular location for short periods beyond posted hours. Such overstays should not be cause for concern.

Chapter 35

Tick pulled into the parking lot at Jackson Falls. He rolled his window down and shut the motor off, then just sat there confused. All morning he had been strangely tempted to return to the bridge in the hope of recapturing a moment. The rational side of his brain said there was no need to relight the flame. The fire still burned, and the memory was still as sweet as ever, wasn't it?

"Yes!" he shouted.

Still, for the mood he was in, what happened at the bridge almost didn't matter. He might as well drive back into Nashville and pull into that same space at the coffee shop, for it wasn't the first kiss that had him all twisted up. It was the second one, the one Cami instigated, the one that straightened his curls and made it hard for him to catch his breath each time he recalled it. That one. Ever since, he had been having difficulty thinking, unless, of course, he counted thinking of her. Actually, that was the problem. He could not think of much other than her. And he was scared. He, Tick Cole, who had never run from anything in his life, was scared—of a girl.

Of course, she was right. This was definitely not the time for romance. How could he shut out any idea of her, though? That was impossible with the memory of how she kissed him still fresh as the morning air.

Tick finally got out of the van. He was about ten miles from this morning's starting point. This spot would do for lunch. There were picnic tables and restrooms. Tick would call the preacher in a minute and let him know. The distant sound of trickling water lured him toward the start of a steep trail. A sign pointed the way to the falls. *Might be something worth exploring*, he thought. His cell phone rang before he could start down.

It was Cami. She had just finished her radio interview in

Columbia. There was an Italian restaurant with take-out across the street. How did spaghetti and meatballs sound for lunch? The carbs would keep Preacher Paul's energy up. She could return to the Trace the way she had come, on state highway 50. The preacher couldn't be too far from the intersection, she said.

"Spaghetti suits me," Tick said. "And you're right. He should be about two miles south of the junction by now. I talked to him half an hour ago. He said he would've made it further, but he got sidetracked. Anyway, I've found a good spot to stop and eat. It's called Jackson Falls. I'd say he'll be here in about forty-five minutes."

"Where's Jackson Falls?"

"Hang a left at the Parkway. You can't miss it," he assured her.

"Okay, I'll be there shortly," Cami said. Her voice changed to a sweeter tone. "It'll be good to see you." Two beats passed. "It's been too long."

Three days, Tick said to himself, not needing to count. *Three impossibly long days.*

"Yeah, uh, same here," he answered, fumbling to push the key to end the call. Grabbing the railing, he levered himself away from the path's edge. "Blame woman!" he said aloud. If his knees came any closer to buckling, he imagined, they'd be changing the name of this place from Jackson Falls to Tick Fell.

Paul felt like he was gliding above the ground. He had his stride down now. The aches and pains in his feet, present the first few days, were gone. His leg muscles were tight and solid, rounding into shape, finally.

Other than meeting an occasional car, hiking here was literally a walk in the park. There were hills, but they were always gentle ups and downs. There were always birds and squirrels. Sometimes, he would spot a raccoon or possum, even a skunk, especially near sunrise or sunset. Yesterday he'd witnessed a covey of quail marching in single file alongside the fence, then disappearing through a gap back into the woods. Once, he spotted a coyote that turned into a four-legged rocket when it realized he was there. He was accustomed to such scenes, for it really wasn't different from home, though with the exception of the coyote, most of the animals seemed tamer or more laid back. They'd raise their head, give him a mildly curious look, then go back to doing whatever they were doing.

Paul felt as if he were walking through a place of solitude meant for only him to see. Green was all around, the grass of the road's shoulders, the weeds peeking over the split rails. Leaves hinted at fall's approach, with some already turned to freckled reds or used-up browns. A few times a day he would catch a glimpse of a dwelling or building through a gap in the foliage. It was enough to let him know civilization was often only steps away. He tried to ignore the evidence, preferring to embrace the feeling of moving alone through wilderness.

A section of the original Trace was just off to the right. Last evening, as he lay in his sleeping bag on a piece of the old trail, it had come to him clearly how he was but one of many who had traveled this route. He had closed his eyes and allowed his imagination to conjure up some of those travelers. Most were walking north—Indians, traders, slaves or those seeking to escape slavery, thieves and murderers, soldiers, Kaintucks returning from long floats downriver, people simply seeking a better place, for the old one no longer welcomed. All had made their way along this winding ridgeline, their path smoothed by countless feet long wearied.

Then he spotted the rabbit—a plain cottontail that paid him no mind as it nipped its way through grass near the fence. Of course, it was different from Sarah's. Its fur was brown, not red. It was small, not huge like Brutus, and it was an actual living creature. Still, the bunnies were similar enough to open the gates to a flood of sad memories.

Paul felt shame as the tide ebbed. He had not said a single word to Sarah this morning, which was when they usually visited. He had not even thought of her. This violated a vow he had made during the first hours of the trek—at least once every day, he would talk to his daughter. He had kept his word until now, sometimes speaking aloud as he walked, sometimes whispering as he sat hidden from prying eyes and ears, but most often inside his head. He had not shared this with Jennie, lest she question his sanity. Perhaps rightly so. Talking to the dead was not an ideal way to convince others one's mind was in balance. Too much had been left unsaid, however, and if he called her name, was she not alive? Some who had walked this way believed so.

Before he knew what he was doing, Paul was walking toward the fence. He passed within ten feet of the unconcerned rabbit, nodding as if it were an old acquaintance, and quickly swung over the rail. Within a minute he found a large oak with a moss-covered spot of ground at its base. A few feet beyond the tree the woods opened to the sky, revealing the edge of a bluff. Paul sat and leaned back against the oak.

"Hello, baby girl," he said, speaking in a conversational tone. "Did you see the little rabbit? Did you ask God to put it there so I would remember our morning talk? I'm sorry I'm late, hon. Poppy forgets things sometimes, even important things.

"This is a pretty spot, isn't it? All the big trees, and the view, wow! It's miles across the valley. This reminds me of where we used to sit beside the creek back home. Okay. I know it's very different. We're up on this bluff here, so things are not that much alike. I guess what it reminds me most of is us sitting under a tree, like our sycamore by the pool of still water."

Paul told her how the woods had sounded the night before with the animals and insects calling to one another, of the antlered deer he had seen framed in the moonlight, how it magically vanished. He described everything he had seen this morning that could be deemed noteworthy, which he knew could be almost anything for a four-year-old. At last, his well ran dry. He sat quietly then, imagining her cuddled against him. It was the most peaceful thing in this most peaceful place. He allowed the minutes to slide by until they began to pile up.

"I don't want to leave here, Sarah. This spot eases my heart, but Poppy has many miles to walk today. I'm going to meet Tick and Cami soon. I will talk with you this evening, I promise. Love you."

Paul made his way back through the woods and swung over the fence again. The rabbit had moved on.

The way ahead soon revealed a large clearing. There was a parking area. Tick's van was there, pulled up near a small building. Cami came rolling slowly past in her car, waving. Minutes later, he neared the picnic table where the pair were arranging lunch. The aroma of garlic-laced food suddenly struck him, and he unconsciously quickened his pace. Tick and Cami appeared almost—almost as if they had been caught doing something they shouldn't be doing, glancing toward each other, their expressions strangely serious. Then they'd look away quickly. Paul managed to hold his smile in check as he wondered, *Do they know yet that they are falling in love?*

Chapter 36

Bob Mendoza grinned, remembering the surprise in Barb's voice when he told her he was in Nashville. He'd been in town for only a couple of hours, doing his thing, following a lead on one of his stories. As usual, this one was about drug smuggling. It was an old subject, but always a fertile one. The problem and its causes never went away. He was more than ready to do something on another subject, but cartel documentaries paid the bills.

Over dinner last evening, he thanked Barb for her call about the walking preacher. She proceeded to fill him in on more details. It was a humanitarian story, a story of faith that could give his flagging independent career a big booster shot. Already he was envisioning a multi-part series on the search for a little girl named Serena. As word got out more concerning what spurred Preacher Paul's walk, any number of reporters would be heading to Brownsville seeking the child. He knew Adriana LaFleur, the network reporter who broke the story. She was a pro, a real bulldog who never stopped digging. There was no time to lose if he was to have a chance at finding Serena first. First was everything. But Bob had a little bulldog blood, himself.

He was uniquely qualified, third generation Mexican American, born in San Antonio, with a knack for languages and a sharp ear for dialects, particularly the dialects found in Central America. These abilities made him attractive to both English and Spanish news networks in the states, for he could switch languages back and forth with ease. Of course, he could do the same below the Rio Grande, blending in without effort whether reporting on television or talking to a peasant growing coca or marijuana.

It was still dark as Bob walked to the window and looked out over the park. He had been awake since 3:00 a.m., his mind on

Barb. She had given him a quick peck on the cheek, a reminder of what was, of what could have been, when they separated on the walk outside the restaurant. Speaking over her shoulder as she walked away, she told him to be sure to keep her posted on how the search was going. Watching her leave, he had promised he would.

Barb is a special lady, he thought as his eyes strained to make out features in the park. They had been very good friends, very *close* friends, when they both worked at the local station where she now hosted the morning show. Hard to believe eleven years had passed since those days. They might have been more than close had her roots in Tennessee not run quite so deep, if his need to climb the ladder had not been quite so strong. She had stayed, and he had climbed. A six-year hitch with CNN had given him the exposure necessary to allow him to branch out with his own production company. Things had been tough lately, however, with the networks almost as tired of airing his drug cartel features as he was of making them.

One more drug story contact to see this morning—the reason he was in Nashville to begin with, he reminded himself—and he would take off on the Serena chase. Before he went to the border, Bob wanted to speak with the preacher. Barb had given him the phone number of the journalism student documenting the journey. He would give her a call to arrange an interview for wherever the preacher happened to be on the Natchez Trace. Barb didn't think the man could be all that far away.

Bob turned from the window and headed toward the shower. He felt enthused, like he always felt when he began a new project. This could be a really good story. Good stories came along fairly often, but usually they involved digging into the past. This one felt like it could be the gift that kept on giving. He could jump on in the middle and follow as it developed, perhaps for months.

Yes, he thought as he turned the water on, *things are looking up.*

Chapter 37

Wrapping up business in Nashville took Bob longer than he expected. It was 1:30 p.m. before he pulled onto the Trace. The low speed-limit made him feel like he was barely moving for the first few miles. Then a strange thing happened. He started to enjoy the drive. Birdsong Hollow was wonderful. He stopped and walked out on the bridge to take in the view. Back on the road, he puttered along, content to check out the wildlife and scenery. There were no tractor-trailers, no wannabe NASCAR drivers zipping in and out, no road hogs riding his rear bumper. He felt more relaxed than he had in a long time.

It was mid-afternoon before he spotted the preacher. Walking stick in hand, the man was swinging along at a fast pace on a level stretch. Bob eased up across from him.

"Excuse me," he said. "You wouldn't happen to be Preacher Paul, would you?"

Paul halted and turned toward Bob.

"Some call me that."

"I'm Bob Mendoza. I spoke with Cami."

"Oh, yes." Paul stepped across the road, offering his hand. "Pleased to meet you," he added. After they shook, he went on. "I've got about four miles to go to reach this evening's campsite. It'll take about an hour and a half. Want to meet there?"

"I was hoping we could walk together. I'd like to film you as we go, if you don't mind."

"I don't mind a bit, if you don't care to have a scarecrow in your movie," Paul laughed. "Sure I look pretty ragged."

"Oh, you're fine. Tell me where you're camping, and I'll drive ahead and leave my car. Then I'll walk back to meet you."

"That would work, but Tick is already there."

"Tick?"

"He's a big fellow with an old green cargo van. My logistics guy. You'll find him somewhere around Swan View. He can run you back. Might save you a few steps."

"That sounds good."

"I'll let him know you're on the way," Paul said, pulling his phone out.

Half an hour later, Tick pulled the van to the shoulder in front of Paul. Bob hopped out, carrying a canvas bag. He pulled a flag-bearer's belt out of the bag, along with a small digital camera and a telescoping pole. In a couple of minutes, he had the belt buckled around his waist, the camera mounted on one end of the short pole and the other end seated in the belt.

Tick got out and stood watching the operation intently.

"I thought you'd have one of those cameras like the news people carry," he said.

"I've got one," Bob replied, "but this is easier for walking."

"Got to be lighter," Tick noted. "Here's you a water," he said, handing Bob a plastic bottle. "And one for you, Preacher," he added, tossing a bottle to Paul.

Tick swung up in the driver's seat and turned the van around. Without warning, Paul started walking again. Bob filmed Paul striding away for a few seconds, then hustled to catch up.

"Alright," Bob said, once he had synchronized his steps with Paul's. "Let's get some baseline stuff. I'm with Reverend Paul Lockhart, walking south on the Natchez Trace, near milepost—" He squinted, trying to read the number on the wooden post 100 yards ahead.

"Three ninety-five."

"You can read that?" Bob was astounded.

"You can't?"

"No."

"Neither can I," Paul laughed. "I remembered the number on the last one."

Bob shook his head, laughing, too. Then he recited the date and time. "Okay, we're in business. This is a great place to walk, Reverend. So peaceful."

"Paul."

"I beg your pardon."

"Just call me, Paul. Reverend is too formal. This is not a place for titles, but it is a place of reverence."

Bob hesitated a minute before speaking, "Yes. I agree. Reverence for the beauty of God's creation is what you're getting at, right?"

"Well, sort of. It is beautiful, but all God's creation is beautiful, I think. I'd say this is more of a place where you can allow your mind to have free rein. That's when answers appear, when you quit straining and the connection with something bigger than yourself takes place without effort or thought. That's true beauty. Walking helps with that—helps you find your way into a feeling of reverence. I walk all the time back home when I'm working on a sermon. My wife, Jennie, says I'm airing out my brain. There's nothing like a stroll in the country to do that."

"Airing out your brain," Bob chuckled. He paused a few moments. "The rest of what you said, well, you've certainly given me some things to think about."

Paul smiled. "That's part of being a minister. Now, I understand you're working on a documentary. I imagine you have a few questions."

"I do," Bob nodded. "I suppose you have repeated your story more times than you care to remember. It must be painful still, but if you would describe the events that led you to where you are now."

"You are right, it still remains very painful for Jennie and me."

Paul recited his stock narrative of what a wonderful child Sarah was, the accident, Serena crying, and finally, the call from God. Bob had the patience not to interrupt. When Paul finished, Bob gave him a moment before making a comment.

"Forgive me for this next question. Do you think there is a link between Sarah's death and your call to go to the border?"

"Are you asking, did God bring about Sarah's death so I would follow His will?"

"Well, yes," Bob replied.

"No. I haven't thought that for one second. I don't believe God works that way. To cause a child to die—absolutely not. What I do believe is that when something happens in a person's life, be it bad or good, to open their heart to His will, God will speak to them. That is what took place with me. Not until I opened my heart, did God call me to do His bidding."

"There are likely some who doubt you heard God speak. Does that bother you?"

"No," Paul instantly replied, catching Bob off guard with his certainty. "Doubt leads to faith. The steps are simple. Question and seek answers. Open your heart and listen. Follow His will."

"You make it sound easy."

"The path may be rocky, but it's straight."

They fell silent as they made their way up a long hill. Bob was soon struggling to keep up with the fast-walking preacher.

"You might want to cut your camera off," Paul said.

"Huh?"

"You're puffing like a steam engine."

"Oh, okay. Right." Bob clicked the button.

In half a minute they were near the crest.

"You know the best thing about walking up a hill?" Paul asked.

"No," Bob wheezed.

"Coasting down the other side."

Several more minutes passed in silence as they descended the far slope. Bob was eventually able to breathe more or less normally. He left the camera off, though.

"You know, Paul, there will be people who think you are up to mischief. For one thing, some may believe your true agenda is influencing immigration policy or maybe embarrassing the authorities. I don't have any evidence of either of those things, but having been on both sides of the border numerous times, I can see where they might become issues. In fact, I expect that'll take place. Just trying to warn you, that's all."

Paul didn't answer for a moment. "It already has, at least with immigration. I had a couple of men tell me as much in Nashville."

Sensing another avenue to pursue, Bob asked, "They get rough with you?"

Paul glanced over at him and smiled. "Let's just say Miss Manners would have given them failing grades."

"Be careful, Paul."

"Oh, I'm certain God will watch over me. I doubt He would send me toward the border and not see that I got there."

"I hope you're right," Bob said, meaning it. This preacher was a good man. He struck him as being a little naïve, however, there was no doubt he believed in his mission. "One more question," he said, reaching up to turn the camera back on. "Serena? She plays such an integral part in all this. What about her?"

Shaking his head, Paul hesitated. "I just want to see her with her mother, safe and happy."

Chapter 38

"I miss you like a pair of tight shoes." Jennie said, beginning their nightly phone conversation.

"I miss you like a mosquito bite," Paul answered.

"I miss you like a runny nose."

"Yuk," Paul exclaimed. "I hate those. Uh, I miss you like drinking some milk, then seeing on the carton that it expired two weeks ago."

"That's just nasty!" Jennie pretended to gag. "I'm switching to something more serious, if you don't mind."

"Sure."

"Remember the time we went walking way, way back in the woods, right after we moved here? It was a chilly day in November. Neither of us had sense enough to wear anything on our head, and it started to rain. We finally found a place to hide under a big cedar tree, but the rain kept dripping through. Do you remember what you did?"

"I took off my jacket, and we held it over our heads like it was a little tent."

"That's the time," Jennie said softly. "We cuddled up, holding each other tight as we could. I was shivering. You pressed your cheek against mine."

"Yes."

"Your skin was so warm. It was like I was sitting next to the fire. I quit shivering. Ever since, when I feel cold, I think of that moment, and the warmth comes back."

"I did not know that," Paul said, emotion making his voice brittle. They were quiet half a minute before Paul added, "And all this time my memory has been that you warmed me.

"Tell me about your day," Paul said after they had held onto the memory a minute longer.

"Same old same old at work. Forms and more forms. Exciting

157

as watching moss grow. Oh, Mary Ellen is pregnant. She told us this morning. On cloud nine."

"I imagine," Paul answered. They both fell silent, remembering when they found out Jennie was carrying Sarah.

"It's still early yet, of course," Jennie was the first to speak, "and I may be rushing things, but there's a tiny hint of change in the woods, I think—some bits of color here and there. I hope it's a pretty fall."

"Me, too," Paul replied, knowing how much she loved that time of year.

"Where are you tonight?" Jennie asked.

"We're at an overlook called Swan View," Paul answered. "I checked it out before dark. It took some searching to find a place to see good, but I finally did. You'd like it. It's a pretty place."

"It's a sweet name. Sounds soothing, somehow."

"Yeah, it does. Haven't seen any swans, but there's a little waterfall across the road. Tick and I went over. Now that was soothing, listening to the water."

"I'll look it up when we get off the phone. I've started doing that the last couple of days. It helps me understand where you are."

"That's a good idea," Paul answered, nodding as if she could see him.

"How's your foot?" Jennie asked, changing rows. "Yesterday you said it was hurting."

"It's fine. I just had that burning feeling for the last mile or so. Everything is good, really. I was thinking this morning that I'm getting in decent shape. For certain, I'm walking faster than I was. It seems like my legs are on automatic pilot now."

"You've covered enough miles to develop some muscle memory," Jennie agreed. Then she changed topics again. "What did you have for lunch? I worry about you eating enough."

"I'm eating like Deacon Henry at a smorgasbord! Today Cami picked up some spaghetti and meatballs. We had lunch at another waterfall—Jackson Falls—and I ate enough for three lumberjacks."

"And for supper?" Jennie asked, laughing.

"Oh, man. Bob Mendoza, that reporter I texted you about, came up with pizzas from somewhere. I ate enough for three more lumberjacks."

Jennie was laughing so hard she couldn't speak. Finally, she managed to say, "Well, I won't worry about you eating tonight."

"You don't have to."

"It's just that I know how you and Tick are. A pack of Nabs and a Pop-Tart are a well-balanced meal."

"Speaking of Tick—" Having cast the lure, Paul let it lay there.

"What about him?" Jennie finally asked.

"Actually, it's what about them?"

"You mean Cami and Tick, and the love stuff?"

"Yes. You see, when I came walking up to them at Jackson Falls, it was like I had interrupted a secret conversation. Then they couldn't seem to look at one another more than— Hold on! How did you know I was talking about those two and love?"

"Elementary, my dear husband. I noticed they were falling in love at the potluck. He kept staring at her when she wasn't looking, and she kept staring at him when he had his head turned. Then when they were close enough to speak, there was just a little too much smiling. The real clue, though, was when they separated. Each one kept glancing back at the other."

"We used to do the same kind of stuff when we first fell in love," Jennie reminded him, "especially stopping talking when anyone came close. We were afraid people might discover our secret. Of course, if they had heard what we were saying—"

"Yeah, I guess so," Paul admitted. "It crossed my mind today they might be falling in love. But you were way ahead of me."

"Any woman could tell there was more than a casual interest."

"Is that so? And any man?" Paul asked.

"Wouldn't have noticed what was happening if you hit him over the head with it."

"That doesn't make me feel better."

"I'm sorry, but the truth is the truth. The good thing is you have a front-row seat to watch love blossoming. That is something special."

"You are right," Paul replied.

"Okay," Jennie sounded ready to move on. "Tell me about the countryside. Are you still walking along the ridge?"

"Yes. It still looks a lot like back home. I'm taking a long stroll through the woods, it seems. I did pass a spot where a branch of the Trail of Tears crossed the road. Funny, when you're walking you go by something slow enough to absorb a little of it. It felt that way to me, anyway. Where the Indians were forced to march through, I sensed—it's hard to describe—but it was like I stepped into a place filled with a great sadness. I said a prayer."

"I'm glad you prayed," Jennie said. "I've never really thought about it, absorbing some of the emotion in a place, but it makes sense, doesn't it? Pain and distress—even great joy, I suppose—may leave traces. So often we pick up suffering in others without a word being said. Why not notice *where* people suffered?"

Both were suddenly thinking the same thing: how it felt to stand by Sarah's swing, to know the pain that lingered in that tiny spot of ground, yet there was also great joy to be found there in the echoes of her laughter. A minute passed in silence before Paul found his voice.

"Don't think I'll push too hard tomorrow, since it's Sunday. There's a place just down the road, something about where Meriwether Lewis died, I think. You know, the great explorer?"

"I've heard a thing or two about him," Jennie, the one with the history minor, replied. "Lewis and Clark. The Corps of Discovery."

"Yes, that Lewis," Paul chuckled. "Anyway, be a good place to get ourselves lined out for the next big push. We've got to do laundry. It's stacking up. Tick's been fussing that the van's getting kind of gamey."

"Shew! I can only imagine," Jennie giggled.

"No, you can't, and be glad." Paul laughed. "Okay, now we need to talk a minute about where I'll be a week from now. I'd like to make some plans."

Chapter 39

"You ought to have that memorized by now," Elsie said, resting a hand on Henry's shoulder. She bent her head down beside his to look at the map spread across the kitchen table.

"You'd think. There's just something about studying out your path and finding what you can see on the way, I reckon."

"I guess so. It doesn't make sense to miss stuff," Elsie said, leaning over further. "What's that by your finger?"

Henry looked down at the lettering.

"Something or 'nother Mound, looks like," he answered, reaching for the magnifying glass. He moved the glass in and out over the map until his hand suddenly steadied, and he announced, "Bear Creek Mound. It's just across the Alabama line into Mississippi. I've noticed there's several of those mounds down that way."

"Indians made them, right?" Elsie asked.

"I imagine," Henry answered. "Remember when we stopped at those over by St. Louis? When we went to see your aunt back in '78?"

"I do remember that," Elsie replied. "Aunt Gertrude, bless her. One of our few trips."

They fell quiet. After a moment Henry looked up from the map. His gaze settled on the far side of the kitchen where the early-morning sun lit up a section of wallpaper and brought life to the old yellow flowers. He finally lifted his glasses enough to rub the bridge of his nose, sort of absentmindedly. "Never took you much of any place, did I?"

"Oh, I don't know about that," Elsie answered, holding her index and middle fingers pressed together as she ran them down the map, following the line of the Natchez Trace. "We went to Florida that time, and we took a lot of little day trips around here."

"Florida," Henry snorted. "What a bust. There three days and it poured rain every second. Might as well stayed home and slept in the tub with the water running."

"We didn't know there was a storm coming," Elsie said. "They weren't good about predicting the weather very far ahead back then."

"Well, I'm sorry," Henry said, turning his face toward her. "I could have done better, took you to some nice places, but I always let this old farm tie me down."

"You've never heard me complaining," she said, still slowly following the route of the Trace with her fingers. "I like it fine right here. It's home." At last, she stopped near the center of the map, her fingertips pressing down lightly on a spot in northeast Mississippi. "Besides, we're a long way from being done traveling. Tomorrow we're going to Tupelo."

"Right you are, gal," Henry smiled. "Heading out with our Jennie at first light."

Elsie suddenly leaned in and kissed Henry on the forehead. "And that's not all. Before Christmas you're taking me to Texas."

"Yes'm," Henry said, moving his great gnarled hand to cover hers. Their fingers intertwined, his thick and rough with calluses, finding the way between hers, so slender and delicate, despite the long decades of hard work. He slowly slid their joined hands down the map until they came to rest, fingertips at the line between Mexico and the southernmost point of Texas. "All the way to the Rio Grande. I promise."

✝✝✝

Paul had been burning up the miles today. Last evening, they had camped in Tishomingo State Park, having crossed from Alabama into Mississippi late in the afternoon. The park, with its full range of facilities, had proved a blessing. Hot water to wash in, a shave in preparation for Jennie's coming visit—the first time he had done that in days—and a fresh change of clothes combined to make him feel like a new man. He and Tick had even indulged with a hot supper at a restaurant in Tishomingo.

Now it was a warm fall day with a light breeze at his right shoulder. The kind of day back home when he could stay out in the fields from dawn to dusk. Work was always something less than true labor then. His legs had responded accordingly, propelling him down the Trace at his fastest rate yet. When he stepped off the roadway at Pharr Mounds for his mid-afternoon break, he had already covered almost twenty miles.

Paul stopped at a display board to read the exhibit information. After a couple of moments, he looked out toward the mounds. They rose in a series, progressing easterly across the wild grasses of the bottomland. It was a quiet place, a place of contemplation. He found a spot of fence rail where he could take a leaning seat and simply indulge himself in looking. Paul found it easy to imagine the flat tops occupied with worshippers. After a few moments, his eyes closed. He offered a simple prayer of thankfulness for having been led here.

Grrrr!

He saw it standing just inside the fringe of mown grass, a sad silhouette of what was once a very big dog. The emaciated creature was staring right at him, all hip bones and shoulder joints and ribs showing like living x-rays just beneath the skin. Its hair was reddish and matted together in clumps of stick tights and cockle burrs. The tail was the worst spot, encrusted with short streaks of dried mud and nests of stick tights and burrs. At the tip a knot of vegetation entwined with what appeared to be green weed-trimmer string to form a lion's tail ball. The head of the beast could only be classified as massive.

"Look at you," Paul said. "Head like that wouldn't fit in a five-gallon bucket."

Grrrr! The dog gave a low growl once more, taking a tentative step the preacher's way. *Woof! Woof!* It barked a little louder than it growled, but the sound seemed dried out and stiff, as if barking hurt its throat.

"I imagine you're hungry. Let's see what I've got," Paul answered, shucking out of his pack.

The dog stepped closer to him. *Grrrr!* It stopped half an arm's length away.

"Patience," Paul said softly. He reached into the pack and fished around for a moment before pulling out a can of Vienna sausage. "I forgot I had this." He popped the can's top and pulled one of the sausages out with his thumb and forefinger. "Here you go."

Glump!

"Careful son, I need those fingers. Want another?" Paul asked, offering a second sausage.

Glump!

"You'll bust a tonsil. Really ought to chew your food."

Glump!

The can was empty.

Grrrr!

"Peanut butter and crackers?"

Apparently, the dog liked them, for two packages disappeared as quickly as Paul could offer crackers. Done, it worked its tongue back and forth to clear the peanut butter and crumbs clump from its mouth.

Grrrr!

"Been so long, you've forgotten your table manners." Paul dug into the pack again. He came out with a honey bun. "This is it," he said sternly, tearing the cellophane off. Then he offered the bun to the dog.

Glump! The dog swallowed it whole.

"Good Lord, Buckethead! You're gonna choke."

Grrrr!

"I told you before you inhaled, I don't have anything else."

The dog stared at him for a long moment, then sat down on its haunches, its face turned to the side. After a few seconds it twisted its head around to stare at the preacher with those big, beautiful, ever so pitiful brown eyes. Paul looked out toward the mounds, trying to ignore the beast, but every time he glanced back at it, the dog was still sitting there, gazing at him as if it could cry, as if it wanted him to cry, too.

"Sorry, buddy. That's all I have." Paul picked up his empty pack and shrugged back into it. "Maybe somebody will come by with a truckload of groceries," he said, reaching more out than down to scratch behind a floppy ear, "but right now, I need to get back walking."

After half a dozen steps, he glanced back over his shoulder. The dog was gone. Then something bumped against his opposite leg. He turned that way to see the creature walking along beside him.

"Go on back now," Paul said, coming to a stop. The dog stopped, too, and sat on its haunches once more. The giant head turned. The pitiful brown eyes stared. "Don't even try that on me."

Paul started off again. The dog followed. Paul walked faster. The dog walked faster. Paul broke into a jog. The dog kept up easily, then suddenly trotted around him, taking the lead. Paul slowed back to a walk. The dog sat and waited for him to catch up. When he stopped beside it, the two, man and beast, joined in a staring contest. After a couple of minutes, the preacher blinked.

"Oh, all right, Buckethead. Let me see what I can do." Paul pulled his phone out.

"What's up, Preacher?" Tick asked after the third ring.

"Need you to find some dog food. Get a big bag—biggest you can find. Got a dog that's dressed up like a Shetland pony walking with me now."

Chapter 40

Bob Mendoza picked up the clipboard from the passenger seat and began to double check the equipment list. As many trips as he had made across the border, he had what he needed down to a science. Nevertheless, he always made this final inspection once everything was in his beaten-up Land Rover. He had been stuck south of the Rio waiting for a part. Things like camera batteries and engine belts could and did bite the dust, but he wasn't going to be held up because he had forgotten to load something that had failed before. As an extra precaution, yesterday a mechanic had gone over the old war wagon from bumper to bumper.

In his apartment on South Padre Island last evening, Bob had double checked another list. This one was for anything having to do with where Serena might be. It included various immigration holding facilities in southern Texas, as well as contacts at some of them. Though the list was incomplete, it was mildly disappointing that none of his sources could report having seen the girl.

The dearth of information was hardly surprising. Searching for particular migrants had never been Bob's main emphasis. Up till now, he had been much more interested in finding out *what*, which was almost always drugs, instead of *who* was crossing the border. That meant he had concentrated on developing information sources—Customs and Border Patrol personnel—at entry sites. He had been successful.

Over the last week, Bob had put out feelers to these contacts, trying to find if any could confirm that Serena had recrossed the border into Mexico. He had quickly heard back from all but one. His contact in Laredo was off on vacation. After his return to duty yesterday, the officer reached Bob with disappointing news. Serena had been sent back across the border in secrecy, transported in a civilian car to Nuevo Laredo six days ago. It was time to internationalize the search. The trail might be cold, but at least he had a place to start.

Back in his apartment, Bob rolled up his sources list and stuffed it inside a half empty box of burritos in the freezer. It was unnecessary—Bob had a memory like a steel trap—but he liked having backup in writing. *Who knows when the old gray cells might start giving out,* he mused? Then he texted a phone number in Mexico. In seconds he had confirmation that his two crew members would meet him at the designated spot in Nuevo Laredo. Time to get moving. Bob pulled his apartment door closed, feeling the heady sense of anticipation he always felt at going below the border.

Chapter 41

Jennie leaned her cheek against the window. The glass was cool. She instantly felt more awake and sat up straight where she could see better. The backseat of Henry's Crown Vic was big enough to stretch out and grab a nap if she wanted. There was even a folded blanket with a thick pillow atop it on the far seat. Yet Jennie did not want to sleep. In fact, she was determined to do the opposite and stay as alert as possible the entire trip. She wanted to see every foot of the way Paul had walked, pretend she was walking along with him. Now, she gazed out the door window, a steno notebook on her lap, and watched the far shoulder of the Natchez Trace slide by. When they passed a spot from where Paul had called her, she marked it in the notebook, jotting down the closest milepost. Somehow, it helped make her feel more connected to him.

She'd left home with Henry and Elsie at the first sign of daylight. They expected to catch up with Paul before dark somewhere north of Tupelo. Henry was driving. The first part of the trip wasn't bad, but as they neared Nashville with its heavy traffic and convoluted road network, Jennie became increasingly nervous. In spite of his age, Henry handled it all with ease. Elsie sat in front with him, making small talk and acting as unperturbed by the cars cutting all around them as if she were seated at her kitchen table back home. The contrast in traffic conditions now was wonderful. They met the occasional driver every minute or two. A couple of miles past the high bridge, a young man in a pickup truck rode their back bumper for a minute. Henry slowed down and the pickup passed them on the first available straight stretch. Now it was quiet and slow, with Henry holding it right on the speed limit of 45.

"This is just lovely," Elsie said, "and relaxing. A true drive in the park."

"Deer." Henry pointed to a spot near the tree line on the right 100 yards up the road. "Makes fourteen."

"Isn't she lovely?" Elsie asked, not expecting an answer, as they rolled near the doe. "There's just something sweet about seeing a deer. Looks like you could walk up and pet them." She turned to watch out the side window as they moved past. "So peaceful here. Just what Paul needed, I'm sure." After a moment she twisted around further to face Jennie. "And you, also."

Jennie smiled back at her friend a moment before answering, "It is peaceful. And you are right, I needed this. I never realized—I feel more at ease now than any time since—"

Elsie managed to reach a hand over the seat back toward Jennie. The younger woman did the rest, lifting her hand to clasp Elsie's. A short squeeze from both said volumes, left their eyes glistening. After a moment, they released their hold.

"How you gals doing?" Henry asked. "About ready for a restroom break?"

"Yes!" both women exclaimed.

"There's a spot just ahead where we can stop and stretch our legs. Called Jackson Falls."

"Oh, I remember Paul telling about it," Jennie said, thinking about their conversation concerning the love birds. The memory brought a wide smile to her face.

Chapter 42

The three of them—Paul, Tick and Buckethead—had made camp last evening alongside a small creek. They ate first, the men dining on bologna sandwiches, the hound gulping down several shovelfuls of dried dog food. For half an hour after eating, Paul and Tick worked at pulling sticktites and burrs from Buckethead's hair. The dog stood still during the tedious ordeal, growling occasionally as they dug out the more stubborn hitchhikers. When they could find no more, Tick pulled off his shoes and socks, emptied his pockets, and then scooped up the creature in his arms. It was a notable feat even for Tick. Amazingly, the dog didn't struggle. Tick carried him down to the creek and carefully stepped off in the water. It came almost to his knees. Slowly, he lowered the dog into the flow, holding on with both hands until it found its footing. A muddy cloud stretched downstream from them for a few moments as the worst of the filth melted away. Tick worked quickly, sliding his hands along the dog's sides and back, its legs and tail, behind its ears, scrubbing a little harder with the bar of soap when he felt a rough spot, pulling the occasional *insect* tick from its skin. Paul stood on the creekbank marveling at his two large companions, one being so easy with each swipe of his hand, the other standing quiet and accepting the care.

"I've been thinking, Preacher," Tick began, using both hands to wipe along the sides of the dog's face from ears to nose.

Paul shook his head. "You just won't call me by my name, will you?"

"Sorry. I keep forgetting," Tick replied, digging a finger inside a dog ear. "Hard to break old habits, especially when *Preacher* is kind of the official name I've always called you."

"I understand," Paul nodded. "We're friends first, though. Besides, there's just the three of us, and I don't think Buckethead cares."

"You're right. All I've heard him call you is, *Grrrr*."

"Exactly," Paul laughed.

"Anyway," Tick tried to get back on track. "I've been thinking about his name. Buckethead's accurate, but it's kind of a mouthful, you know. I think we need to shorten it up. Maybe give him a nickname"

"Okay. Got any ideas?" Paul was trying not to laugh at Tick's serious demeanor.

"How about Buck," Tick said, glancing at Paul. "He's big as a deer and looks wild as a buck."

"Perfect," Paul smiled.

Tick lifted the dog's face to look at him. "What do you think, Buck? Like that?"

Buck's tongue shot out and gave Tick one giant slurping lick from Adam's apple to hairline.

Tick sputtered and spat, then finally ducked his face in the stream.

"Ooh, nastiness. I can't stand nastiness," he said, shaking water from his face. He didn't seem to be that bothered, though, giving Buck a good scratching behind his ears.

Chapter 43

The tarpaper shack was on a dirt road in pine woods outside Meridian, Mississippi. It didn't look like much, and it wasn't. Odd-sized strips of tarpaper were missing. There were only a few windows. Each had at least one broken pane. A slanting brick chimney, with black slits where mortar had fallen out, thumbed its nose at gravity above the rust-covered tin roof. A narrow porch ran across the front, its roof sagging to trap the screen door ajar.

A vehicle had left tracks of mashed down weeds on what passed for the front lawn. Along the sides, pines crowded up to the building. Where sunlight found open patches, saplings poked up like crazed stick people, their skinny arms waving in the breeze. An electric line drooped between a gray-weathered pole and a riser at the rear. Ten paces from the back door, a board outhouse patched with Pennzoil signs and Texaco stars, canted heavily to one side, a hard sneeze from falling into the hole it was built to shelter.

A small green car came chugging up the lane, laying a smoke screen of dark curlicues. It rolled into the weeds on the left and stopped. Jones exited the passenger side, a plastic grocery bag in each hand. Smith got out from behind the wheel. He tried to close his door, but it caught halfway, making a loud pop. Smith kicked it until the stubborn thing was almost closed. Then he threw his weight against the side and pressed it flush, but it wouldn't latch. Giving up, he headed toward the *safe house*.

"Piece of crap," Smith said at the door, glancing back toward the lane. "Blind man could follow us. Look at that cloud. No wonder. We burned fourteen quarts of oil between here and Nashville."

"Can't afford no better," Jones replied, not looking. He stepped inside the doorway and set the bags on the little square of counter next to the pock-marked sink. "Least the radio works. We can keep up with the preacher."

"Yeah boy," Smith grunted. He shuffled past Jones and made his way to his cot. Sitting down, he surveyed his surroundings. Jones' cot was a couple of paces away, toward the front. In between, a broken dresser drawer partially covered a hole in the floor. A vine grew from the hole, ran across the floor and up the rear wall to escape outside where a pane was missing from a window. The ratty blanket was still in place where they had hung it, blocking the one interior doorway to help hold some heat in. From an outlet near the sink—the only one in the house that still worked—an extension cord ran to a small electric heater. On the counter on the other side of the sink, a microwave was plugged into the same outlet. A sudden racket made him jump. Jones was dumping ice in a plastic cooler.

"Beer's chilling," he announced. Then he dug into a bag on the counter and started lifting out small white cartons. "Want any of this Chinkle Chow?"

"What I want is the money for that preacher video in Nashville," Smith fussed as he rose from his seat. "'Course, you had to let that gorilla smash your camera. No video, no money—and now no job."

Chapter 44

Jennie twisted around in her seat until she could see out the back window. The Whitleys and Marian Cole were close behind. They saw her looking and waved. She waved back, then turned to face forward again. Jennie was getting excited. They were close. Tick had called a few minutes ago and said everyone was at the Visitor Center.

"There's the sign. One mile to go," Henry said, glancing at Jennie in the rearview mirror.

"Yes," Jennie replied in a whisper. She leaned to the right so she could see better between Henry and Elsie. Less than two weeks ago Paul set out. It seemed like two years. The nightly calls helped—where would she have been without them?—yet they weren't enough. She made it fine the first few days, quickly establishing a solitary routine: work, dinner, dishes, and a few minutes of housework after eating. Then a bit of TV or reading, prayer, and sleep, with the call from Paul falling in the list somewhere.

But this week had been horrible. Sleep would only come in fits and starts, interrupted by dreams of the accident. Jennie was always alone, sitting on that sad spot of ground, holding her daughter, the undeniable God-awful certainty of knowing Sarah was dead tearing her to shreds. Every night since Sunday, Jennie had awakened screaming. Paul knew nothing of this, for she feared the keen edge of telling him might be as sharp as the event itself. But she would tell him tonight. Jennie would tell him, and he would hold her as she cried—oh, how she needed to cry with him—and everything would be better. It had to be. It simply had to be.

Paul stood in the Visitor Center parking lot, leaning against the side of Tick's van, afraid to sit down lest his legs cramp up. He had already made over twenty miles today and intended to go another three. Tick said that would get them to the motel, so he needed to stay limber. More important, though, was the knowledge Jennie was only moments away. He knew he wouldn't be able to resist running to her.

The unexpected meeting with the black minister and his choir director had just concluded. Reverend Horace James did most of the talking, extending an invitation to attend that night's revival service. He was a smaller, much older man, gregarious, laughing a lot and promising a joyful fellowship. With a twinkle in his eye, he informed Paul he should expect a true blessing before the evening closed. It happened all the time at his church, he said.

Choir director Clarence Harlan, however, was the minister's opposite. He was young, soft spoken, and exhibited a seriousness that seemed to make him more likely to simply smile than laugh. Paul noted Clarence was listening intently when he spoke, turning his head slightly to one side and leaning toward him.

When it came to size, the director was on a par with Tick. The two seemed to each recognize something in the other, the director lingering to talk with Tick for a few moments after the minister departed. They took turns scratching behind Buck's ears as they talked. The dog's response was to shove his head against whichever man happened to be scratching at the time.

Suddenly Paul straightened up. Two cars he recognized, one following the other, had turned off the Trace and were headed in his direction.

†††

Chief Ranger Herbert sat in his office chair, looking at the parking lot. Hidden in the shadows cast by the half-open blinds—a spy driven by happy curiosity—he had been watching the meeting between the preacher from Kentucky and Reverend James. It appeared all went well, for the two ministers smiled and laughed a lot. *Good.* Herbert had not taken part in the meeting. His role had been to set it up. That was enough. Tonight, however, he would meet this walking preacher in person and wish him a safe journey.

With the meeting over, the chief watched Tick and Clarence getting acquainted. It was a pleasant thing to see, the making of a friendship. Like Paul, he smiled as Clarence and Tick took turns scratching the huge red dog. Finally, the chief rolled closer to the window and reached for the rod to close the blinds. A car easing to a halt in the middle of the lot made him hesitate. The preacher went running toward it as the rear door swung open, his open arms extended toward the young woman springing from the back seat. The chief hesitated only a moment more, then he closed the blinds with a quick twist. It felt wrong, somehow, watching two people so obviously in love shedding tears as they embraced.

Chapter 45

Jennie and Paul held hands as they strolled. Now that they were in each other's company, there was no need to hurry. Indeed, it was the last thing either wanted. The Trace ran through a stand of woods here. Though sunset was still a couple of hours off, the light was dim, sliced into narrow slivers that fell through the timber at shallow angles. It was quiet, except for the slow *swooshing* of tires on pavement as an occasional car rolled past.

"It feels old here," Jennie said, her gaze sweeping through the trees. "This is an ancient place, almost sacred it seems. I can imagine eyes following us. Perhaps even ghosts."

Paul turned his head toward her. "We're not very far from Tupelo, where Elvis was from. Maybe it's him."

"Oh, don't be silly," Jennie fussed. "I'm trying to tell you something serious."

"Sorry," Paul answered, instantly contrite. "I'm listening."

"I feel a warmth here, a presence. It's as if others are walking beside our path, watching over us. We are safe. I know that. And the quiet—it gets inside you. That's the sacred part, more than anything. Do you feel it?"

Paul waited a moment before answering. "Yes. I've been feeling that a lot."

"So, I'm not crazy?" Jennie asked, reaching across with her free hand to grab his arm and pull them closer together.

"Anything but," he said, turning his head to give her a quick peck on the lips. "It seems like the further I go, the stronger the feeling gets."

"Like you are not alone?"

"Exactly," Paul replied. "I usually can sense I'm walking with God. Like you said, there's this warm presence, and I know I am not only safe, but I am doing His biding." He hesitated a few seconds. "Sometimes, though—this sounds crazy, but sometimes it's something, I mean it's someone else."

"Sarah?"

The name stopped him like a blow to his chest. "Yes," he whispered. "Sarah."

Paul felt Jennie drop his hand, saw her rush ahead of him. He stood rooted in place as she turned onto a path to the left and broke into a run. Only then did he move, flying after her. They were out of sight of the highway, deep into the woods, before he caught up. She tried to push him away, stumbling backwards, finally coming to a stop with her back pressed flat against the trunk of a great oak.

"I'm so sorry, Paul," she cried, her hands still raised to ward him off. "I thought tonight we could talk, but I can't hold it in another second!"

One arm reaching toward her, Paul took a careful half-step. The tears were pouring from him, also. He inched forward another half-step, felt their hands touch, felt his fingers glide between hers. Suddenly, she was pulling him in, holding him so tight he couldn't breathe.

"Jennie, Jennie, Jennie," he whispered, his lips brushing against her ear.

For a time, they stood there beneath the great oak, neither willing to let go or stop crying. Jennie, the first to start, was the first to stop.

"I've been having these horrible dreams," she managed to say.

"I want to know," Paul said, pulling back enough to look into her eyes.

"Most of the time it's about the swing—that God-awful swing. I'm holding her—I'm holding her after *it* happened, and I look down at her face. She looks so peaceful with her eyes closed, like she's asleep. Suddenly her eyes pop open, and she starts speaking. I see her lips moving, but I can't hear her voice. And I keep saying, 'Mommy's here. You can tell me, baby.' I never hear a word, though, and I wake up screaming, 'Tell me! Just tell me!'"

Jennie made it through without breaking down. All Paul could say in response was, "Oh, my love."

For a few moments they pushed back against their raw emotions. Then Jennie asked, "And you?"

Paul took a deep breath. "I promised to talk with her every day. Several days ago, I saw this wild rabbit. That made me realize I hadn't spoken with her. I even asked if she had God send the rabbit to remind me."

"How sweet," Jennie smiled.

"Yeah." Paul hesitated, remembering. "Anyway, I walked into the woods, and I found myself at the edge of a high bluff. I sat down by a big tree, and we snuggled while I told her about the things around us, and what I'd seen that day. Sometimes, we hold hands while we walk. I can feel her little fingers in mine. At night, though—I dream. I see her reaching up to me as I reach down for her. We can't quite make the stretch, however, so we never touch. It seems to go on for days, our hands only a breath apart, before God finally grants me mercy and I awake."

Jennie said nothing, simply pulled his head down and pressed her cheek against his. For a minute, neither moved.

"I thought I was stronger now," Jennie broke the silence, "that enough time had gone by to put the worst of the pain behind me. I was wrong."

"Me too," Paul replied, leaning back from her. "After the calling, I guess I just figured everything would kind of take care of itself."

"It was never going to happen like that, Paul. Sarah and the calling are inseparable. The most important thing we can do, though, is share our pain with each other."

"You are right, of course," Paul replied.

"All the way down," Jennie continued, "I felt so guilty, like I was holding you back. But I couldn't wait to see you, either. This flood was rising inside me, and I had to be with you to let it go."

"I was in the same shape. I needed to cry a river, but I couldn't without you."

After several moments, Jennie spoke, the strength in her voice returned. "Okay, I am better now."

"Me, too." Paul nodded. He paused before adding, "Well, I guess we better get going. Got a revival tonight."

They held hands once more as they made their way back along the path. Just short of the Trace, they stopped to share a long kiss.

"Tell me, Reverend Lockhart," Jennie said as she pulled back to look in his eyes. "Did you miss me?"

"Like a hole in the head. And you, Mrs. Lockhart? Surely you missed me?"

"Like a toothache, dear sir."

Chapter 46

Paul and Jennie had just enough time to shower and wolf down sandwiches before leaving for the A.M.E. Church in Mantachie. They would have had more time, but Paul had to shave off his ragged beard. Jennie said it got in the way of their kissing.

The entourage left in a convoy for the twenty-mile ride to Mantachie. Jennie and Paul rode with the Jacksons, Cami with her parents and Mrs. Cole climbed into the old van with Tick and his new best friend, Buck. Tick led the way, having scouted the route. They arrived at a packed building minutes before services were to start. Reverend James greeted them at the door, then led them to a front and center pew. From beside the pulpit, a third man walked over to huddle with Paul and Reverend James. Reverend James introduced Paul to Dr. Wardlow. After a few moments' conversation, Paul handed his walking stick to the doctor. He inspected it closely, nodded, then passed it back.

Paul and Dr. Wardlow took seats behind the pulpit. Reverend James stepped forward and called the service to order. Then he led the congregation in prayer. Next, the choir, sang "How Great Thou Art," with Director Harlan's deep bass voice guiding them. At the hymn's conclusion, Reverend James stepped to the pulpit again.

"My friends, last evening I told you about a minister from Kentucky who would be passing through today. We met this afternoon. Two seconds into our conversation, there was no doubt in my mind that standing before me was a true man of God. He walked twenty-five miles today, still Preacher Paul Lockhart readily agreed to join us tonight. Thank you, Paul," he added gesturing toward him with an upturned hand.

Applause erupted across the congregation, punctuated with exclamations of "Amen" and "God bless."

"I promised the preacher there would be a true blessing tonight because those happen at our church all the time. I made that promise without a clue as to what the blessing might be, of course, but I knew we would all reach out to the Lord, and He would make it happen. Can I get an Amen to that?"

The members of the congregation responded as one with a loud, "Amen!"

"Praise the Lord!" Reverend James shouted, his face breaking into a wide smile. He waited for things to settle. "As I am certain you noticed, there are other new faces here. Some are traveling with Paul to support his mission. Some are family and friends from Kentucky who have driven down to share this weekend. I leave it to him to make their introductions. Please welcome my friend, Reverend Paul Lockhart."

Paul took his feet to a round of sustained applause and made his way to the pulpit. He brought his leaning stick with him and rested it against the choir railing. When the applause died down, he turned sideways to address the two ministers seated behind him.

"Thank you, Reverend James, for inviting us here to worship this evening. Like you, when we first met, I knew instantly I was with a man of God. It is my honor to also call you my friend. And thank you, Dr. Wardlow, for graciously allowing me to delay your message a few moments. I look forward to hearing you speak."

Both ministers nodded in acknowledgement. Then Paul turned back to the congregation.

"I look out at this wonderfully full house of the Lord on a Friday evening, when there are thousands of other things demanding your time, and I know what it is to be with people who believe. What a blessing."

A roomful of smiles answered.

"Now, I'd like to introduce our group. Please stand as I call your name." Looking at them, he thought of deer in the headlights. "Cami Whitley. Cami is traveling with us. She is a journalism student at Western Kentucky University and is handling the press side of things. She also blogs about this 'great trek,' as she has christened it. Visiting her are her parents, Frank and Rachel.

"Thomas Cole, or Tick as we call him, drives our supply vehicle and handles any logistical needs. We're still waiting for him to get his growth."

At the sight of Tick's size when he rose, laughter rolled through the assembly.

"With Tick is his mother, Marian. We are fortunate to call the Coles our neighbors. The Jacksons, Henry and Elsie, are also our neighbors." Paul paused to allow the older couple to stand. "They are two very special people. We rely on them for everything. Henry is one of our deacons. He is also our community music critic. Not long ago, he said my singing was so bad it made his cows quit giving milk."

The ripple of laughter grew to a roar when Henry spun around and shouted, "It's true! I swear!"

Elsie looked down and shook her head. As the roar subsided, her stage whisper filled the room. "Be quiet, old man."

Paul waited for the new round of laughter to subside. "God bless you, my friends. Please, everyone, take your seats."

He waited for the group to settle before saying, "Jennie." Rising, she turned and gave a quick wave to the congregation. Facing back to him, she stood straight and composed, the hint of a smile on her lips.

"You know I may embarrass you."

"Been there," she answered, her voice carrying. "I am not afraid."

Paul hesitated several seconds, the tension building. "My prayer," he began, his gaze sweeping over the congregation, then returning to her, "is that each man and each woman here find in their mate the things I have found in you: love and respect; a true conscience to follow when their own needs mending; a pure soul to restore one's faith when it wavers; a best friend."

He smiled, letting her know he was done. She blew a kiss his way, then resumed her seat.

"I am so blessed," Paul smiled, his eyes moving across the gathering once more, lingering an instant when he found someone nodding agreement. "Back home I serve as pastor for a church that is small in size, but huge in the faith of its members. I have a fantastic wife and wonderful friends and neighbors. So, what in the world would make me decide to walk halfway across the country?"

Speaking in a matter-of-fact tone, Paul spent several minutes relating the loss of Sarah, his blind anger at the sight of Serena crying for her mother, his awful night in the wilderness, the call at dawn.

"And the most amazing thing of all, I believe, is not one person questioned that I had been called. Instead, they all immediately pitched in to help. What a testimony of faith."

A chorus of "Amen" and "Praise Jesus" rose from the congregation. Paul waited for quiet before speaking again.

"One other thing I will tell. Early in this journey, on a hot afternoon in Tennessee, I met an elderly man named Raymond. He invited me to sit with him in the shade and share a cool drink. He soon got on me about not having a walking stick. Then he gave me this one." Paul stepped over, took the stick in his hand, and held it up so all could see. "Raymond said this is a *leaning stick*. Then he added that its official name is a *Jesus Stick*. All you have to do when you get weary is lean on it, just like Jesus."

Once again, many voices rose in agreement.

"Now, will you please join me in a moment of silent prayer, for the children?"

Many people saw Paul grasp the sides of the pulpit before they bowed their heads. Only Clarence Harlan kept watching, noticing how the preacher held on with a hard, determined grip, as if he would fall if he dared loosen his hold. The choir director knew he should close his eyes, also, but that did not keep him from praying as he looked toward the pulpit.

✝✝✝

"Yes, my friends, it is faith that will carry us through," Dr. Wardlow said. "As Preacher Paul told us, all we have to do is lean on Jesus. He will hold us up whenever we grow weary. Give us the strength, Lord, to never forget His promise. Amen."

"Now," he continued, "will the choir lead us in singing the invitational?"

Dr. Wardlow turned toward the spot where Clarence always stood when directing the choir. Clarence wasn't there. He glanced toward the closest choir member, but she only shrugged her shoulders. The doctor looked over at Reverend James, who lifted his hands, palms up, in confusion.

Suddenly the door to the fellowship hall swung open. Clarence came slowly walking through. In his hands he carried a large aluminum pan. A white towel was draped over one arm. He carefully made his way across the front of the sanctuary until he arrived before Paul. Bending over, he placed the pan on the floor, then slowly dropped to his knees.

†††

Paul didn't know what to think when he saw Clarence untying his shoe. Suddenly both shoes and socks were gone, the cool air moving over his skin. Then he realized his feet were being gently lowered into warm water. He glanced up to see Reverend James beside the pulpit, hands clasped before him. Tears rolled down his cheeks. It took a moment for Paul to realize the reverend was mouthing something. The words finally came clear.

"I told you so. I told you."

Chapter 47

"You didn't find anything at all?" the thin man asked, his eyebrows arching upward as he spoke into the phone.

"The man's clean as a whistle. Her, too," the male voice replied. "Believe we spoke with at least half the locals. Followed our normal routine posing as journalists. Ran into plenty of actual reporters beating the bushes: one with the biggest paper in the state; another with CBS, Childers; independents looking for an angle that'll sell."

The thin man knew about Childers. *Just great*, he thought. She had been an ongoing pain since the start.

"They're exactly what they seem to be: a rural preacher and his wife," the voice continued. "They pay their bills on time, help their neighbors, visit the sick, all that country stuff. He farms. She's a bookkeeper for a second-generation family outfit. Legit as they come.

"Anyway, everyone acts like they hung the moon, even those who don't go to their church. They all buy his call from God story. In fact, they seem proud of it. A couple even said it was because Caney Creek is a God-fearing place."

"Well, we're not going to find anything in Podunk Holler," the thin man said. "I think we need to spread out. Family, college, whatever. Give it a shot."

"Your dime," the man's voice said, not sounding enthusiastic. The phone went dead.

The thin man was hardly surprised by the report, nor was he particularly disappointed. Sometimes you just had to dig a deeper hole to find the crap. Something was always there. The man had told him one thing he was concerned about: real journalists were onto the story, so it would not disappear anytime soon. In fact, it would grow. The journalists could be countered, of course—he had people in several news organizations that would put out whatever he said—but doing so had limited usefulness. He needed real dynamite if he were going to change minds. He'd give his guy a chance to come up with something salacious. Then he'd have a real story that would spread across the media on its own. The thin man smiled, remembering streams of crocodile tears pouring down as their owner admitted, "I have sinned."

"Yep. Everybody has," he said aloud.

Chapter 48

The evening at the Mantachie church had been trying. Though he left out many details related to Sarah's death, talking about it was hard on Jennie and him both. That night as they lay cuddled in bed, Paul made a vow to himself that he would not speak of their personal loss to such a degree again. It was too painful, and almost as bad, it felt as if he were seeking to stir others' emotions based on their daughter's death. He did not mention he also feared going to that well again without having Jennie there to hold him up.

Then there was the foot washing. It made him uncomfortable. He brought it up to Jennie.

"I think I get it why Clarence washed my feet. He is a very humble young man. You realize that in a few moments of conversation. There's also no doubt his heart is full of love. I believe he felt compelled to exhibit that love. Don't you? It made me feel kind of weird when he was doing it, I don't know, like he thought I was something more than I am."

Jennie brows pinched together in concentration. A minute passed before she spoke.

"You are right. Clarence is a very humble man, and his heart is filled with love. I think you may be missing the point, however."

"Oh?"

"Jesus washed the feet of his disciples as a lesson in humility. You are the one receiving the lesson. Humility must reside in your heart if you are to carry God's message. Even the thought that another may see more in you than what you are must be guarded against." She looked up at him. "I'm sorry to sound harsh, Paul, but we've always been honest with each other. I can't escape the feeling that you are but the vessel."

Paul smiled at her. "You are so right, my love," he said and bent down to kiss her.

✝✝✝

They ate a late breakfast with the Caney Creek group. Henry kept insisting he had seen Elvis the night before in Tupelo. Elsie finally told him to shut up. He did, for about two seconds, then started in about seeing Bigfoot on the Trace. Tick said he and his mom were going to take a ride south to look around the countryside and scout ahead. Cami reported she had been on local television the day before, as well as on an early morning Christian radio program that day—*Wright with the Lord*, because the host's was named Wright. She added they were all invited to meet with a group of ministers at a church on the south edge of town at noon. There would be a potluck meal. They all agreed to go. After all, as Henry noted, there was free food involved.

Henry and Elsie drove Paul and Jennie to the meeting. It was at a large white-brick church set on the crest of a modest rise. Gray smoke floated upward in the still air, carrying the wonderfully blended scents of charcoal and barbeque sauce from an assortment of grills and smokers. The older couple struck out on an inspection tour of the scores of dishes on long rows of tables.

Families had spread blankets on the ground or placed canvas chairs in circles near the tables. A low roar of conversation came from the gathering, but as the Lockharts approached it began to die away in stages until the only sounds were the high-pitched screams and giggles of children at play. The relative quiet held through a short period of recognition, then the murmurs of overlapping conversations returned.

Paul turned toward Jennie. "Ummm. That fried chicken smells good."

"Baptist DNA," she laughed. "You're like a hound dog, always sniffing."

As they turned toward the church grounds, Paul noticed a group of men and women coming down the hill toward them. As they neared, he began to recognize faces. Reverend James and Clarence were in the group, along with Jim Hardesty from Nashville and several members of the *Disorderly Order*. A tall, bald-headed man took the lead in two long strides, extending his hand as he came to a halt before Paul and Jennie. The others eased up a pace behind him.

"Brother Will Young," he said, grasping Paul's hand. "Welcome to Trace Baptist. We're proud to have you."

"We're happy to be here. My wife, Jennie," Paul replied. As the tall minister took Jennie's hand, Paul added, "This is quite a gathering."

"The Lord put out the call and Tupelo answered."

"Yes, indeed." Paul nodded his agreement.

"Let me step out of the way so you can meet the rest of our ministerial group."

Paul started on the left, Jennie holding at his side. Reverend James was the first in line. "It appears we have another miracle with such a crowd," Paul said, taking the minister by both hands.

"Yes, we do, my friend. Yes, we do," the reverend answered with a grin. "The Lord sows ripe seeds in Mississippi."

Clarence was next. He and Paul exchanged handshakes and nods. Then came Reverend Hardesty. "Great to see you, Jim. You all have traveled a long way."

"We figured it was about time for a road trip," Jim smiled. "Give Nashville a break. I also have something I want to discuss with you after," he said, giving Paul's hand a hard squeeze before releasing it. "You remember Rabbi Moser," he said, turning to the next person from the *Disorderly* group.

Near the end of the line, an older lady wearing a plain black coat and white minister's collar took his hand in both of hers. "Gail Humphrey, Jackson Street Lutheran. We pray for you every service, Preacher. What a blessing the Lord has given you with His call."

"Yes, He certainly has," Paul nodded. "Thank you for your prayers."

She smiled and nodded in response, then turned to Jennie. Jennie reached for her hand, but the minister opened her arms wide instead, stepping forward to wrap them around the younger woman's shoulders.

"Come here, my child. Only a hug will do for us." Jennie immediately threw her arms around Reverend Humphrey, hugging her in return. Paul had to look away when he heard the minister say, "I pray each day that God gives you strength and comfort." A long moment passed before the women released one another.

"Paul." It was Brother Young speaking. "Would you all please come with us to the speaker's stand?"

As they neared the simple wooden platform, Brother Young explained the short service they had planned before the meal. With a wave of his upturned hand, Brother Young invited the others to find seats on the folding chairs arranged along the back, then stepped up to the podium and adjusted the microphones so he wouldn't have to bend down to speak. Clearing his throat first, he began.

"Welcome! Welcome, my friends!" The noise from the crowd began to fall away. "Thank you for joining us in this celebration of faith." Only the cries from a few small children could be heard now. Brother Young smiled in their direction, and the little ones, quickly corralled by their parents, fell silent. "We have gathered here in fellowship, not espousing any one denomination, but simply as believers who wish to acknowledge one who has answered the Lord's call. That person is Preacher Paul Lockhart. He is here from Kentucky with his wife, Jennie, whose sacrifice in fulfillment of God's mission for her husband, in no small way matches his own.

"In a few moments we will partake of this wonderous bounty placed before us, but first we will have an opening hymn sung by Clarence Harlan of Mantachie A.M.E. Church. Then Preacher Paul will make some remarks before our blessing. Clarence, if you will."

As Reverend Young stepped away from the podium, Clarence took his place. Without preamble, without the accompaniment of a single instrument, Clarence began to sing.

"Amazing grace, how great thou art," his great bass voice rolled down the slope.

"That saved a wretch like me.

"I once was lost, but then was found,

"The hour I first believed."

Clarence sang only the first verse, but that was enough to alter the crowd's mood. A newfound feeling of reverence seemed to permeate the air.

191

Paul took the podium next.

"My friends, what a joy, what a blessing, it is to be a part of this gathering. On behalf of my wife and myself, I say thank you, Tupelo, thank you, Mississippi, for your many kindnesses, but especially for your prayers. We feel them this very moment."

Paul allowed his gaze to roam over the assembly for a few seconds, amazed at its size—at least a thousand people—and gathered from it the strength he needed to go on.

"I trust you are familiar with the events that led me here, so I will not go into great detail. Simply put, I failed our Lord by lashing out in anger. Not until I gave myself up to His service did I find relief. Then, in His wisdom, He called me to walk to our southern border and pray for the children. I ask that you join me now in silent prayer, for the children."

Like so often, many of those close to Paul noticed how his hands clutched the sides of the podium, seemingly needing the support to stay upright. As the seconds ticked by until they filled half a minute, then a minute, some dared to lift their faces and peek. Most quickly looked away or closed their eyes, surprised, even ashamed of witnessing the man's obvious vulnerability, his struggle. Then Paul said, "Amen."

"Amen," the congregation answered. The sound came back to him like an undulating breeze. He was not surprised by its warmth.

People were gathering up their dishes and lawn chairs, making their way down the hill to the flat parking area at the bottom. Paul shook one last hand, then turned to locate Jennie. He spotted her sitting beside Reverend Humphrey under the sparse shade of a tall, ragged pine. He grinned, seeing them both laugh. Footsteps approached from behind. He turned to see Jim Hardesty. Jim wasted no time.

"Paul, have you had any trouble? Anyone give you a hard time?"

"Not really. I had a guy speak ugly to me in Nashville, but I don't think he was all there," Paul replied, shaking his head. "Why do you ask?"

"It's something we've picked up on. Not everybody is on your side. Some pastors, some churches, are criticizing you, saying you're just going to the border to stir up a mess."

Paul shrugged his shoulders. "It's a free country, Jim. People can say what they want."

"Sure, they can. I'm not worried about what people say. I'm concerned some may think they hear a call to action, a call to stop you. Just be careful. We live in crazy times."

"Thank you, my friend, for caring."

Chapter 49

Cami's Blog

It is already three days past our reunion weekend in Tupelo. I can't begin to describe how wonderful it was to see family and friends. We parted with promises of meeting again as soon as possible. Now we are on the Great Trek once more. Preacher Paul has increased his pace. During the first stage traveling through Kentucky and Tennessee he averaged twenty miles a day. Since leaving Tupelo, he has raised that to almost twenty-five. He attributes the increase to a combination of flatter terrain and the strength he gathered by seeing his wife and friends. He also admits his feet needed a short break.

I stayed the last two nights at a sorority house at the University of Mississippi in Starkville. Thank you, ladies! Tonight, I will stay with the family of one of my sisters in French Camp, where I will meet up with Preacher Paul and Tick. I am anxious to hear from them about the latest phenomenon. As he neared Nashville, people would sometimes wait along the street to see Preacher Paul and wish him well. That is still happening some, though so far there have been few communities of size near the Trace, other than Tupelo. A handful of people may simply gather at a country crossroads and wait for him to pass. Since leaving Tupelo, however, there have been instances where people will join with the preacher, walking along with him. At times, it is a single individual, but most often the walkers show up in a group. This morning the preacher reported the largest group so far, some thirty people, men and women, black and white. He said they were primarily college age, though a couple were at least in their fifties. Most of them, he thinks, were from Ole Miss. Go Rebels!

Chapter 50

Droopy McNaughton dug the binder out of his briefcase. He flipped it open and thumbed through the pages until he came to the song he had started in Nashville. Looking over the lines, Droopy mused about his writing process. Sometimes a song came to him practically all in one piece, but most often, over time he tacked on a bit here, stuck on some more there, or scratched out a line or two and came up with something that wasn't even close to the original. This song was following the later method. A cobbler, he called it.

He had made progress, though. All he needed were a couple of closing lines. Surely, he could get those down today, he thought, knowing at the same time that pushing things didn't usually work out well. He read through what he had already, then read through it once more, allowing the rhythm to come through and carry the words. That part at least, the rhythm, had come early. His fingers moved of their own accord, strumming the strings of an imaginary guitar.

Of course, he realized why he had to get the binder out. Strange how things worked sometimes. Last Friday he was on his way from Birmingham to Memphis on Interstate 22 when his bus blew a tire. Waiting in the shop while a new tire was mounted, between requests for autographs from staff and patrons alike, he had watched a replay of Cami's morning interview on a noon show in Tupelo. She reminded him of the preacher, and remembering the preacher reminded him of the song. It was enough to get him back to thinking about how to wrap up the lyrics. Now, after three shows in three days—two in Memphis and one in Little Rock—he was on his way home to Fayetteville with nothing else to do as the familiar Arkansas hills sailed past his window.

Droopy rose from his seat and made his way along the narrow

aisle back to where his guitar, *Sweet Thang*, lay on an empty bunk. He took it out of its case and carried it to his seat. Being such a big man, even in his customized captain's chair, it took him a minute to get situated with his feet propped up and *Sweet Thang* resting on his thighs. Then he began to play, singing the completed lines softly, slowly, like an old-time hymn—"Rock of Ages," maybe—feeling the lilting flow of words and music find their way inside his heart. He soon came to the incomplete final verse. Droopy tried a new line.

As I walked with You, my Lord.

No, that wasn't it, but *walking* had to be in there. He tried again, hanging onto the theme.

Walking along with you, God.

Closer. Droopy sensed it was coming. Something was turned around, though. What if he, the preacher, was relating what the Lord had said to him in His calling? The lines came in a rush.

Walk with Me, son, preach My word,
Pray the children's cries are heard.

He repeated the last line, softer and slower.

Pray the children's cries are heard.

Sid, the driver, knew to never interfere. Yet now, from the front of the bus came a single word.

"Amen."

Chapter 51

The border guard was walking up to a car stopped in an inbound lane. It took Bob Mendoza aback at how his contact had aged since the last time he laid eyes on him. His hair was gray. He had developed a noticeable paunch—not beer belly size, but a definite change from the flat stomach Bob remembered from four years back. They hadn't met in person since. Things had changed, the officer said at their last meeting. Bob's face was getting too well known, and the guard had too much time in to risk losing his pension.

Crossing the border had been uneventful. Bob made his way through Nuevo Laredo, keeping to Highway 85, until he was almost out of town. It was just after 1:00 p.m. when he spotted the modest sign across the front of an ageless, stucco-covered building. *RAMONA'S*. He pulled into the dirt lot. His two-person crew—Miguel and Carlos—were leaning against the side of their banged-up Bronco, smoking cigarettes. They waited until Bob got out of his vehicle, before striding toward him, smiling.

"Amigo," Miguel said, clasping Bob's hand.

"Amigo," Bob answered, tightening his grip. "You look well, my friend."

"Better than him." Miguel laughed, nodding toward Carlos.

"You need a mirror." Carlos frowned. His face instantly broadened into a smile as he took Bob's hand in turn."

"How are you two?" Bob asked.

"Good. Very good," Carlos answered.

"Hungry," Miguel replied, rubbing his stomach.

"He's been chewing on the steering wheel since we got here," Carlos deadpanned.

"Then we better eat." Bob smiled.

In a minute, the three were seated around a back-corner table. Food and cold beer were ordered.

"I know it's only been a few days," Bob said in Spanish, to keep from drawing attention from the other patrons. "Had any luck?"

"No," Carlos answered for both. "We sniffed around Reynosa a little. Nothing."

"Here's all I know," Bob started. "They reunited Serena with her mother. Then within the hour they sent them back over here." He paused while the waitress set three bottles of beer on their table. "I want to talk to the girl, but the mother has the full story."

"I doubt they're still around Nuevo Laredo," Miguel said, picking up his beer and taking a pull. "Most likely, they're still close to the border. They sure as crap don't have the money to head back to Guatemala."

"I agree," Bob nodded. "I know a priest in town that can probably help."

"Of course, he does," Carlos grinned at Miguel. "Man knows more priests than the Pope."

"He just tells one sin when he goes to confession," Miguel said with a straight face. "Doesn't want to weigh them down."

Bob shook his head. "I've missed you two."

His friends flashed wide, toothy grins. Miguel spoke first.

"They picked a good place to send them over. There's nowhere close to cross back. It's about fifty miles south to the next spot, and Eagle Pass is even further going north."

"And no towns close to the Rio Grande," Carlos nodded. "At least down south there are towns."

Bob casually glanced about the room. It was an old habit to check for eavesdroppers. After a minute he was satisfied. "I think they're down south, Reynosa or Matamoros, probably in one of the camps. But since we're here, where they crossed, we need to check. While I'm talking to the father, you two nose around town and see if you can catch a scent. Tomorrow, we'll look along Routes 1 and 85. If we don't find anything, then we'll head downriver."

"It's not much of a plan. The good thing, I don't think anyone will be shooting at us this time."

Miguel and Carlos flashed wry smiles. That was a very good thing.

Chapter 52

Paul was swinging along at a good pace. The latest group from Starkville had turned off at Highway 82 a few moments earlier, heading home. Walking with them had been entertaining. They kept up a lively conversation, even debating Bible passages. When some of the more energetic ones dared him to a walking race from milepost 206 to 205, each step hitting heel and toe, Paul managed to beat all but two, unless one counted Buck, a skinny male student of nineteen and a lady of fifty-seven. The lady finished first, then broke into a gyrating victory dance that had everyone cracking up. Buck stood ten yards in front of her, turned sideways and watching with his head canted to the side, as if to say, "Why are you dancing? I won."

Now, it was only Paul and Buck, at least until Tick met them at the next crossroads with lunch. The big dog was getting bigger, thanks to Tick giving him shovelfuls of food. He appeared to have put on several pounds since he showed up. Paul could still count his ribs, but they didn't stand out like a picket fence any longer.

"Well, Buckethead," Paul said, reaching over to pet the massive head, "I was beginning to think you'd forgotten me. I understand. Tick cleaned you up, and doctored you, and he's been feeding you like a horse, not to mention riding you around in his van. Y'all are tight. Right?"

Buck looked up without breaking stride, his huge eyes seeming to say, "So?"

"What I thought," Paul nodded. Buck turned to watch a dove that had whirred off in the woods. "I just want to know," Paul persisted, "do you still love me?"

The dog did not look around, nor break stride. It did, however, sidle over against Paul for a few paces, so that it rubbed its side against his leg. "Okay," Paul smiled. "I'll take it."

It all made for a fine morning. The sun was warm. No sound of civilization intruded through the trees. He had a good dog to keep him company. Paul felt energized and upped his pace. Somewhere in Buck's drive train, a gear kicked a tooth forward, and the beast adjusted without apparent strain.

At lunchtime, Buck, per his habit, decided to ride with Tick in the van. Paul waved them off and fell into an easy stride, helped along by a breeze at his back. It was a good time to commune with God. On the quiet Trace, Paul spoke aloud.

"Jennie keeps reminding me that I'm not the important one in this mission. I know she is right. I feel it. You have something important to make known through me, however. That's part of why these people show up along the way, isn't it? To keep me humble. You sent Clarence to wash my feet. I see that now, Father.

"I also noticed that in Nashville and Tupelo both, there were ministers of many faiths present. You said it first with Raymond: denomination doesn't matter. We report straight to You. That's what prayer is about, isn't it? You have been guiding me all along with this preference for silent prayer. I think I see why now. You want, You expect us to come to You, individually."

With each question, he sensed the Lord responding, as if nodding in agreement. There was something about the solitude here that seemed to open his mind. He felt as certain of his faith as he had ever felt, but now he sensed strength. When he stopped talking an indescribable feeling of peace settled over him. Jennie would understand this. He was anxious to discuss it with her, but she was still at work. Tonight then. He couldn't wait.

As he strode along the road, the forest suddenly opened up. Paul stopped so quick he rocked forward. Just ahead was an expanse of ground between the Trace and the village of French Camp. Several hundred people were gathered there on the grass.

Chapter 53

The crowd was filtering out of the packed church in French Camp, heading to their cars in the shadows of the gravel lot. Paul continued visiting at the foot of the steps, not unlike how he did in Caney Creek. Buck lay spraddled on the grass off to the side, in happy land with two young boys rubbing his belly. Cami and Tick watched from under a dim streetlight a hundred feet away.

"I think his pattern's pretty well set," Tick said.

"Yes," Cami agreed. "He talks about the call and the leaning stick. The other ministers do the peaching."

"Right," Tick replied. "Have you noticed how people react when he calls for silent prayer?"

"You can't help it. A lot hesitate to bow their heads at first, as if they were expecting him to say more, something profound. And they always stare at how he holds onto the pulpit."

"It's like he's afraid of falling off," Tick nodded.

"Or he's trying to pull himself up higher."

Tick didn't reply. He finally turned his head toward her and nodded his agreement. "I never thought of it like that. I believe you're right. Preacher is reaching for something higher."

Cami gave a slight smile in return as she watched Paul and the other ministers. They were mixing with people in the pool of light spilling out the church door. It was hard not to compare. The church was somewhat bigger, and so was the village, for that matter. Still, the people seemed much the same as the hard-working rural folks of Caney Creek. They took their worship seriously. She had no problem imagining certain ones having an exact double back home.

"It's a nice evening." Tick broke into her line of thought. "Still warm. Feels good, doesn't it?"

"Yes," Cami replied, turning away from the church. Across the

Trace all was dark, the woods a high ragged wall, barely discernible, but above it— "It's a beautiful night. So many stars."

Tick spun around. "The sky's full to the brim. Whup! There goes a shooter."

"I saw it!"

"Aren't you supposed to make a wish or something?" Tick asked.

"Sure. Let's both make a wish."

"I wish, I wish—"

"Wait!" Cami interrupted. "You're supposed to keep it a secret, right?"

"I don't know." Tick chuckled. "Maybe. I guess it can't hurt," he hesitated. "You ought to at least be able to give a hint, though. It takes the fun out if you keep it to yourself."

"Well sugar!" Cami smiled at him. "You can't take the fun out. We can give a little hint, I suppose."

"Good."

"Now, let's close our eyes tight," she said, "and say the magic words together. I wish, I wish, upon—I don't hear you saying anything. Let's do it together."

"Oh, yeah. I wish," he began. Cami quickly took the lead. Tick stumbled along half a beat behind, finishing with, "upon a star." At that instant she surprised him by taking his hand.

Neither said anything for a few moments. Finally, they turned to face each other. "Let's hear yours," Cami said.

"Nope. Ladies first."

"Just a clue, like we promised. Mine has to do with finding love and happiness."

"Hmmm," Tick nodded. "Like everybody wants, I guess?"

"Of course, like everybody wants," Cami smiled up at him. "Now you."

"Okay. I wished you and me would grab that old army blanket out of the van and go off over there in the short grass toward the Trace. Then we could lay on our backs and look for more shooting stars and make a bunch more wishes."

"Thomas Ivy, that's the whole kit-n-kaboodle!" Cami giggled.

"I didn't tell everything. We might see fifty more shooting stars, maybe a hundred, and I didn't tell a single one of all the other wishes I've got lined up and ready."

"You won't do." She giggled again. "Let's get something straight first. Do you promise—do you cross your heart and promise—to behave yourself? Remember, we made a deal. No hanky-panky."

"You want *me* to promise? That's a good one. Back in Nashville, it was you that slung me around like a rag doll. I've still got a crick in my neck."

"Do you promise?" she pushed, the faint light catching the impish grin on her face as she looked up at him.

"Yes, ma'am. The question is, do you?"

"I'll be good as gold. Cross my heart."

Minutes later they lay on their backs on the blanket, close but not touching, gazing at the sky. Neither said anything for a few moments.

"I like it here," Tick said, breaking the silence. "It's a neat place. Even the name's cool. French Camp."

"I know. It's pretty. It was fun looking around this afternoon."

"Wasn't that old chief's carriage something?" Tick asked. "It's still in pretty good shape, considering. Can you imagine riding all the way to Washington and back in that thing. Man, that'd be rough."

"And he did it twice," Cami added.

"Right, and the roads were nothing but ruts. They'd jar your teeth loose."

"I'd like to come back here sometime," Cami said, her voice taking on a whimsical tone. "Take my time driving the Trace. Stay here a few days, perhaps. Soak it all in, you know?"

"Sounds like a plan," Tick agreed. "Who knows. If, uh, things work out, maybe you and— There's one! See it?"

"Yes!" Her hand found his again. "Ready?"

"Yep."

"I wish, I wish upon a star," they chanted together, but this time they didn't release their hands when they finished.

"You first," Cami instructed. "Remember. Just a hint."

"Man, this hinting around stuff is hard on my system." Tick hesitated a few moments. Finally, he rolled onto his side, facing her. "I know we're on some kind of probation," he began, his tone sincere, "but I, it just seems like we ought to be able, you know, 'cause if we were really careful like, maybe, and didn't get all carried away, surely we could, don't you think?"

Cami rolled onto her side toward him, so that their faces were only inches apart. "Oh, Tick, forget trying to hint. Just say it."

"Steal a kiss!"

"Hmmm." Cami didn't say anything more for a minute.

Tick couldn't stand it any longer. "Just a little one," he said, lifting his hand before her eyes, thumb and forefinger almost touching together.

"I'm not certain we can share just a little kiss," she said, staring straight into his eyes.

Tick stared back, unblinking. At last, he spoke softly. "I hope we never can."

Cami squeezed his hand in response. She brought her other hand over to touch his arm lightly at the elbow, then slid it up to rest at the back of his neck. "So much for your promise to behave," she said.

"I know," he replied, his free hand moving across the narrow space between them, finding a spot above her hip to hold. "I've been trying as hard as I can, I swear, but you've got me so knotted up and twisted around inside I don't—"

He quit speaking because her face was moving toward his. Their lips met, and they each pulled the other in tight. For half a minute there was only their kiss.

Slowly, reluctantly, they each drew back until their lips barely touched, keeping the moment alive that one last, glorious instant. When the awful parting came, they held still, their faces inches apart.

"You didn't ask about my wish," Cami whispered, her fingertips drawing circles on the back of his neck.

"What was it?" Tick whispered back.

"That we would share a kiss."

She leaned in, ever so slowly, until their lips touched once more, seeking.

"Ow!" Cami exploded, jerking backward. "I'll slap your face!" The hand so recently massaging Tick's neck was drawn back, poised to strike. "You pinched my butt. How dare you!"

"I never touched your butt. I—Ouch! Don't have to jab your nails in!" he exclaimed, not noticing her hand was no longer at the back of his neck. "Ouch! Quit it!"

They leaped to their feet as one, each breaking into a St. Vitus dance. Both were smacking at various parts and trying to rub at other parts at the same moment, but their hands never seemed to make it where they were most needed before another spot burst into flame.

"They're all over me!" Cami yelled. "Ow! Ow! Get 'em off!"

"I'm on fire!" Tick hollered.

Then Cami let loose with a run-for-the-hills banshee scream so high-pitched Tick froze in mid-vaulting goose step to cover his ears.

"They're in my hair!" she cried, splitting the night air into echoes.

Flashlight beams suddenly caught them like searchlights, both swatting and bouncing about so wildly it looked as if they were illuminated by strobes, instead.

"Stay back, Preacher!" A sharp voice warned. "Keep a hold on that dog!"

Buck was tearing at the ground, threatening to drag Paul into the spasmodic melee.

"Nothing like fire ants to inspire a fella," a second voice added with a rusty cackle. "Look there? Pitched that blanket right atop a mound."

Chapter 54

Paul liked having the big red dog walking beside him. Buck pushed him to step faster, and he pushed back, trying to take the lead.

"You're not bad company," Paul said, managing to stay even. He reached over and gave the spot between Buck's ears a quick scratch. "My daughter had a huge stuffed rabbit the same color as you, named Brutus." Without breaking stride, Buck turned his great head to glance up at Paul as if he expected him to say more. When the preacher didn't oblige right away, Buck looked back to his front. "He was a good rabbit, wasn't he, Sarah?" Paul finally whispered, his gaze sweeping across the branches arched above the road. "Got us a pretty good dog here, baby," he said. "Want to pet him?"

Buck cocked his head toward Paul, as if listening in. After a second, he gave a slight nod, followed immediately with a gentle *woof.* The sound was so low Paul almost didn't catch it. Then he reached over and stroked the dog's back. "If only," he said. "If only."

A few moments later, the sound of Tick's old van made him shift his gaze to the next curve. It didn't take long before he rolled into sight. Tick stopped beside them. Buck stood up on his hind legs, tail wagging a mile a minute, forepaws pressed against the door, and stuck his head inside. A tongue the length of a razor strop shot out.

"You got me right on the eyeball!" Tick exclaimed. "Love you, too," he said, a big hand appearing from the window to rub Buck's head. "What about it, Preacher? You getting hungry?"

"Yep. I believe I could fall off the wagon today. Got a place in mind?"

"There's a restaurant a few miles down in Kosciusko. Everybody says it can't be beat. Mark your spot and we'll see."

Paul walked to the forest edge to find a suitable stick. He brought it back close to the pavement and stuck it in the ground, marking his progress.

Standing to one side as a precaution, Paul swung the passenger-side door open. Buck vaulted past him and landed with a thud between the seats, rocking the van. Then he tried to turn around, his wildly wagging tail catching Tick across the throat.

"Dang it, boy! Right on my Adam's apple!"

"That thing's like a bull whip." Paul laughed as he climbed in.

The van continued to rock until Buck got his bed made. He sat on his haunches then, with his head on the level with the men's heads, staring out the windshield.

"You say there's good food up here, huh?" Paul asked.

"Yep. The word's not to wait too close to noon. We're in good shape. It's just after eleven now."

Tick quickly found a spot to turn around and headed back toward Kosciusko. After half a mile, Paul asked, "How're your critter bites? They still stinging?"

His jovial face suddenly stone, Tick turned toward Paul. "I don't care to talk about it."

Paul swallowed his smile, but it almost choked him.

The people Tick had talked to were right about the restaurant. Though they arrived well before noon, a line was already forming. It was a quick and efficient operation, however. Customers filed by steam tables filled with various vegetables and meats as ladies on the other side passed plates from one to the next, hesitating only long enough to ladle on big helpings of whatever a person indicated. At the end, one paid and picked up their plate. The two men found a corner booth. They ate without conversation. The food was that good and both were that hungry. The instant Tick shoved in his last bite, however, he attempted to speak.

"Uh, Preacher, I want to say—" He got that far and fizzled out.

"What's on your mind?"

"I just, well—"

Paul remained quiet, waiting for his friend to find his way. A few seconds passed and Tick took another stab.

"About last night—"

"You mean the fire ant incident?"

"Yeah." Tick met the preacher's gaze. "We, uh…we certainly didn't mean to stir up a ruckus like that."

Paul hesitated before replying. The sorrowful look on Tick's face was too precious to quickly chase away. "I've got to say, that was impressive. I didn't know you could move like that, nor did I suspect Cami could, either."

"What I'm trying to say is," Tick plowed ahead. "I'm sorry I embarrassed you. It was my idea to lay there and look at the sky. Thought we, uh, we'd see some shooting stars."

"I see," Paul answered. "And did you? See some shooting stars, I mean?"

"Felt more than I saw," Tick answered, his tone too serious for Paul to laugh. "Blame! Those things mean business."

Paul forked his last bite, but before he could taste it his laughter got in the way. Once he started, he couldn't rein it in. Finally, he managed to throttle back enough to speak.

"You didn't embarrass me, Tick. People in love put themselves in, how shall I say it? Dangerous predicaments."

The expression on Tick's face was as close to fear as Paul could imagine. This time he didn't leave the younger man hanging.

"You didn't know?" Paul asked.

"What?" Tick sounded lost.

"That you're in love? Anyone can see. Jennie was the first to notice, probably about the same time as Cami's mother. Your mama, too. And back at Tupelo, Elsie—"

Paul was suddenly afraid to go on. Tick's face was the color of molten metal.

"I guess everybody in Caney Creek's laughing at me by now!"

"It's okay, my friend. Being laughed at kind of goes with being a man in love." Tick did not look convinced. "A man can't fight it. Women always have the lead in these matters."

That dimmed Tick's cheeks a few degrees.

"If it makes you feel any better, everybody sees that Cami loves you back."

Tick didn't respond, just looked off to the side, but over the next minute his skin slowly returned to a level near its normal shade. At last, his voice that of a small boy, he asked, "They really think so?"

"Yes. We all believe she loves you."

Paul watched Tick's transformation. It came on the young man at a crawl, one tiny facial muscle at a time rearranging itself. He managed a broad grin, finally, but almost immediately started to slide back.

"I don't understand what's happening." He glanced at Paul. "I've never been so addled."

"Don't worry about it," Paul smiled, bringing his last forkful to his mouth. "It comes with the territory. I've been in the same boat since I first laid eyes on Jennie." He shoved the bite in. Tick just sat there watching Paul chew. At last, the preacher swallowed. "Tick," he said, "there's only one thing I understand about a man and woman being together. If they don't respect each other, whatever they have between them is not love. It's something so dry and brittle it'll never grow into anything worthwhile."

Tick sat up straighter.

"Do you respect her?" Paul asked, surprising his friend with a hard stare.

"Yes, sir."

"It'll work out then."

Paul took a long drink, then casually asked, "How's Cami's wounds?"

Tick hesitated. "I don't know," he finally managed to answer. "She won't answer her phone. When she went stomping off last night, she said she never wanted to see me again."

Paul slid out of his seat and stood. He twisted back and forth a moment, working the kinks out. Then he reached across and laid a hand on Tick's shoulder. "Yep," he said. "Sounds like love to me."

From across the room an older woman yelled, "I know you! You're that Preacher Paul!"

Chapter 55

A handful of people followed the preacher out of the restaurant. The ensuing meeting lasted only minutes. They asked God's blessings for his journey. Paul then led them in a short prayer for the children. Now he stood in the parking lot with the last member of the group. A slender young man of college age spoke of how he had recently felt called to be a minister.

"I just want to be certain. You know?" the student said.

"It's not for me to say if you actually heard God, if that is what you are asking."

"I believe it was God," the young man nodded emphatically. "It seemed like it."

"Thinking on it now, does it still feel right?"

"Yes! Absolutely."

"But you have some doubt?" Paul asked.

The student shrugged his shoulders. "I would call it confusion."

Paul thought a couple of moments before continuing. "Prayer is the only answer. Go to the Lord. Listen closely. He will not lead you down a path other than the one He has laid out for you. If He wants you to spread His gospel, you will hear His call again and again, until you surrender to His will."

"So, you're saying a true call is not something I can ignore?"

"Yes. The Lord is persistent."

The young man smiled at the preacher's words and nodded.

Paul smiled back. "Mind if I pray with you?"

"Please."

Paul laid a hand on the young man's shoulder, then bowed his head. "Father, we come to You asking that You give this young man guidance. If it is Your will he devotes his life in Your service, give him the strength of purpose he will need. In Your name, we pray. Amen."

"Amen," the young man repeated in a low voice. Then he lifted his eyes and met Paul's. "Thank you, preacher."

"Good luck, uh…."

"Lucas."

"Okay, Lucas. Forgive me, but I must get back on the road," Paul said extending his hand to shake. The sudden clatter of worn-out engine parts in a knock-down-drag-out fight made both men turn toward the street, only to have a cloud of oily black smoke block their vision.

"Wasn't that just precious," Smith said, his eyes on the rearview mirror, trying to find the preacher and the young man in the swirling exhaust as he and Jones chugged down the street. "Having a little prayer with his driver before they get going again."

"This'll be a piece of cake," Jones said. "Neither one's big enough to swat a fly."

"Nope," Smith chuckled. "Let's head down the road and figure out where they'll be tonight. That gal on the radio said he's making twenty to twenty-five miles a day, so another ten or twelve miles should do it."

The two would-be secret agents were a little short on their calculations. That didn't matter, though. It wasn't like there were a lot of places to camp along that part of the Trace.

Then there was bad timing. Smith and Jones were watching the preacher instead of the van when Buck raised up from eating. Of course, feeding the beast was why Tick was also in the van. He was stretched out beside Buck, trying one more time to get Cami to answer her phone.

Chapter 56

Late in the day, Paul came ambling into the River Bend picnic area. He had put in a good day's walk—thirty-one miles, his top distance. Now his feet and legs were complaining. Sleep would come early, he hoped, unless Tick got wound up again asking questions. Paul had to laugh. The poor guy had a bad case of Cami-itis.

Paul glanced down the line of picnic tables and spotted Tick's van parked at the far end. Tick was standing on the riverbank close to the water, phone to his ear. Buck was only a couple of paces away, sniffing along the muddy edge. Suddenly he raised his head and caught sight of Paul. Here he came galloping, a whirl of legs driven by that propeller of a tail, stumbling to a slobbering halt with his forepaws, mud and all, on the preacher's shoulders.

"Easy there, big head," Paul warned, falling back a step. He kept his face turned to one side, trying to avoid being licked to death. "You'll knock me in the river."

Hearing the commotion, Tick turned and waved. Paul managed to get Buck wrestled down to all fours. Then four very distinct words carried back from Tick, "I love you, too." Paul smiled to himself, assuming Tick had been speaking to his mother. As the men grew nearer, Tick's voice came to him again. "Cami says hi. She'll be here in a few minutes with supper."

"Good," Paul replied, surprised. He took a seat at the picnic table beside a cooler.

"She's bringing meatloaf from a place in Jackson."

"Now you're talking." Paul nodded.

"Can't beat it," Tick agreed.

"So, you two are speaking again?" Paul asked, rummaging in the cooler for a drink.

"Yeah. We sort of made up."

"I'm glad to hear it," Paul grinned.

"She said once her bites cooled down to a simmer, she thought it over and figured we were both to blame."

It was 4:30 a.m. when Smith began to inch forward in the full moon's light. Rounding the turn by the restroom building, he could see the line of picnic tables. There was the van, backed in by the last table. He eased ahead another ten yards before he spotted the bulky forms on the ground. That had to be their sleeping targets. Dropping to a knee, he waved Jones up. Seconds later, he whispered, "See?"

"Yeah," came the low reply, and the two began to creep forward, each bent low and holding a baseball bat in one hand. In his other hand, Jones carried a metal can of gasoline. Their plan, like them, was simple. Beat the preacher and the driver with the bats, then use the gas to set the van on fire. They figured that would be enough to send the two back to Kentucky to stay. And, of course, the thin man would be so thrilled he'd put them back on the payroll. That was their only goal. There was nothing personal about the attack. There never was.

Halfway there, Smith held up a hand, signaling a halt. Jones stopped beside him.

"When we get to the front, I'll circle 'round. You take this side," Smith whispered. "Lay into the first 'un you see. Remember, don't whack 'em on the head. I ain't going to prison for killing no preacher."

As they started forward again, Smith's knee bumped into the gas can Jones was carrying. The sound was small, metallic.

"Look out, idiot," both men said, trying to whisper but missing by a few decibels. Jones had enough sense to carefully set the can down then, before he dropped it or worse.

Tick and Buck awoke to the metallic noise. Buck growled, low and throaty. Tick had his hand over the dog's mouth in an instant. Lifting his head a few inches, he looked past Buck's nose and saw bent shapes in the moonlit drive. Knowing you could make out things better at night by not looking directly at them, Tick adjusted his line of sight off to one side. Two men were crouched over, each carrying something. *Weapons?*

Working his bare toes to catch purchase against the fabric, Tick began shrugging out of his sleeping bag. He was clear in seconds. The shapes grew closer, then disappeared behind the van. Tick managed to get to a knee, holding Buck with one hand and keeping his other over the dog's mouth. He leaned down to the dog's ear.

"I say *go*, bite somebody," he whispered.

Tick stilled his thoughts. Ideally, he would awaken the preacher. But the man might startle and cry out, costing them surprise. Buck was quivering so hard he didn't know how much longer he could hold him back. Any second now. Tick focused on the near corner of the van, suddenly saw movement.

"Go!"

Chapter 57

Tick sprung forward, bringing his left hand up from the ground with all he had. He wasn't exactly certain where his fist might land, but he knew it would land somewhere in the man's middle. He could see enough of an outline to be sure of that.

Kerrack! Oomph!

The sounds were a nanosecond apart, yet Tick heard each one clearly. It felt like he was punching a hole through a bag of pretzels. Things, hard and brittle, snapped and gave way. The second sound sent a familiar burst of air in his face. It wasn't the first time he had knocked the wind out of someone. He leapt after the attacker, right fist cocked to finish him off. Somewhere to the side, he heard a voice screaming bloody murder.

Tick didn't have to swing. Smith was down in the shadows. Suddenly he crab-crawled into the moonlight. A hand extended, grasped the baseball bat lying in the dirt. Tick swung his foot. The attacker flipped onto his back with the impact as the bat went *whizzing* into the darkness and banged against something hard. Digging his heels in the ground, Smith tried to push away on his back, but he couldn't gain any real distance between them. Tick saw him move a hand to his midsection and made ready to kick again, thinking the attacker was reaching for a gun, but suddenly realized the man was clutching his side.

"How them ribs feel, sonofabitch?"

Tick took a quick step forward. One hand caught Smith at the belt buckle, the other his shirt collar. In a flash he had the man above his head as if he were no more than a broomstick. Pivoting toward the river, he took a step forward.

Smith screamed, "No!"

Light suddenly enveloped the pair.

"Don't Tick!" The preacher was on his feet, shining a flashlight. "Put him down."

Tick rolled his wrists forward and dropped the still scream-ing attacker from seven feet in the air. The man bounced off the bank and landed in a mat of lily pads. Flailing arms and legs sent showers of muddy water and torn vegetation sailing through the flashlight's beam.

"Get him out of there!" Paul ordered sharply. "He'll drown!"

Squatting down at the water's edge, Tick reached out to grab a foot, but Smith was suddenly a human motorboat. He shot onto the bank fifteen feet away and was gone like a rabbit into the dark woods.

"What's that racket?" Paul asked, spinning around. His light fell on the source. "Lord God!"

Buck had his teeth sunk into Jones' buttocks and was swinging him from one side to the other as if sweeping the floor. The man was screaming like crazy.

"Buck!" Paul yelled. "Let him go."

The dog ceased his swinging and cut his eyes toward the preacher.

"Let him go," Paul repeated.

Buck seemed to think about it, then with a half-hearted growl, he abruptly released his bite. Jones landed with a thud. Buck didn't walk off, however.

"Good job, boy," Tick said. "Come here."

Jones laid flat on his stomach for several seconds, until the dog sat down beside Tick. Suddenly he was on his knees. A moment later he took off like he'd been shot from a cannon, the beam from Paul's flashlight illuminating his bare hind end where Buck had ripped away the seat of his pants.

"Come on, Buck. We'll catch him," Tick said.

"No," Paul ordered, dropping the beam to form a circle around their feet.

"We've got to find out who they are," Tick insisted.

"Let them go, Thomas." Hearing his given name, the authority in the preacher's tone, pulled Tick up short. "We can't be beat-ing people up. That's not what we're about," Paul continued in a no-nonsense tone.

"I know it," Tick replied, "but those two meant to hurt us. Wait a minute! What's that shining out there?"

Paul swung his light about and quickly spotted the can Jones had left in the lane. "Stay," Tick told the dog. Then he walked over and picked up the can. Undoing the cap, he took a quick sniff. "Gasoline! They meant to burn us up!"

"We don't know that for certain."

"Paul, I don't get you," Tick shook his head, forgetting in his exasperation that he never called the preacher by his name. "They had baseball bats, and this can of gas," Tick added, his voice rising. "What more do you need? They came here to kill us! Let me and Buck go after them, or we'll never know who they are."

"I already know."

Chapter 58

The sun was beginning to throw light through the windows as Paul and Tick stood up to talk with the park ranger again. Paul had finally given in to Tick's pleading and agreed to report the incident. Since the attack had taken place on Parkway grounds, it was a federal incident and thus the ranger's to investigate. At this hour, these three were the only people in the waiting area for the hospital emergency room in Jackson, Mississippi. The ranger had escorted them into the treatment area long enough for Paul and Tick to identify the injured men as their attackers, then he had sent them out while he interrogated the culprits. Now the ranger was back. He motioned the two to follow him outside.

"Doc said he used a gallon of disinfectant to rinse out the punctures on that one fella," the ranger said, stopping off to the side of the entrance. "They've given him all kinds of shots, too, aiming to kill everything from lockjaw to the blue jungle crud. Doc said he will be alright, but he'll probably sleep standing up for a while.

"Other fella has three broken ribs. There's not much they can do but wrap his middle in one of those big elastic bandages to hold him together. He'll take six or eight weeks to heal." The ranger looked straight at Tick. "You sure all you hit him with was your fist?"

"Yes sir," Tick nodded. "I kicked that baseball bat out of his hand and slung him around some, but I only hit him that once."

"Hmmm," was the ranger's only response as he continued to stare at Tick. Finally, he turned toward Paul. "That dog must be something."

"He is," Paul answered. "Big as a racehorse."

"I gathered as much, looking at those bite marks," the ranger said. "You say he's in your van?"

"Yes," Paul answered.

"Let's take a look at Kujo. I have to make sure it's not foaming at the mouth.

Moments later, Tick let Buck out of the van. He scratched behind the dog's ears, keeping him close. Wagging his tail, Buck looked up at the ranger as if to say, *Aren't you going to scratch me, too?*

The ranger made no move to do that, however. He simply looked the dog over for a minute before asking, "Where's his leash?"

"He doesn't have one," Tick answered.

"You have a thick rope, maybe a log chain, anything to keep, uh—"

"Buck," Paul gave the name.

"That's short for Buckethead," Tick added.

"It fits." The ranger nodded without smiling. "What I was getting at, don't you have anything to keep this creature under control."

"No sir," Tick replied. "We just tell him what to do, and he generally does it."

"Generally?"

"He's been like that since he showed at Bynum Mounds," Paul offered. "The only thing he's ever refused to do was leave."

"Huh," the ranger shrugged his shoulders and simply stood there staring at the dog for a minute. At last, he spoke, "Well, that has to change now."

"What do you mean?" Tick cut in before Paul could open his mouth.

"We've got a huge dog here," the ranger replied, "that's viciously attacked a man. I can't just let you take off with him. What if he decides to do it again? He might kill somebody."

"He didn't do it on his own," Tick spoke up. "I told him to."

Now it was time for the ranger *and* the preacher both to stare at Tick. "You deliberately had him jump that man?" Paul asked sharply.

"What was I supposed to do?" Tick responded, his tone strong and certain, as if there was no reason for argument this time. "As soon as I woke up, I could tell those guys were carrying something. I didn't know what, and there wasn't time to wake you without tipping them off, so I told Buck when I said *go* to bite somebody. Then they split up. I waited until they were right on us before I gave him the word. He took the one on the right, and I took the other guy."

Neither the ranger nor Paul spoke for a moment. Finally, the ranger said, "All that may be, but I don't have a choice here. The procedure is to put the dog up long enough to see if he has rabies or something else bad. We've got a vet we work with here in Jackson. That's where the dog is going until the lady says otherwise."

Paul answered quickly, "I understand. Do what you have to do."

Tick didn't say anything. After a few seconds he nodded his head once, sullen like.

"All right then," the ranger said, sounding a bit relieved. "We'll drop the dog off first. Doc Vincent gets in at the crack of dawn. Should already be there, unless I miss my guess. Then I need you to follow me to the office, so I can get the charges typed up. After that, we'll go back to River Bend. It'll be light enough by then to show me where everything happened."

"I have a question," Paul interrupted. "What if we don't press charges?"

"Well, uh," the ranger stumbled in surprise. "They might go free, I imagine, like nothing happened."

"I'm inclined not to push for anything," Paul said.

"You shouldn't get in a rush here, Reverend," the ranger quickly replied. "Those two may not be the shiniest spoons in the drawer, but that doesn't mean they aren't dangerous. The one with the busted ribs admitted right off that they belong to a radical group called the *Pat Henrys*. Who knows what they may do next?"

"That may be, but here's how I look at it," Paul began. "They were probably intending to do us harm, but neither one actually did, and I don't believe they'll be in a hurry to try anything again. The one Buck chewed up has learned his lesson, I'll bet. If it were me, I'd be waking up screaming for a long time to come. The one with the broken ribs—I've had broken ribs. They let you know about it every breath until you're healed. He'll have thousands of painful breaths to remind him of his mistake."

The ranger simply stared at Paul for a long stretch before he finally turned to Tick. "And how about you?"

"I'm with Preacher."

The ranger shook his head. "I can't make you do anything, and

I certainly can't speak for what the judge might say, even if it gets before the judge without you. I seriously recommend you think long and hard before you walk away, though. We get to River Bend you need to talk it over with the chief ranger. He's going to meet us there."

"I will be glad to talk with him," Paul replied, "but I don't imagine I'll be changing my mind."

"Whatever," the ranger shrugged. "Let's go check this hound into the hotel."

Chief Ranger Herbert was there with Cami, waiting to meet them, when they returned to River Bend.

"Hello, Reverend," the chief said. "We met briefly at my church in Mantachie."

"Yes, I remember. Please leave the reverend stuff aside. I'm Paul."

"And I'm Langston."

Despite dropping titles, the chief was no more successful than his ranger at convincing Paul to press charges. Finally, he said, "Alright, Paul. Let's all have a seat and go over what has to happen from here on.

They found seats at a picnic table.

"First," he said, directing his gaze at Tick, "I don't think you did anything wrong. You were defending yourself and Preacher Paul."

He turned toward Paul. "Second, this incident has already drawn media attention. I just heard from the office that we're getting calls. This will escalate quickly, therefore, it is imperative that any question about charges or arrests, anything having to do with law enforcement, is directed to me.

"Third, we don't know if this attempt was the work of a couple of, shall we say, misguided good old boys, or if it involved an organized group. It sounds like an organized group, but nobody seems to know anything about the *Pat Henrys*. Anyway, this is not something you should respond to, if asked. Like I said, the legal stuff is for me. From now on, however, you must keep a sharp eye out. If you see someone suspicious, or you are threatened personally, or you are made aware of threats against Preacher Paul, contact law enforcement immediately. That's one of my rangers as long as you are on the Parkway. You have to be careful. Okay?"

All three nodded their agreement.

"I will be meeting with the U.S. Attorney and federal law enforcement agencies in Jackson shortly. Now, I know this may seem like making a mountain out of a mole hill, but I can't ignore that the culprits came prepared to do serious harm. The fact of the matter is that we live in times when a lot of people can't simply disagree with others. Anyone who thinks differently from them is an enemy. So, at least one ranger will always be near until you make it to Natchez. That includes all of you, even Cami. That's the way we're handling it.

"Finally, we will have a press briefing in Jackson at 10:00 this morning. Paul, if you agree, I would appreciate it if Cami could participate. She is much better prepared to answer any questions regarding your walk."

"That's fine with me," Paul agreed. "Cami?"

"Sure. Just tell me where to be."

"Thank you," Chief Herbert said. "We will get you there. Our approach, Cami, will be to relate everything in as straightforward a manner as we can. We are simply trying to get ahead of this thing. We will, of course, avoid speculation on motives. Are there any questions?"

"Not from me," Paul said. Cami and Tick shook their heads no. "We are grateful for your efforts, Chief. Hopefully, this will be the end of it. I was wondering, could I have a quick word with you."

The two men walked away from the others, coming to a stop at the edge of the water.

"I underestimated the impact this would have on your organization," Paul said. "There's something I have to tell you. I have seen those two men before. They verbally accosted me in Nashville."

Chief Herbert managed to keep a straight face. "Where and when did this happen in Nashville?"

"It was in front of the Union Station Hotel, on the morning of, let me think, I believe it was the fifth day of the Trek. Cami will know the date. We had just participated in a press function at the state capitol."

"Okay, I'll ask her." The chief paused for a long minute. "Paul, I've got to say, I don't like the sound of this. It makes me think this morning's attack will not be the end of it. I can't stress my belief enough that you and your team are in danger. I ask you to please help us pursue charges."

"Thank you, Langston. I see your concern. Please understand mine. I can't get involved in anything that will delay or take me away from answering my calling."

Chapter 59

That day Paul only walked twenty miles. The short night of sleep and the late start, as well as the stress from the whole mess had him out of sorts and out of rhythm every step, it seemed. He had finally made it to Jackson, when a ranger pulled up beside him and said there was a parkway information cabin a little way up ahead that would be a good place to camp. Paul thanked him and called Tick to meet him there. Neither one had any idea the chief ranger had communicated to his officer that this was where they would stay because it would be easy to keep a watch over them.

†††

Tick lay on his back looking up at the full moon. Sleep seemed out of the question. After what Paul had said to him over supper, he wasn't sure he wanted to sleep. Things had gone off course on the ride back out to River Bend this morning. Paul made it plain he was upset over how Tick responded to the would-be attackers. And the way he had spoken to him was as distressing as his language. Paul never raised his voice, never indicated by gesture or expression that he was angry or put out with him in any way. He simply let his words convey what he felt.

That's the way Tick's daddy had been when he was peeved, speaking as smooth and easy as anything, yet his words might as well have been razor blades, their meaning cut so sharp, so deep. Tick had a thousand times rather his daddy whip him than talk to him that way. After this morning's chewing from the preacher—if it could even be called that—he had rather Smith and Jones had beaten him with their bats.

Tonight it got worse as they concluded their spartan supper. The preacher started out saying they were going to the border in response to God's call to pray, how there was no place anywhere in what they were doing for violence, no matter the threat. What really twisted Tick into a knot was when Paul put his drink down and stared at him straight in his eyes.

"I knew how you were, Tick—a man with a hair-trigger temper and hammers for fists. Knocking the other guy flat is how you've settled problems ever since your father passed. My fault, this time, though," Paul shook his head. "I've been aware since Nashville there were people out there who stood against us, although I can't claim to understand their reasons why. Anyway, I knew there could be trouble again, though I believed it would just be talk, and I didn't say a word to you about how important it was to not respond in your usual way, about how we would just have to turn the other cheek. I should have explained. There's plenty of good in you, Tick. You've got a heart as big as Christmas. Jennie and I have seen it, and believe me, we are forever grateful. I can tell you feel bad, but you shouldn't. I let you down."

Yeah, Tick thought, his gut aching as he remembered, *a ball bat upside my head would have been better.*

So, he stared at the bright moon and tried to let the waves of anger and irritation finally come to rest. It wasn't easy. Old habits are hard to break. Right after he and Buck stopped the attack, he felt good. No. It was more than that. He felt flushed with the righteous satisfaction that the warrior can only find by prevailing in battle. Had he not saved them? They could have died! Yet Paul made it clear there was something inherently wrong in what he had done. His taking the blame only pulled the mantle of shame further over Tick's eyes.

It all amounted to tons of stuff heaped upon his head—a head, as the preacher said, not disposed to thinking before acting—but it was nothing compared to the realization of what the consequences of his actions might yet be. Paul said it this morning, almost in passing, as they readied themselves to leave River Bend. They had to overcome this somehow, or the mission would be in jeopardy. It seemed a stretch when Paul spoke, but now, at last, Tick could see what the preacher was driving at. That he had only thought to protect them didn't matter. Another danger was even greater.

Still staring at the moon, it came to him. There was only one thing to do. He would have to call it quits. No matter what Paul said, he was the one who had put them in this mess. Tick glanced over at the preacher. He was lying on his back, hands locked behind his head, apparently staring at the moon, also. Tick pushed himself up into a sitting position, then scooted around a little sideways to face him better.

"Preacher," he began, surprised at the emotion welling up in his throat. "I'm sorrier than I can say. I didn't mean—well, I'm heading back home in the morning. It's all I know to do, and I think it's what I should do. That ought to take the monkey off your back."

Paul did not reply. Tick waited a few anxious seconds, hoping, in spite of what he had just said, that the preacher would tell him that it would be alright, that they would get through the mess together.

His voice low, tired sounding, Paul finally answered. "I'm not the one you hand your resignation to."

"What do you mean?" Tick said, confused.

Again, Paul was slow to reply. Then he spoke, lower than before, almost mumbling, "Think back to when you first realized you should go with me."

The moment came back instantly, the flood of questions rushing in as he sat on the pew in church, and the answers to those questions right on their heels. He remembered explaining it to his mother. What had he said? *It was like he was being sent*. Yes!

Tick didn't answer for a few moments. At last, he sought confirmation about what Paul was getting at.

"So, you're saying I should talk to God, right?"

His answer was the soft flutter of Paul's snoring.

Chapter 60

Paul reached Natchez at mid-afternoon of the fourth day out of Jackson. He walked downhill through a series of lazy curves, the slope quickening his steps, until suddenly the Trace came to an end, and the city was right there in front of him. He hadn't expected it to be an emotional moment, yet it was. The Trace had been a comfortable place, other than the time of the attack. Indeed, though people often walked with him, or at least came out to meet him earlier in the journey, since the news got out about Smith and Jones, he had seldom been without companions. Many openly declared they were there to protect him. The latest of these—a half dozen young men and women who joined him at Washington—held back now as he took his last step on the Trace, sensing that this might be something special, the crossing of a line for him. That step taken, they rushed forward as one to shake his hand and wish him safe travels.

Paul walked alone along Liberty Road thinking he had indeed crossed a line. The Trace had been an easy stroll in a number of ways, compared to what lay ahead. The traffic had been lighter and slower than the first leg on regular highways to Nashville, with no winds from big trucks threatening to toss him airborne. The parkway's shoulders had been wide, usually offering room to step off to the side when a vehicle approached. Now he sensed the almost worshipful feeling of walking through a park was over. It was highways from now on.

It took him less than an hour to reach the visitor's center. He found Tick there, sitting cross-legged on the grass, gazing out on the Mississippi River. Paul placed a hand on the big man's shoulder to steady himself as he eased down beside him. Neither man spoke, each content to simply feel the warm afternoon sun on his face as he gazed upon the *Father of Waters*. It was an arresting sight.

"That's a lot of water," Tick broke the silence after a few minutes.

"Yes," Paul agreed. "Gathered here before us from lands near and far."

Tick looked over at Paul for a moment, a mischievous grin spreading across his face. "You know, sometimes you talk just like a preacher?"

Paul had to laugh. And he couldn't seem to stop once he started. The *like a preacher* line was hardly heehaw funny, but it struck him that way. Tick joined in after a moment, cackling loudly, matching Paul. The thing was, they both needed to not just laugh, but to laugh together. Since River Bend there had been a painful tension between them. Even earlier that day, as they ate their sandwiches, staring up at the massive bulk of Emerald Mound, they hadn't shared a dozen words between them. Now, however, the strain at last relieved, they grew contentedly still.

A couple of quiet minutes passed before Paul spoke. "Give it a try."

"What?" Tick turned to face him.

"Say something like a preacher might."

"You've been out in the sun too long," Tick replied, his crooked expression seeming to dismiss the idea.

"If I can do it, anybody can," Paul persisted. "It doesn't have to be religious. Maybe something about the river."

Tick replied with a chuckle, but almost immediately his face took on the appearance of one lost in thought. Paul watched in amusement. As the moments clicked by, however, seeing the younger man drop his eyes groundward, seeing he was really trying to come up with something, his smile faded. Finally, Tick lifted his face toward the Mississippi.

"The least drop fell, raced down the bank to find comfort with the others, and a mighty stream was born." Tick twisted his head around to look at him. "Kind of weak," he said, apologizing.

Paul didn't respond. Tick's words had carried him back. He was in the caneland at home, kneeling on the damp bank of the creek. Pleading. Seeking. Each tear sounding a solitary *plop* as it struck the earth.

"I wouldn't make much of a preacher," Tick interrupted his reverie.
Paul reached out and squeezed Tick's shoulder.
"Don't sell yourself short," he said. "You're way ahead of me."

Chapter 61

"**I** don't know about this, Sarah girl," Paul said aloud. He came to a halt after a single, tentative sidestep along the narrow catwalk, just as he moved out over the water. He was on the bridge crossing the Mississippi River between Natchez, Mississippi, and Vidalia, Louisiana. The muted hammering of a towboat's diesel engine came drifting in from a few hundred yards upstream as it pushed a tow of barges northbound. Watching from a distance was kind of cool, the boat's exhaust pouring from the stack, blue-gray and heavy, trailing in a slowly unraveling rope over its wake.

Looking straight down was another matter. His stomach turned over at the first glimpse. How far was it to the water? Maybe a hundred feet? Or two hundred? A mile? He glanced off in the distance again, fighting back the nausea. It took him a few moments to steady himself. Then he forced his eyes to turn down again. This time was a little better. Grabbing the wet handrail with both hands helped. The rhythmic sound of the tow's white-fringed wake slapping against the rocks along the shoreline was mesmerizing. Driftwood lay amid the rocks, broken and bleached, piled in tangled heaps. He wrinkled his nose at the strong smells of dead fish and dank wood hanging in the humid air. These scents of decay were familiar. Had he not smelled a milder form a thousand times along the creek back home? Moving water not only brought life, but it also carried death away.

Paul said, "I do not like high places, and this thing is way up in the air. Phew! It must be nine miles long." He turned his gaze toward the Louisiana side. "It'll take us a week to get across." He thought about his estimate for a minute. The exaggeration was too close to a lie. "On second thought, it'll take at least a good half hour."

Still, he didn't take a step further out over the water. Finally, he took a deep breath, then let it bleed slowly across his lips.

"I know, we need to get moving," Paul said. The message seemed to get lost on the way to his feet. Then he thought of Sarah outside the church, her arms around Tick's neck as she told him it was alright. "Okay, hon. Hold my hand, so Poppy won't be quite so afraid." He reached out with his left as he imagined her reaching up and grasping his fingers. His right hand slid along the wet handrail as he started. The metal was slick and cold from the fog, as if he needed more to make him nervous.

He—or they—moved slowly at first, but Paul became less nervous the further he went. The fog around the bridge was thinning, down to narrow slivers that drifted after the tow of barges. The improvement in vision helped, though it revealed just how high up they were, as well as how far from either shore. He could at least see where they were and where they were going. Still, it seemed easier to Paul if he kept his eyes turned toward the river. That view was simply majestic. Mississippi lay on the right, Louisiana on the left, with both flat for miles in any direction. The impossibly wide river lay flattest of all, right up to the feathery wall of fog. About the midway point he came to a stop. He edged around, still gripping the handrail tight, until he faced the water.

"Something to see, isn't it?" He allowed a few seconds to pass. "Humbling. It tells just how small one truly is. You could drop a rock from here, and you wouldn't even hear the splash."

Paul fell silent for several moments.

"You know?" he started up again. "I've been over thousands of bridges in my life, just about all of them in a car, especially the bigger ones. Driving doesn't get it. You can't get an accurate feel for what's below. Looking here, the Mississippi's not only huge, it's, I don't know... Inevitable? That's close. There's a certainty to this flow, with its untold numbers of Caney Creeks pushing together. Tick said it right. 'A mighty river was born.'"

He looked down at the fast-moving current, at the spinning swirls and eddies being constantly drawn and erased. "See how brown the water is? Muddy. That's what they call this, hon, the Big

Muddy. A long piece of driftwood came floating beneath them. An instant before it disappeared beneath them, Paul realized it was a large tree. Upstream, the towboat, a tiny toy now, was silhouetted against the fog. As he watched it was silently swallowed whole. The long, lonely moan of its foghorn came drifting softly to his ear. *Woooooooooo*. Such a sad sound. He waited half a minute for it to come again, but there was nothing other than the *clack, clack* of traffic rolling over joints on the bridge. At last, he started walking toward the Louisiana shore. When his feet touched land, he came to a halt.

"Thanks, hon, for guiding me across," he said. For a moment longer he stood still, just in case something came in answer. Nothing did. He imagined her smiling up at him, though, because he needed that, then he started moving once more.

Paul hadn't gone a block when he noticed a policeman propped up against the side of a patrol car. As he got within a few yards, the man suddenly stood up straight and turned to face him. His hand came up to shake Paul's.

"Welcome to Louisiana, Preacher. If there's anything you need, anything that seems out of the ordinary, just let us know."

Paul was a little taken aback at the greeting. "Thank you. I appreciate the welcome. Seems like a nice town."

"That it is, sir, and we aim to keep it that way. Like I said, just give us a shout."

Though Vidalia did not appear to be more than a few thousand people, it still took Paul another hour to get through the built-up part. Twice, small groups met him along the way. A few minutes here, a few minutes there, and he was on his way again. He was finally walking in flat countryside when Tick phoned to let him know he was turning back to Mississippi. A ranger had called with a request to meet back on the Trace. When Paul asked what was up, Tick gave a vague answer, saying it was over something they'd lost.

Despite traveling on a regular road again, the walking was still easy, the shoulders flat and wide. There were no hills. The traffic had been a little disconcerting while he was crossing the bridge, but Paul was growing accustomed to vehicles moving by at speed.

The day was sunny and warm. Occasionally, someone would slow down and blow their horn as they passed. These instances were more than simple greetings. The horns were usually accompanied by a waving hand, and sometimes he would hear something along the lines of, "I've got your back, Preacher."

The miles and the minutes slid by. Paul was almost to Ferriday when a vehicle slowed to a halt alongside him. He glanced over and recognized Tick's van. Sitting in the passenger seat was a dog with a head as big as Saturday night.

"Buck!" Paul exclaimed, moving to jerk the door open. The dog was ahead of him, however, vaulting through the open window and knocking him winding.

Tick eased the van onto the shoulder. In no time he was back to where the preacher and the dog were getting reacquainted. Paul was sitting cross-legged on the ground, his face turned to one side as he hugged the dog's neck. Buck, for his part, was wagging his tail hard enough to knock fenceposts out of the ground as he mopped Paul's face with his tongue.

"Same way he did me," Tick said, stroking Buck's back. "That tongue's like sandpaper. I won't have to shave for a week."

"Me either," Paul laughed, using both hands to push the massive head away from his face. "Okay. Easy big boy. Sit down now."

Using a combination of coaxing and rubbing, the two men finally got the dog to sit.

"I thought he had a few more days in the slammer," Paul said.

"When we met up, the ranger shouted, 'Take this bucking bronc, please!' Buck was about to tear his car to pieces. The man was laughing, though. He said the vet told him if this dog was sick, he'd hate to feed him when he was well. Buck was eating them plumb out of their budget."

"He does look like he's filled out some," Paul laughed, running a hand down Buck's flank.

"Yeah, he might have picked up twenty or thirty pounds," Tick grinned, reaching to scratch behind Buck's ears. "Were you hungry, buddy?" he asked. Then he turned to Paul. "Speaking of food, how are you doing?"

"I could eat."

"I'll scout up ahead," Tick said, straightening up. "Should be a town soon. Do you want to keep the horse with you? Let him burn off some of that crazy energy?"

"That'll be fine," Paul replied. "Glad to have his company again."

Chapter 62

The thin man finished his call with the investigator and laid the phone down. Although the man had dug deep for any dirt in Kentucky, this Preacher Paul was proving a hard nut to crack. The preacher wasn't the only one without a skeleton in the closet, he reported. Everyone around him was without sin. How was it he had phrased it? "Place is cleaner than the board of health." *Great. No sense throwing more money away.* He told the detective to drop the job.

All he wanted was a little something to blunt the preacher's appeal before he got going too strong. He had Smith and Jones to thank for screwing up things. Those two ignoramuses! Now the whole country knew about the preacher. People were forming patrol groups and walking teams to protect him. Last evening, he'd heard there were even a few militia boys taking part. What the hell was that all about? Some kind of screwed up God and country thing? Where was their loyalty?

As to Smith and Jones, good riddance. He was done with them. What was he thinking? You didn't need I. Q. tests to see those two didn't have enough sense to tie a shoe. Their latest cockamamie idea proved that.

Okay. At least they were back in their shack near Meridian, nursing their wounds. As far as he was concerned, that's where they would stay. That door was slammed shut and nailed to the frame. He had half a mind to give them a special mission, however, a suicide mission, if the preacher ever headed to Mexico. It was so much easier to get rid of someone south of the border. Hmmm. Something to think about.

Yes, something to think about. The Cowboy lived in Mexico. Using him was not out of the question. It was a bit desperate to think this way, he knew, but he didn't like the odds of what might happen once the preacher got to Brownsville. On his own, he could sink the cause. It was better to have a plan in place ahead of time.

He picked up his cell phone and keyed in a text.

`Call when you get to Mom's.`

Chapter 63

In mid-afternoon, Tick happened upon the minister at a little Baptist church close to Wildsville, just as the man was finishing mowing. The minister readily agreed they could stay the night. Twenty minutes before dark, Paul and Tick wiggled into their sleeping bags. Both went out immediately and were thus spared the sometimes unsettling sounds of creatures and critters conversing and cursing along the nearby Black River.

Paul and Buck had just crossed the bridge over the Black early the next morning when Tick came circling back.

"I found a good spot for breakfast a couple of blocks ahead. Big John's," Tick said through the van's window. "Y'all hop in." Paul laughed to himself as he opened the van's passenger door. Tick must be starving. All they'd had before leaving was a banana apiece.

Big John's didn't look particularly fancy, but Paul knew from the smell as soon as he got out that it had good food—country food. One step in, a quick glance at the plates before a couple of customers, and he knew his companion had found a good spot. Paul wound up with a soup bowl of grits, swimming in butter, two fried eggs, five pieces of bacon, and biscuits and gravy, not to mention two cups of coffee and a glass of orange juice. Tick had the same things, other than three scrambled eggs instead of two, and an extra serving of biscuits and gravy. They placed a to-go order for bacon to mix in Buck's dry food.

The two ladies had their operation down. The older one, maybe the mom, did the cooking. The younger woman took orders, delivered food and bussed the tables. Other than a handful of older men hanging around a liar's table, the place was empty by the time Paul and Tick finished. The young woman pulled up a chair at their table.

"Y'all get enough?" she asked with a smile.

"Lord, yes," Paul replied. His plate was clean.

She glanced over at Tick. He seemed to be contemplating more. With a shrug, he finally said, "I reckon so. That was very good," he added.

"Yes, it was," Paul agreed. "Thank you."

"You're welcome," she smiled. "Where y'all from?" Somehow, her question didn't seem nosy. The men would have asked the same thing of her had she shown up back home. New faces in a small town merited curiosity.

"Kentucky," Paul answered. "Little place called Caney Creek. About fifteen miles from Bowling Green."

"I know Bowling Green. Been by it on the interstate." A few seconds passed and she said, "And?"

"As in where are we going?" Paul asked back. "Texas. Brownsville, Texas."

"All the way to the border," Tick chimed in.

"Where my boyfriend's from," she nodded. "Brownsville." She stared at Tick for a few seconds, then glanced over at Paul for a few seconds more before she spoke. "You're that preacher, aren't you? You're going down to pray for the babies."

"Yes ma'am. That's me."

A chair scraped across the floor behind him, but Paul paid the noise little mind.

"I've heard about you. We've been following y'all and praying for you at our church."

"Thank you. We appreciate it more than we can say."

"Ah, excuse me," a man's voice said from over his shoulder. Paul twisted around to see an old man wearing a ball cap and a long-sleeved checkered shirt. Paul rose, and they shook hands. Then the man stepped around the table to greet Tick.

"This is Brother Hiram Jeffries." The lady did the introductions. "He's a retired minister. Brother Jeffries, this is Preacher Paul—I'm sorry. I don't recall your last name."

"Lockhart."

"Preacher Paul Lockhart. He's from Kentucky."

"Your reputation precedes you, sir."

"I hope that's a good thing," Paul smiled. "Please join us."

"No. I'm not going to keep you. I've got to get home and paint the porch. I heard—please forgive me for eavesdropping—but I heard you and Rolonda talking. I was just going to check on your route for the day."

Paul glanced over at Tick for an answer.

"Well, sir, we're heading west on 84 from here for eight or ten miles. Then we're hanging a left on 28 and going down to Alexandria. It's too far to make in one day, so I'll have to scout out a place for us tonight."

"Okay," Brother Jeffries nodded. "I imagined that's how you'd go. I would. There's not much of anything that way for a long stretch, though, and enough wild stuff in the Catahoula to chase a herd of elephants off. If you don't mind me butting in, I could make a recommendation."

"Please do," Paul said quickly, glancing at Tick.

"My baby brother, Harve, has a little church on 28 a touch over twenty miles from here. It's got water and bathrooms. I'll call and let him know you're coming, if you're interested."

"Yes, sir," Paul replied, rising to his feet. "We would appreciate that very much."

"Alright then," Brother Jeffries said, taking Paul's offered hand. "My brother can be cantankerous, but he's a good man. He'll fix you up."

Chapter 64

Twenty-three miles from Wildsville, Tick found the church. It stood on a half-acre of squishy ground carved out of the wilderness. Across the road was Catahoula Lake, one of those swampy places like in the movies, where thick timbers draped in Spanish moss grew straight out of coffee-colored water. He imagined alligators floating to the surface, their vacant eyes seeking anything within chomping range.

Tick parked in a patch of gravel-speckled grass behind the church. Before he opened the door, he swept his eyes over the ground, checking, his worry having changed from gators to snakes. He half expected to see a water moccasin curled up like a pile of fat garden hose. For an instant, he wished Buck was there. The red dog was with Paul, though, walking through this alien territory beside the Catahoula.

Tick stepped out of the van and eased over to a pair of picnic tables. The woods stood dark and thick a few paces past them. Midway between the tables was a low mound of pale-gray ashes, the remnants of a campfire. Stepping carefully, he cast about until he found a fallen branch about the length and girth of a baseball bat. He picked it up and settled it in the crook of his arm. Then he began gathering dead limbs for firewood. He dropped the first armload atop the ash heap, then made a teepee of twigs and small sticks in a gap at the bottom. One match and a moment to make sure the fire was catching, and he moved out to the woods' fringe, where the pickings were more plentiful. In minutes he had a pile of wood big enough to last for hours.

He was seated atop one of the picnic tables, sipping a coke, when an ancient Cadillac came flying into the drive. The contraption was as big as a house, its whitewall tires ripping gravels loose from the lot as it bounced to a stop ten feet from him. Tick thought of old Ms. Kirby back home. That was the way she came in for a hot landing. Then he saw a man in a flat-brimmed hat behind the wheel. As the driver's door swung open, Tick set his drink down and slid off the tabletop. He simply stood there in an easy stance, loose but ready, his *bat* leaned up against the bench an arm's length away.

The hat appeared above the door. A weathered face—seventy at least—tanned into crinkled leather, stared back from beneath it.

"You a preacher?"

"No, sir."

"Well, I'm looking for a preacher. Fella from Kentucky, they say. If you're not him, who are you?" Leatherface asked as he stepped around the open door.

Tick scanned him quickly. No obvious weapons. Laced up boots, military style, jeans, wide belt, long-sleeved shirt with snaps instead of buttons, like a rancher might wear. He was an average-size man, no bigger than Paul. That is to say, physically, he didn't appear threatening.

"They call me, Tick," the younger man said, extending his hand to shake as he stepped forward. "I'm traveling with a preacher from Kentucky. Paul Lockhart."

"He there in the van?" the man asked, taking Tick's hand like he wasn't sure it was a good idea. His shake was quick—two pumps. "Harve Jeffries. Minister here." He jerked his hand back and gave a half wave toward the building.

"Pleased to meet you, Reverend," Tick nodded. A moment later he added, "No sir. In answer to your question, Preacher Paul's still walking. Be here in thirty minutes, give or take."

"I'll wait him out. My brother called and said y'all might want to camp here tonight. Not sure that's a good idea."

"The gators and snakes are bad around here, I bet."

"I've got a shotgun in the trunk if any show up. I just need to talk to that preacher 'fore things get riled."

Tick wasn't sure what might get riled, so he changed the subject.

"Are you thirsty?" Tick asked. "I've got sodas, tea, what have you."

"You got any sweet tea?

"I sure do," Tick replied, starting toward the van. "Be right back."

"Obliged," the minister answered, settling down on a bench at one of the tables.

Suddenly a fireball of red-haired lightning came skidding around the corner of the church. Seeing the strange man, Buck slammed on the brakes and hunkered down. Then he started in with his low grumble that signaled confusion.

"It's okay, boy," Tick called. "He's a friend of mine. Reverend, meet Buck."

The reverend didn't hesitate, holding his hand out toward the dog, palm up. Buck still crouched in place, though, staring a hole through man.

"Come on," Tick encouraged him.

Then the reverend clucked his tongue a couple of times. Buck took a tentative step toward him, then another and another, until the proffered hand could reach the backside of an ear and begin scratching. Jeffries gave him a good wooling, switching from one ear to the other. Buck at last pushed his big head up against the man's side, nuzzling in, returning the favor.

"Yeah, he likes that," Tick grinned.

"I've never known a dog that didn't," the reverend nodded, obviously enjoying the scratching as much as Buck. "How many head of cattle does this boy go through in a week?"

"We've been weening him. He's down to one full-grown steer a day," Tick deadpanned.

Both men and the dog were so distracted, they didn't notice Paul's approach until his feet started crunching through the loose gravel behind the Caddy.

"Evening," Paul said. "I didn't know we had company."

Tick got to his feet.

"Preacher Paul, Reverend Harve Jeffries," he said, gesturing toward the older minister. "This is his church."

It took Jeffries a few seconds to swing his leg back over the bench seat and get to his feet. Finally facing Paul, he reached out to take his hand.

"Pleased to meet you," both men said in the same breath. Each smiled at the accidental parroting.

Tick had been a bit nervous about how things might start out between these two, especially with the way Reverend Jeffries had come flying in, all no nonsense and ready to lay the law down. Maybe scratching old Buck had helped ease the man's mood.

"Ready for something to drink, Preacher?" Tick asked, taking a step toward the van.

"Sure. I'll take a water," he answered. For a few seconds, the two ministers simply stood facing each other. Paul broke the silence. "I hope you don't think I'm being unmannerly, but I need to sit down. My feet are saying *that's it* for today. We covered a fair piece."

"Only twenty-three miles," Tick yelled from the van's open door.

"Oh sure. Have a seat" Jeffries replied, motioning to the other side of the table. They sat down, facing one another over the gray boards. "That's a good stretch. Is twenty-three about your usual?"

"Yeah. Some days are better than others. The afternoon piece was kind of tough. A little change in scenery helps keep you distracted from the aches and pains."

"I imagine," Jeffries nodded. "It is boring. Seen one mile along the lake, you've pretty much seen them all."

"I believe you're right," Paul laughed, reaching to take a bottle of water from Tick. He took a long swallow. "Umm. That hits the spot," Paul said, setting the bottle down.

"It's the simple things," Jeffries said, pausing to take a sip of his tea.

Tick was getting Buck's food and water dishes out, but he kept an ear tuned into the ministers' conversation.

"That was your brother we talked to?" Paul asked.

"Yeah," Jeffries nodded. "He gave me a call. Why I came over."

There was something in the tone of the last sentence that caught the attention of both Paul and Tick, like maybe Jeffries had to do something he didn't really care to do.

"Oh," Paul said, wondering where this was going.

"You see," the minister began, "we're just a small country church." The minister was obviously uncomfortable. Paul spoke up, not trying to do anything other than give the man a moment or two to get his thoughts lined out.

"Our church is, too. Looks like they're about the same size. If we get seventy-five for preaching, it's a red-letter day."

Jeffries nodded. "Same here." He hesitated again before taking another stab at explaining. "We're pretty set in our ways. Real conservative, guess you could say? We don't hold for all these immigrants, us taking care of everything, like we took 'em to raise. And what you're doing, heading to the border, something about it doesn't sit right. Sounds like stirring just to be stirring. Follow me?"

"Yes, I do," Paul replied, following all too well. This was sounding like what Jim Hardesty had spoken of in Tupelo. "It's not what you—" he started to explain. That was as far as he went. Then he shook his head, as if clearing it, before adding, "The last thing we want to do is cause problems. We'll just move down the road and find another other spot for the night."

Tick had just dropped another stick on the fire. Now his head jerked up in surprise at Paul's easy capitulation.

"It'd probably be for the best. I appreciate you understanding, Paul."

"No worries, Harve."

Tick caught the shift. No pretense of formality anymore. It was as if they were simply two friends who had recognized a potential conflict and agreed on how to defuse it. And though Tick understood—or at least thought he understood—what the men were doing, something about their agreement irked him. He was surprised to hear his own voice.

"It's not about immigrants."

Both men glanced toward him, each taken aback that he had decided to put his two cents worth in. The silence that ensued stretched out several moments before Tick found his voice again.

"With respect, sir," he said, looking straight at Jeffries. "I've been with Preacher Paul from the start. I've never heard him so much as mention the word immigrants. What he's doing is about children."

Tick stopped there, embarrassed that he'd said as much as he had, but relieved he had spoken up, just the same.

"I'm confused," Jeffries said, looking at first Tick, then Paul. "On the radio, they said you were going to the Mexican border to pray for the immigrants. Well, they might have said *children*, too, but it was plain they were talking about immigrants, whether they were kids or not. So, what is it?"

"Children!" Tick popped off. "Doesn't matter where they're from."

Paul raised a hand, palm out, toward Tick. Then he smiled to let him know he wasn't upset. Paul closed his eyes for a minute. When he opened them once more, he began speaking.

"Thank you, Tick," Paul began, "for clarifying our mission. You are right. It does not matter where a child is from. All babies are our responsibility, for they are the truly innocent." He turned to face Jeffries. "When God spoke to me, He said I was to walk to the border and, *Pray for the children*. He did not offer me a choice of one group over another. How we mortals might decide to sort and label are not considerations in His plan."

This time the silence stretched out past uncomfortable, until the only sounds came from the evening calls of birds and the hum of insects warming up for their night's work. At last, Reverend Jeffries began to untangle his legs from the picnic table's bench. He took one step away, then turned back toward Paul.

"Y'all like jambalaya?"

Paul smiled. "Only had it once, but it was really good."

"What is it?" Tick asked.

"Cajun food," Jeffries snapped, sounding like a drillmaster. "You're in Cajun country now, so you might as well eat what we eat. My Ruthie's the best cook in the parish, and she just made a big pot of jambalaya. I'll be back with some before you can shake a stick," he added, turning toward his car. He hadn't gone two steps before he stopped and twisted around again.

"Y'all might as well figure on staying here tonight. Won't feel like moving after you eat."

The minister held in place, apparently lost in thought. After a few moments, he added, "You've set me to thinking, about the kids I mean. I had you pegged wrong. I'll pray for your safe journey, and for your work when you get there."

Chapter 65

"Welcome back Alexandria to K-N-O-W, channel 27, where Central Louisiana turns for all the news worth hearing. You are watching *In the KNOW*. I'm your host, Brett Delacroix. Still with us is Cami Whitley, media liaison for Reverend Paul Lockhart. As Cami told us in our first segment, in response to his calling, Preacher Paul is walking from Kentucky to the Mexican border to pray for the children. Preacher Paul will pass through Alexandria today. Right Cami?"

"Yes, Brett. Last night he and Thomas stayed a few miles outside of Holloway. They should be in Alexandria by noon."

"Now Thomas handles the supplies and transportation needs, as you explained earlier. He goes by a nickname, though, doesn't he?"

"Yes," Cami smiled. "Tick. What everyone back home calls him."

"I love it. Great Louisiana name, too. I know a couple of guys that go by that," Brett grinned. I believe your group has one other member—a dog?"

"Yes, Buck just showed up back at Pharr Mounds—which is in northeast Mississippi and—as the preacher likes to say, adopted them. He's been part of the group since."

"Buck is also a nickname, isn't it?"

"Yes," Cami smiled at the camera, showing her dimples. "His name is actually Buckethead because, well, his head is as big as a bucket. He is a very large dog."

"Heard it takes a lot to feed him," Brett said.

"Tons," Cami laughed.

"You may be wondering why I'm asking so much about Tick and Buck," Brett spoke to the camera. "It's because these two disrupted a would-be attack on Preacher Paul. Cami, please tell us about that."

Cami hesitated a moment, then launched into her spiel about

the attempted attack by Smith and Jones. As Paul had his standard explanation regarding Sarah's death and how it led to his calling, Cami had quickly developed hers for what happened at River Bend. She got through it quickly, giving a simple recitation of the events without elaboration or conjecture.

"Thank goodness Tick and Buck were there to stop those men before something truly awful happened." Brett shook his head. "Didn't they have a can of gasoline?"

"Yes, they did," Cami nodded. "And I agree, thank goodness nothing worse happened."

"And I hear the two attackers were injured?"

"That's true. One suffered some broken ribs when Tick stopped him, and the other was bitten by Buck. I understand he needed stitches."

"So, what happens now? I assume the attackers are being prosecuted?" Brett continued to dig. "People who attack a man of God ought to be put under the jail. Right, Alexandria?" he added, glancing at the camera.

"I don't know where the investigation stands," Cami replied. "The incident occurred on the Natchez Trace, thus Parkway officials are in charge. I'm afraid I must refer you to them," she concluded, not having risen to the bait about what should happen.

"Well, we are just glad Preacher Paul is okay, and, of course, we wish him a safe journey the rest of the way. The Great Trek. What an incredible story. Thank you, Cami, for being our guest on *In the KNOW* this morning. It has been a true pleasure."

"Thank you for having me."

Twisting around to face the camera again, Brett said, "And thank you for joining us. Remember, to find out what's happening in central Louisiana watch *In the KNOW*. This is Brett Delacroix turning it over to Stacey Yarmuth with the K-N-O-W midday news."

Chapter 66

It was mid-afternoon on Paul's second day out of Alexandria when the soldiers showed up. There were half a dozen of them jogging toward him on the shoulder of the road. They came to a halt a few steps short of meeting. Most seemed closer to Tick's age, except for one, a tall, rangy man who appeared to be closer to Paul's years. Though the day was on the cool side, they all wore tee shirts and jogging pants stenciled with *U. S. ARMY.* The tall one extended his hand.

"Sergeant Mike McManus."

"Paul Lockhart," Paul replied, shaking hands.

"I thought you'd be along about now."

"Oh, you did," Paul answered, wonder finding its way into his voice. "Am I in trouble with the Army?"

"Not hardly," Mike laughed. He held off saying more while the others stepped up to introduce themselves and shake hands. The last was a female, a petite brunette who rolled Paul's knuckles when they shook. He thought he had managed not to wince, but he wasn't certain.

Greetings over, the soldiers began to pepper him with questions. "You walked all the way from Kentucky?"

"You're going to Brownsville, Texas? To the border?"

"How many days have you been on the road?"

"Where's your dog? I heard you had a big dog."

"Did you have some trouble back in Mississippi?"

"I love that walking stick. Make that yourself?"

"You Baptist or Methodist?"

"Easy gang, easy," Mike finally cut in. "Give the man a chance to answer."

Paul chuckled before he started speaking. "I've walked all the way from Caney Creek, Kentucky. That's close to Bowling Green, which is about an hour's drive north of Nashville. I'm going to Brownsville. This is my twenty-seventh day. I'm close to the halfway point. I guess it'll take somewhere around thirty days more. Houston will slow us down. We do have a big dog. His name's Buckethead—Buck for short. He put in the morning with me, but he's riding with Tick now. Tick is our—" he stopped while a log truck thundered past. "Tick's our transportation and supply guy. I'm Baptist. I did have some trouble back on the Trace, but Tick and Buck took care of it. This stick is a leaning stick, or a Jesus stick. Just lean on it, like Jesus, when you're weary. A friend in Tennessee—a Korean War veteran—made it for me. What have I left out?"

The soldiers laughed at his question. Then Mike spoke up.

"Very impressive, sir. Good briefing. One more question, if you don't mind. You're going to the border because you were called by God? All that way? That's a pretty strong calling."

Paul took a minute to rest his eyes on each soldier, in turn, finishing up with Mike. Everyone met his gaze without flinching. "It is a strong calling, but if there are people who can understand an undeniable call to act, I would think it'd be folks like you."

No one said anything, but a few of the soldiers nodded ever so slightly.

Just as the silence was beginning to stretch, Paul spoke again. "So, tell me, how is it that a group of our nation's best should wind up out here on this empty stretch of road?"

"Well," Mike began, "we're from Fort Polk, just south of here. We had an early start and finished ahead of time, so we thought we'd get in a little P. T. before calling it a day. I live in Leesville, five miles down the road. I'll drop out there. The rest will circle back to Fort Polk."

"Okay," Paul answered. "Just wondered. So, if I followed you right, we're all headed the same way now?"

"Correct," Mike nodded. "Shall we get to stepping?"

"Absolutely," Paul laughed.

For the next hour they walked together, though the troops soon began to wander ahead. All but Mike. He and the preacher struck up a conversation. In a brief lull, Paul smiled to himself about this chance encounter, about how the two of them quickly eased into calling each other by their first name as if they had always been friends. His biggest surprise was learning the sergeant was eight years older than him.

Still an hour out of Leesville, the others made their way back to the pair and huddled up. "Sergeant," the female said, "we thought we'd jog on in."

"Sure," he replied with a nod. "Everybody have a good weekend and stay out of trouble."

Before the soldiers took off, each one made a point to shake Paul's hand and wish him well.

When they reached Leesville, Paul's legs felt like they were good for a few more miles, yet he didn't hesitate to take Mike's offer to camp overnight in his back yard. It simply felt like he should. A few blocks into town, they arrived at Mike's home.

"Bethany!" Mike yelled as he swung the front door open. "Brought some company home."

From back in the house came a woman's voice. "Which one of your sorry army buddies is it this—" Rounding a doorway into the living room, Bethany froze when she spotted Paul. A confused smile instantly lit up her face.

"Hon," Mike explained, choking off a laugh, "this is Paul Lockhart—Preacher Paul Lockhart. He and his friend are going to spend the night. They're camping out in the yard."

"O—kay." Bethany replied. There were some missing parts in that bit of information, but that went with being an Army wife. One adjusted and overcame. "Pleased to meet you," Bethany said as she stepped forward to offer her hand. "Wait a second. I've heard of you. Where was it?" She hesitated a moment. "Oh yes, that girl on the morning show yesterday. Cami. That's it, the young lady who is traveling with you. Solves that. Anyway, welcome to our home, Reverend."

"Paul. Just call me Paul, please, and thank you for the welcome."

"Okay, Paul," she agreed, though she didn't sound certain.

"He might be thirsty, hon," Mike said, leaning in to kiss her on the cheek. "He's walked about twenty-five miles today."

"Why yes, I should have realized," Bethany exclaimed. "What

may I get you, Paul? A soda, iced tea, a beer? Oops, you might not want a beer."

"Water's fine."

"Speaking of water," Mike cut in, "I'm jumping in the shower. We've got a second bathroom, Paul, if you want to shower, too. Make yourself at home."

"Thanks. I'll take you up on that once Tick gets here. He's got our clean stuff."

"Sure," Mike said and disappeared down the hallway.

"Let me get your drink," Bethany said, turning the opposite direction through the doorway. She immediately stuck her head back in. "Ice?"

"No thanks," Paul answered.

She did not turn to leave this time. "What did you have for lunch?"

"Well, let me think. Tick found us some sandwiches somewhere. Some kind of Cajun aquatic thing, I believe, and a banana MoonPie for dessert."

"For heaven's sake," Bethany shook her head. "Look here." She ordered him to follow her with a crooked finger. "Other bathroom is down that way," she pointed, "second door on the right. Wash up, and I'll get you a bite to tide you over. Supper's not for a couple of hours yet."

"This ought to hold you," Bethany said, placing a huge piece of pecan pie topped with a scoop of vanilla ice cream before Paul. "Give it a minute. I heated the pie. The filling will blister the roof of your mouth. It's better, anyway, once the ice cream's about half melted."

"Lord, have mercy!" Paul exclaimed, his eyes growing wide. "I can't believe the table's still standing."

"Don't worry about the table. I'm worried about putting some meat on those ribs. I can count each one. I can't imagine what those people in Mississippi fed you, but you're in Louisiana now, and we know how to cook."

Paul nudged off a bite with his fork and put it in his mouth.

"*Mmmm, mmmm.* Yes ma'am, you do know how. This is so good."

"Thank you," Bethany smiled.

He almost told her about Elsie back home, and her delicious pecan pies, but he didn't think she would care to know she was tied with another cook for making the best thing ever. Instead, he ate like he'd had nothing all day. It wasn't difficult. He thought about licking the ice cream dribbles off his plate, but reluctantly pushed back. Bethany picked his plate up and carried it to the sink.

"I'll have us some coffee ready in a second," she said.

"Sounds wonderful. I love smelling it brewing."

"I do, too. Looks like we've got enough," she said a couple of seconds later, sliding the pot out and filling two cups. She brought the cups to the table and placed one before Paul, then the other before her spot. At last, she sat back down across from him.

"Reverend," she began.

"Paul," he corrected.

"Okay," she said, appearing to consider if this was something she could be comfortable with. "Paul," she finally said. "We heard what happened to your daughter. Mike and I talked about it last evening. I am so sorry."

"Thank you, Bethany. That means a lot."

"I know."

Her words threw him for a minute. Then a flash of understanding came.

"Oh, no," he began. "Not you, too?"

"We lost our son, our only child, five years ago. I'm sure Mike didn't tell you." She added, moisture gathering in her eyes.

"No, he didn't. Perhaps it's too painful."

"Yes, it is. Mike is such a strong man. He keeps things tied up inside, though, things he should let out. Oh, I'm so awful to bring this up. You lost your baby girl such a short time ago."

"It's okay," Paul nodded, and it was. This wasn't the first time he had found himself in a new place and suddenly realized he was meant to be there. Then he heard her give confirmation.

"It's just that when I heard who you are, I knew—I knew God had sent you."

"Or maybe," Paul hesitated a moment while his mind absorbed a second idea, "God put Mike on my path this afternoon to help me."

Bethany met his gaze and held it for several seconds before she nodded. "Perhaps. Or so we could all help one another."

"Yes," Paul answered, shifting in his chair. He could see the pain in her eyes, the terrible need to unburden. "What happened?"

He expected a flood, but her recounting came in a cool stream, as if her grief had long ago thundered down the mountain and now only trickles of emotion meandered through the flat caneland, tired and all but spent.

Chapter 67

Mike dropped another chunk of wood on the fire, sending a brief shower of sparks up into the night, then returned to his chair beside Paul. A few yards beyond the fire, three rolled sleeping bags stood on end. One each for Paul, Tick, and Mike.

"I go in to get a cold one, and Tick and Cami disappear," Mike said, looking about the backyard as if they could be hiding in a dark corner.

"They're around front," Paul answered. "Said they were going to listen to music in the van."

The fire gave enough light for Paul to see the grin. "Good excuse as any," Mike said, sounding more serious than his grin implied. "Unless I miss my guess, those two aren't listening to much of anything. Especially Tick. He's been hit over the head."

"With a Louisville Slugger." Paul chuckled. "Cami, too, I think, but she hides it better. Tick, though, he's plumb addled."

"Ah, me," Mike said with a shake of his head. "Nothing like young love."

"Yeah," Paul agreed. "I remember when Jennie and I started getting serious. We used that listening to music excuse a bunch of times." He fell silent with the realization those days were already ten years behind them.

"Me, too," Mike seconded. "We'd use any reason we could think of. Once—" he had to stop to laugh. "Her daddy was a farmer, see. I was visiting one evening about sunset, and he said something about needing to put down new bedding in the horse's stall. I volunteered, just to show I was a nice guy and he could trust me. Well, Beth followed me to the barn. Before you knew it, we were rolling around up there in the loft, hugging and kissing. It was dark time we got back. We didn't realize till we stepped under the

254

porchlight that we had stuff all over us. Then the door opened and there stood her daddy."

"Uh oh." Paul laughed. "Did he have a shotgun?"

"No, thank God, but there we were, picking straw out of each other's hair like two monkeys. He just stared at us, seemed like fifteen minutes. Finally, he said, 'Hope you left some in the stall.' Then he turned and went back in. Bethany always said she was glad to be the youngest of seven sisters, because by the time she came along her folks had seen it all. Otherwise, she might have wound up a widow before I proposed."

"That's a good one," Paul laughed. He waited a few moments before asking, "How long have you been married?"

"Seventeen years. Seventeen mostly good years," Mike added. A second later he said, "I didn't mean for that to sound like she hasn't always been a good partner. That's not the case. Beth has always been a princess. It's just that, well, there's been a rough patch or two."

"We all have them," Paul said. "You know about our worst one."

Mike shook his head. "Horrible. Simply horrible."

"Bethany told me about yours."

Mike cut his eyes toward Paul and held them on him for a long moment. There was no anger in his gaze, nor surprise, just something vacant and lonely. Then he looked down toward the ground. "Our son was a good kid. He knew how to love. Just riding his bike and a drunk driver—" Paul gave him time, sensing more was coming. A full minute passed before Mike spoke again. "It's not right, Preacher, when things happen out of order. It should have been me first, especially with the business I'm in. I guess she told you I was in Afghanistan when it happened?"

"Yes. And she said it took days for you to get home. That had to make it even worse."

"Lord, did it," Mike replied, his whole being seeming to sag. "You've been there when the flames are eating you alive, when each second goes on for an hour and every hour takes a week. To tell the truth, the hardest thing was knowing Beth didn't have me by her side. I still feel like I let her down."

"I think you know that's not true," Paul said, his words sounding sterner than he meant.

Mike waited long moments before answering. "It's hard to say. I don't know what's true about most of that time. I remember some of the drinking. Some. I stayed soused for months. That's reason enough to feel guilty. I wasn't exactly what she needed to lean on."

"You're being too hard on yourself," Paul said, shaking his head. "That's not what she told me. In fact, she said she didn't know how she could have got through it without you."

Mike raised his head to stare at Paul again. Once more, a spell of silence hung heavy as a damp quilt. Finally, he found his voice.

"That'd be just like her, saying that. Huh." Mike hesitated several seconds before continuing. "You know, I've wondered a lot over the years how I came to luck out. Bethany's way more than I have a right to."

"I'm in that same boat with Jennie. Of course, the Lord always gives us more than we deserve."

"You said that last part just like a preacher would."

"Thanks," Paul laughed.

"Well, speaking of the wife," Mike said, stretching his arms above his head, "I wonder what she's up to. Thought she'd be out to join us by now."

"She might still be on the phone with my missus. They started talking after I told Jennie good night."

Mike nodded. "I'd say that's a good thing."

"Yeah," Paul nodded back. "They're probably best friends by now."

"No doubt. I hope they talk the whole night through. Imagine they both need it."

"I wouldn't mind if you and I did the same thing," Paul said.

Chapter 68

The good news was there wasn't much traffic on this road. The bad news was the road was two-lane with narrow shoulders, so much of the time was spent walking on the hot pavement. To Paul's surprise, a couple of miles outside of Leesville, a sheriff's deputy pulled up alongside him. Paul slowed to a stop. The door window made a *whirring* sound as it came down.

"Morning, Preacher. How you doing?" the deputy asked from behind mirrored sunglasses.

"I'm doing fine," Paul replied, leaning down toward the window. "How about yourself?" he asked, moving close enough to read the officer's nameplate. "J. T., is it?"

"Yes sir. J. T. Ferguson at your service."

"I'm glad to meet you."

"And likewise, I'm sure," J. T. answered. "Just wanted to let you know you're my assignment today."

"Oh?" Paul was perplexed. "You making sure I don't steal anything?"

"No. We thought with you being a preacher, you wouldn't try to pack off too much." J. T. laughed. "I'm your escort, till you get to Texas, anyway."

"Well, I appreciate it, but I don't think that's necessary."

"I have my orders," J. T. held up both hands. "Don't worry, I'll keep out of your hair. The main thing to watch for is the timber trucks. I'll turn my lights on when I see one coming. That'll slow them down. For your part, just get off the pavement the best you can till they get by."

"Sounds like a plan." Paul smiled, patting the door.

"That's up to you, Earl," Lidge Clairborne, Vernon Parish sheriff and deacon at the New Canaan Baptist Church, said to his counterpart across the Sabine River in Texas. "I'm just telling you what I've done. It doesn't mean beans to me what you do. Chuck him off in Toledo Bend if that's what suits you. He's Baptist. I imagine he can take getting wet."

"I don't know," Newton County, Texas, sheriff Earl T. McCall answered, his voice sounding serious. "Folks around here might not care for that. He might mess up the fishing."

"You won't do, Earl," Sheriff Clairborne laughed.

"Neither will you," Sheriff McCall answered. "About what time you think he'll get here?"

"I'd say mid-afternoon. Want me to give you a buzz when he's a couple of miles away?"

"That'd be helpful," Sheriff McCall replied. "It'd let me have someone at the river when he crosses."

"One other thing you might want to know, Earl. Couple of militia types tried to attack him back in Mississippi."

"Ain't that a load?" Sheriff McCall groused. "Okay. Thanks for the heads-up. If you're not going to let this preacher get run over, then we'll do our best to keep him from it, too."

†††

It was 2:00 p.m. on the nose when Paul spotted the metal-truss bridge up ahead. There in a sandy pull-off on the right just before the bridge, were Tick's van and Cami's car, with the pair perched on the car's hood. Seeing him approaching, they both jumped up and started waving. Paul waved back and quickened his pace.

"Imagine meeting you two here," Paul said with a grin when he drew close.

"Wow, you've made good time," Cami said, returning the grin.

"I've been moving along okay. Just took a short break around 11:00."

"She just got here," Tick said, jerking a thumb toward Cami. "Guess what? She's brought us a bucket of chicken from the Colonel. There're some picnic tables across the river, if you want to go over there and eat a bite."

"That sounds good. Let me say goodbye to my escort first," Paul said, turning to wave the deputy on up to them. "Do you have a drumstick in there, Cami?"

"Sure," she answered and started toward her car to get the bucket. By the time she had a drumstick out, J. T. was pulling up beside them. Paul quickly introduced everyone. Then he turned to Cami.

"Let's give him that piece of chicken, Cami," Paul instructed her.

"Oh, I can't take that," J. T. tried to wave her off.

"Of course, you can." Paul insisted. "Everybody loves fried chicken."

"Well…" J. T. hesitated, then his hand started slowly reaching toward the piece of chicken Cami was offering.

"Thank you, J. T." Paul said, stepping around Cami to clap the deputy on his shoulder. "You've been a big help. And thank the sheriff, too, please. You be careful, okay?"

"I'll do that. You have a safe trip, preacher." Even though he was gnawing on the drumstick, J. T. had the cruiser turned around and headed back in seconds.

"Alright, gang," Paul said, stepping past Tick. "Let me take a quick gander at this river. Then I'll meet y'all in Texas for lunch."

Cami glanced over at Tick as they headed for their vehicles. He wore an expression so sad a stranger might have wondered if he had lost his wallet. She had to laugh, which made him turn toward her.

"It's okay, hon," she assured him. "Even with the piece I gave that officer, Paul and I can eat two pieces each, and you'll still have five left for you."

In a flash, Tick's expression changed to a wide toothy grin. He was still smiling a minute later as he slowly drove across the bridge. Then it dawned on him that Cami had called him, *Hon*, and he almost wrecked the van.

Chapter 69

Bob Mendoza parked near a refugee camp in Matamoros. Miguel and Carlos were working separately, checking other camps. It had been a month since the three had convened in Nuevo Laredo and started their quest for Serena. If his priest contact there had not been so adamant about the Guatemalan family traveling south to Matamoros, Bob would have given up searching the area already. It was his only decent lead, however, even if it had gotten him exactly zilch. He couldn't make it on zilch much longer. Math was math. If he didn't find her soon, he'd have to pull the plug.

Then a chance meeting with an aide worker from Rio Bravo sent him back to this camp he had checked out weeks ago. The rumor was the family was laying low. They were terribly frightened of being discovered and sent to who knew where this time. He could understand. In fact, he had made up his mind before he crossed the river that he would not reveal where the child was once he found her. There was another reason, a simple business one. He wasn't about to share his scoop.

So here he was, Bob Mendoza, intrepid reporter, peering through binoculars at a boy of fourteen or fifteen sitting on an upturned plastic bucket at the entrance to a refugee camp. He was probably a guard, which wasn't unusual. Child lookouts were often preferred. They moved about without attracting attention, disappeared easily into a crowd, etc. Suddenly a young man wearing a backwards ballcap moved into view. The young man stopped beside the boy and handed him a small bag, then walked away.

So, what have we here? Drugs?

The boy opened the bag and glanced inside. Then he hopped up and started walking down the main *street* of the camp. All at once he stopped and thrust his hand inside the bag. Bob dialed the binoculars and was just able to make out something in the boy's hand when he pulled it out. A Butterfinger? A small brown hand appeared, reaching up for the candy. The boy passed it down, then bent to receive a quick hug around his neck. For an instant, before the recipient hurried off, Bob caught a full view of her face. Then Serena disappeared into the warren of ragged tents and sagging clotheslines.

Chapter 70

"This fooled me, Sarah girl," Paul spoke aloud. "I never thought Texas had much in the way of trees, but that road to Jasper sure did, all those tall pines. It looks like timber's a big business around here.

"My feet hurt. That stretch of two-lane with no shoulder about got me. I must have jumped off in the weeds five hundred times because of traffic—and does it fly! The speed limit's seventy! I'm just glad I didn't land in a hole and twist an ankle. That looks like a roadside park up ahead. We'll stop and rest.

"This morning old Buck kept me scared half silly, the way he was wandering from side to side. I worried for nothing, of course. He always jogged over in plenty of time to keep from getting hit. I know you love him. He does you, too. You can tell by the way he swings his head your way when you scratch behind his ears. He can sense your presence as well as I can.

"I've been wondering about some things I might have done differently. We should have gone exploring more. You loved it, and your mama and I were always so tickled when you made a new discovery. No excuse. I let life get in the way, and we were all cheated because of it.

"Remember that time you took off running across the church parking lot. I grabbed you by the shoulders and shook you so hard. It scared you something awful. You cried and cried. I'm sorry. Poppy was afraid. Miss Kirby can't half see, and she drives like a maniac. I handled that wrong. I told you I was sorry then, but I don't think you understood, you were so upset.

"One more thing and I'll hush. I should have gotten you a dog. Imagine if you had one as big as Buck, you and Brutus could have ridden him like a pony. Every child deserves a dog, with ears to scratch, and a tail that wags like crazy when he sees you, and who'll give you a big, wet kiss when you're feeling low. We all need it, Sarah, someone special of our own to love without question and be loved by in return. Someone to watch over us. Maybe, if you'd had a dog—"

Sometimes guilt just jumped up and grabbed him. Paul stopped talking. He stopped walking, too. Staring down at the ground between his feet, he concentrated on breathing deeply. A few moments crawled past, and the sharp edge dulled.

He looked up. "Hey, there's Tick's over at the park. Lookout! Here comes Buck!"

A minute later, as Paul knelt running his hand down the length of the dog's back, Buck turned his head away and held it cast down at an angle, leaning into something. He heard the deep bass *grrrr* of contentment coming from Buck's throat. Paul smiled. He could almost see little fingers digging behind big ears.

Chapter 71

"Y ou boys get enough?" the red-headed waitress asked. "Little more sweet tea?"

"Thanks, I'm fine," Tick answered. "How about you, Preacher?"

Paul suddenly covered his mouth with his napkin, stifling a burp, as he raised his other hand, palm out, in a universal *wait a minute* sign. After a few seconds, he managed to speak. "I couldn't eat another crumb. That was great. I thought I was at a potluck back home."

The waitress stepped half a pace back from the table's edge, their ticket still in her hand, and stared at Paul. "Preacher?" she finally said. "You've had me scratching my head since y'all came in. You from Kentucky? The one that's praying for the kids?"

"Yes," Paul replied, his eyes meeting hers.

"Debbie!" the waitress bellowed as she turned toward the cash register. "Brenda! Jonell! Somebody holler at John and Rosa!" she yelled, as if they couldn't possibly hear her locomotive horn of a voice. "Everybody come over here."

Paul and Tick looked at each other, only slightly embarrassed. Such reactions had become commonplace.

"It's that preacher we saw about on TV."

The others came closer, moving tentatively, as if they weren't quite certain how to respond. Then one lady took Paul's hand, then Tick's in turn, wishing them a safe journey. The rest of the staff followed suit, wishing the same or a muttered, *bless you,* until only Rosa, a short Hispanic lady remained. She removed her apron and folded it neatly. "Momento," she said. With care she laid the apron on a table to one side. Still, she hesitated, her eyes cast downward. For an instant Paul thought she was simply shy, then, seeing her lips moving, he realized she was praying. She looked up slowly, her

264

expression one of grace as she stepped forward. Catching his hand between hers, she pulled it to her lips and softly kissed it. "Vaya con Dios," she said.

"Gracias." Paul nodded, knowing for the first time since settling in his seat what it was to be truly full.

Eating alone at a small table near the stairs, a man lifted his head just enough to see from beneath the brim of his battered Stetson.

"Misspoke there, senorita," he mumbled to himself. "Gone to God, not go with God, is what we'll be saying soon enough."

Chapter 72

"I'm not believing this," Paul groused. He was seated on the floorboard at the van's open rear doors. Lying in the dirt nearby, Buck lifted his head to look.

Tick came walking back, "Don't believe what, Preacher?"

"I've got a blister on my heel," Paul answered, not trying to hide his exasperation. "Already busted."

"Yep," Tick said, bending over to look. "That'll need some doctoring."

"My first blister since Tennessee. I expected foot problems back then—my feet were still toughening up—but after all these miles."

Tick shrugged, "Did you notice it yesterday?"

"My heel felt a little warm the last mile or so, but I didn't think it was a blister."

"I'll get the first aid kit," Tick said. He was back in a minute. As Paul dug out what he needed, Tick spoke. "I know what caused it. You do, too, if you'll just think."

Paul threw him a questioning look. In answer, he received a wide smile. "Okay, what's so funny?"

"Well, I wouldn't say it's funny now."

"I'm all ears," Paul grumbled.

"That buffet yesterday. You're not used to packing the extra weight." Tick chuckled.

Paul frowned for a moment. "That might be it." A smile slowly spread across his face. "We didn't even eat supper last night, did we?"

"Nope. You crawled in your sleeping bag right after we stopped. Snoring two seconds later. Of course, I was right behind you."

They both laughed, then shifted their conversation to the day's plan while Paul continued to doctor his heel. Suddenly Paul looked up.

"Oh shoot! If I went to sleep right after we stopped, I didn't call Jennie."

"Relax, Preacher. You called her while you were still walking."

"Oh." Paul hesitated. Bits of conversation came drifting back. "You're right. She just heehawed about all the stuff I ate."

Paul carefully worked his hiking boot on, then stood. He took a few tentative steps to see if the bandage offered enough padding.

"Okay. I hope that holds. So, what's our first town today."

"Buna. We should be able to find something for lunch there."

"I'm not sure I'll be hungry after yesterday." Paul chuckled, dropping a couple of drinks and an orange into his pack. He glanced down at the dog. "What about it, boy? Ever been to Buna?"

Cami had just finished an interview on a morning show in Beaumont—in fact, was still in the station's lot—when her phone rang.

"Hello, this is Cami," she answered, hoping it was her dad. He always got a kick out of how she gave her name when she answered now.

"Ms. Whitley, this is Marguerite Merriweather with the Sunrise Cathedral in Houston."

Cami smiled to herself, thinking *Ms. Merriweather could work at the White House switchboard, or maybe Buckingham Palace, with such an inflated manner of speech.* She didn't bother to ask how the lady had obtained her number, for she had given it out dozens of times.

"Good morning, Ms. Merriweather. How may I be of assistance?"

"Please just call me Marguerite, dear. May I call you, Cami?"

"Certainly, Marguerite," she replied, thinking it hardly lowered the sense of formality.

"Thank you, Cami. May I assume you are familiar with our Sunrise Cathedral?"

"Oh, yes," Cami replied, remembering how it looked on TV with its huge yellow-glass windows behind the choir bathing everything in the cathedral's signature golden sunrise glow.

"We understand," Marguerite plowed ahead, "that Reverend Lockhart will be in or near Houston this coming Sunday. Reverend

Michelson wishes to extend an invitation to Reverend Lockhart to present a sermon at the Cathedral that morning. May I report that he gladly accepts?"

"I will relay the reverend's gracious invitation to Preacher Paul and get back to you shortly. I must tell—"

"Oh." Marguerite cut her off. "I assumed you could answer for the—preacher."

Cami nearly laughed out loud. *Nice dig*, she thought.

"The nature of the journey," she started again, throwing an explanatory shovelful back, "often results in fragmented communications. It is possible Preacher Paul has made other arrangements for Sunday. I will track him down and get back to you as soon as possible."

"Please do, dear," Marguerite replied, thick vines of condescension coiling about the last word. "We would so love to have him."

"As to the preaching," Cami said, "should he attend, I doubt he would actually deliver a sermon. His usual course is to make a few brief remarks before leading the congregation in prayer for the children. I simply want you to be forewarned."

"I appreciate that," Marguerite answered, sounding anything but appreciative. "We certainly hope he presents a sermon. Every minister who comes to our church just can't wait to lead a service."

"I'm certain. I will call you back shortly."

"Thank you so much, Ms. Whitley."

"My pleasure, Ms. Merriweather."

"You did fine, Cami," Paul said into his phone. "I'm still reluctant to deliver a full sermon. It would inevitably bring attention to things other than our mission. Please inform your contact that I would be delighted to lead a simple prayer service for the children."

"I felt sure that's what you would say. I'll call Ms. Merriweather right now."

"Very good. And one other thing while we're talking."

Paul hesitated so long Cami said, "Yes," to be certain he was still there.

"I'm sorry. Just trying to reason something out. Uh, the Cathedral presents the opportunity to reach a great many people—not only in Houston. Their services are broadcast nationwide. It is important, however, that what we are doing isn't seen as only a mega-church effort."

Paul hesitated again, lost in his thoughts. Cami remained quiet.

"Find us another church in Houston, a much smaller one, a church with a Hispanic membership. We will also go there Sunday."

Chapter 73

Paul kept his eyes closed throughout the choir's amazing rendition of "Go Tell It on the Mountain." He opened them to the sight of thousands of people, all bathed in the soft golden light pouring through the stained-glass windows of the cathedral. His church wouldn't fill the space between him and the congregation. Three semi-circular carpeted tiers descended in order, with the lowest level ending an arm's length from the front row of worshippers. There was no pulpit, no communion table, only a simple wooden lectern occupying the center point of the lowest tier. It held an open Bible.

Sensing movement, Paul turned his head to see Reverend Michelson rising from his throne-like chair. The reverend bent slightly to pat Paul's arm, then made his unhurried way down toward the congregation, coming to a halt half a pace behind the lectern, where the rays of sunlight were focused. Paul followed the reverend's words. First, he praised the choir. Then he introduced Paul.

"We have a special guest with us today, the Reverend Paul Lockhart. Most of you are doubtless aware, Preacher Paul, as he is known, in answer to a call from God, is walking from his Kentucky home to the southern border to pray for the children. When we asked him to give today's message, he graciously declined, saying he preferred to simply lead us in prayer. Preacher Paul, would you please come forward to lead us now?"

Paul rose from his simple chair and followed the same path forward as Reverend Michelson had, stopping behind the lectern as the reverend discreetly stepped to one side. Paul's clothes were what he wore on the road on cooler days like today: a flannel shirt, jeans, hiking boots. As his hands grasped the edges of the polished platform, he caught a snippet of conversation. A man's voice. "If that's his Sunday best." A woman quickly answering, "Shoo!" Paul didn't try to locate the speakers. He simply allowed his gaze to sweep slowly over the countless rows, taking in the full gathering. A thought flitted through his mind—*You ain't in Caney Creek anymore, son*—and left him smiling. This was by far the largest group he had ever addressed, yet he was not nervous. He always made eye contact and spoke to one person at a time. Besides, he was confident the Lord would provide words if he faltered.

"Good morning, my friends," Paul began, instantly relieved the wireless microphone on his collar was working. A low murmur of *good morning* came back. "Thank you, sir," Paul said, facing toward the other minister, "for your kind invitation to join in worship." Reverend Michelson dipped his head in reply. Paul turned to the choir and brought his hands together before his heart in a sign of prayer. He inclined his fingertips toward the group as he spoke. "As the reverend said, thank you for your glorious singing. My goodness," Paul added, pivoting back to the congregation. "I imagined I had happened upon the gates to Heaven and heard the angels' voices coming from inside."

"Amens," lifted from many voices. Paul settled his focus on an older, white-haired man seated straight ahead on the front row. The gentleman was resplendent in his gray suit. The corner of a red handkerchief, pressed flat and sharp, protruded from his breast pocket. With his eyes locked on Paul, he nodded.

"Reverend Michelson," Paul began, "related that in response to God's call, I am on a journey to the border to pray for the children. You would be right to ask, *What does that mean? Pray for which children and pray for what, exactly?* Did He mean I should pray no child ever go hungry? Or they shall always have safe shelter? Did He mean I should pray they never suffer serious injury or illness? Or should I ask that their parents are forever near to hug them tight when storms rage, to kiss them when their eyes grow heavy, so they fall asleep knowing they are loved? I don't know. The Lord was not specific about *what* and *why*, only *who* and *where*. For now, I walk, at ease in my faith and the knowledge that His will shall be done."

Paul paused, his gaze roaming over the congregation as he allowed his words to sink in. He noticed the television camera rolling closer but paid it no mind. At last, his eyes met those of the old man again. Again, the man nodded at Paul in agreement.

"Back home, I often ask our members to join me in silent prayer. All that means is that each person goes directly to the Lord. I may suggest what to pray for, and I will do that here. This is something we can ask for children, all children, at the border or otherwise." He paused a moment. "There is one great trial I believe we have all gone through, something, my brethren, we would not want to befall the least of these. Please think back to when you were a child. Something happened that frightened you beyond anything you had ever known. What it was does not matter, only the fact that you were so scared you could not cry, or speak, or draw a breath. Remember?" Again, he hesitated. "Go back to that instant when the icy claws of fear gripped you so hard it was all you knew and ask God that no child ever experience what you felt."

Paul allowed half a minute to creep by in the eerily quiet sanctuary, his hands clutching the edges of the podium, his face lifted toward the beams of light converging in front of him.

"Please stand," he said, his arms rising, palms out, "and take the hand of your neighbor."

After a moment, he allowed his arms to drop partway until his fingers suddenly closed, as if grasping the hands of unseen neighbors at his sides. A few astute observers noted his left hand was somewhat lower than his right, as if he were holding the hand of a child.

"Let us speak with the Lord," Paul said. Then he bowed his head.

Chapter 74

Paul hopped out of the van and hurried toward the church. They were running behind, despite Tick's best efforts to quickly negotiate their way through Houston. He looked up to see a young priest standing outside the weathered front door.

"Welcome to St. Ignatius," the priest said, a smile stretching his face as he moved down the handful of steps toward Paul.

"I'm delighted to be here," Paul replied as the men grasped hands. "So sorry we're late. Houston takes a while to get across."

"Don' I know it?" the priest laughed. "I'm Manuel Diaz. Father Manny to my small flock."

"Paul. Preacher Paul to my modest congregation. Oh, here comes our logistics guy." He gave Tick a few seconds to catch up before making the introductions.

"There is also a lady with you?" Father Manny asked.

"That's Cami," Paul nodded. "Our press person. She will be here shortly with some reporters. I trust that is alright?"

"No problem. She mentioned reporters when she called." He turned and gestured toward the steps. "Shall we go inside? Mass just concluded. Everyone is waiting to meet you."

†††

The sanctuary was small, with seating that would be less than a single row in Sunrise Cathedral. It was an old church, with an old church's smells of candle smoke, scrubbed stone, and wooden pews worn slick with use. Countless human steps had ground paths into the floor. From behind the pulpit, a carving of Jesus on the cross, its paint faded and flaked, hung on a column. There were a handful of modest, gold-framed paintings between the sconces along the side walls: Jesus with a crown of thorns; Mary holding her infant son.

273

"Buenos dias," Paul said as he stepped up to the pulpit. "I apologize for being late. I promise not to keep you long."

He briefly reviewed some of the events leading up to the trek, concentrating on Serena being separated from her mother and God's call to him.

"What God has sent me to do is simple. I am to pray for the children at the border in Brownville. As our Father instructed, I walk the same distance Serena walked from Guatemala so I may understand something of the difficulties she and so many others faced to get to the border. May God watch over all who go through that struggle. Now, I ask that you bow your heads as I lead us in prayer for the children."

"Our Father, we come to You in gratitude for the miracle of children. What a privilege to hear their laughter and see their smiles, to receive their unquestioning love, to follow their progress as they grow into adults, and most importantly, to then see them set the perfect example for their children by always doing unto others as they would have others do unto them. These things are among Your greatest blessings.

"We come to You today, asking that all children always know they are loved, that they have their parents and families close by, ever ready to guide and protect them, that in Your good time they come seeking Your love and understanding, and that they return that love to others tenfold. We ask these things in the name of Your son, Jesus Christ. Amen."

"Amen," the parishioners echoed. Then they filed forward to meet him.

The people were friendly, yet somewhat reserved in how they individually approached him. There was a formality to their actions. The men shook his hand as anyone might, though their expressions were serious, as if this were a solemn moment. Most of the women grasped his hand with both of theirs and simply held it for a minute, some squeezing it lightly as the hint of a smile warmed their expressions. None of the adults said the usual *hello* or *buenos dias.* Instead, they said *gracias* or *thank you.* The last in line was a white-haired lady, bent with age. She approached without diffidence and reached up to his face with both hands. Then she pulled him down close and kissed his forehead.

Paul was amused by the teenagers. The boys did their best to look as stern as their fathers, while the girls cast shy glances and whispered thanks his way. Strangely, the smaller children were absent, other than a handful of toddlers brought forward by parents.

Father Manny came up to him when the greetings were completed.

"I appreciate you coming here today," he said. "We will continue to pray for your safe journey and for the success of your calling." The priest paused a moment. "There is something I should tell you."

"Yes," Paul answered.

"Not all Hispanics are—how shall I say it? There is some suspicion about your reasons for going to Brownsville."

"Really?" Paul was surprised. "Why is that?"

"Some may harbor distrust because it is a white man talking. They question if you really mean what you say? There is also a feeling with a few, that anyone wishing to come here should go through the same types of difficulties they or their parents had to go through. In other words, nothing should be handed to them."

"I see," Paul said. "These are things I had not considered. The greater issues around immigration are not part of my calling, however. It is centered solely on the children."

"I understand, and you have my support." Father Manny nodded. With a smile, he added, "I look forward to us meeting again."

"Nothing would make me happier." Paul smiled back, reaching to take the priest's hand. After a moment he said, "I guess I better find the rest of my gang. Tick's disappeared and Cami never did show up."

"Come, my friend," Father Manny said. "We will search together."

As they stepped through the front door, they discovered the *gang*. Tick had transformed into a living jungle gym. He was making grunting, growling noises as he trudged about the dusty lawn, festooned with small kids. A boy rode atop one foot, a girl the other, both holding onto his legs. One boy was suspended by his hands from each of Tick's extended arms, as if hanging from a limb. A fifth child, a girl, rode him piggyback, her brown arms wrapped around his neck.

Cami stood near the street in a row of laughing parents. Buck lay on his back at her feet, happily undergoing a rub and scratch work over from other children. Two still photographers and a TV cameraman circled about Tick and his young climbers. Paul and Father Manny stopped at the head of the steps and joined in the laughter. After a moment, Tick spotted Paul.

"Hey," he said. "Y'all want to meet the preacher?"

The children dropped off Tick one by one and timidly came forward to stand in a tight group at the foot of the steps. Paul walked down and knelt before the closest child. He offered his hand to shake. The boy seemed perplexed, canting his head to one side and staring. He suddenly shot forward and wrapped his arms around Paul's neck. All the other little ones rushed to join him. Adults and teenagers instantly started taking pictures with their cell phones. The still photographers and the cameraman moved to take shots from every angle.

Much of the professionals' work made its way into TV news reports and morning papers. They were all usurped by a girl of fourteen. She was only a few paces away when the children's stampede occurred. Raising her phone, she snapped three quick photos. It took her but seconds to select the one she liked best—Paul's laughing face afloat in a sea of children. She posted it on social media. Within the hour, it had gone viral.

Chapter 75

Reverend Micah Michelson resisted the urge to slam the door shut behind him. Instead, concentrating on the iron self-control he prided himself on, he eased it shut and walked around his desk to plop down in his padded leather chair. So, this Preacher Paul, who had not wanted to preach to the Sunrise congregation, had managed to do just that, and do it quite well with an enviable economy of words. Then he, the resident minister, had found himself scrambling and stretching for points in his own sermon just to stay in the ballpark. It was embarrassing, but being a seasoned pro, he knew he had managed to do a good job of covering.

"Whew," he exhaled slowly. It was time for some self-reflection. In his mind, he ticked off the things that had led to the need.

1. He had been enthralled by the idea of the preacher's walk since he first heard about it, instantly realizing the great P R potential.

2. He had closely watched Paul since, noticing, even within the Cathedral membership, that he was winning a growing following.

3. Reports were consistent in the assessment that Paul seemed to be genuine.

4. He had anticipated some of the Preacher's attraction rubbing off on him. Any benefit there was yet to be seen, but by giving the man a national platform it seemed inevitable, unless, of course, Paul made a major misstep.

"Okay," the reverend said aloud. "No harm." Then he reverted to speaking to himself. *I'll keep an eye on Paul. If he doesn't mess up before he gets to the border, we'll make our presence known there, too. It should look like we're close, but not too close. Anyway, we are both men of God, sworn to spread His message. I'm not too big to ride on someone's coattails if it means reaching more people.*

The last sentence seemed to grate. He decided to add an explanation.

Yes, Lord, I know I have an ego as big as Texas, but I really mean it. I ask Your guidance.

A soft knock at the door broke his chain of thought.

"Yes."

The door swung open a bit, and the head of his personal secretary appeared.

"Come in, Marguerite. What's up?"

"Initial ratings report," she said, passing him a single sheet of paper.

He looked at it for three seconds before glancing up. "Is this real?"

"Absolutely. I double-checked everything myself. Notice how it climbs from the moment Preacher Paul started speaking and stayed up right through your sermon."

The reverend was staring at the page again. A huge grin spread across his face.

"We have been blessed," he said.

"Blessed indeed," she nodded, the corners of her mouth lifting in a smile.

Chapter 76

"Welcome back, Houston," the co-host said. "As promised, we are returning to our lead story about Preacher Paul Lockhart, who is walking from the tiny community of Caney Creek, Kentucky, to Brownsville, Texas. Our on-scene reporter, Tina Dickson, is in Sugar Land. Tina, looks like a steady stream of people walking by."

"That's right, Ron. They're following Preacher Paul as he heads out of the metro area." The camera zoomed in on a sign carried by a tall, gaunt man. *Prayer is the Answer,* it read. "It's difficult to give an accurate count, but it's certainly in the thousands."

✝✝✝

Newspaper reporter Brady Vinson was struggling to keep up with Paul. The preacher had hit *road gear,* as he called it, the point when the aches and kinks from the day before melted away and he found his optimum stride.

"Think you could slow down a little?" the reporter panted, glancing up from his old-fashioned tape recorder.

"No," Paul replied. Chuckles rose from the knot of fast walkers close behind.

Brady shot Paul a hard look, thinking the preacher was messing with him.

"Hang that thing around your neck," Paul said without looking his way. "It'd make it easier, wouldn't it?"

"I guess so," Brady replied. He tried to loop the recorder's strap over his neck without stopping but couldn't. Stepping out of the flow, he got the gear straight, then stole a glance back at the undulating line.

"The line stretches back as far as you can see," Brady said, hustling to fall in stride beside the preacher again. "You've become quite the celebrity."

Now it was Paul's turn to give a hard look.

"That's the last thing I am or ever intend to be."

Brady grinned. "Yesterday you spoke at one of the largest churches in the country. Afterward you went to a small Hispanic church. Nice balancing act. Where this was taken," he added, holding his phone in front of Paul.

"Aren't they beautiful?" Paul said, smiling broadly at the photo of children hugging him at St. Ignatius. "The innocent love of children. There's nothing sweeter."

"That picture's gone viral."

"What Cami said."

"The first thing I thought," Brady hesitated a moment, "was it was staged."

"No," Paul replied.

"Is that all you have to say?

"Yes."

Brady waited for more, but when Paul didn't add anything, he switched subjects.

"Yesterday at the Sunrise Cathedral, you asked people to pray that no child would live in fear. If I'm correct, all along you have been saying that you are making this walk to the border to pray for the children, but you've never stated any particular thing they might need. You kind of let the cat out of the bag yesterday, though, didn't you, talking about fear?"

"I'm not sure what you're looking for," Paul replied. "The list of children's needs is endless. I suggested one possible topic at the Sunrise service. It happened to be something that many people have in common."

"Why did you suggest *fear*?"

"I'm not certain," Paul answered, his brow wrinkling in thought. "I didn't know I was going to until I said it."

"Are you saying the Lord told you what to say?"

"No." Paul answered immediately, then hesitated. "Maybe He did. Who knows? The truth is—I imagine this happens to most people—sometimes something just pops out without me thinking. Have you ever done that?"

The question caught Brady off guard.

"Yeah. Yeah, sure. We all do sometimes."

They walked on in silence for a hundred yards before Brady glanced back at the line.

"Wonder how far they'll make it? Most will probably give it up before evening," he added, answering his own question.

"Perhaps," Paul nodded. "It is a long way to Brownsville. Over three hundred miles."

"So, what happens when you get to Brownsville?"

Paul glanced over at Brady, his eyes narrowing, "I'll pray for the children."

"Okay," Brady said with a wry smile. "I've got that part. I mean where will you stay? How long will you be there. What's the schedule of events? That kind of stuff."

"Events! Where did that come from?"

"I didn't mean anything by it, Preacher—"

"Paul. Just Paul."

"Okay, uh, Paul. A plan, that's what I mean."

"I don't have one."

"Come on, Paul, you must have some idea."

"No."

"Really?"

"Really. I'm to pray for the children, and the rest, well, it's a matter of faith."

"Okay, I give," Brady shook his head. They traveled in silence for a few minutes before he spoke again. "I kind of pushed you a little hard. Nothing personal."

"You are a seeker of truth," Paul replied instantly, "as am I. I have never found anything offensive in that."

At Rosenberg, Brady said goodbye. By 11:30 a.m. he was back in the office and had filed his story. The headline read, *A Seeker of Truth.* The article did not include his speculation that most of the walkers would give up by evening. He would admit to that thought in his column the next day, when he wrote about the 3,000 people who had gathered in an encampment with the preacher, most sleeping on the ground, that first night out of Houston.

Chapter 77

Droopy McNaughton, in Houston for a series of concerts, was one of those who read Brady's columns and watched other local news reports about Paul. He was troubled by a recurring theme. Here were thousands of people, most of whom had not walked a mile in years, pushing themselves past their limits and risking their health staying out in the elements overnight, not to mention there were no provisions for feeding them. Some press members were already calling it a disaster in the making. Droopy picked up the phone and selected a number from his contact list. His call was answered on the second ring.

"What's up there, old man?"

"Rent and taxes, Lucky. Just a wondering," Droopy headed right for the point, "if you've seen much about this Preacher Paul fella who's walking to the border."

"I've been picking up bits and pieces. Interesting. It sounds like he's got a real crowd following him."

"Yep, a big one and it's growing fast. I'm down in Houston, and the press is going half nuts saying there's going to be a calamity if something's not done. You know how things get blown up—people on the march getting sick and starving and maybe dying? That sort of stuff."

Lucky didn't say anything. Finally, he cleared his throat. "Yeah. They can get a little sideways sometimes, but there might be a kernel of truth there. That's gnawing at you, isn't it? That kernel?"

"Yep," Droopy answered. Lucky always could see straight through him. "All those people—" He left the fragment hanging, not caring to run down the list of what could go wrong.

"It seems to me like this preacher is the real deal. He's going down there to pray for the kids, right?" Lucky was surprised by the sudden chill that came with his question. Then he thought, *strange how hearing you're about to become a grandfather can impact a man.* "What do you know about him?"

"I've been keeping up the best I could since he passed through Nashville. He walked right past my motel there. Everything I've heard says he's a true man of the Spirit. Shoot, I even wrote a song about him."

"You did now, did you?" Lucky smiled to himself. If Droopy McNaughton, his friend since they met on the practice field in Fayetteville over twenty-five years ago, had written a song about the preacher, then the preacher was a true man of the Spirit. "Baptist, isn't he?"

"Yes," Droopy replied, smiling, knowing the question came from a deacon at the largest Baptist Church in Fayetteville.

"Well, I don't see how we can call ourselves good Christians," Lucky spoke slowly, "if we leave a preacher and his flock on their own smack dab in the middle of the Texas wilderness. So, let's see what we need to get rounded up."

They spent less than five minutes discussing needs for food, shelter, and transportation. Lucky agreed to handle things from the northwest corner of Arkansas, which happened to be where a giant retail chain had its headquarters. Less well known, the headquarters of several other Fortune 500 corporations were also based there—businesses that produced and processed food, as well as moved goods from Point A to Points B through Z around the country. Lucky was the founder and CEO of one of those truck lines.

For his part, Droopy would start working his contacts in country music, where generosity was part of the gig. He would make the first move, himself, sending three of his buses from Houston down the road to wherever Preacher Paul and his followers were, picking up stragglers along the way. Lucky promised to, "Aggravate half of Arkansas," to get what was needed, logistics-wise.

"You reckon we ought to call the preacher?" Droopy said as they wound down. "Let him know what we're up to and ask for his ideas?"

"It might be a good play," Lucky chuckled. "We don't want to scare the man. Can you set up a three-way for tomorrow morning?"

"Sure," Droopy replied. His publicist could handle it. "Lucky," he began, then stopped.

"Yeah, Droop."

"You know, once we start, we're in it for the long haul."

Lucky chuckled again. *In it for the long haul* was his company's motto, emblazoned on every tractor and trailer in the fleet. The mirth was gone from his voice, however, when he spoke. "Imagine that's what the Lord expects, my friend."

"Amen," Droopy replied.

By sunup the next day, having departed from widely scattered points, a fleet of passenger buses was on the road heading for south Texas. Another fleet, this one of semi-trucks, was headed to the same area, carrying everything from tents and cots to field kitchens and enough food to feed an army on the march.

Chapter 78

The thin man stared at the picture on his phone a moment longer before finally closing the news app. The sight of Preacher Paul kneeling, beaming from ear to ear while half a dozen brown children hugged him, was burned into his mind as vividly as the sight of the preacher praying in the Sunrise Cathedral.

He fumed over how quickly things had escalated. For a couple of months, stories of the preacher had held to an even keel, for the most part as only brief progress reports. Friends in the media had worked the angle that the man was a heartbroken father to be pitied, downplaying his stated purpose for traveling to the border as something akin to lunacy. Then came Houston. Only four days ago the preacher had appeared on Sunrise Cathedral's morning service with millions across the nation tuned in. Then the photo with the little children went flying like a rocket through the ether. Probably half the population had it saved on their phones. Suddenly everyone knew of Preacher Paul and his mission.

There were hordes of people following him under the bright Texas sun, as if he were Moses heading for the Rio Grande, intending to smack the thing with that stupid-ass stick of his and cut a four-lane highway through the water. These kiddie lovers were coming from all over, obviously hoping to be the first to moon walk across to Mexico so they could get a bucketful of chimichangas without getting their backs wet. As if that weren't enough, that country music buffoon, Droopy McNaughton and his Nashville buddies, were sending buses to haul them around, along with a great caravan of semi-trucks carrying everything imaginable. It was a moving city, rolling inexorably south, toward the border.

Hadn't he seen the danger coming? Hadn't he looked out his

hotel window in Nashville, looked straight at the man only yards away on the sidewalk, and known he was trouble?

But the Big Guy hadn't taken his warning seriously.

Until now.

"Do something!" The petulant prince had screamed moments ago, plainly oblivious to the fact that he, his most insightful adviser, had recommended action way back in Nashville, when the preacher was hardly a blip on anyone's radar. "He's a threat to everything I've accomplished! To national security! Shoot the sonofabitch!"

The thin man had known that last bit was coming. The Big Guy often ended his diatribes by screaming the line.

So, his boss wanted the good reverend shot? He would start the wheels rolling then, not because he always listened to what the Big Guy said, but because in this instance he happened to believe the man was right. Anything that might engender sympathy for immigrants had to be thwarted, lest the gates be swung wide open and America overrun.

He punched the keys and hit *send*.

Dad called.

Chapter 79

One of the instructors had told him the first day of training, "Look the part, act the part, you are the part." Today he was a cowboy. His wide-brimmed hat, rolled into loose semi-circles on the sides, was stained from sweat and grit-laden wind. His long-sleeved shirt had snaps instead of buttons and pocket tabs that curved down to points. The cuffs of his denim jeans were worn to ravelings. Sharp boot toes of scuffed leather made trowel-shaped tracks in the dust of the crossroad. Holding everything together, in true Texas style, a belt-buckle the size of a MoonPie, etched with the head of a long-horn steer.

His ride was an old Chevy pick-up sprinkled with rust and manure, along with a few deep dents where bulls had butted heads. He leaned against the driver's door, looking across the hood at the distant, rolling wave of people walking his way. A sporty red convertible with the top down stopped across from him. The driver, a man in his early twenties with gold-tinted sunglasses and long blond hair hanging over the back of his collar, stared at the crowd for a moment before turning toward the cowboy. In that short interlude, the cowboy had pulled the front of his hat lower and pushed up on the nosepiece of his sunglasses. His index finger was still there, so his hand obscured most of his face.

"That the preacher that's on the news?" Preppy Boy asked. He turned away an instant later. Working men, especially disheveled working men, didn't merit a longer look.

"Yeah," the cowboy answered with a drawl despite having grown up in Detroit.

"Crap, I'll never get through that mess," the prepster fussed, already backing into the crossroad. He was gone in seconds.

"Neither will a bullet," the cowboy muttered, his attention back on the approaching gaggle. That was an overstatement. He could thread a round through a keyhole at 500 yards. It was the getting away afterward. Out here there were few good places to hide and fewer roads, not to mention prying eyes, human and electronic. To punctuate the point, a news helicopter suddenly appeared, flying above the column.

He got back in his truck and pulled out, heading away from the marchers.

They should have given the green light while he was still in East Texas. At least there's real trees to hide behind there, instead of this damn scrub.

Oh well. It would just take a little more planning, but the outcome would be the same.

Chapter 80

It was midnight. Paul's eyes would not stay shut. Things were very different since Houston, especially when the quiet of evening should be luring him to rest. Sounds came from every direction. Voices—some laughing, some scolding—called out to others. Footsteps crunched through dead grass, hurrying to the banging-door porta-potties set up in the brush. In the distance, singing. Punctuating everything, the sounds of others who *could* sleep snoring like buzzsaws. *Good grief!*

For two months he had known the luxury of solitude, of free time to think during the days. Evenings were relegated to calls with Jennie and conversations with Tick. Then he would tell Sarah good night. Sleep came early and easy. It was wonderful.

Now the established patterns and rhythms of the trek were gone. He seldom had a moment to himself. He had tried to adjust his walking, to speed up enough to stay out in front of the throng, but no matter how he pushed someone was always right at his shoulder. Everyone had something to say or ask. Most often it was words of encouragement or maybe a simple blessing. Yet some wanted him to pray for someone in particular. Him? As if he had some special insight or ability? He prayed, just the same. He listened closely and did his best to offer comfort, as a minister should, and tried hard to be patient.

Those who came to him while he was walking were much the smaller group. When the day's trek was completed, he scarcely had an opportunity to put his feet up before the people with harder stories began to come to him. Theirs were tales of relatives or friends missing, forced into smuggling drugs, imprisoned, sent back to where they had fled, only to be persecuted or even killed. But the stories of children—pawns of governments or gangs or twisted individuals, abused and raped and sold into only God knew what—cut him deeper than anything imaginable.

Paul lay on his back, looking up at the stars, and tried to digest all these things. He felt guilty over his struggles to offer answers. But what could he do, other than pray? So, he prayed. He spoke to God for wisdom, for the ability to tell those who came to him how they might make things better, for empathy and understanding, and most of all, for strength. And when he was done, Jennie's words came to him in a soft whisper. *You are but the vessel.* Imagining her breath against his skin, his daughter's warm face burrowed into the crook of his arm, Paul closed his eyes and with his last conscious thought whispered, "Good night, my sweet girls."

Chapter 81

The calls all came within an hour. Cami couldn't set her phone down before it rang again. Finally, she rushed through the camp, searching for Paul. She found him sitting cross-legged at the far edge of a lake, watching the sun go down. Buck sat next to him. Tick stood twenty yards beyond, lazily skipping rocks across the water.

"There you are," Cami said, jogging up to Paul. "Dang, let me catch my breath."

Paul looked at her. "Slow down. You look like you've been in the Derby."

"I feel like it. I've got some news. Let me get Tick over here. Tick!" she yelled. "He'll want to hear this."

Paul smiled at her excitement while they waited.

"Well, come on," Cami urged.

"What's up?" Tick asked, as he ambled over beside Buck.

"I just spoke to a lady who works for a country music star," Cami said.

"It must be important then." Paul laughed.

"We're setting up a video-conference call first thing in the morning." She rushed ahead, ignoring Paul's wisecrack. "The lady said she's got some people offering to help."

"Sounds good," Paul said. "Always use a hand."

"And I spoke to Reverend Hardesty, and Chief Herbert, and Clarence."

"What's Clarence up to?" Tick asked.

"He's—all of them, they're coming." Cami beamed. "Understand? They're going to Brownsville with us."

"Heehaw!" Tick yelled.

Paul didn't say anything. A smile began at the corners of his mouth, though, and slowly spread until it reached from ear to ear, as bright as the sun setting across the water.

Paul marveled at what a difference the last few days had made. When Droopy and Lucky offered help in that initial meeting over the phone, he truly had no inkling what it might entail. The two men started out by asking what was needed. Cami and Tick offered their thoughts, along with Paul. Then Lucky, showing his CEO skills, began making two lists. One for *Immediate Needs*. Another for *Goals*.

By mid-afternoon of *Day 1*, Droopy's buses, filled with stragglers, reached the night's campsite. Semi-trucks began rolling in right behind the first bus, including one carrying a field kitchen. Supper was hastily prepared. It was not enough, but it was a start.

Throughout the second day more trucks passed the line of walkers, headed to that night's campground. Seven more buses joined Droopy's three, picking up stragglers. Once these people arrived at camp, they formed themselves into groups and went to work on whatever was needed—laying out the campground, setting up lights and tents, helping prepare a meal. Shortly after midday a communications van arrived. That was Lucky's doing—one deacon talking to another who had a sister-in-law who knew who to call. After dark, one last bus out of Nashville arrived. Paul was there to greet the first person to exit.

"Hello, Jim," he said. "Proud to see you."

Now, early on the afternoon of the third day, Paul and Reverend Jim were walking at the head of the column. Jim glanced toward his friend.

"You can feel it, can't you?"

Paul gave a slight smile.

"I've been feeling it since that first step away from Caney Creek."

"Yes, I imagine so." It was Jim's turn to smile.

"Have you ever seen so many happy people?" Paul shook his head. "It's like they've discovered something special about themselves."

"Yes. They've discovered faith in action."

Paul looked toward him and nodded. When he turned back to the road, he noticed Cami and Tick coming their way.

"Hey, y'all," Tick said, as the couple fell in step. "We just left the Comm center. Talk about people who know what they're doing! They've got everything figured out. Food, tents, cots, medical, fuel, even where the campsites will be for the rest of the trek. Everybody's flying in circles. It's like sticking your head in a beehive."

"They've even got a press room," Cami said. "I just did a live interview from there with a radio station in Corpus Christi. You've got to see it."

"I'll do that this evening," Paul promised.

"And the nicest thing," Cami continued. "They treat Tick and me like we're in charge or something. Everybody wants to know what we think."

"Y'all are in charge," Paul answered with a smile.

"Yeah, sure." Tick made a goofy face, then changed the subject. "We've got to go in a sec. Doing a little inspecting."

"Inspecting what?" Jim asked.

"Tonight's campsite, first. It's by the San Antonio River. Cool, huh?"

"It sounds like it," Jim nodded.

"Then we're driving down to the next spot at Refugio," Cami added. "We'll try to get a good idea how many people are there already."

"There shouldn't be that many, should there?" Paul asked. "Didn't think it was a big place."

"It's not huge," Tick replied, "but it's one of the spots where a road comes in from San Antonio, like where we will be tonight. We've also got the same San Antonio connection where we're stopping later, down close to Corpus Christi."

"I'm missing something," Paul shook his head. "What's the big deal about San Antonio?"

"San Antonio is a whopper, Preacher. Roads run from there straight up through Austin and Waco, and on to Dallas and Fort Worth. Don't forget, they're still pouring out of Houston, too. If you slow down, they'll run you over."

"I think Tick's saying a great many people are headed our way." Reverend Jim laughed.

Paul looked dazed. "How many?"

"Thousands," the young couple answered as one. "Multitudes," Tick added with a laugh. A minute later he said, "We need to scoot."

"See you tonight." Cami smiled as she turned to leave with Tick.

A minute later, Jim realized Paul wasn't walking beside him anymore. He stopped and turned around. Paul was thirty feet back, standing still as a post.

"Coming?" Jim asked.

Paul's eyes locked on Jim's. "Lord," was all he got out.

"Yep," Jim chuckled. "He's sure got things hopping in Texas."

Chapter 82

Tick and Cami were following a large van pulling a box trailer. It slowed and turned in near the Comm center. They kept following. The *Center* was where they would report on their scouting trip. The van stopped in front of the center's steps just as Paul and Jim came walking out.

"There's the preacher," Cami said. "He'll want to hear."

"I'm sure," Tick answered, then turned his attention back to the van. "Come on, buddy, Pull up a little."

The driver's door on the van swung open. A large black man literally vaulted out and hustled over to envelope Paul in an embrace.

"Clarence!" Tick yelled, scaring Cami. He slammed the gearshift into Park and jumped out, rushing to his friend.

"It's so good to see you," Tick said, taking his turn hugging Clarence.

"It's good to be here." Clarence smiled.

"My turn," Cami said, stepping up, arms open.

"How's Reverend James?" Paul asked as soon as the hugging stopped.

"Fine. He said to tell you to keep up the good work."

"We're doing our best." Paul grinned.

Tick suddenly punched Clarence on the shoulder.

"So, what are you up to?" he teased. "Didn't expect you this soon."

"Well," Clarence hesitated, "we've been following along on TV, trying to keep up. I kind of got an itch, I guess, like maybe this was where I was supposed to be."

"I know what you mean," Tick replied. "Welcome to scratchers incorporated."

Clarence laughed, "Anyway, yesterday morning I told Reverend James I was heading down. The next thing I know, he's calling people all over Mississippi and half of Alabama, gathering equipment. That trailer is full to the gills with microphones and amplifiers. We figured they'd be handy once you start holding services."

Placing his hands on his hips, Paul stared at Clarence for a long minute. Finally, he turned to Jim. "What do you think? Do our first service this evening?"

"Yep," Jim answered. "Never a bad time to gather. I was looking at this open spot over there." He pointed. "The way it slopes up, you could seat a ton of people."

Paul nodded. "You're right. We could have our pulpit down in the low end. That'd work."

"We'll set it up," Tick promised. "What time are you starting?"

"Hmmm," Paul mused. "We need to give folks a chance to settle in and grab a bite. I'd say 6:30. What about it, Clarence? We could use a music director."

Clarence simply smiled and nodded in answer.

Tick and Cami headed toward the Comm center as the two ministers huddled with Clarence. Paul heard the door creak open and looked up.

"Hey Tick!" he called. "You didn't say how many people are coming from San Antonio."

"Aw, there's about a thousand already at Refugio. We swung up to Beeville, also, and saw a steady stream heading toward Corpus Christi. A deputy there said he figured at least four thousand had come through already. That was what, two o'clock?" Tick asked, turning toward Cami.

"Yes. He said he didn't expect a letup until dark."

Jim and Clarence both started chuckling at the change in Paul's expression.

"Lord," was all Paul said.

Chapter 83

The music was slow and easy. The kind that helped one ease a day's aches and troubles to the ground. A young man had arrived unbidden, guitar in hand. He set up a folding chair before a mic and started strumming. Paul stepped up on the flatbed trailer and moved over beside Jim. Clarence and Tick, along with a couple of techs from somewhere, were at the far end, making last-minute connections to some amps.

"You mind if I have a seat?" Jim asked. "I didn't walk half as far as you today, but my feet are killing me."

"I understand." Paul smiled, passing a folding chair, then grabbing one for himself. Before he sat, he picked up another. "We need one for Clarence, too."

"Jim nodded. "It looks like we'll have a full house."

"Yes," Paul agreed, looking at the people moving onto the slope. "You know, I was thinking, we need to include leaders from other religions. I know some are here."

"You're right. How do we find them?"

"I'll make an announcement at the end of services each night, inviting any leaders to come meet with us afterward."

"Simple enough," Jim said. "We need them all. This thing is going to keep growing."

Paul nodded in agreement. "Okay," he said. "It's almost time." He caught Clarence's eye.

"We're hooking up this last speaker," the music director yelled over the rumbles of the crowd.

Two minutes later, Clarence stepped up to the pulpit, a long crate set on end. "Testing, testing." The crowd began to settle. Clarence lifted the mic from its holder. "Good evening." A few people answered. "Let's try again," Clarence said, sweeping his hands upward. "Good evening!" The reply from the crowd was much louder. "Lots better!

"Okay. First, thanks to Truman Jones for getting us in the right mood with his beautiful guitar playing. Take a bow, sir."

Truman bowed and waved to the crowd, then hopped down from the trailer.

"We're going to sing a couple of songs now," Clarence announced. "I have a rule, though. If you know the words, sing along. If you don't, or if you claim you can't sing—" He made a point of turning to stare at Paul. "Make a joyful noise. The Lord is listening.

"Here we go. *Jesus loves the little children, all the children of the world.*" Thousands joined in. "*Red and yellow, black and white, they are precious in his sight. Jesus loves the little children of the world.*

"Good! Let's do it again," Clarence shouted.

Paul and Jim exchanged glances as the voices grew ever louder, amazed at the change that had come over Clarence. He was marching about the stage, slapping his thigh in time. When the song ended, Clarence yelled, "Amen!" The crowd answered with a roar.

"That was wonderful! One more" he said. "We'll slow it down a notch." Then his fantastic voice began, "*I walk through the garden alone, while the dew is still on the roses, and He walks with me, and He talks with me—*"

The crowd joined in, but they were more subdued this time, as was appropriate for the hymn. When it ended, he said, "It's my privilege to introduce Reverend Jim Hardesty." Jim rose and walked slowly to the podium.

"Please stand." He waited a few seconds for the crowd to rise. "Let us pray. *Our father who art in heaven, hallowed be Thy name. Thy kingdom come. Thy will be done, on earth….*" Thousands recited the Lord's Prayer with him.

"You may be seated," Jim said at the prayer's conclusion. Again, he waited a few moments. Then he said, "Preacher Paul."

Light applause started as Paul rose from his seat. It grew ever stronger as he walked to the pulpit, becoming a cascade of sound. People leapt to their feet, many shouting, "Amen!" Paul froze in place. This was not what he had expected—or wanted. He began to wave his hands back and forth, calling for quiet. The noise slowly diminished, yet Paul waved until not a single pair of hands could be heard clapping.

He grasped the edges of the pulpit. If a man could be seen to be thinking hard, then he was that picture. His eyes closed and his head bent forward, Paul remained in that pose for half a minute, obviously in prayer. Then he lifted his head and looked out over the crowd, slowly turning his gaze from one side to the other.

"My friends, I am only the minister of a small church in Kentucky. There is nothing noteworthy about me. I am but the vessel—as my dear wife, Jennie, has so often reminded me—the carrier of a message from God. I ask you to remember that each of us, no matter our station in life, is no more and no less, than one of His humble servants.

"How mighty is the Lord. Look to your neighbors for evidence of the wondrous palette He employs. He has painted us in all colors, formed us into all manner of shapes and sizes, not to divide, but to show that each one of us is unique.

"Say hello to your neighbors, and you will hear replies in a number of languages and accents. Some may be difficult, even impossible to understand, yet God hears and knows all we say. Ask your neighbors what denomination or religion they follow. Once again, you may receive a host of replies. Yet God loves every one of us, asking only that we believe in Him.

"Through faith, I am led to believe we are all equal. It cannot be otherwise if we are made in His image. Yet God does not stop there. He is in everything: the breeze that cools your skin on a hot summer day; the sweet notes of a little wren's song; your heart as it fills to the brim when you see a child's smile or hear a baby's laughter.

"But all He gives does not come free. He expects us to act as He instructs. His trumpet call is a command to move. All of us heard it, followed by the same words spoken by God as He charged us with our mission. *Go to the border and pray for the children.*"

Paul let his last words sink in. Then he said, "Let us bow our heads in silent prayer, asking the Lord to keep our faith strong as we answer His summons."

†††

The two men standing a few yards to the left of the stage had walked up seconds before Paul begin to speak. Rather than push their way into the crowd, they stopped where they were. At least they could see the minister. When he said the line, *God as He charged us*, Lucky turned to Droopy and said in a low voice, "We are where we need to be."

Bowing his head, Droopy replied in a whisper. "As we answer His summons."

Chapter 84

"It's hard to believe it's only been four days," Tick said.

Clarence nodded. "It seems like weeks. Man, there's a lot going on."

"Yeah. Things have really changed since Houston. It's kind of exciting, but I've got to admit, I miss the old days."

"How's that?"

"Preacher and I had our routine. I'd go ahead on the road every day, scouting for food and a place to camp that night. Sometimes I'd leave the van and hike back to him, you know, just to walk together for company. At night, we might talk before we conked out."

"What did you talk about? God?"

"Some. I've never come forward, been saved, you know. We might talk a little about what that means, but he wasn't pushy. We'd discuss other stuff, too."

"Like what?"

"Oh, sports. Preacher's a big basketball fan, though you'd never know it. University of Kentucky. He hates to miss a game."

"I'm that way about football." Clarence laughed. "Ole Miss, Mississippi State. I pull for both unless they're playing each other. Then it's State."

"I'm split between UK and Western Kentucky. Western's next door, so it's my home team."

"What else did you talk about?"

Tick looked away a second, then turned back. "Women."

"Would that be one particular woman?" Clarence asked, a wide grin on his face as he leaned in. "Name starts with a C?"

"Uh, yeah," Tick answered, managing to keep a straight face for all of three seconds before he burst into laughter.

Clarence joined him. After they quieted, he asked, "This getting serious?"

"It's been that way for a spell."

"Really?"

"We're cooling it for now," Tick replied, "what with the mission and all. But it's rough. I stay tied up in knots."

"A woman will do that to you." Clarence chuckled.

"Of course, when we got that sign from God, it made it easier to behave."

"What in the world?" Clarence asked, genuinely surprised.

"We were down at French Camp. I had this old blanket, so I asked Cami if she wanted to lay out and watch for shooting stars."

"I've used that line myself." Clarence laughed.

"Ha! Anyway, we got to making out. All at once she yells and threatens to slap the snot out of me. She said I pinched her, which I didn't. Then it hit me, too, like a branding iron. Next thing you know, we're both break dancing and whacking ourselves over the head like a couple of nuts. Fire ants!"

Clarence exploded in laughter. When he finally quit wheezing, he said, "That wasn't a sign from God. That was the devil!"

"Whoever, we got the message. We've been scared to do more than smile at each other since."

Chapter 85

The cowboy made a mental *X*. Anywhere along the empty stretch south of Kingsville was out of the question. Climbing a giant wind turbine was about the only place to get a clear shot. Height wasn't a bother, but getting down in a hurry was. There were few escape roads here, and helicopters were following the preacher—news and cops—almost constantly. Of course, the cop choppers had infrared, so forget it.

He took the exit for U. S. 77 where it split off from I69E. He was glad to be out of Kenedy County, with its towns mostly those of the one-horse variety. Now he was finally heading back into a metro area. Cities gave him something to blend into. He could hide better and breathe easier. In Raymondville he eased over to a bodega and bought a bottle of water.

He sat on the tailgate and drank as he planned the rest of his day. Looking as he went for good vantage points, he would drive all the way to the river. It would take the preacher and his crowd another week to reach the border in Brownsville, so he had time to pick and choose.

†††

The thin man was no trained sniper, but he didn't have to be to understand the cowboy would almost certainly not risk a shot anywhere in the scrub lands of Kenedy County. As if to prove his hunch, the TV picture switched to a high angle as the helicopter climbed, with the on-board reporter even remarking on how few roads there were in the area. Then the cable news show switched back to a scene of a patrol boat cruising along the Rio Grande.

He sat staring at the screen, not paying attention anymore. Suddenly he slammed his fist on the desktop.

Sonofabitch! That's perfect! An international incident would get folks riled.

Tonight, he would send a secure message to the cowboy. A line popped into his head.

A shot of tequila helps with Montezuma's revenge.

Chapter 86

It was an hour before the evening service. Underneath a tent, Paul sat on a bale of straw. Cami and Tick shared another, Buck napping at their feet. They were only a few steps from the Comm center. Suddenly, the trailer door swung open, and Droopy stepped out, followed by Lucky. They headed for the tent.

"Preacher Paul, the home stretch is going to be rough," Droopy got right to the point, "so we've got to do something about all these people following you."

"I worry about them," Paul agreed. "So many have to ride the whole way. Then today, the temperature shot up. Cami tells me even some of the better walkers were feeling it."

Droopy nodded. "Serious problems, alright, but we have some proposals that will help. It's a matter of logistics. Lucky here, is one of the best in the business at managing that."

"Transportation, distance, shelter, food. These are the primary factors we have to deal with in moving the fifteen thousand plus that are with you now." Lucky paused.

Paul shook his head. "I hadn't realized it was that many."

"*Plus*, with more coming every hour. Here's the breakdown. You're a hundred and twenty miles from the Rio Grande. The next seventy-five miles are practically unpopulated, with few places to shelter. It's not the Sahara, but they're kin."

"Tick said it's an empty, dry stretch," Paul noted.

"Yes sir," Lucky nodded toward Tick. "And Cami's right about the weather. It was nine degrees above average today. That figures to hold for the week.

"We've been keeping an eye on the marchers. Only about a thousand are maintaining pace with you. That number's consistent. These are your hardcore, your better athletes. We can supply and shelter that many across those worst seventy-five miles. It looks like another twenty-five hundred to three thousand are in their own vehicles. Some of those can take extra passengers. That leaves us transporting eleven to twelve thousand, along with our support personnel. We have forty-three buses, but that's not enough to move everybody to Brownsville in one day.

"So, we switch to plan B. We haul them part of the way. There's a good camp location on this side of Lyford. It will take most of tomorrow to move everybody there. My guy, Tommy, is in Brownville now. He may be able to round up a few buses to help, but we can't count on it.

"By the way, Tommy just confirmed that he and Reverend Hardesty have secured us a large spot on the west side of Brownsville. They're cutting the red tape now. Those two are a dynamic pair—kind of dangerous, actually."

"No doubt." Paul grinned. "That's fantastic about Brownsville." He paused, his expression becoming serious. "Okay. It sounds like you've got a handle on the move. I appreciate your hard work."

"Thank you," Lucky answered. "One other thing. If you'll call on me during tonight's service, I'll explain how the shuttle will work."

"I'll do it," Paul replied.

Chapter 87

Jennie walked toward the Jackson's back door. Though it wasn't late, fall's short days had already brought on the dark. A rectangular pool of yellow light spilled through a gap in the curtains, illuminating the doorstep. She raised her hand to knock but hesitated. Henry and Elsie were seated at the kitchen table, heads bowed, holding hands around the dishes as they prayed. Jennie waited until they looked up before rapping on the glass. Elsie took a moment to make it to the door, her steps noticeably slower than they had been only a few months back. Jennie felt a pang with the sad realization.

"Get in this house, child," the older woman exclaimed as she swung the door open.

Jennie stepped inside quickly, the cool air seeming to push her forward. Elsie shut the door, then turned to give her a good hug.

"Grab you a plate, gal," Henry ordered. "We just sat down."

"I got it." Elsie waved her hand. "He's not about to get up. Already stuffing his face." She reached inside a cabinet and pulled out a plate. "Here. Chicken and dumplings, green beans, and cornbread," she announced. "Help yourself."

"I didn't come over to eat," Jennie replied. But Elsie's chicken and dumplings were to die for. She glimpsed the piece of fat back floating in the beans. *Mmm!* And that cornbread—Lord! It'd melt in your mouth cold. Jennie filled her plate. Before she could take a seat, Elsie handed her silverware and a glass of tea.

"You're doing me a favor," Henry said, cutting a chunk of dumpling with the edge of his fork. "She's been shoving those beans down my throat for a week."

"First complaint he's had," Elsie said without changing expression.

"I'm not complaining." Henry shook his head. "I never fuss about your cooking, it's just that my skin's taking on a greenish tinge."

"I believe you're right," Jennie laughed.

Henry nodded, then stabbed another dumpling. He didn't bring it to his mouth, though.

"You got the word, didn't you?" he asked.

Jennie glanced at them both before answering. "Yes! They'll be at the border the day after tomorrow. I fly out of Nashville at 9:15 in the morning. Paul doesn't know I'm coming. I'm so excited!" she said, unable to contain herself another second.

"We'll get you there." Henry grinned.

"I hate to get y'all up at the crack of dawn, but they want me there two hours early, so you've got to pack and everything tonight."

"Don't you fret." Elsie shook her head. "He's been packed since Monday, when you said it'd be toward the end of the week."

Henry made a hurt face. "So have you," he mumbled around a dumpling.

Jennie laughed out loud. "Are y'all driving straight down after you drop me off?"

"Nope," Henry answered with a wink. "The woman wants to see the Gulf of Mexico."

"We thought we might stop by the ocean for a day or two," Elsie explained.

"And I'm wading in it," Henry vowed, "even if it's chock full of grape jellyfish."

Chapter 88

Spud Murphy popped the top to a can of beer, and took a long swallow.

"How many does that make?" his girlfriend, Minnie, asked, her upper lip twisting in a snarl.

"It's seven, but who's counting," the young man snarled back.

He was good at making faces, his grandmama always said. Nicknaming him *Spud* had been her doing. "Head like an Irish potato," were her words on seeing him the first time. By his fourth birthday she was adding, "and about as much sense."

"The cops," Minnie retorted. "Gonna get busted."

"Ain't no cop messing with me." He paused, squinting through the windshield at something straight ahead, something rapidly growing in size. "What the hell," he got out before a patrol car blasted past, lights and siren going, followed an instant later by a second cop.

"*Yiiiii!*" Minnie screamed, covering her ears. "I told you the cops would get you."

"Hush! They're after somebody else. Besides—now what's this monkey shit?"

"Slow down! You'll hit somebody."

Spud did ease off the gas some, but more out of curiosity about the walkers than any safety concerns.

"Here you go, Preacher," Tick said, tossing a bottle of water Paul's way. Buck sat beside him, his great head turning to follow the bottle through the air. "Come get it! Got plenty!" Tick yelled to the crowd.

As Paul uncapped his drink, he glanced back at the throng behind him.

"Yes, come get a drink," Paul called to the closest walkers. He still wasn't accustomed to being first in line, but no one else would come forward until he had something. It had been like that since Houston. The others would simply stand in the bright sun with arms folded, patiently waiting on him.

As Paul strolled past the van, Cami moved over to walk beside him. He glanced down at the water in her hand and stammered. "I ought to be ashamed. I completely forgot our escort."

"No worries. This is hers." Cami smiled.

Before they could make it to the patrol car, it suddenly shot ahead, swung wide off the shoulder, accelerated through a U-turn, then raced back toward them. With a screech of hot rubber, it skidded to a stop next to Paul.

"Bad wreck at Norias," the officer spoke in a rush.

Then she was gone, siren wailing. In no time the sound faded to nothing. Paul and Cami strolled a few steps more, stopping once they were far enough from the throng to have a conversation.

"The *Movements* crew is meeting us in Raymondville," Cami said, glancing at Paul.

"Oh me," Paul replied, rolling his eyes.

"I told them you don't stop walking for interviews. They're just going to film some. The reporter, Clifford Cumberland, wants to talk to you tonight, maybe tag along in the morning."

"Whatever you say, boss," Paul answered, flashing a brief smile her way.

✝✝✝

"Somebody left the looney bin unlocked," Spud fussed.

"It's that preacher," Minnie said, pointing ahead.

"Preacher my ass. Can't be backing up traffic."

"What traffic?"

"You just watch," he warned, rolling to a stop on the shoulder opposite Paul and Cami.

"Spud—" Minnie reached for his arm, but he was out in a flash, the half-can of beer still in his hand.

"Preacher!" Spud barked. "What the hell you doing, crowding people off the road?"

Paul lifted his voice in reply. "I'm sorry to cause trouble."

"I got your trouble!" Spud's beer can came flying. It bounced off the pavement in front of Paul, spewing beer. He was instantly wet from both knees down.

For a couple of seconds all was quiet. Then a low murmur began to sweep along the line. Buck joined in, the sound of his growling rising as he edged toward Spud. "Buck. Here boy," Tick said calmly, one hand slapping against the side of his leg as he came walking toward the preacher. "Sit," he ordered, and Buck did, though his eyes never left Spud.

"You, okay?" Tick asked, halting in front of Paul, his back to Spud.

"It's nothing. My pants are a little damp. That's all."

"Hmm." After a moment, Tick turned toward Cami. "Get any on you?"

"Not a drop."

"Hmm," Tick said again. "Good."

Tick squatted down ever so slowly and wrapped his fingers around the can, then turned it upside down and shook out the few remaining drops. He rose at the speed of bread baking, muscle and bone straining against his clothing, until he stood straight and tall once more. Then he turned to face Spud.

Paul read it all, sensed the power and menace in that first unhurried stride Tick made across the roadway, knew the determination to do something in the roll of his shoulders.

"Tick," Paul said.

His friend did not slow or turn in response.

"Tick!"

The big man's open left hand came up, remained there at shoulder height—a signal for quiet. Paul and Cami simultaneously drew in their breaths, fear of something awful about to unfold stretching out time.

The expression on Spud's face screamed, "Run!" Yet, somehow, his feet held still. Tick halted half a pace in front of him. His right hand rose slowly, clutching the empty can, and came to a stop inches in front of Spud's eyes. Tick's fore and middle fingertips crooked over the can's top. His thumb braced the bottom. There was a slight crinkling sound, then a pop, followed by a louder pop. Crunching sounds rolled over one another as the can became progressively shorter, until at last Tick held an object the size and shape of a drink coaster pinched between fingertips and thumb.

"This yours?" he asked.

Spud didn't answer. His face was so screwed up with fear he seemed incapable of answering.

Tick lifted an eyebrow a single millimeter.

"Uh, yeah," Spud managed to croak.

"It's against the law to litter."

As if his arm were straining against a great band of rubber, Spud reached out and carefully took the disk from Tick's grasp. He quickly backed up a couple of steps, then turned and hustled around to the truck's door, his boots kicking up puffs of dust. The sound of Minnie's wild laughter hung in the air as the pickup sped away. A loud cheer arose from the crowd.

Only then did Tick come walking back to a stern-faced Paul.

"I don't know why he didn't stay and visit," he told the preacher.

Paul looked as if he were about to say something, but he finally turned on his heel and walked toward the van.

"What gives?" a puzzled Tick asked a frowning Cami.

"Simian," she answered, then turned her back.

Chapter 89

Paul had to give it to Clifford Cumberland, the reporter for *Movements*. For a man of sixty, he was doing a good job keeping up. A small truck was leading them. A cameraman, as well as a sound man with a boom mic, rode in the back.

"So," Clifford said, "almost thirteen hundred miles walked, and tonight you will sleep beside the Rio Grande. How does that make you feel?"

"Glad, apprehensive," Paul answered with a quick glance. "Sore," he chuckled. After a moment he said, "Most of all, ready to give thanks."

The crowd filled the sidewalks and the better part of the road, leaving only a single lane straddling the centerline. Instead of clapping or cheering, most people had their hands folded before them in the sign of prayer. Many bowed their heads as he passed. Paul couldn't look at them eye to eye. He was right on the verge of tears as it was, knowing the reverence they were expressing was not for him. *For what God has sent me to do,* he recited to himself over and over.

Clifford knew they were close to the river, and the walk's end. With a subtle hand signal, he motioned the truck's driver to pull to the side and let Paul by. The reporter slowed, allowing the preacher to walk ahead alone. Without the truck to part the seas, the lane shrank to half its original size, then a quarter, until there was only a path.

"Hold my hand, Sarah. I'm smothering," Paul whispered. "Show me the way."

Above peoples' heads, he could make out where the brick walls of storefronts ended, revealing a swath of blue sky. Paul increased his pace. He found himself crossing a wide street. Then he was in a park, heading toward the tall metal pickets of the wall. A young woman stood in profile next to it, gazing at something he could not see. His mind would not register. Then she turned to face him, her eyes glistening wet in the light. He ran the last steps.

"Jennie! Oh Jennie!" he cried as he lifted her in his arms.

Chapter 90

"Y ou awake?" Jennie breathed against Paul's chest.

Paul felt her words arrive in minute puffs on his skin. He turned his head, his chin brushing her hair, and whispered back, "Yes."

She snuggled deeper into the crook of his arm, felt his fingertips tracing circles on her shoulder.

"Have you slept at all?" she asked.

"Some. And you?"

"A little. I've been awake a few minutes, listening to you breathe."

"I've been doing the same thing with you," Paul said, smiling to himself. Suddenly he felt a twinge of apprehension. He hesitated a moment. "Last night, afterwards, I guess I passed out. Forgive me?"

"There's nothing to forgive. I think I did, too. Or perhaps I drowned. All I remember was us loving."

They fell silent for a few moments. Then, as if on cue, both spoke at the same instant, "I missed you."

Without warning their dams burst, releasing floods of tears. All they could do was cling to one another, certain they would be swept away if they loosened their embrace.

Minutes passed and the floods abated. They lay quiet, secure in one another's arms. Eventually, as the first light began to play at the curtain edges, Paul spoke.

"If we had gone through a longer period, had a chance for our mourning to run its course—I don't know. It seems unfair, not only to us, but to Sarah."

"I have fussed with God about that," Jennie said, her admission surprising him. "So many times since you left, I tried to pray about it, but I always wound up complaining. I would twist and turn in that bed and yell at Him. How could a child so sweet have been taken? And you weren't there. I needed you, and you weren't there."

"Jennie, I am so sorry. I didn't—you didn't say—"

"I need to get this poison out of my heart, Paul. Please let me."

Paul didn't say anything, though he turned on his side toward her.

"I'm confessing. I'm telling the man I love, the man I know will understand, among all other people on this earth, that I was angry with God. I *wanted* to be angry! So help me!

"And it wasn't only because Sarah had died. Before I could even begin to think clearly again, He sent you away. Who ever knew quiet could have weight? That a broken heart could house a prison?"

She stopped. Paul started to speak, but something told him to wait, to make certain Jennie was finished. A full minute passed before she started to talk again. Her voice was different, the hard edge gone.

"When God called you, all I asked was that you phone me every day. Thank goodness you did! I love you more for that. Your voice, no matter what you said, kept me from going completely mad. It gave me the strength to hang on and seek a way out of my whirlpool of self-pity. At last, I turned to God and surrendered, I suppose something like you did in the cane." She hesitated. "Well, not quite. My plea came on the porch steps with me wrapped in a blanket, gazing at the stars. He said my purpose was clear, if I would only look."

Jennie rolled toward him. Enough light was flowing around the curtain edges now to illuminate Paul's features.

"This is not a visit, Paul, like Tupelo. It is a reunion. I am here to stay for as long as God sees fit. He has work for me, also, with the children.

"Seeing how this is between God and me," Jennie said, her voice suddenly light, "you don't officially have a say. However, in the interest of maintaining good marital relations, I will at least ask if you agree."

She watched the smile spread across his face.

"I do," Paul said.

Chapter 91

Bob Mendoza stepped out of the Land Rover and pushed his hat back on his head. He wanted his eyes to be seen. Half a block ahead, a boy was walking toward him, carrying a small bag. He had been right. The teenager had been going to the bodega when he passed by ten minutes earlier. Bob moved up to the front corner of the vehicle, pulled a Marlboro pack from his shirt pocket and shook a cigarette out. He lit up, then leaned forward over the hood and rested on his elbows. The boy was close now.

"Buenos dias, amigo," Bob said, smiling. He kept his elbows on the hood. No sudden moves. Everything depended on him appearing non-threatening.

The boy stopped short, cutting his eyes from side to side. He even took a long look behind before settling his gaze on Bob. "Buenos dias," he answered weakly.

"Pardon me," Bob continued in Spanish. "I am looking for someone. I was hoping you could help me."

No reply.

"I am an American reporter. I will not cause trouble. You have my word."

It wasn't much, barely perceptible, but the young shoulders relaxed.

"You are a good man to bring her candy."

That struck a nerve. The teenager did his best to hide his reaction, but the alarm in his eyes gave him away. Suddenly, he was walking again.

"Please, hear me out."

The boy hesitated, then stopped straight across the hood from Bob. "I don't know what you are talking about."

Bob took a draw on his cigarette, exhaled a stream of blue smoke.

"I only want to send her family a message. I would like to talk with them, but I will never tell where they are. You have my promise."

The boy didn't say anything, but he didn't walk off.

Bob nonchalantly lifted his hand and shoved the cigarette pack in his shirt pocket. When he pulled his hand out, the folded paper cupped in his fingers was noticeable to only the boy.

"I can help them. Will you take a message?"

A minute passed with no response. Then a curt nod.

"Thank you," Bob said, extending his arm across the hood. The boy hesitated. "Shake my hand."

For a long moment it seemed the boy wouldn't do it. Then he suddenly took Bob's hand. As he turned to walk away, he slipped the paper into his pants pocket.

"One moment," Bob said. The boy stopped and looked back. "There is money in there. Two bills. One for them. One for you. Comprende?"

"Si." The boy stared at him, his brown eyes growing soft. Bob was not surprised when he started speaking in English. "Life is hard. Harder for them than me. I'll give them both bills." With that, he turned and walked away.

Bob looked down, dropped his cigarette and ground it out. He'd told himself his hide was tough for so long he had come to believe it. "Never assume," he mumbled to himself, reciting one of his mantras as he slid behind the steering wheel. He popped the glove box open and snatched a crumpled handkerchief out of the mess of maps and papers, but he didn't bring it to his face. Somehow, he'd managed to blink away the tear.

Chapter 92

Paul followed Jennie into the noisy tent. A dozen people were working at tables, some on laptops, others on phones. Paul guided her toward a man their age at a card-table in the back.

"Jennie, this is Jim Hardesty. He's the minister at Third Christian, Disciples of Christ in Nashville, and our chief of staff."

Jim dropped the paper he was studying, hopped up from his folding chair, and hurried around to Jennie.

"No, a handshake won't do," he said, brushing her hand aside. "From you, I need a hug." He embraced her for a moment, then took a half step back and gently took her hands in his. "These last few months must have been very hard and lonely. You have been in my prayers since I first heard of the—the tragedy."

"Thank you," Jennie said, forcing a smile, "for your concern and your prayers. Paul tells me you are an absolute Godsend."

"Aw, I just stir up a little dust here and there," Jim answered with a quick laugh. He released her hands and looked over at Paul. "I know you're tickled to have this sweet lady here for a visit."

Paul shook his head. "She's not visiting. My partner is here to stay."

Open mouthed, Jim looked from one to the other. "Alright!" he finally exclaimed.

"Now," Paul said, "if you don't mind, please give us the nickel tour of our set-up."

"Yes, sir," Jim said, quickly casting about and finding two more chairs. Reaching out, he caught the tent flap and pulled it aside. "Let's step out back to my private office, where it's quieter, and I'll give you the low-down."

†††

"That's all I can think of for now," Jim said, leaning back. He'd been speaking for almost twenty minutes, with only brief interruptions from Paul and Jennie.

"I knew there was a significant mission presence at the border already," Paul said, "but I had no idea it was this extensive."

"Yes." Jim nodded. "And the minister list part of that is growing. There were quite a few to begin with, but there are all kinds showing up now. Many seem intent to be a part of whatever is happening with you. Others—well frankly, there's some looking to ride your coattails."

"There's no need to worry." Paul shrugged. "God has a job for everybody."

"Exactly, and this thing is going to have an old-fashioned camp revival feel, no matter."

"Hmmm," Paul said, looking toward the sky. "That might be what He had in mind."

The thought made them all pause for a minute. It was Jennie who broke the spell.

"I want to hear more about these aid groups, especially the ones who deal with children. I would love to do some work there."

"Okay." Jim nodded. "I know a guy. We'll set up a meeting right away."

"Thank you." Jennie smiled, reaching over to give Jim's hand a squeeze.

The men sensed the importance of her gesture. It left them quiet.

"I want to see the meeting site," Paul finally spoke.

"Sure," Jim agreed. "We can head right over."

"We'll need Clarence and Cami, and also Tick," Paul added.

"I'll run them down. Anything else you can think of?

"A million things." Paul rolled his eyes. "First, you need some help."

"I'm fine. I've got some of the Disorderly Order on the way down from Nashville."

"Good," Paul said. "It's all so much. You said there're still thousands more people on the way."

"My friend." Jim leaned forward. "You were not the only one to hear His call."

Paul stared back a moment. "I knew that. Thanks for reminding me, though."

The men made to leave, rising from their chairs. Jennie looked up at Jim.

"I noticed your wedding ring," she said. "Do you have children?"

Jim paused. "No. That hasn't—she—we have miscarried twice."

"I am so sorry," Jennie replied softly, glancing away. When she turned back, their eyes locked. "Please give your wife my thanks for enduring loneliness while you are here."

"Oh, Ruth's probably glad to have a break from me," Jim laughed.

"What a perfect name for a woman of God," Jennie smiled. "I doubt very seriously she's glad to have you gone. Quite the opposite. I'm certain Ruth is a kind and loving mate. She's obviously very smart—a person who makes wise decisions."

"That's a wonderfully accurate description. Woman's intuition?"

"Yes, based on who she married."

Chapter 93

Paul climbed to the top of the little hill. Immediately to his front was a huge natural amphitheater, its northernmost reaches near the road, two hundred yards away. *Like an oriental fan,* Paul thought, *spread wide and held by a great hand here at the hinge, the hill.*

Above the fan's right border was a large, flat expanse holding thousands of tents in all sizes and colors, with archipelagoes of motorhome islands scattered throughout. Smoke drifted up from cooking fires. People moved along the *streets.*

The ground to the far left, the west, was decidedly different, with erosion scars culminating in a delta of gullies. These became progressively deeper as they neared the bottom. Tents stood on the few flat spots.

The most intriguing view was from the rear, where the Rio Grande cut west to east, bordered by banks of lush green reeds and grasses. Across it, in Mexico, people could be seen walking beneath the scant trees. Cars cruised silently. Buildings revealed bits of wall. A playground seemed to grow out of the earth, its brightly colored equipment devoid of children.

And here, on the American side, the wall. It stretched both directions into the distance, a line of perfectly upright steel pickets, each locked arm in arm with its neighbors by horizontal bars of more black steel. Paul saw the pickets as skeletal soldiers in a minimalist painting, aligned for battle. Then he had another thought. *Was a river not line enough between friends?*

Paul walked to the rear of the hill, where the ground dropped at an abrupt angle. For the last fifty feet before the wall, it flattened out. Past the wall, the bank fell away to the river. Seeing Tick and Clarence climbing toward him, he felt his spirits lift. Buck was in front. He rushed up to shove his head against Paul's thigh. Paul found an ear to scratch.

"Morning, Preacher," Tick said.

"Good morning!" Clarence practically shouted.

"And to you." Paul smiled.

They moved to the hill's front edge. Paul gave them a chance to look around.

"I can't believe we're here," Tick said. "Wow! You can finally give your feet a rest, Preacher." He turned around. "And that's Mexico. A whole other country. Wow!"

"I've got to agree with you, brother," Clarence laughed. "I love this spot. It's not all that high—maybe fifteen feet—but I bet the acoustics are great." He began to sing. "Blessed be the tie that binds, our hearts in Christian love."

Paul saw Jennie and Cami turn from halfway up the fan. "Sounds great!" Jennie yelled.

"Fabulous acoustics." Clarence beamed. "Man! This place will hold an army."

"It is a good spot." Paul nodded. "A very good spot." A few minutes passed, each man taking in the view, before he asked, "So, what have you all been up to?"

"We've just been nosing around, getting the layout," Tick replied. "People are already naming things."

"Really?" Paul asked. "Like what?"

"That's Gabriel's Gulch, where it's all washed out."

"Gabriel?"

"Somebody heard a trumpet over in Mexico." Tick shrugged. "You know? Gabriel blow your horn?"

"And over there," Clarence started, "where it's so flat. That's the Plain of Abraham. Putting up street signs right now."

"No kidding?" Paul laughed.

"If you're looking for a name for this hill—"

They turned to see Jim come trudging up from the rear.

"I say we call it Paul's Pulpit. Preacher Paul's Pulpit."

"You need to leave my name out of it," Paul shook his head.

"People are already calling it that," Jim laughed. "You might as well get used to it."

"Good grief," Paul answered in a tone that said he'd heard enough.

After a moment, he changed rows. "We were just talking, Jim. You and Tommy did a fantastic job picking this spot."

"Thanks, I guess. We were sort of led here."

"What do you mean?"

"It's the first and only spot we looked at."

A grin spread across Paul's face. He patted Jim's shoulder as he spoke. "It's a great place to worship." They moved to the front edge, stopping beside Tick and Clarence. "Welcome to our new church."

"Yes, our church." Jim nodded. "It's up to you to give it a name."

Paul turned in a slow half circle, stopping when he faced the river. "Riverbank. Riverbank Church."

Chapter 94

"Worthless bastards!"

The shout blew through the open doorway, followed by a crash. It didn't sound as bad as usual for one of the Big Guy's tirades. Maybe he hadn't broken the TV again. The thin man pushed his chair back. He took a step, then halted to open a desk drawer and extract a new remote.

Inside the office, the thin man found the TV still on. He extended his hand as he drew close, passed the new remote to the Big Guy, and turned to face the screen. Preacher Paul was on his knees, head bowed. *So, that was what set him off.*

"What's he done now?" the thin man asked. "Turned the Rio Grande into wine?"

"It's that same old praying crap. On every damn network. How can I get my message out?"

The thin man didn't reply, knowing he wasn't expected to, knowing the man didn't have an actual message, nor would he be able to stay on point if he did. It was up to him, the one here with sense enough to focus, to see that messages were properly crafted and presented. The Big Guy might think he was captain of the ship, but he was only its foghorn—someone to blare from inside the mists and draw attention away from the great storm coming.

"Don't think I've forgotten your promise to do something about this preacher boy."

The thin man cringed inwardly. Just because the boss had removed the recording system, did not mean others weren't listening. He lip-synched, "*Soon.*" For once, the dunce seemed to get it, giving a goofy grin in return.

"I heard something break. What was it?"

The thin man had no more than said the words when he spotted the pieces of black plastic at the foot of a bookcase. The top shelf held a framed photograph. It was turned askance, its protective glass spiderwebbed into a thousand cracks.

"*Hee-hee.*"

Did the man have to laugh like a little kid?

"I Oswalded that smirking jackass!" Another string of *hee-hees* followed.

The thin man walked to the bookcase and carefully picked up the photograph of JFK.

"I'll have it repaired."

"Yeah, you do that," the Big Guy answered, flipping channels. "You believe this shit! Nothing on now but that school shooting."

Chapter 95

"It's about time," Jennie whispered in Paul's ear.

"Please excuse me," he said to the circle of ministers sitting cross-legged on the ground. "It's time to go to the river, if I can straighten my legs out."

"When you get to motivating, give this old man a hand up, would you?" Henry asked. He and Elsie had pulled in late last evening, both looking refreshed and happy. And did Paul dare say it? In love.

Once outside, Jennie and Elsie linked arms and walked two by two as two sisters might. Jennie glanced back at him and smiled a smile that told him they were still in love, too.

"So, preacher," Henry said as they started down the slope, "why we going to the river? Li'l baptizing, maybe?"

"We can't get to the water for the wall, so baptizing is out. Basically, we're still doing the same brief service we started on the road. Several ministers pray. Clarence leads us in a hymn or two, and Jim gives the Lord's prayer. Then I say a few words and have a final prayer."

"You do a silent prayer?" Henry shot a glance toward Paul, his great, bushy eyebrows going up.

"Yep. Then Clarence leads us in a closing hymn. I usually pick it out."

"That's it? No hellfire and brimstone?"

"No."

"Sounds boring." Henry appeared disappointed.

Paul chuckled. "Might be. On Sundays one of the other ministers gives a morning sermon. Truth be told, there's no end to the preaching. We have tons of ministers here. Any time of day, somebody's liable to set up."

"Is that so?"

"Yeah." Paul nodded.

"Back to these services, you do sing an invitational, right?" Henry pressed. "There's bound to be bunches here that haven't come to the Lord."

"No. Others might do that. Not when I'm leading, though."

Henry fell quiet for a few steps. He suddenly came to a stop. Paul noticed a pace further on and turned back.

"Are you okay?"

"I reckon. It's just that—"

"What is it?" Concerned, Paul took a half step closer.

"I don't get it," Henry said. "I mean, look at the gobs of people. There're thousands."

"They calculated somewhere north of fifty thousand last count." Paul agreed.

"Goodness gracious!" Henry said no more, stunned into silence. It didn't last. "So, you've got a whole city's worth of souls, and you're not even inviting them to come down and be saved? What kind of revival are you running?"

A big smile spread across Paul's face. "That's just it, Deacon," Paul said, clapping his old friend on the shoulder. "I'm not holding a revival. This is a prayer meeting."

† † †

Tick and Cami were forty yards behind Paul and Henry, moving in the flow of humanity toward the river. Once, when she got bumped pretty hard, she rebounded Tick's direction, and he caught her by the elbow. He almost allowed his hand to go sliding down her forearm, but then awareness hit him. No way he could hold hands. The way her fingers felt intertwined with his, her skin all soft and warm, and the way she smelled when she moved closer, were wonderful, but also scary.

As if she could see inside his mind and knew any first move fell to her, she grabbed his hand in hers and went marching straight ahead, like such a thing was as natural as scratching and wouldn't twist a man all up inside and make him sweat oceans. It took him a while to say anything. Even then, not trusting himself, he was careful not to speak about her, so he nodded toward the preacher.

"I don't get him."

"What do you mean, hon?"

Hon? Now that was deliberate. She had to know what a word like that did to his nerves.

"He's confusing. After that deal with the beer thrower, know what he said? 'You're doing a little better.'"

Cami thought a minute before cutting her eyes his way. "Yes, you are. And I'm proud."

"Thank you for that." He hesitated, unable to hold her gaze. Man could get lost in those eyes. "Probably should have let it go at that, but I didn't. Guess I was kind of fishing for a bigger compliment, maybe."

"Oh?" She drew her head back in mock surprise. "What did you do?"

"I just said, you know, not whacking people was hard on my system."

"I'll bet he shook his head, didn't he?" Cami said, shaking hers.

"Yeah. Is that goofy or— Wait! How did you know?"

Cami came to an abrupt halt. With a jerk, so did Tick. He had to. She had him by the hand. He thought, *How can a woman so small throw such an anchor?* People went streaming around both sides of their little island.

"Oh, hon." There, she did it again! He had to kick both feet to keep his head above water. "You are doing better, but your heart is still not where he knows it can be."

"You'll have to explain."

"You crushed a beer can between your fingertips."

"That's right. I did a full Budweiser like that once. Soaked Howie Johnson. 'Course, he wanted to fight. I had to whap him over the head to make him sit down."

"Good grief." Cami shook her head. "Let's get back on point, shall we? When you crushed the can, were you trying to tell that man something?"

"Sure," Tick said, smiling. "He better behave."

"And if he didn't, were you going to *whap* him, too?"

"It wouldn't have taken but one lick."

"Tick—that's enough. Think. The preacher was saying you have to turn away from violence altogether. Even threatening you might do something is still wrong."

Tick didn't answer. Finally, crinkling his nose up like something smelled awful, he said, "Sounds like I can't even look cross-eyed at somebody?"

"That's not exactly how I would put it," Cami answered with a quick nod, "but yes." Then she changed rows. "Come on," she said, pulling him forward. "Don't want to be late."

He was as confused as buttermilk, but he didn't resist. After all, she was holding his hand.

Chapter 96

"Oh sister, come on down, come on down."

Everyone was singing the old spiritual as they walked into Riverbend. It was not a song meant to lift the rafters. Instead, the effect was soothing.

Paul came to the wall at the rear of the hill. He reached out and grasped a steel bar with each hand, then pulled himself forward until he felt the cool metal against his cheeks. For a time, he simply looked through the gap at the eddies and swirls on the water. He shifted his gaze, took in the long grasses and rushes of the far bank waving in the afternoon breeze. People were there, too, gathered in the thousands at the top of the bank. Paul swung his attention to where the crowd thinned out, then further, until all he could see was a single person lying in the shade beneath a tree. *Good place for a siesta*, he thought.

He pushed away, for the first-time noticing people were lined up along the wall in both directions as far as he could see. They were also pressed against the bars, looking across the river. His steps slow, deliberate, Paul started climbing to the pulpit. He lifted his eyes and saw Jim atop the mound. A few feet in front of him, Clarence was leading the singing, his voice riding over the sounds of countless feet shuffling into place. Suddenly there was no other sound but singing. Clarence brought the hymn to a close.

"Down to the river to pray."

The filthy man beneath the tree stirred. Groaning and mumbling to himself about the pain in his head, he finally managed to get propped up on an elbow. Dressed in ragged clothes, there was nothing to indicate he had anything worth stealing. Squinting, he lifted the empty bottle before his face, then dropped it on the ground in disgust.

The cowboy didn't have to move to see on this, the Mexican side. He shifted his gaze across the water and was relieved to see the preacher climbing to the top of the little rise. Of course, at two hundred fifty yards, he couldn't make out anything about the man's face, but he didn't need to. He already knew his gait, his height, and posture.

Today's scouting mission was to check out the shot. At this oblique angle, he had feared the wall would rule it out. From straight across the river, he could put a hundred rounds between the vertical bars without scratching the paint, but from this spot the wall might as well have been one solid piece of metal because the bars lined up in such a way as to eliminate any gap.

When Paul was on the mound, though, the angle worry disappeared. The preacher stood head and shoulders above the wall's top edge. From this range, the cowboy knew he could put ten out of ten in the bullseye. Not that he needed ten. One would put an end to the preaching.

Tomorrow. The Cowboy nodded to himself.

Chapter 97

The pulpit was a simple wooden lectern constructed of two-by-fours and plywood. With several microphones clamped to the book rest, it balanced perilously on the rough ground. Folding chairs were provided behind it for Paul, Jim, and Clarence.

Jim stepped up to the lectern first. Looking out over the congregation, he saw a huge host of people seated in camp chairs or on cushions. Many simply sat on the ground.

"Let us bow our heads," Jim began. "Our Father who art in heaven, hallowed be Thy name. . ." Clarence and Paul recited along with the congregation. "For thine is the kingdom, the power, and the glory forever. Amen."

Paul waited for Jim to come back to his seat before taking his place. He rested his walking stick upright, using a notch in the side of the bookrest. Grasping the edges of the pulpit and leaning forward, he spotted Jennie in the center of the front row. Henry and Elsie were with her. Cami and Tick sat cross-legged on a patch of grass immediately to their left, with Buck on his haunches between them. To his surprise, he saw Chief Herbert in the row behind them. The two men exchanged nods. Paul swept his eyes over the crowd before speaking.

"My friends, how wonderful to see you here on this gorgeous day the Lord has provided. The harsh edge of the afternoon's heat has drifted away on the breeze. Soon night will come, and with it rest. We will dream of what this gathering is stirring within our hearts. Perhaps God will whisper to us in our sleep and provide His guidance for the morrow. Isn't that what we seek?"

A chorus of shouted, "Amens," swept across the church.

"It has been a long journey. So many people have helped. I wish to take a minute to recognize two special people who have been with me every step of the way. Tick, Cami, would you please stand?"

Cami quickly rose, but Tick tried to get by with simply lifting his hand. A punch on the shoulder from Cami got him standing. They had hardly sat back down when Buck stood and let loose with a bark that echoed like a cannon shot.

"I'm sorry," Paul laughed. "I didn't mean to leave you out. Folks this is Buck. He joined us in Mississippi. You can be seated now, boy."

Laughter rang out when Buck promptly sat down.

"Up here with me are two other very special people who joined us along the way. We were just led in the Lord's prayer by Reverend Jim Hardesty, minister of Third Christian Church, Disciples of Christ, in Nashville, Tennessee. Clarence Harlan, music director at Mantachie A.M.E in Mantachie, Mississippi, fills that role for us here with his wonderful voice. Thank goodness, because I can't sing a lick. I may suggest a closing hymn to Clarence, but that's as risky as I'll be.

"There's one more person I want to recognize. My wife, my partner, my love, Jennie," he said, motioning for her to stand.

Jennie rose and turned toward the congregation, then gave a brief wave. Sustained applause followed her as she sat back down.

"Okay," Paul began as the congregation quieted. "A few words as to how we will conduct our gatherings. This is *not* a revival. It *is* a series of prayer meetings for the children.

"Near the close of each meeting I will ask you to join me in silent prayer. This is something I frequently ask of our congregation back home. I believe it is a wonderful practice, one that can be used anywhere, anytime. It helps one be comfortable with going to the Lord. We will hear many exquisitely beautiful prayers delivered, I have no doubt. However, when I call for silent prayer, it's because I want us to go to God individually, so He hears all our prayers.

"I trust you know the story by now. God called me to Brownsville to pray for the children. You heard His voice, also, else you would not be here. We were not the only ones. Reverend Hardesty told me this morning that tens of thousands of others are coming to join us. They are coming from all over America. They are coming from other countries. Like us, they are journeying here for one reason only, to pray for the children. To that, I can only say, amen!"

Shouts exploded like thunder. Paul waited for the outburst to die down.

"There's one thing everyone should understand. It's true, I am the pastor of a small Baptist church, yet this is not a gathering of Baptists. Indeed, it is not simply a gathering of Christians. I met with leaders from a dozen different beliefs this afternoon. All the world's major religions are here, and many others. I would be proud to see any of these leaders standing where I'm standing. I expect they will because they have come for the same reason you and I are here. We welcome everyone. The Lord, in His call, did not place restrictions, nor shall we.

"Earlier today, Jennie and I came here for the first time. I discovered certain areas have already been named. The huge expanse of flat ground to my right, where so many of you are camped, has been designated the Plain of Abraham. This gullied area on my left is Gabriel's Gulch.

"And behind this rise of ground is the Rio Grande, the border with Mexico. As the old hymn goes, we have gathered at the river. We come to such places to cleanse body and soul, to marvel at the flow ever returning to the sea, to understand something of our Father's genius in His creation of the lifeblood of all living things—water.

"This morning, I stood here with friends looking out at this great natural amphitheater, imagining it filled with people, as you fill it now. The thought dawned on me that this bowl, this deep dent in the Rio's bank, is more than a place to gather. In reality, it is our church. I shared the idea. Reverend Jim said it was up to me to give this sanctuary a name. Riverbank is what came to mind. Riverbank Church. Call it a synagogue or mosque, a temple or cathedral, or any name that designates a place of worship. The second part does not matter quite as much. Riverbank is the important term, for it is always a riverbank where we gather to drink from the flow of life and to pray.

"Tonight, I will talk about responsibility. Before I begin, I ask

Reverend Jim to lead us in prayer again, imploring God to open our hearts to the needs of the children."

Chapter 98

"As Reverend Jim said, children are the innocents among us. To be innocent is to be free from guilt or sin, to be unknowing, to be an angel. Is this not how we think of a child?

"Sadly, we live in a world where blame is often assigned through association. Children are despised based on nothing more than their race or color. How can that be fair? It does not matter if a child is red or yellow, black or white, if we are to live the words of the song we so happily sing. They are all precious in His sight. Nor does it matter where they are from, whether they are short or tall, have a disposition that is sweet or sour, are quick to give a hug or shy away.

"Likewise, the culture they are born into has no bearing, nor does their religion. It does not matter if their family is poor, or if they are orphans living on the streets, forced to be old beyond their years. These things should not determine how we see a child. Judging one a victim is never cause to convict."

Paul hesitated a moment. A blockbuster *Amen* from below smashed the quiet, triggering a dozen more, followed quickly by a hundred, then a thousand. Looking down, he saw Deacon Henry, arms folded across his chest, nod his way. Paul smiled at his decisive friend.

"So, you ask, what do these things have to do with *responsibility*? Now there is a weighty word. A word too great to hand over to an unknowing child. How can a little lamb be expected to bear the awesome burden of such a term in this world of lions? The answer is a child cannot.

"Responsibility is something we start expecting of children as they move into their teens. However, it is the act, or a way of acting, that we can only truly expect from adults. Being responsible is how we get things done—done in the right way. It starts when one person stands up and says, 'The burden is mine.'

"I think I should have phrased that differently. I do not wish to give the impression that responsibility is a requirement placed solely on individuals. It may be in certain situations, but that depends in large measure on the magnitude of the issue. For instance, an individual may be responsible as the owner of a business, the head of a family, the minister of a church. To succeed in any of these roles, or to fail, scarcely causes a ripple in the grand scheme.

"One thing is so great, though, so important, that no one person, or select group of people, can be expected to carry the full responsibility. A few, working together, can never hope to succeed. That can only happen when each and every adult steps up to share the burden of caring for all children."

Paul stopped and looked out over the congregation. It was perfectly quiet, no amens or shouts of hallelujah. Even Deacon Henry was still, other than another quick nod of affirmation.

"We speak with such easy conviction about our children. 'They are our future,' we say. I have said that myself, many times. Now I think I have never uttered anything more asinine. Of course, they are our future. What we fail to realize, however, is that they are our *now*, as well.

"Anything we may work for or plan on concerning our future pales in comparison to the importance of how we care for our children. I would go so far as to say, any debate or discussion, any plan, any commitment of funds or effort that does not consider first and foremost the effects it may have on our children is an abdication of responsibility. Nothing else is worth considering if we don't predicate our actions thusly. The stakes are simply too high. It does not matter if you have children of your own or not. Each and every adult must see themselves as responsible for each and every child. And *every* is exactly what I mean. No excuses allowed."

Paul hung tight to the sides of the pulpit, his head tilted down. Waves of applause and shouts of *Amen* washed over him. When the waves began to die, he looked up.

"My friends," Paul started, his voice having lost much of its force.

"Hope can only exist for children if adults take responsibility for their well-being. I have spoken of this first because without it nothing else we might imagine as worthwhile has a chance of going far. For now, I ask you to join me in silent prayer, a prayer for our children. And a prayer for us adults that we find the strength in our hearts to meet the tremendous burden God has placed on our shoulders."

He let go of the sides of the pulpit and took a step to the left. Without warning, he dropped down to his knees in the dust and bowed his head.

Chapter 99

"I don't like this," Henry's voice came through the gloom.

"What are you fussing about now?" Elsie asked, her voice full of sleep.

"Sleeping in separate beds, that's what."

"It's all they had."

"Let's find another motel."

"Henry, you know good and well there's nothing within fifty miles."

"Then I'm getting a tent. We'll make us a pallet on the ground and sleep there."

"Sleep on the ground! Come morning, neither one of us will be able to move."

He didn't say anything for a moment. "Might be right," he agreed, reluctance plain in his tone. She heard the rustle of bed covers, felt the familiar presence of his body against her side. "Scoot over."

"Henry, what are you doing? Trying to knock me to the floor?"

"I'm getting in bed with you."

"There's not enough room. It's a single bed."

"If we both sleep on our side, we'll fit," Henry insisted. "Let me get my pillow on here."

"I'm hanging off the edge!"

"I got you," Henry said, draping his arm across her. "See? Now, let's talk a—"

It happened in an instant. The weight of his arm vanished, the mattress sprung up on his side of the bed, and there was a tremendous *boom!*

"Henry!"

No answer.

"Henry?" A low moan. "Oh Lord! Are you alright?" Her hand shot out in the darkness, searching for the lamp switch. An eternity

341

later light flooded the space between the beds where Henry lay wedged in a tangled-up wad. "Where are you hurt?" Elsie cried.

Long seconds passed. "Well, I don't rightly know. See any blood?"

"No!" She took a moment to look him over, top to bottom. "I can't see any."

"There's none on my head? I popped it pretty hard."

"Let me feel," she said, reaching down and gently touching the back of his head and neck. "It's not damp or anything."

"I think I ripped a toe off."

Elsie smiled to herself as she checked, knowing he was trying to joke.

"You've still got ten," she assured him. "Where else are you hurting? Got to be something. You hit like thunder."

"It feels like I broke both hips and my right arm. That's all," he said, giving her a weak grin. He began a slow struggle to untangle himself, moving in small, measured increments. Suddenly he moaned loudly and stopped.

"Don't move!" She reached for the phone. "I'll get some help."

"You'll do no such thing!"

"Henry!"

"Just give me a hand."

"You're as stubborn as Uncle Bob's mule," Elsie complained. She swung off the bed, though, and managed to work a foot in on each side, so that she was straddling him.

"Watch your back," Henry cautioned as his upper half started to rise, him pushing and her pulling. Finally, he managed to lock an elbow atop the mattress and get his knees under him. Half a minute later, with a couple of loud grunts thrown in, he was on his feet. Winded, Elsie plopped down on her bed.

"Thank the Lord!" she exhaled.

Henry slowly twisted from side to side, bent forward slightly then straightened, turned his head this way and that, all without complaint. He took a couple of test steps out to the foot of the bed, did a little more twisting, a little more bending.

"Well?" Elsie asked, having watched every move like a hawk.

"Everything seems to be working. Give me a minute to walk it off," he added. He began moving about the room, twisting and turning more as he walked. After a minute he returned to his bed and sat down facing her way. "If that don't beat all. Nothing feels broke."

"It's a thousand wonders," she said, shaking her head. "I told you it was foolish."

"Foolish!" Henry bellowed. "Since when is it foolish for a man to sleep in the same bed with his wife?"

"There's not room."

"How long we been married?" he demanded.

"Since the Civil War."

"Right, and we've slept in the same bed every single night."

"Except for when I had my gall bladder out."

"Technicality," Henry growled. "Hospitals don't count." He leaned across and patted her knee to show he was playing. "Besides, you'll remember I slept in that old broken-down recliner right next to your bed and held your hand all night long."

"I remember." Elsie smiled. "That was sweet."

"Yeah, it was." Henry smiled, too.

"I have to go to sleep now," she said, starting to lay back.

"Not yet," he cautioned, getting to his feet. Without warning, he began stripping the covers from his bed. "Come on, get yours off."

"Uh-huh. I knew you busted your head open. Your marbles fell out."

"I've got an idea."

It wasn't like her to give in easily, but it was past their bedtime, and she was too tired to fight. Before she knew it, Henry had both mattresses lined up side by side on the floor. Three minutes later they were lying next to each other.

"You happy now?" Elsie asked, snuggling up against him.

"Plumb tickled," he said, squeezing her shoulder. "We've never missed a night sleeping in the same bed—other than that gall bladder deal—and we're not about to start now. As long as we've got a mattress, the floor will do."

Elsie burst out laughing.

"What's so funny?"

"Our wedding night. Remember? Mama gave us that old bed and a feather mattress. My brothers brought them over on a wagon."

"I remember!" Henry chuckled. "Rascals didn't bring the slat boards. Done it on purpose, of course."

"Of course. They stood there grinning like possums, waiting for you to fuss. But you didn't. You just snatched that feather mattress up over your head and slung it straight on the floor inside the bedframe. What was it you said?"

"We got it from here, boys."

"Oh, that embarrassed them." Elsie giggled.

"They had it coming." Henry chuckled again. "That old mattress didn't have a dozen feathers and everyone flat as a flitter."

"I don't recall you complaining that night," Elsie teased.

"Nope," Henry smiled at her in the half light. "Never have and never will."

Both contented at last, sleep came at them quickly, yet not before a few words about the meeting at Riverbank slipped out.

"What did you think of our boy, Paul, this evening?" Henry asked.

"He was wonderful. The whole thing was just wonderful. Everyone was moved," Elsie said. "How did it strike you?"

"He hit the nail on the head. Grownups have to step up."

"I'm so proud of him," Elsie whispered, her eyes fluttering closed.

"I couldn't be prouder if he were our own son," Henry replied.

Elsie's eyes flashed open. It was only a way of talking. She knew Henry had not meant for his words to sting, and they didn't, not much, not after all these years without children of their own. Still, if only. Their son would have been like Paul's twin. She knew that. They would have seen to it. A soft *whoo*, a sleeping sound, came from Henry's mouth. She leaned in and kissed his cheek, then closed her eyes.

Chapter 100

Chief Herbert was surprised by the early morning call. He wasn't accustomed to receiving breakfast invitations from FBI agents. He agreed to meet her, though she didn't say what she wanted. As he stepped into the hotel dining area, a hand lifted above a booth in the far corner. He walked over.

"Hello, I'm Cathy," the agent said. She extended her hand. In her other hand she palmed her identification, *Catherine Blackstone*.

"Pleased to meet you. I'm—never mind." He grinned. "Still half asleep. Mind if I grab a cup?"

"Sure," Cathy answered.

Chief Herbert was back in a minute with coffee. He sat down and took a quick sip.

"It's good," he smiled at her, setting the cup down. "I need my caffeine fix."

"I understand. I'd join you, but I'm already past my limit."

The chief nodded, electing not to ask why she called. Besides, he was ninety-nine percent certain he already knew.

"I'll get right to the point," Cathy began. "You know this Preacher Paul Lockhart."

"I do. We met when he came through Tupelo."

"And you spoke with him as part of your investigation of the attempted assault on the Natchez Trace?"

"Yes."

"You also spoke with the attackers?"

"That's true. I interviewed both," the chief answered.

"What was your assessment of them?"

"Not enough sense between the two to open a can of corn."

"You saw them as acting on their own?"

"I didn't say that." He shook his head. "Just because they're

345

imbeciles doesn't mean someone wasn't using them. That was my concern, my primary reason for going to the U.S. Attorney in Jackson. As you've seen in my report," he noted, "this was not the first time they've accosted the preacher. I strongly encouraged him to press charges. I didn't believe we'd get to the bottom, otherwise. But he elected not to push it."

The agent stared at him for several seconds. At last, she spoke.

"You were right to be concerned. We have uncovered a link between the two *imbeciles,* as you appropriately termed them, and a third party. This third party is also in contact with a more *competent* threat."

There it was. The chief kept a straight face. Confirmation his professional intuition had been correct gave a minute degree of satisfaction. It quickly evaporated.

"You know the man," she stated. "Do you think he will work with us to protect him?"

The chief shrugged. "He is as sincere as he seems. Nothing will divert him from his calling. He may not flat out oppose protection, but I wouldn't expect him to make it easy."

Moments of silence passed before the agent spoke.

"I noticed you took vacation time to come here. That wasn't because you were concerned about his safety, though, was it?"

"No. At least not altogether. I see something in him, in what he's doing. It's hard to explain, but I want to be here, be part of it, somehow."

"I see," she said, for the first time the hint of a smile lifting the corners of her mouth. "He has that effect." After a moment, the agent continued. "You think he'll come to a security meeting?"

"Probably. Just don't expect much."

"We have to try, Langston. We have to try."

He felt his stomach turn. Her last words hammered home the seriousness of the situation more than anything else said. Agent Blackstone was frightened, and now so was he.

"Who's calling the shots?" Langston asked, instantly regretting his choice of words. "Can you say?"

The agent hesitated. "No. I'll just say someone high up."

Chapter 101

Alejandro, Bob's teenage contact, met him at Holy Spirit Church. He led the way inside to a small alcove at the rear of the sanctuary, where they met Father Andres. The priest also knew Serena and her mother and did what he could to aid them. He had spoken earlier to the mother, Juanita, and Bob separately, first to make certain the mother was willing to tell their story, and second to see if he thought Bob could be trusted. Satisfied he could be, Father Andres nevertheless warned that Juanita was very leery. Bob should approach her with care.

Father Andres led Alejandro and Bob to another room. He invited them to sit down at a simple table, then stepped to another door. In moments Juanita and Serena entered. Juanita was very reserved, but at the priest's urging, she took a seat across from Bob. Serena, however, flew to Alejandro. He tried to introduce her, but the child clung to him, offering the reporter only a shy smile. That was okay with Bob. It was Juanita he needed to hear from.

Her family's experience was one more sad story in a town brimming with sad stories. Juanita related it in a monotone voice, never changing expression. Robert had seen this behavior before. Sometimes a victim spoke in such a dry, straightforward manner the horror being described came without color, like it was written in gray ink on gray paper. *That,* he thought, *might be the greatest horror of all.*

"My husband was a good mechanic. He could fix anything. He had a shop next door to our house. People brought their cars to him from all over Guatemala City.

"One day a man, a gang leader, brought his car to the shop. My husband repaired it. As the man started to leave, Serena came running in. Her father picked her up and hugged her. The man said, 'What a pretty girl. I have a place for her to work when she is older.' My husband understood the devil's words and told him not to come there anymore.

"That night we talked about what had happened. It was one more sign the city was too dangerous. The police could not protect us. The gangs controlled everything, and now this devil had threatened our daughter. Such things did not happen in America, my husband said. Serena would be safe there. We agreed we must leave. The next morning, my husband went to his shop. Later, I took him some food. He was not there. I asked the neighbors. No one had seen him. I looked everywhere. I begged the police for help. *He has a girlfriend*, they said. *Don't worry. He'll come back.* This was not true. I never saw my husband again.

"Life became a great burden. I worked as a seamstress all day, every day, yet I still did not make enough.

"A month after my husband disappeared, a man came to the door. 'Where is the mechanic?' he asked. 'He has such a beautiful daughter.' At that moment, Serena came into the room. 'Ah, there she is!' the man shouted. 'More beautiful than ever. If she needs anything, let me know. I will take care of her.' Then I knew this monster had killed my husband.

"The next day Serena and I started to the United States. We soon joined with many others. Always walking. It was very hard. Every day, so many difficulties."

"What was the worst thing?" Bob asked.

"The border," Juanita answered. "They ripped my daughter from my arms. She is a little child, my baby. She was screaming for me. Comprende? She was screaming!" Her face still showed no expression, but tears were rolling down her cheeks. "And so was I," she added, her voice beyond tired. "I did not know where they took her. I did not know if I would ever see her again. I was ready to die. 'Please, God,' I prayed. 'Take me. Take me.'"

Chapter 102

"Good evening, America. I'm Clifford Cumberland. Thank you for joining us for this special two-hour presentation of *Movements*. This evening we are in Brownsville, Texas.

"A week ago, we were with Preacher Paul Lockhart of Caney Creek, Kentucky, as he took the final steps of his nearly thirteen hundred-mile trek to Brownsville. To recap why he walked this far, Preacher Paul says it was in response to a call from God to come here to the border and pray for the children.

"On the west side of town, there is an area alongside the Rio Grande where over eighty thousand people are camped beside a large, natural amphitheater. We will go on a video tour of that camp tonight and hear from some of the people who have joined the preacher to pray. We will also hear from others who question the preacher's motives.

"This gathering is not only about prayer, though Preacher Paul terms it a Prayer Meeting. It has become a magnet for people of every faith, of every walk of life, from all fifty states and from many other nations.

"There is a commercial side of this to consider, also. At more than one location we saw Bibles, Korans, and Torahs for sale, along with other holy books, on the same table. Some things border on the irreverent. We found a Tacos for Jesus stand, among dozens of vendors. And, of course, there are souvenirs. Coffee cups with Preacher Paul's likeness, refrigerator magnets in the shape of Texas with a cross instead of the usual lone star, and as one would expect, tee shirts. A popular version has a pair of praying hands in the center, with *PRAYING WITH PAUL* in an arc of letters above. We point out, the sale of anything here is not approved by or affiliated with Preacher Paul.

349

"You will see an interview we conducted this morning with Paul and Jennie Lockhart about a great personal loss they suffered and about the extraordinary movement manifesting itself here, when we return from a short break."

The picture started high, taking in the amphitheater and a slice of Mexico across the Rio Grande. It zoomed in close to a blue canopy on the pulpit, then switched to another camera.

"Hello, America," Clifford Cumberland said. "We are atop a little hill on the bank of the Rio Grande. With me are Paul and Jennie Lockhart." He turned toward the couple. "Thank you for joining us."

"Our pleasure," they replied in unison, then glanced at each other and laughed.

"How long have you been married?"

"Eight years in February." Jennie smiled.

"The 14th," Paul added.

Clifford's eyebrows went up. "Valentine's Day?"

"Yes," the couple answered in unison again, managing not to laugh.

"One could get the impression you are still very much in love."

"Absolutely," Paul replied immediately. "Jennie will always be my valentine."

Jennie laid her hand atop Paul's and squeezed. "And Paul will always be mine."

Clifford smiled at them, then glanced down at his notes. A couple of seconds later he looked up. His expression had changed, like he had something to ask, but didn't really want to.

"These last few months have been a rollercoaster for you," he began, moving his focus from one to the other. "Many of our viewers may not have heard how this began. I know this is painful to discuss—" He settled his gaze on Paul. "Could you please explain the events that brought you here?"

"Our daughter died in an accident."

Both men were surprised to hear Jennie speaking.

"Sarah was four, going on forty." Jennie gave a quick smile. "She was into everything imaginable, forever asking questions, precocious to a fault. Our daughter had an innate ability to sense when others were hurting, and—this was her most important trait—she knew how to help them feel better. If they needed a hug, she would hug their neck. If they needed a kiss on the cheek, she kissed them. Hers was an extraordinary gift of compassion."

Jennie sucked in a breath before continuing.

"Sarah wanted a swing. Like any good father would have done, Paul hung her a tire swing in the big maple tree in our front yard."

"Jennie," Paul interrupted. "I'll—"

"No," she cut him off. "You've had to tell this too many times already." Jennie paused a moment, then looked straight into the camera. "Sarah had her favorite stuffed animal, a big red rabbit, on her lap while she was swinging. She dropped it. When she couldn't reach it, she let go of the rope and leaned down further. That's when she lost her balance and fell. Her neck...."

An audible gasp came from a crew member. Jennie turned toward the sound, her eyes big and round with a mother's concern. Then she glanced at Paul. He made to speak, but she shook him off.

"As with any parents who have lost a child, we were beyond heartbroken," Jennie explained. "We drifted apart, lost in our sorrow. Then one night we saw a little girl on the news. Her name was Serena. She was bawling her eyes out because she had been separated from her mother at the border. We saw her, and we saw our Sarah."

Jennie turned to Paul then and nodded.

"That's when I lost it and crushed what was left of Jennie's heart," he said. "I spent the night in the cane thicket near our house. I pleaded and complained and argued with God. Finally at dawn, I surrendered to His will. He told me what to do. I was to walk here, to Brownsville, and pray for the children. Now, here we are."

"Thank you, Jennie, Paul." Clifford shook his head. "That had to have been very difficult. So, as you said, Paul, here we are, on top of this little mound in Brownsville, a huge natural amphitheater on one side and the Rio Grande on the other. I understand people call this mound, *Paul's Pulpit*."

"Oh, I wish they wouldn't do that." Paul frowned. "Just call it the pulpit."

"Whatever the name," Clifford said, "it's located in an arresting spot."

"It is beautiful. We call this place Riverbank Church," Paul said, raising his arms wide to take in their surroundings, "or Cathedral, Mosque, Synagogue, House of the Lord. Whatever name suits anyone."

"Yes," Clifford nodded, turning his eyes toward the river. "Riverbank is a perfect name."

He returned his attention to Paul.

"Let's touch on something now that must bother you. Some people doubt you heard anything from God. The charge He supposedly gave you sounds too vague or too small to them. They believe you have an ulterior motive. There must be more than just *pray for the children*."

"Doubt does not bother me," Paul replied. "I see it as a good thing. It's the first step of the journey to faith, to trust and belief in God. It is doubt that leads us to question, and in our questioning, we find answers that reveal the way.

"As to whether God spoke to me. When I was lost in the caneland, God told me to go to Brownsville, Texas, and pray for the children. His words were perfectly clear. If anyone wishes to question whether that happened, it is their prerogative, yet it cannot change what I heard. The miracle of this great gathering is that many thousands of others must have heard God say something similar to them.

"Ulterior motive? I would simply point out that I am literally following my marching orders. Any motives which gave rise to those orders are not mine, but God's.

"Finally, as to whether His charge is too vague, or too small, I would ask, what is more important to pray for than our children? There is only one answer to that question. Nothing."

Chapter 103

Tick was at a loss. He missed being responsible for important things on the trek. He missed the talks at night with Paul. They were fun and interesting. He admired the man. Paul was close enough in age to see him as a big brother, and old enough to have Tick's respect.

Of course, he had known it would all come to a halt one day. As they got closer to Brownsville it had set in that their days together were almost done. He still went through the motions, but the reality was he didn't have much to do. Then Brownsville, with Jennie and Paul reuniting, and Tick was suddenly as alone as when his father died. It felt like that, like a death. If not for Cami—

They had grown closer, but she was much busier now. She wasn't just scheduling interviews for Paul and herself. Now reporters and news agencies had established residence. Her phone was ringing constantly. Somehow, she still wrote her blog. A chain of small newspapers was publishing it as a regular column. All of it meant long days and late nights for her, and way too much time alone for him.

At least he had Buck! They had toured the Plain of Abraham today, sampled the fares at several food vendors, even listened to a roundtable discussion. He visited with a dozen people, all of whom were more interested in the dog than him.

It was mid-afternoon. They had grown tired of the crowded camp. Ambling alongside the border wall, dog and man kept their heads canted toward the river. At the rear of Paul's Pulpit, they came to a stop. Tick had a sudden, powerful urge to go fishing. He looked through the bars. His first cast would go where those bushes trailed in the water. Any self-respecting fish would hang out there. Buck might have been thinking the same thing, for he stuck his big head as far as it would go between the bars and started whining.

"Sorry buddy," Tick said. "Shame, we can't even get our toes wet."

Buck pulled his head back and turned toward Tick as if waiting to hear more.

"I promise you, once we get back home, we'll go down to the creek, and you can jump in up to your elbows. Turn that tail into a propeller and go running wide open, chasing fish and frogs and mud turtles till you can't go another inch. Okay?"

"*Woof! Woof!*" Buck replied, bouncing his front paws off the ground.

Tick laughed and grabbed the dog by the head. He proceeded to give both ears a good scratching. They soon tired of the game. Somehow today, it wasn't much fun. They resumed their sauntering. After ten feet, Buck hopped toward the wall. In a flash, he was digging like his favorite bone was buried where the thick bars disappeared into the ground, sending dirt and rocks flying out between his rear legs in a dusty rooster tail.

"Quit it!" Tick snapped, grabbing a handful of red hair and pulling the dog backward. He started digging in the new spot, though, each stab at the ground pulling them closer to the wall. "Dang it! Gonna get me arrested! Stop!"

And Buck stopped. The way he twisted his head sideways toward Tick said he didn't understand. This was good digging dirt.

Tick suddenly realized the dirt was loosely packed. A hole had been filled in here. This was a way out, or more likely, in. He leaned forward to look. Three inches down, the bars had been cut away, leaving an opening big enough to crawl through. Panicked, Tick began to rake dirt back in with the side of his foot. He almost had the surface flat and even again when someone shouted, "Tick!"

He spun toward the sound.

"Chief Herbert!"

"What are you up to, son?" the ranger asked from atop the Pulpit.

"Uh, Buck started digging here and found a hole. Somebody's cut big chunks out of the bars, I guess so people can slip through."

The chief squinted at the spot a minute, then nodded.

"Okay, I'll tell Border Patrol. Can you come up here? We've got stuff to talk about."

Chapter 104

Cami was flustered. She needed to concentrate on the reporter's question, but thoughts of Tick popped into her head without warning. Other than a quick cup of coffee at 6:00 a.m., they hadn't seen each other in two days. It wasn't enough for two young people in love. Cancelling their hoped-for romantic dinner last evening didn't help the situation, but her interview on a Christian radio station was important.

"I understand," she answered the reporter. Fortunately, he was long-winded enough for her to still catch his drift. It was more of a complaint, anyway. "We would love to give each reporter more time in the one-on-one interviews," Cami said, "but Preacher Paul has so many demands on his time. We are exploring ways to improve access. I ask for your patience."

She glanced down at her list.

"Okay, our final item for this morning's briefing is Droopy McNaughton. As I'm sure most of you know, Mr. McNaughton is a hugely successful country music artist with a long list of number one songs and a host of awards. What you may not know is he has been instrumental in supporting the trek. From just south of Houston, he supplied buses that transported literally thousands of people here. We are eternally grateful for all he has done in donating his time, funds, and energy. Now I'd like to turn the mic over to Krista Koslowski, public relations manager for Mr. McNaughton. Krista."

"Thank you, Cami," Krista said, turning to beam at the crowd with her flashing green eyes and perfect white teeth. "First, one thing I would like to correct about Cami's remarks. We never call Droopy, *Mister*. He says it makes him itch."

Laughter swept through the tent. Krista waited for the noise to settle down.

"When Preacher Paul walked through downtown Nashville, Droopy was staying at a hotel there. Watching a morning show, he saw an interview with my friend, Cami, about the Trek and the events that led up to it. This was followed by a live report from the state capitol as the preacher prayed with a group of ministers. On a hunch, Droopy looked out the window. Preacher Paul was walking by. Inspiration struck. Droopy immediately started work on a song.

"Last month in Nashville Droopy recorded that song, titled, "Walk with Me, Son." It is being released this morning. Handouts of the lyrics are on the table here.

"Droopy has made the following stipulations. All proceeds will be divided equally among the charities listed on the handout. You will note, each is concerned with the welfare of children in southern border communities. Further, he will waive any and all fees and restrictions for any artists wishing to cover this song, provided the proceeds are donated to these or other children's welfare agencies operating in border communities.

"Finally, under the direction of Music Director Clarence Harlan, Droopy and the Children's Choir—should I tell them about the choir, Cami?"

"Please do."

"The Children's Choir consists of one hundred children. Some are from this area. Some journeyed here with their parents. At tonight's meeting, the choir will make its debut, joining Droopy in singing, "Walk with Me, Son." It promises to be a special evening."

Chapter 105

A fire officer waved Paul into the classroom. Then she stepped inside and closed the door behind her. Paul noticed shoulder patches from Customs and Border Patrol and the Brownsville Police Department on others, as well. He moved toward a chair between Chief Herbert and Tick, across from a woman in her early forties, dressed in a business suit.

"Thank you for coming, Reverend Lockhart," she said, rising to shake hands. "I'm Special Agent Cathy Blackstone of the FBI."

"Are we expecting a fire?" Paul smiled, hoping to ease the palpable tension.

"They're also emergency medical," Tick answered. "Case it's worse than River Bend."

Paul looked like he had been slapped.

"My friend has a way of getting to the point," he said, recalling not only Tick's statement just then, but the words he had used earlier in convincing him to come.

Paul, you're not thinking. If you're in danger, then so are others.

"I understand you believe I'm in danger," Paul continued. "I will listen to what you have to say with an open mind, because Tick has rightfully pointed out to me that others might also be threatened. Of course, I want them to be protected. In this you have my full support."

Paul moved his gaze along the line of officials, then back to Agent Blackstone.

"Reverend Lockhart," she began. "Or do you prefer, *Preacher*?"

"Paul is fine."

"Very well, Paul," she answered. "Please call me, Cathy," she added, hoping the informality would make the meeting go smoother. "I can tell you this much. A known assassin came to this area at the same time you arrived."

"Okay."

"He crossed to Mexico, then back into Brownsville," the border patrol chief offered. He didn't mention their new facial-recognition software was incredible, when it was working, which it hadn't been for a three-hour stretch the day after the last sighting. Software glitch. They didn't know if the assassin had crossed back into Mexico during that period, but no law enforcement agency had spotted him in the U. S. since, and they had been looking.

"Okay?"

"There's more," Agent Blackstone nodded. "We've intercepted communications between the assassin and an individual who is much opposed to your mission."

She left out that the individual was a high government official, and that his boss had been on a rampage about Paul lately.

"And?" Paul asked.

"These things may not seem convincing to you, but we have other information, corroborating information, we cannot share." She frowned. "Please trust me. There is cause to be concerned. We need you to work with us on some protective measures."

"It depends on the measures, I guess," Paul flashed a smile back.

"For starters, we think it necessary to provide you a security detail, twenty-four seven. It'd just be a few plainclothes officers. We'd also like for you to wear a bullet-proof vest," she added. "And we'd like to place some clear shielding on the pulpit area, especially around the lectern."

Paul shook his head, "I've had cameras on me every step since Houston. I suspect any reporter would notice the security detail in the first five minutes. The same goes for a bullet-proof vest. People could see it under my shirt from a mile away. And the shields? There's no hiding them, either. So, I have to say no to all those things."

"Please reconsider, Paul." Agent Blackstone leaned forward. "This is very serious."

Paul held up his hand. "I know I sound unreasonable. I'm well aware that my stubbornness, or foolishness, if you wish to call it that, makes each of your jobs more difficult. I ask you to try to understand my calling. I am not a brave man. What I have instead of courage is certainty—certainty in my belief that God has led me to this place to deliver His message of prayer. Should I do the things you suggest, I would be saying I have no faith in God to protect me. Worse than that, it would give the unmistakable impression that my personal safety is more important than His message. Nothing could be further from the truth."

No one replied, unsure of what to say. Finally, Paul cleared his throat.

"I said I would listen to ideas about how others might be protected."

The officials pitched several suggestions over the next few minutes. Paul agreed to plain-clothes officers in the congregation, at the entrances to the church, and along the border wall. He had no problem with firefighters continuing to provide first aid and standing by with ambulances. Given the growing crowds, they were already looking to increase their presence. He rejected metal detectors and patrol dogs as too obvious. Finally, he agreed to the hidden installation of armor plate in the speakers around the pulpit. It could block shots from certain angles.

"Thank you, Paul," Agent Blackstone said, ending the discussion.

"My thanks to each of you," Paul smiled as he rose to his feet. "I'll pray for your safety."

The agent sincerely replied, "And we'll pray for yours."

Tick followed Paul out. Chief Herbert rose to leave, too, but Agent Blackstone said, "Please stay," so he remained by his chair.

"You were right, Langston," she said. "He's not making it easy."

"Think he's looking to be a martyr?" the CBP supervisor asked.

"No." Chief Herbert shook his head. "He's simply doing as he feels led."

"We'll keep people in his vicinity," the agent said. "We just can't crowd him." She looked at Herbert. "You're around him a lot. Can you increase your time?"

"Sure."

"Carrying your service weapon?"

"I can," he replied, thinking it probably wouldn't be much use in stopping a sniper.

"Please do." She turned to the CBP head. "Julius, I think it's time we talked to our peers across the river."

"I'll make the call."

Chapter 106

Paul and Jennie made their way down the long, central aisle of Riverbank Church. The meeting would not begin for half an hour, yet the crowd was already huge. Attendance was expected to approach a hundred thousand. The Comm center said the numbers of people heading to Brownsville were increasing. There were at least fifty thousand on the road south, with Father Diaz and Reverend Michelson jointly leading a contingent of ten thousand from Houston.

A few individuals spoke words of encouragement as they made their way. Paul leaned on his walking stick. Jennie clung to his arm. Occasionally, a man's hand thrust out for Paul to shake. With Jennie, a few women reached to lay a comforting hand on her shoulder, her back, this mother of a child lost. For the most part, though, people kept their distance. Many simply raised their hands before their hearts in the symbol of prayer.

Here was the prayer gesture again. It made Paul uncomfortable. Then he remembered something Henry had said. "You are the middleman." The symbol was not for him, but God.

As they passed the lower sections, Paul slowly swept his eyes over the pulpit area. Much had changed in the two days since he last spoke. Rows of folding chairs had been added for the choir. As if to confirm, Clarence appeared at the head of a stream of children. The pulpit was no longer a spindly stand. A six-by-six post, concreted in the ground, had replaced the original two-by-fours. Three large amps now flanked each side. Paul and Jennie swung left to make their way around a TV camera platform. As Jennie slid into her seat with the other folks from Caney Creek, Paul lifted his hand in acknowledgment of a friend seated behind them.

"Chief Herbert," Paul said.

"Preacher."

"Long time, no see," Paul joked.

With a wave to the group from home, Paul headed around the left flank of the Pulpit. When he reached the backside, he walked over to the wall. As before, he pushed his face forward until it touched the bars and looked across to Mexico. The crowd on that side looked much larger than before. Cami had told him a jumbo screen TV system had been installed there.

Paul closed his eyes and pushed his face harder against the bars, feeling the warmth they harbored from the afternoon sun. "Father," he whispered. "Guide me, as always, I pray. Amen."

He turned around and strode toward the steps cut into the slope, not bothering to look left or right. Had he looked he would have seen that those who peered through the bars now formed a mass four and five deep that stretched out of sight both east and west. Had he been listening closely he might have heard their prayers.

Near the pulpit's front, the three guest ministers had finished praying. Paul touched hands with each as they met at the steps. Clarence was surrounded by children six to eight years old, a mix of colors and races. Paul smiled at them as he worked his way through the crowd. Reaching his chair, he noticed Tick and Buck were busy on the other side. Tick was swinging kids on each arm, like he had at St. Ignatius. Buck was giving out face slurps to first one squealing child, then another, while a gang of gigglers rubbed him every which way a dog could be rubbed.

"Hey preacher," Clarence called. "How about our choir?"

"It's wonderful!" Paul yelled back.

"All right, gang," Clarence's voice boomed. "Everybody find your place. It's time to get started." Suddenly kids were running everywhere, kicking up dust as they formed into a long, looping line. Clarence raised his arms. All grew quiet.

"Jesus—" he began, and the children sang with him as they paraded in serpentine fashion around the front half of the Pulpit. "—loves the little children." Many in the congregation joined in. "Red and yellow, black and white." Suddenly Clarence jerked his arms down in a chopping motion. The choir members immediately stopped singing and marching. A handful of individual voices in the congregation stumbled on for a minute, then they also went still. Clarence crossed his arms over his chest in a hugging motion. Two hundred little arms crossed one hundred little chests. He gave a nod. "*We* are precious in his sight!" shouted the children. "Jesus loves the little children of the world," they continued, resuming their marching.

By the time of the second rendition, most of the adults in the congregation had caught on and did not sing the *We are precious* line. But children throughout the church jumped to their feet and sang along.

The choir went through the song five times before Clarence had them switch to "This Little Light of Mine." Again, the children of the choir and of the congregation joined together, singing the song as they danced in place. When Clarence signaled an end, the church erupted with a tremendous round of applause punctuated by shouted *amens.*

As the noise died, the children formed into semi-circular lines behind Clarence. He picked up a microphone and took a step forward. "Just as I am, without one plea." The sound of his voice as it carried across Riverbank seemed to be something palpable, something one could hold in the palm of one's hand and marvel at its magic. "And that thou bidst me come to Thee." Then the high-pitched voices of the Children's Choir swept in. "Oh Lamb of God, I come. I come."

"Oh, my Lord," Paul said.

"Yes. Oh, my Lord," came the reply from beside him.

Paul turned to see Droopy McNaughton beaming at him. Their hands clasped. Leaning back to see better, Paul checked out the guitar the big man held by the neck.

"I hear you're going to sing, too."

Droopy nodded.

"Good!" Paul couldn't hide his excitement. He had a weakness for Droopy's music. "What? Mama's Boy? Drifting Down the River?"

"No. I thought I'd try something new. It's about a friend of mine."

Reverend Jim approached the pulpit and led the congregation in the Lord's Prayer. Afterward, he addressed the gathering.

"There have been many people who have provided help on this great trek to the border and who continue to give aid in countless ways. I did not know this man a few weeks ago, but today I am proud to call him my friend. His faith is unshakeable, his generosity unmatched. Droopy McNaughton."

Cheers and deafening applause arose as the big man moved forward, working his way around the seated choir. As he neared the pulpit, he raised his free hand palm out, then brought it down over and over in an attempt to quiet the greeting. The congregation soon grew silent. Droopy stepped up to the microphones.

"A couple of months ago, I looked out my hotel window in Nashville and happened to see Preacher Paul walking down Seventh Avenue. He has walked many, many miles since. All of us here this evening felt compelled to join him because we, too, heard the call. That morning in Nashville, I started writing a song about his journey."

Droopy strummed his guitar. For several moments that was the only sound. Then he began to sing. "Walking down this endless road, burdened by my heavy load—" Such was the power of that perfect voice, ranging high or low as the song called for, no one clapped or cheered. "Why Lord, why did Thou choose me? Because you came on bended knee."

People became aware, in the way one suddenly realizes warm air is flowing across one's skin, that the Children's Choir members were all on their feet, humming in rhythm with the music. Droopy played on, his eyes squeezed shut as if in prayer. Surely in prayer. He was singing more than a song. It was a worship service in itself. "Walk with Me, son, preach My word." The choir's voices, high and bright as a hillside of wildflowers, were suddenly there. "Pray the children's cries are heard." Then slower, with emphasis on each word. "Pray the children's cries are heard."

"Amen," Droopy said, opening his eyes. Then he turned and walked toward the rear of the pulpit.

Chapter 107

"Good evening, my friends," Paul said, resting his Jesus stick against the pulpit. Hearing the echo of his words coming from across the river made him pause an instant. "My goodness! What about our Children's Choir? Are they not fantastic?" he asked, clapping his hands.

All joined him. Shouted *Amens* rose above the din. Paul waited for the noise to die.

"Clarence, thank you for sharing your wonderful voice. Droopy—your music gives me chills. And your song—I believe it is for everyone here. We have all walked that endless road to come here and pray.

"My thanks to the religious leaders who offered prayers to start our meeting. Here at Riverbank, we know, regardless of one's religion, every time we bow our heads and go to God in prayer, we are heard. God listens to all His children.

"We have established a schedule of sorts," he announced, gripping the sides of the pulpit. "Every other night, I will speak briefly on a topic that I believe is important to children. Other leaders may speak on the nights in between. Every night people of different faiths will come forward to pray for the children. We welcome each of these voices. To hear someone of another faith praying for the same thing I am praying for is one of the most confirming things I can imagine. It is too easy to find reasons for separating beliefs, one from the other. *Why?* I ask, when we are all joined by one thing more powerful than any list of negative reasons. Prayer! Prayer is what unites us!"

"Amen!" Henry shouted. He was on his feet, fist in the air. Thousands of others were suddenly on their feet, also, shouting and waving.

Again Paul waited for the noise to subside. "My friends," he began, his fire damped down. "I have heard this gathering called many things. I'll be clear, this is not a revival. It is not a celebration of one particular religion. It is quite simply a prayer meeting." He twisted halfway around and pointed at the choir. "And here is who we are praying for, our children, red and yellow, black and white, each one precious in His sight, because—because God said they need our prayers."

"But—" he waited a few breaths, letting the tension build. "What are the specifics? Do we simply pray for children's welfare? I hope we do that much—send the Lord a nice, general request for their safety and well-being. At least the little ones are on our minds. God hears those prayers, too.

"That shouldn't be all we do, however. Put in a little research. Look and listen. One cannot turn on the TV or drive along the streets or roads in certain sections of any community without seeing the needs of children. Listen to what they are praying for. Then ask Him for guidance on how best to help.

"He will answer. When that light comes on in your heart, when you suddenly know there is something you can do, it is God responding to your prayers. Then it is time to act. Get up! Get out! And get involved!"

The congregation exploded with shouts of *amen* and *hallelujah.* After a few seconds the voices began to recede, giving way to something else. Paul heard it coming, like the drumbeats of an approaching army. *Clap, clap, clap, clap.* He looked across the congregation, saw people rising to their feet, until it seemed all were standing. They were bringing their hands together with the same slow, deliberate cadence. *Clap, clap, clap, clap.* He glanced down at Jennie, saw her smile and point toward Mexico. Paul caught it then, coming over the water, that same measured beat. The sound was everywhere. *Clap, clap, clap, clap.* It felt like he was inside a great, rolling storm cloud. He made no move to stop it, so the beat went on for two, three, four minutes. At last, he raised his hands.

Paul allowed his gaze to wander back and forth over the congregation until it appeared the last person had taken a seat.

"My goodness! What a start," he said, smiling broadly. A wave of laughter came back from the congregation. "I do believe that was heard in heaven." That brought on another wave of reaction.

Paul paused, giving people a few moments to settle. Glancing down at Jennie, he got a wink to let him know he was on the right path.

"My goodness." He waited a breath. "I don't say that enough. My dear mother said it all the time, for anything that required an exclamation. Think about that phrase. There is something good God placed inside each of us, something we can summon at will. Our goodness."

Paul smiled. He lifted his eyes skyward until he felt the words welling up.

"Two nights ago, I spoke on the responsibility of adults, of how we must embrace our roles of watching over all children. Tonight, I wish to talk about an area where children need security. Family.

"The greatest guarantee that a child will succeed and know happiness, is for him or her to be raised within the arms of a loving family. The key word is *raised*. It means lifted up, taken to a higher plane. It is the perfect word to describe what we seek to do when we go about meeting our responsibility to children.

"Providing family is not a part-time job. Notice I said *providing family*, not *providing for family*. Too often we get lost in the latter, at the expense of the former."

Paul waited a moment for that to sink in while a thousand voices said *amen* in agreement.

"In providing family, there are no vacations nor holidays. The work is a constant, ongoing commitment to put family above all other interests but God. Of course, in these times when single-parent families are so common, it is easy for the non-custodial parent to take a back seat, to ignore their responsibility. That will not do. A child is brought into the world by two people and deserves nothing less than the best efforts of both.

"Most of all, parents and child should never be separated. Man has no right to tear asunder what God has blessed."

"You have probably heard the story of the little Guatemalan girl, Serena, who was taken from her mother at the border. When

Jennie and I saw her on TV our hearts were torn in half. 'Mama! Mama!' she cried. No! She bawled, 'Mama!' She was so pitiful. I have thought of her mother many times since. Was she crying, too? 'My baby! My baby! My baby!'"

Paul lowered his eyes. Those seated close could see his knuckles were white as they gripped the pulpit. A full minute passed before he looked up.

"A few weeks ago, I spoke at Sunrise Cathedral. I asked everyone there to recall their worst childhood fear. Now, I ask you to do the same. Close your eyes and remember a time when you were so frightened you could not rest, you could not breathe. Maybe all you could do was cry. Something dark and terrible sent sharp, stabbing pains through your stomach. You knew your world would end if this awful thing did not go away. Take a moment to remember."

Paul slowly swept his gaze over the congregation. He saw some people swipe at their cheeks or give a sob or two. Finally, he spoke.

"Remember how horrible that time was? Now, ask yourself if your experience was as frightening as Serena's, or her mother's, must have been when they were torn apart?"

An eerie quiet fell over Riverbend. Paul waited a minute, then two, before speaking.

"Let us go to God in silent prayer for the children." He stepped to the left side of the pulpit and fell to his knees. Then he bowed his head.

The cowboy was not happy. *Where did those kids come from?* he asked himself. They were bad enough, but somebody had placed giant amplifiers on the hill. He was patient, moving around a few feet this way or that, but between kids and speakers, he couldn't get a clear shot.

Now where did the preacher go? It took the cowboy a minute to spot him. The man was on his knees beside the pulpit. He caught a glimpse of hair past the front of one of the speakers. But you couldn't kill hair. There was nothing to do but find a better angle.

Upstream a hundred yards, the river bent north. That might work, provided there was good cover. He started that way.

Speaking of cover, the cowboy thought, coming to a sudden stop. He pulled out his tequila bottle, unscrewed the cap, and took a long pull on the water inside. Then he spun the cap on and dropped the bottle in his rear pocket. He only wobbled a little as he walked. He wasn't worried about the cops stopping a drunk wandering the riverbank. And without patting him down no one would find the well-padded pieces of a high-powered rifle hidden under his loose clothes.

In a few minutes he found a great new position. Now he could shoot straight at the side of the preacher, instead of at an angle.

Only trouble was, the preacher was gone.

Chapter 108

After breakfast at Ruth and Naomi's—a popular feeding spot on the Plain of Abraham—the Caney Creek contingent retreated to Paul and Jennie's tent. Cami's parents and Tick's mom had arrived together the evening before. Henry and Elsie rounded out the group. Cami and Tick sat across from one another, laughing at Henry's stories and Elsie's pretended fussing, trying hard not to stare at each other and thus give away their feelings. They fooled no one.

It was pure torture for Tick. He had rather jab toothpicks under his fingernails than sit there, looking at Cami, and not be able to at least hold her hand. So, when Cami's dad pushed up from his chair and announced he would like to tour Riverbend, Tick shot up like he had sat on a thumbtack and volunteered to show him around. Ten minutes later, they were standing behind the pulpit's hill, staring through the bars at the river.

"I thought it was bigger," Frank Whitley said after a few moments.

"Me too," Tick agreed.

Whitley shook his head. "You can't really tell on TV. I always imagined a wider river, like we've got back home. The Ohio or the Mississippi, maybe. Huh. So that's Mexico?"

"Yes, sir."

"It doesn't look much different."

"Nope." Tick shook his head. "It threw me the first time I laid eyes on it. Another country's supposed to look way different, how I figured. Preacher says it doesn't matter. People aren't different. Everyone wants the same things, especially for their children."

"I can't argue with that."

The men grew quiet. After a minute, Tick caught movement out of the corner of his eye. Cami's father had turned from the wall and was pointed toward the steps at the rear of the hill.

"Mr. Whitley!"

Tick asked himself a rapid-fire question. *Did I shout?*

"Yes." The man turned around.

"Well, sir, uh, I've got something I need to say. That is, if you've got a minute?"

"I've got one or two," Whitley replied, moving to ease a shoulder against the bars.

"I don't know exactly how to say it."

"Since you look like you're about to choke, you might ought to hurry."

"Okay then."

That was as far as he got. Tick just stood there staring at the older man, praying for the relief a direct hit by lightning would bring.

"Tick?"

"I'm in love with your daughter! Cami's the sweetest, smartest, kindest, prettiest girl ever, and I can't live without her."

Mr. Whitley smiled but didn't say anything in return.

Is he laughing at me? Tick asked himself.

Before he could go further down the rabbit hole, Mr. Whitley spoke.

"How's she feel about you?"

"She loves me. Loves me with all her heart, she says."

"I see." her father nodded.

It took a moment for Tick to realize the other man was waiting for him to say more. When he raised his eyebrows, Tick finally got the message. "Sir, I'm asking your permission to marry your daughter."

"You think she'll say *yes*?"

"Uh yeah, I sure hope so," Tick replied, then sucked in a deep breath. Oxygen was suddenly in short supply.

"Couple of questions," Cami's father said as he pushed away from the wall. He stood up straight, facing Tick head on. "What about your drinking?"

"I quit. I haven't had a drop since I told Preacher I was going with him."

"And how about your fighting? I heard you had a bad scrape in Mississippi."

"That's the only time since way before we left home. Those fellas had it coming, but I hope that was my last time ever. Preacher's been working on me about it. I'm trying hard."

"Good," Mr. Whitley replied. He seemed to be thinking. "And you love her with everything you've got?"

"Yes, sir, Mr. Whitley. Everything."

"Frank," the older man said, extending his hand as he stepped toward Tick.

"I beg your pardon," Tick replied, taking his hand.

"Call me, Frank, seeing as how we're practically family. You have my blessing, Thomas."

"Whew!" Tick said, blowing out a lungful of burnt nerves. "Well, uh, *Frank*, I sure hope we'll be family soon. Now, if Cami will just say yes."

"I expect she will. Before y'all left home, she told her mother she was going to marry you one day."

Chapter 109

The Big Guy was speaking to the camera. His face was beet red, his voice loud, just below shouting. He had been calm at first, as befitted someone in his position. However, he soon became animated, and now, after ten minutes of increasingly acidic half-truths and lies, he was almost apoplectic.

"I've fought to keep us safe from the flood of savages besieging our border. Trust me, we are in the midst of a true national crisis. We've caught every kind of monster you can think of trying to sneak into America. Criminals so bad their own countries threw them out. They steal across in the dark—terrorists, rapists, killers, thieves—hunting for their next victims.

"There are those who claim there's nothing to worry about. They would swing the gates wide open and proclaim, '*Come one, come all. We will feed you, give you a home, give you some American's job.*' And who is going to foot the bill? You, of course, the brow-beaten working men and women who built our nation and kept her free.

"This is a crisis unlike anything we've ever seen. We are at war—at war to save our jobs, at war to protect our very way of life. Thank God for you patriots fighting beside me. It's up to us to turn back the tide.

"I'll close with a final warning. Beware of false prophets, my friends. Beware of false prophets. Just because a man goes on a long hike does not mean he has been sent by the Lord."

The Big Guy stepped to one side and struck his Mussolini stance. Finally, he saluted the camera. Then he turned away. The large double doors seemed to open of their own accord. He stepped through and disappeared down a long hallway.

The thin man stood with the press secretary and the national security adviser. As the Big Guy approached, the press secretary said, "Great job, sir. I'll get a list of talking points out immediately."

More fawning, the national security adviser added, "Perfect! Simply perfect."

The Big Guy looked at the thin man, raising an expectant eyebrow.

"Very good," the thin man said without enthusiasm. "I was wondering if I could speak to you?"

Taking the Big Guy's peevish expression as their key, the secretary and adviser quickly disappeared. "Sure," he said, turning toward his office. Once inside, he headed straight to his chair and plopped down. He did not offer a seat to the thin man. "You didn't like it?"

"The standard crisis at the border stuff was fine. You could have left out the false prophet bit. Everybody knows who you were talking about. We have no need to antagonize his followers. There'll be well over a hundred thousand in Brownsville come Sunday—probably twice that a week from then. People are flocking to him from everywhere."

"I've already heard your numbers," the Big Guy replied. He spoke with a no nonsense, *I'm the boss* tone. "I had to act before this crap gets any bigger. That's why I spoke at the same time he was speaking tonight. Why I spoke at all. You think I don't have anything else to do? Of course, if your man—"

The thin man hesitated a moment, then nodded.

"Heard anything?"

"No," the thin man answered. "Standard procedure."

"Well," the Big Guy said, his voice dropping to a growling whisper. "Standard procedure's not getting it. Give him a wake-up call, dammit!"

Chapter 110

Bob tried to remain cool. Since the setup call to Cami, that had been difficult. He sat in his vehicle, a block from the border crossing, and watched. Then he saw it come through, a black VW beetle. As it rolled past, he made out the Lockharts crammed in the back seat. For the next few minutes he followed, but never too closely, trying to determine if anyone was tailing them, as well as him. It took concentration, but this wasn't his first rodeo.

His phone rang. "Si," he answered. A moment later he said yes again, still in Spanish, letting Miguel, the VW driver, know all was clear.

Up ahead, the VW swung right onto a cross street, passed a nodding Carlos, and eased over to the curb beside Holy Spirit. Bob drove a few car lengths beyond, then parked, keeping watch in his mirrors as the Lockharts extricated themselves. They could have been tourists, with their big hats and sunglasses. In seconds, they ducked inside a rear entrance. Bob waited a full minute, making certain, before getting out. Another minute and he was inside.

"That was interesting," Paul said. "Sure all the cloak and dagger stuff was necessary?"

"Yes," Bob glanced his way.

Paul wrinkled his brow, but before he could say more, Bob motioned them down the hallway.

"First door. Just knock. We're expected."

Paul started to raise his hand, but the door swung open before he got there.

"I heard your footsteps," an old priest said. "I'm Father Andres. Come in, Reverend," he added, taking Paul by the arm and gently pulling him inside a small meeting room. "And you must be Jennie," he went on, guiding her in. "Hello, Bob. Good to see you. Get the door, please."

An oblong table of rough wooden boards, gray with age, surrounded by half a dozen simple chairs, filled the room. The priest didn't offer anyone a seat, however. Instead, he moved to a second door and opened it.

"Juanita," he said.

A Hispanic woman in her twenties stepped through. For a few seconds she simply looked at the group. Suddenly, she came striding across to Jennie and took her by the hands.

"Sister," she said in heavily accented English. "I pray for you."

"And I for you." Jennie smiled.

Paul started toward the women, but Father Andres suddenly appeared with a little girl. She ran to Juanita and grabbed her skirt. Her mother smiled and lowered her hand to caress the child's hair. The girl beamed back. After a moment, she looked up at the new lady.

"Jennie," the mother said, then added a few words in Spanish.

"Our friend is a mother, also," the priest added. "You can hug her."

The girl stepped forward as Jennie knelt down to meet her. While they hugged, the child gave her a kiss on the cheek.

Paul had held it together until he saw the kiss. Then the water came. He looked away, but it didn't help. He blinked and saw a pair of small hands reaching up. Paul found himself on his knees, little arms around his neck. Soft words in Spanish came to his ear.

"It's alright," the priest translated, his old voice cracking. "Serena says, 'It's alright.'"

Paul and Jennie were on a park bench on the Mexican side of the river, a hundred yards downstream from Riverbank. Bob sat on the grass across from them. The breeze caused spots of light to filter through the sparse shade and dance on the ground. No one spoke. The meeting had left them spent. Bob finally broke the silence.

"Sorry I had to keep it a secret. I promised Juanita."

"I understand," Jennie said, showing a timid smile.

Paul glanced upward. "I didn't think I would ever see her," he whispered. "Not in person. I see her all the time in my dreams, or she'll pop in my head when I'm walking. Not once have I pictured her without thinking of Sarah."

Jennie reached over and placed her hand atop Paul's. "Me either," she said. "I've thought about this day. How would she react? How would I feel? I knew I would be relieved that she was safe, of course. Turns out there's more to it than just relief. It's like God picked up a piece of the puzzle for my heart and slipped it into an empty space."

"What a beautiful way to put it," Paul said, looking in her eyes.

They fell quiet, the stillness stretching out until Bob spoke again.

"Paul, back when we first met, do you remember what you said you wanted for Serena?"

"Yes," Paul answered sitting up straight and smiling. "I said I wanted to see her safe and happy, reunited with her mother. Thank you, Lord, for answering my prayers."

"And thank you, Bob, for never giving up on finding her," Jennie added.

"What I do," Bob answered, flashing a smile.

"So," Jennie began. "What happens to them now? Father Andres said they're living in a camp."

"Yes," Bob replied.

"How long can that go on?" Jennie pressed.

"Years."

"That's horrible."

Bob simply nodded. He turned to look at the river. The silence stretched out again, longer than before. Paul and Jennie were surprised when he started speaking, still looking at the water.

"In my business you never want to become part of the story. I've managed that very well over the years. With this one, I was doing fine until I met Serena and her mother. Not like I haven't heard a thousand similar stories. My God, there are a million of them here. But Serena and Sarah, those two little girls, have touched a lot of hearts, mine included. So, I've decided to get involved."

Jennie and Paul glanced at each other.

"This may take years, too," Bob said. "There are ways, legal ways, to get them across the border. Maybe a sponsorship. I've got a lot of research to do, so I can't claim to know where to start, but I'm finding out. And if I can't get it done, I've got reporter friends who will help keep the story alive until somebody makes the right thing happen, even if it's just so we'll shut up."

"That's wonderful!" Jennie said, clapping her hands.

"Fantastic!" Paul agreed. "We'll help in any way we can."

"I knew you'd say that," Bob answered. "What you're doing is too important to get caught up in politics, though. No doubt, some people would try to use you that way."

"Children are our only concern," Paul asserted. "Others can worry about politics."

"Preacher, sometimes you're so naïve I have to wonder."

"Take it up with the Boss," Paul laughed. "Just following His orders."

Bob could only chuckle.

"How do you see this working out?" Jennie joined in. "Where will they go? What will they do?"

"Juanita's a seamstress. She might get by almost anywhere until she finds something better. My idea of a good spot, though, is Middle Tennessee. I've got a place north of Gallatin, up on the ridge. I've decided to settle there. It's not far from Kentucky. We could be neighbors." Bob laughed. "Anyway, it's big enough. Plus, I've got a good friend who lives close by. She would be a great help. I just need to ask her a question or two first."

"What's her name, this Mrs. Mendoza to be?" Jennie winked.

"Whoa now," Bob said, throwing up his hands. "I didn't say anything about marriage."

"Yes, you did. And don't ask Paul for help. This is out of his league, other than the ceremony."

"I'll give you my friends and family discount," Paul promised.

"Barb." Bob grinned. "Her name is Barb. And it's no guarantee she'll say yes. For someone who makes a living asking questions, I've taken way too long getting around to asking her."

"It'll be fine," Jennie said. "You're a catch. Ah, love. The love shown by two little girls, and shown for them, is stirring more love in others. What a blessing."

"Yes," Bob nodded. He paused a minute. "Well, I guess we better get you back across. Imagine you have a lot to do," he said, looking at Paul.

"The list never ends," Paul nodded. "I need to take a little walk. Work on an idea for tomorrow's meeting."

"You know your theme yet?" Bob asked.

"I think I'll talk about love," Paul replied, pushing to his feet.

"Barb?" Bob said into the phone.

"Robert? Is that you? Kind of late, isn't it?"

He could hear the heaviness of sleep in her voice.

"Yeah, uh…"

"Why—I mean, I didn't expect to hear from you. Are you in Nashville?"

"Matamoros."

"Mexico?"

"I found her. I found Serena."

"Fantastic! Is she okay?"

"Yes. She's with her mother. I want to bring them here, I mean, to Tennessee."

"Alright."

"Will you help me?"

"Of course."

"Thank you, Barb. Thank you so much."

Quiet seconds ticked by.

"Is that all, Robert? You know I have to be up in a couple of hours."

"No. Yes. I mean I know you have to be up soon, but no, that's not all. I need to ask you one more thing."

"Please do," she said, yawning loudly into the phone.

"I'm—of course you can't see—but I'm on my knee."

"Oh, Lord!"

"Barb—I should have done this years ago—

"For heaven's sake, do it now!"

"Will you marry me?"

"Yes!"

"Really!"

"Yes, really! I love you, Robert."
"I love you, Barb, with all my heart."
"Goodnight, darling."
"Sleep tight, my love."

Chapter 111

Cami was stunned. *Protesters! At a prayer meeting? Are you kidding?* Tick estimated three hundred. She found them on the trail leading from the plain to Riverbank. It was a perfect location to disrupt the flow of worshippers. They were marching in a circle, carrying signs and chanting. The signs and chant were the same. *Preacher Paul is a false Prophet.*

As upsetting as Cami found the sight, she was not surprised. Hearing of the rant on TV by the highest official in the land, she had pulled it up on her phone. There it was, bold as the blazing sun—speech meant to suppress freedom to pray and worship. Now, strutting with their signs before her, were fruits born of the poison tree.

She walked away from the noise and called Paul's number.

"Yes, Cami."

"We have protesters. Hundreds."

"That's what I hear."

"But, well, they'll disrupt the meeting."

"We will pray for their enlightenment. Then we will invite them to pray for the children with us."

"The greatest of these is love."

Paul looked out over the crowd. Riverbank Church was full to the brim. The comm center reported attendance would top one hundred thousand. On the plain beyond, he could make out protesters waving their signs like guidons. *They can not still His voice, however,* Paul thought. *The Lord will not be shouted down.*

"My friends," Paul began. "Those who agree with the purpose of this meeting and those who have something else to say are both welcome here." A roar of affirmation arose from the congregation, drowning out the protesters. Paul waited for it to die down. In the ensuing vacuum, a handful of protesters could still be heard. "I must admit, I am in agreement with our guests." That brought the chanting down to a murmur. "I am a simple country preacher answering a straightforward call from God to pray for the children. This evening, I wish to begin by leading us in prayer. I ask that each of you stand and join hands with those beside you. Reach across the aisles and to the other rows. We want everyone joined with everyone else."

As the gathering settled, Paul grasped the sides of the pulpit.

"Let us pray." All bowed their heads with him. "Our gracious heavenly Father." Across the congregation, many heads momentarily lifted. It was the first time they had heard Preacher Paul pray aloud. "We come in answer to Your bidding, our hearts full of love, determined to raise our voices in prayer for the children. Guide us, Father, as we seek to act as You would have us act. Help us find ways to reach out to those who have not heard Your call, so that they, too, will have their hearts filled to overflowing with love. We are here, Father, from every corner of this earth, representing every manner of belief and worship, ready to march to the sound of Your trumpet, armed with the greatest of these. Love. Use us, Father, we pray. Amen."

†††

The tiny concrete-block building stood forty feet back from the river's bank. The roof was gone, as was the door. High on the right-hand wall was the only window, its glass missing, other than a few jagged shards clinging to the frame. Weeds and vines sprouted from the uneven layers of dirt and debris on the floor. In one corner, a pair of slender saplings brushed against the top blocks. On the outside, vines snaked over the flaked dusting of paint like camouflage netting. Saplings and weeds formed a thick perimeter on all sides.

A step outside the door, the cowboy stopped and took a last drink from the tequila bottle. Then he tossed the empty into weeds. He cast glances around to see if anybody was close. Finally, he began fiddling with the knot on his rope belt, before hurriedly stepping through the threshold, thumbs locked in the waistband of his pants. The apparent drunk smiled to himself, knowing anyone watching would almost certainly turn away from nature's urgent call.

Inside, he took three careful steps toward the window, each step landing in a clear spot he had made by moving old cans and bottles to one side. No sense stepping on something that might rattle or clink during his escape. At the window, he laid a folded bandana over the bottom of the metal frame. Then he reached inside his pants and withdrew the two rifle barrel sections from the sleeves hanging from an inner belt. He screwed the sections together, then rested the barrel atop the bandana. In quick order, he removed the remaining rifle sections and fitted them in place.

Looking through the scope, he determined all the primary factors that might influence the shot were unchanged. He could not see where the preacher would stand, other than a corner of the pulpit. The huge amplifiers were still there. But the cowboy was not interested in where the preacher would stand. He could plainly see the area to the left of the pulpit where Paul always knelt. The man would stay there unmoving for minutes. Wind was the one factor he could do nothing about. He would take it into account when it was time to pull the trigger. It was not an easy shot, but in Iraq he had made over two dozen kills at longer distances.

The cowboy carefully laid the rifle atop a strip of cardboard on the floor. Using more scraps of cardboard, he covered it. The bandana went back in his pocket. Then he sat down, his back against the wall, and dropped his chin to his chest. Should someone happen by all they would see was a filthy drunk sleeping off another bottle.

Half an hour passed before he heard the Lord's prayer in Spanish, coming over the jumbo TV monitors. There would be music, the man would speak, then more music. After that, the preacher would drop to his knees, and he would drop the preacher.

Chapter 112

Tick had volunteered to stay close while Paul was speaking from the pulpit. There had been resistance from the professionals in the morning briefing, but Tick's logic won out.

"I won't draw attention. Everyone's used to seeing me around him. And if it comes to something physical, I can handle myself. Just ask that yahoo in Mississippi."

Chief Herbert had to smile.

"Besides, I'll have Buck. Use a police dog and everybody knows something's up."

Tick could read the worry on their faces. Obviously, they had received some scary news. He wasn't scared, however. Arrogance? Confidence? Some of both. After all, he usually won his fights. This evening? Tick had known from the first moment that protecting the preacher was his job. He'd be where he was supposed to be.

So, late that afternoon, he sat on the dirt with Buck, half a dozen feet to Paul's right, his gaze slowly sweeping across the crowd.

"Love," Paul said. "Of all the things children need, what is the most important? Food? Shelter? Security? The list goes on. There is only one thing, however, that is truly above others. Love. Love sustains a child as much as food. Love shelters a child better than any roof. Love gives a child something to cling to in the darkest hour.

"Then there's the happiness that comes from sharing love. Have you ever felt joy at seeing a child's smiling face? Have you laughed when you heard a child laugh one of those great, falling-to-the-floor belly laughs, or marveled at their wide-eyed wonder? If you have, you know what it is to share love with a child.

"Showing children love can be as simple as acknowledging their presence. Say something funny to one. Brag about her singing in church or say you're proud of his good grades. We all want to be told when we've done a good job, right? Notice their kindnesses, especially, like when he holds the door for an older lady, or she rushes to take the handles of a man's wheelchair. Tell them you appreciate what they did. And when you see a child in distress, remember nothing beats a hug.

"When I was nine, I received what may have been the greatest compliment of my life. I came riding up on my bicycle as our neighbor, Mr. Doolin, was trying to start his old car. All it would do was grind. *Rar, rar, rar, rar.*

"Now Mr. Doolin was seventy, and his car was somewhere close to that, which meant to me that both were older than dinosaurs. Anyway, I was standing there, straddling my bike, when he hopped out and slammed the door hard enough to crack walnuts. Here he came, marching straight at me. My first thought was I had Mr. Doolin all wrong. He could still step 'em off."

Light laughter rolled across the congregation.

"'Paulie,' he said. 'I can't get this thing to start for nothing. What do you think is wrong?'"

"Hold it right there! See the compliment? Mr. Doolin asked *my* opinion. He asked me, a nine-year-old, what I thought.

"Well, the importance of what had just transpired didn't get past me. I puffed up so much it's a wonder I didn't pop. Then, after due deliberation, I gave him my opinion.

"Reckon she's out of gas?"

Laughter thundered in response.

"Only thing I knew about cars was they needed gas." Paul shrugged, once things quieted.

"'Shoot fire!' Mr. Doolin said. 'Hadn't thought of that.'

"We headed back to his car. After he slid in behind the wheel, he turned the key enough to make the gauges work.

"'Look here,' he said. 'She ain't got a drop. That needle's so far past *empty* it can't stand on its toes and reach bottom. Thank you, Paulie. You saved me a lot of trouble.'

"I went strutting back to my bike like I'd won first place."

Good-hearted laughter floated up from the gathering.

"There's a lesson in how to build adults. We have to make children feel good about themselves by showing them respect. It is important that we ask their opinions and then thank them for sharing. That's love, too."

"Before we pray, I'm going to reference two Bible verses.

"Matthew,19:14—*Jesus said, Suffer little children, and forbid them not, to come unto me, for such is the kingdom of heaven.*

"And last, I'll return to where I started. In First Corinthians, 13:13 we find that faith, hope, and love abide, *but the greatest of these is love.*"

An outburst of *Amens* followed. Paul looked over the congregation as it grew quiet. No one shouted or spoke. No one chanted anything about a false prophet. Finally, his eyes settled on Jennie. She winked.

"Let us ask that all children always know love. Will you please join me in silent prayer?"

Paul stepped to the right, toward Tick, and dropped to his knees.

"Wrong side!" The cowboy thought, looking through the scope. The support post for the pulpit was in the way. He slid to the right. Checked again. Two inches clearance. Plenty. No wind. No worries. Crosshairs on the mark. He squeezed the trigger.

The evening breeze blowing up from Mexico wasn't much. Little wonder the cowboy couldn't feel it inside the hut. It was stronger over the Rio Grande. From this angle, the bullet passed above the cool water for three hundred yards, plus.

The shot drifted left.

A spray of red. The preacher pitched forward, out of sight. Something else caught the cowboy's eye at the moment of impact. *There! The post.* A sliver of wood was gone from a corner. The projectile must have struck it. No worries. The spray told him all he needed to know. He carried the rifle to the corner with the saplings, laid it on the ground and covered it with a couple of sun-bleached pieces of cardboard. Then he headed out the door.

Tick saw the blood fly and the puff of dust where the bullet dug into the ground at the same instant. Ignoring the hornet sting to his own thigh, he leapt to his feet. He caught Paul under his arms from the left side, deliberately placing himself in the line of fire, and rushed for the front slope. Half running, half stumbling, he managed to get to the bottom. Jennie met him there, with others from home rushing up behind her.

"Paul! Oh my God, Paul!" she screamed, putting her hands to his forehead, trying to stem the flow. A firefighter/paramedic was beside her in a moment.

"Let me see," he ordered, gently pushing her hands aside. "ABD pad."

His partner was already ripping the paper off a pad. He handed it to the first firefighter, then passed him a second. The firefighter stacked them over the wound. Blood still soaked through. He called for a third pad. As he held pressure, his partner wrapped gauze around Paul's head to hold the dressings in place.

"Need to get him to the unit," the first firefighter said.

"It'll take forever to get a gurney down here and back," his partner answered.

"We've got him," Droopy said, sweeping in from behind with Clarence. Each man slipped an arm under one of Paul's armpits and grasped the other by the elbow across Paul's back. Then they caught him with their free hands, one under each leg, so that they held him sitting up in their arms.

"Let me in there," Tick demanded, grabbing Clarence's arm.

"You're hurt, man," Clarence said over his shoulder. Then he and Droopy started jogging up a side aisle of Riverbank leading to the plain, toward the ambulance staged there, carrying the preacher between them. Jennie, the front of her dress red with Paul's blood, followed close behind.

"Sit down, Tick," Cami said, her tone pleading. "You're bleeding! Jesus Lord! Something's stuck in your leg!"

The firefighters had started after the men carrying the minister, but they heard Cami and stopped to look back. Both saw the sliver of wood protruding from Tick's thigh. It moved, just a quiver. Then it moved again, and again, apparently in time with Tick's pulse.

"Oh crap!" The first firefighter said, stepping toward this new-found victim.

"I'll make the calls," his partner replied, reaching for his radio as the first firefighter started working with Frank Whitley and Deacon Henry to lay Tick down.

"Don't you dare move this leg," the first medic told Tick. "Okay men, let's get it elevated. Gently! Don't touch that splinter! I have to immobilize it."

Suddenly Buck was there, nuzzling Tick's neck. Tick grabbed an ear, pulled the big head close to his lips.

"Catch him," he ordered.

The second firefighter thought a moment about how to describe Tick's injury before keying his mic. Plain English was usually best.

"Medic Six to Dispatch.

"Dispatch, Medic Six."

"Impaled wooden object, quarter inch by ten inches, upper inner thigh, obvious movement on patient's pulse, no exit wound. Request Life Flight.

"Break. Medic Six to Medic Three." He called the second ambulance crew, who were stationed on the plain above."

"Medic Three."

"Transport the head injury. No apparent skull penetration. Civilians carrying him up."

"Ten-Four Medic Six. We've got him.

"Break. Medic Six to Engine Seven."

"Engine Seven.

"Need assistance by the pulpit."

"Engine Seven is already moving. ETA one minute.

From another staging area across the road, came the unmistakable sound of a helicopter engine revving up.

"Dispatch to Medic Six."

"Medic Six."

"Life Flight enroute. ETA two minutes."

"Ten-Four," the firefighter answered, pulling a blood pressure cuff out of the trauma kit. *Hope this guy's got two minutes,* he thought as he moved to check Tick's vital signs. *If it punctured the femoral—*

Chief Hughes, gun out, hustling after the dog, was amazed by how fast it was digging beneath the wall. Suddenly Buck rammed himself under, leaving knots of red hair caught in the bars. A heartbeat later, he launched himself into the river and began swimming toward Mexico.

The helicopter landed atop the pulpit. Firefighters carried Tick to the open door and placed him inside. As the machine lifted off in a cloud of whirling dust, dozens of religious leaders remained on their knees at the foot of the hill, heads bowed.

The congregation had also stayed in Riverbank. Some protesters were still present, though their signs had long since been scattered. The groups had mixed. It was impossible to tell whether any individual belonged to one or the other. They all had their heads bowed. The picture went out on a national network feed as Clifford Cumberland spoke for the first time in several minutes.

"Our prayers join with the thousands here and across the Rio Grande in Mexico, and with the millions praying around the world." He paused a long breath. "We will return."

On the Mexican side of the river, Bob was seated near one of the jumbo TV screens, video recording Preacher Paul, when he heard the shot and saw Paul pitch forward. He was on his feet and moving toward the shot's origin while the sound still echoed. In less than a minute, he spotted a patch of weeds and saplings near the top of the riverbank. Bob stopped. Something wasn't right. After a few seconds he realized he was looking at the fractured outlines of a small building inside the thicket. He hesitated for only a moment before heading off through a scattering of trees toward the building's front. At least they provided some cover.

From behind, he heard the sounds of running footsteps and the word *quiet* hissed. He turned to see a handful of others joining him. Using only hand signals, this ad hoc posse fanned out to cover all sides, then cautiously approached the hut.

Suddenly a wet blob splash-landed atop the riverbank. Buck gave a quick shake, flinging a cloudburst. Raising his head, he sniffed, then loped toward the building and disappeared inside the door. There were scratching sounds, a loud bark. Buck shot back out. Nose to the ground, he trotted toward a street in a direct line with the building.

Bob spotted a man on that street, walking into town. Even at a distance, he seemed unsteady.

A member of the posse stepped to the door.

"A rifle!" the man exclaimed. "There's a rifle on the floor."

"Don't let anybody inside," Bob ordered, then turned back to find Buck. The big dog suddenly let loose with another high-pitched howl. Then he was off at a hard charge, heading straight toward the wobbly man. Bob broke into a run after him. He couldn't keep up, but the sounds coming from Buck told him he had to try. The dog was no longer a dog. He was the ancient lone wolf in deadly pursuit, his continuous high-pitched howling a signal to his prey that its time was near.

A couple of police officers came trotting toward him. He waved them on. "This way!"

Up ahead, the unsteady man broke into a run, turned a corner and vanished. Seconds later, Buck tried to turn the corner, too, but he was going so fast he couldn't keep his feet under him. He rolled out into the street in front of a car. Screeching brakes, the blare of a horn, and Buck was up and gone.

Bob and the officers reached the corner at the same time. The officers motioned him back as one risked a peek. He quickly waved the others up, but the man had disappeared. They moved single file, the officers leading, guns out, covering each side, waving people back. In the middle of the block there was an empty space. It held only a dumpster reeking of things long rotten, and a huge red dog. Buck paced beyond the stinking container, then quickly came back to it. He started growling, canines bared. All at once he was on his hind feet, the sliding door's handle in his teeth. Buck jerked and it moved. He jerked again, the opening growing wider, then he vaulted inside.

Explosions of sound erupted. There were screams and curse words and desperate outbursts of pitiful begging, things ripping and tearing, being crunched. Then, like a switch had been thrown, it stopped. The men looked at each other. After a moment they sidled up to the opening. Buck stood astride the cowboy, his great mouth holding the man by the throat.

"Should we shoot the dog?" one officer asked, fearing it would not let loose, otherwise.

"No. We don't want to make him mad," his partner explained, not sounding like he meant to be funny.

"I've seen this guy around," the first officer said. "Just another drunk."

"Strange looking underwear," Bob noted.

"Yes," the first officer agreed, staring at the pouches and slings attached to an inner belt around the man's waist.

His partner leaned in a bit closer. "Looks like they're made to carry stuff."

"Like parts of a rifle," Bob added.

"Amigo," the first officer said, pointing his pistol at the cowboy's face. "You will do exactly as I say, or I let the red wolf eat you—alive."

Chapter 113

Cami's Blog, Day 1, Post Shooting

It is very difficult to write this, for the events described herein have had a great emotional impact on me personally.

It is now 5:00 a.m. At approximately 5:00 p.m. yesterday, a sniper shot Preacher Paul Lockhart while he was on his knees praying at Riverbend Church in Brownsville, Texas. Thomas Cole, logistics manager for the preacher, was also injured in the attack.

I have received permission from the families of both men to report their medical conditions. Preacher Paul suffered a grazing wound to the forehead, which resulted in significant bleeding. He also has a hairline skull fracture. Scans do not reveal any brain damage or swelling. Over the next several days, he will be closely monitored and retested to ensure he remains stable. His was one of those wounds where a fraction of an inch in the wrong direction could have resulted in tragedy. Fortunately, he is expected to make a full recovery.

Thomas Cole suffered a life-threatening wound. A pencil-length wooden splinter was sheared off the podium's support post, likely by the same bullet which struck the preacher. The splinter struck Cole's thigh, where it remained impaled, and damaged his femoral artery. Led by a vascular surgeon, the surgery team at South Texas General Hospital repaired the artery. Though his healing period will be longer than Preacher Paul's, he also is expected to make a full recovery.

The families of both men wish to extend their sincere thanks for the immeasurable numbers of prayers lifted for their loved ones. They also wish to recognize the life-saving actions of the para-medics from the Brownsville Fire Department, who immediately provided emergency care for both men and transported Preacher Paul. In addition, they thank the crew of the med-evac helicopter who treated and transported Thomas Cole, as well as the surgical team and Emergency Room staff at South Texas General Hospital.

At 10:00 a.m. today, a press briefing will be conducted at the hospital.

The shot, according to U. S. law enforcement authorities, appears to have been fired from across the Rio Grande. Within minutes of the attack, a suspect was arrested by local police in Matamoras, Mexico. Initial reports state he is an American citizen. A press briefing addressing these aspects of the attack will be held at Matamoras City Hall at noon today.

Thank You, God.

Cami

Jim and Clarence walked out of the hospital in the early morning light, so tired and emotionally drained they could scarcely put one foot ahead of the other. Voices called to them from across the street. Other people who had spent the night praying wanted to know about Paul and Tick. As Jim walked toward them, he thought about giving a brief medical update, but when he started to speak, all he could say was, "They live. Thank God. They Live."

Chapter 114

Day 2, Post Shooting

Jennie pushed Paul's wheelchair up to the door for Tick's room and leaned over to knock.

"Come in!" Tick boomed.

The door swung open to reveal a tearful Cami holding the handle.

"I'm so glad you're here!" she exclaimed, bending toward Paul. "Okay to give you a kiss?"

"Please," Paul replied, offering a cheek, "if you don't mind smooching Frankenstein."

Cami kissed him, then embraced Jennie. As they hugged, Jennie whispered, "You okay?"

"I'm good," Cami whispered back. "I'll explain in a minute."

Jennie nodded. Both turned to watch the reunion in progress.

"Preacher," Tick said from his bed, "you're a sight. Two raccoon eyes and a fat turban on your head. Whoa! Where's my sun-glasses?"

"Good to see you, too, my friend," Paul said, reaching out to grip Tick's hand. "What everybody says. I'm afraid to look in a mirror."

"Say, y'all didn't bring any groceries, did you? I'm starving. Meals here wouldn't keep a leprechaun alive, and they won't put biscuits and gravy in my IV. I'd go fix some myself, but they claim I need to lay still."

Cami shook her head.

"Tick, I just brought you a Subway sandwich, and breakfast was only an hour and a half ago. I think you've got a tapeworm."

"I don't know about that, Hon, but this laying around thinking really burns up the calories."

Paul and Jennie picked up on the *hon* and exchanged amused

glances. Then Paul turned serious. He reached out and grasped Tick's hand again.

"I want to thank you for saving my life."

Tick looked away for a long moment. Then he looked back, locking eyes with Paul. "I'm the worst excuse for a bodyguard there ever was. I'm sorry."

"There's nothing to be sorry about. You carried me to safety. I saw it on the news. You risked your life to save mine. We are forever grateful."

"Forever," Jennie said, wiping her eyes.

The men finally relaxed their grips. Jennie and Cami found seats, one on each side of Tick's bed. For a minute, the enormity of what they had been through filled the room like hot smoke. Finally, Tick could stand the silence no longer.

"Enough of this serious stuff. Cami, you want to tell them?"

"Yes!" she exclaimed, jumping to her feet. "I said, *yes!*"

Jennie understood immediately and jumped to her feet, also. The women met at the foot of Tick's bed and hugged.

"Congratulations," Paul said, squeezing Tick's shoulder. He twisted around to face Cami. "To both of you."

"They'll be dancing in Caney Creek," Jennie sang. "Have you set a date yet?"

"Soon." Cami beamed at Tick. "As soon as he heals."

"I'm the luckiest guy in the world," Tick beamed back at her. "I had it all planned out. Getting on my knee and everything. I already asked her daddy. Then this."

He reached across to the nightstand and picked up a clear plastic bag holding a pencil-length sliver of wood. One end tapered down to a fine point. "Thought I'd save it for a souvenir, especially since it just barely nicked the artery. The doc said God was watching" he added, handing the bag to Paul. The preacher gave it a close inspection.

"That's a mean-looking piece of wood," Paul said, handing it back.

"Not how I see it," Tick said. "You've got your Jesus stick. This is my *deciding stick*. I've been laying here staring at it, and I finally decided something. I want you to baptize me. I want you to baptize me before Cami and I tie the knot, and I want you to do it in the Rio Grande."

"That last part might take some finagling," Paul said with a huge grin, "but I'll be proud to do it. God bless you, Tick."

Jennie came over beside Tick's bed. "I couldn't be happier," she said and bent down to kiss his forehead. "Does your mother know?"

"Yep. That big, *Glory hallelujah,* that rattled the windows a while ago came from her."

"I heard that!" Jennie laughed. "Oh my. What a wonderful morning."

"Absolutely," Paul nodded. "It's enough to wear a person out."

"Are you getting tired?" Jennie asked. "I guess we better take you back." She moved behind Paul's chair.

"Just a minute," Tick said. "I've got one more thing. Cami's the only one that knows this. I told her just before y'all came in. That's why she was crying."

"They were tears of joy," Cami explained.

Tick drew in a long breath, visibly composing himself, then turned toward Jennie and Paul. "I saw Sarah. It was dark. Then it started getting lighter and lighter till it was so bright it dazzled. Suddenly, she was there, coming toward me through that white glow, plain as anything. She hugged my neck tight, like always. Then she pushed me away."

The parents didn't react how he had expected they might. Each broke into a huge smile.

"That's our girl," Jennie said, squeezing Paul's shoulders. "She knows."

"I don't understand." Tick frowned. "Knows what?"

Paul leaned over close. "You have more to do here, my friend."

The cowboy didn't care for *solitary*. Still, it was better than the last place, a large, open room where the first prisoner to approach punched him in the mouth. So did the second. The other prisoners began forming a receiving line, but the guards got him out while he still had teeth. No worries. The thin man would spring him before anything worse happened. Were he privy to a certain conversation taking place in Mexico City at that moment, however—

†††

On orders from Washington, the U. S. ambassador demanded that Mexico hand the cowboy over for prosecution. The Secretary of Foreign Affairs explained that the individual in question had carried out his crime on the sovereign soil of Mexico, and therefore, he would be tried in Mexico. The secretary did offer her nation's sincerest regrets for the injuries sustained by Reverend Lockhart and Mr. Cole. She also assured the ambassador that in no manner whatsoever did the government of Mexico condone attacks across their common border. When the ambassador asked for an audience with the president, so he might personally press his complaint, the secretary rose and offered her hand. In the diplomatic language equivalent of *go fish*, she replied, "My dear friend, I am afraid that is a non-starter."

†††

Chicken and grits. Strange that he loved this combination. Growing up in Georgia, he ate enough chicken to depopulate a county's worth of chicken houses, along with tons of grits, but never the two in the same dish. He loved *Mama Betty's*. No one came up to him here to pitch an idea or bug him about making an introduction to the Big Guy. He paid his bill, left a decent tip, and headed out the door. The two men in dark suits walking his way—one black, one Hispanic—did not set off alarm bells. Probably just a couple of bureaucrats, who like him, wanted an out of the way place to eat. He was surprised when they split up, one to each side, and none too gently took hold of his elbows.

"Delane R. Wallace?" the black man asked.

"If you know who I am, you should know better than to grab me," the thin man warned.

"I'm Special Agent King, FBI," the agent said, flashing his credentials. "This is Special Agent Castille."

"You are under arrest," Castille said. "We are going to handcuff you for our protection. Then I will read you your rights."

Once handcuffed, Wallace waited impatiently while the agent read. When he was finally done, Wallace burst out, "What's the charge?"

"Something about conspiracy," Castille replied. "They'll explain back at headquarters."

The agents started to frisk him. It was embarrassing. People stopped to watch. It wasn't every day in D. C. that you saw a black man and a Hispanic man in suits emptying the pockets of a handcuffed white man, also in a suit.

"This government issue?" King asked, holding Wallace's cell phone.

"Leave that alone. Matter of fact, uncuff me and give it here. I'm calling the boss on you two bozos right now. You'll be sucking blubber in Nome by midnight."

King looked at Castille. "I guess he didn't see the press conference."

"The one where they announced his dismissal?" Castille asked.

In the back of the agents' car, Wallace mentally reviewed the conversations between him and the cowboy. They had always spoken in code, so no worries. Then it dawned on him. Sometimes it wasn't what you said, it was who you said it to.

Chapter 115

Paul and Tick were in wheelchairs on the sundeck outside rehab. Tick's chair had a special attachment that stuck straight out, supporting his wounded leg.

"If I have to stay this way long, I'll end up walking like a zombie."

"That'd be cute," Cami said. She was seated at a patio table, scrolling through her messages.

"Umm, that morning sun feels good." Paul said.

"It sure does," Tick replied. "I was about to freeze in there." A few seconds passed quietly before he mused, "Wonder how old Buck's—"

"There you are!" Chief Herbert shouted his arrival. Suddenly a great beast leaped over the decorative fence and headed for Tick like a blazing meteor.

"My leg! Watch my leg, boy!" Tick tried to warn Buck, but Cami and the chief quickly jumped in and managed to keep the dog off of him. He still suffered a slurping lick from chin to hairline. "Ah, I missed you, too, buddy," he said, digging hard behind Buck's ears.

"He's in seventh heaven now," Paul observed.

Without warning, the dog had its forepaws on Tick's leg, readying himself to jump. Cami and the chief came to the rescue again, wrestling him down. Cami finally snapped her fingers and yelled, "Buck! Sit!" Buck listened. Calm as anything, he moved over to the spot where she was pointing and dropped down on his haunches. "Now you two get on each side close enough to pet him." Tick and Paul maneuvered their chairs into position. "Hello Chief," Cami said over their heads, smiling at Langston. "So good to see you." Then she walked back to her chair and resumed looking through her messages.

"Whew," Tick whispered. "I guess that's a lesson for me."

"I heard that," Cami said. Glancing toward her, they saw she was laughing.

"Didn't mean to cause a ruckus," Langston apologized. "Just thought you'd like to visit."

"Yeah," Tick answered, smiling.

"Glad you brought him," Paul agreed.

Both men were stroking the dog's long hair. Langston watched quietly.

"You're petting a genuine hero," he finally said. "Old Buck caught the bad guy."

"What?" Paul and Tick asked in the same breath.

"Quite a story. Tick, remember that place where somebody dug under the wall?"

"Yep. I thought they fixed it."

"They did, until Buck decided to dig it back out. I saw him. Dirt flying everywhere. It didn't take him two seconds. Then he swam the river and found where the guy shot from, and his rifle."

"Wow!" Paul said.

"There's more. He tracked the man down and caught him in a dumpster. Jumped right in and tore him a new— Let me put it this way. That nut on the Trace looked like he cut himself shaving compared to the shooter. You know Bob Mendoza?"

"Sure." Paul answered.

"He's got most of it on video. Police in Matamoros aim to give Buck a medal."

"I knew you were a good boy," Tick said, scratching behind an ear and grinning.

"Yes, he is." Paul nodded.

"Oh, I almost forgot." The chief took a step back to the decorative fence and bent down. "Thought you might want this," he said, handing Paul his walking stick.

"Oh yes! Thank you. I didn't feel right without it."

"There's something you ought to know. Look about a third of the way up, where that knot is."

"Okay," Paul answered, sliding the stick through his fingers. "Huh, that wasn't there before."

"I know. TV cameras and cell phones caught the whole thing. The FBI has fantastic forensic people. They've measured the pictures from any angle you can imagine, straight back to where the shooter was, and they've got everything figured out.

"Paul, you know how you always stand that stick up against the right side of the podium?"

"Sure. I'm righthanded, so it's natural, and there's a little notch there on the edge to hold it."

"There was one bullet," Langston began. "It hit the support post first and knocked a sliver off. I've seen the piece flying through the air in slow motion, till it strikes Tick. That didn't turn the bullet at all. Then it hit your stick dead on the knot and cut that place. The knot turned it just enough. If it hadn't—"

No one said anything.

At last, staring into the distance, Paul spoke.

"I'm looking forward to visiting a friend in Middle Tennessee. He makes walking sticks to God's exact specifications."

Chapter 116

One Month, Post Shooting.

P aul and Jennie's tent on the Plain of Abraham came to within a few feet of the wall. No other campers were within thirty yards, a result of their neighbors' desire—these *plain folk*, as they had taken to calling themselves—to grant the couple privacy. Paul rose at first light and slipped outside into the cool air, being careful not to wake Jennie or trip over the extension cord that provided their power. He sat down in his camp chair, the fabric damp with dew, and gazed through the bars of the wall at the Rio Grande. A great blue heron glided silently eastward with the current, inches above the water, and disappeared below the lip of the bank. On the Mexican side, he could see glimpses of movement as Matamoros kicked off the bed covers.

It would be a busy day. He had Tick's baptism at 11:00, Cami and Tick's wedding at 2:00, and the prayer meeting at 5:00. In between would be the usual meetings with other religious leaders. Also, Jim wanted to review plans for new camping areas. The numbers of people continued to grow.

The tent flap rustled. He turned and saw Jennie smiling in the opening.

"Hello, handsome," she said.

"Hello, beautiful," Paul answered. "Looks like you got up on the right side of the bed."

"I did, indeed." Her smile widened. "Coffee will be ready in a minute. I'll bring you a cup."

"Great." he said, rising to drag her chair close. His phone beeped as he sat back down. He glanced at the screen. The text left him smiling.

A couple of minutes later, Jennie stepped out, a Styrofoam cup in each hand. As she walked up, he reached for the closest cup.

"A kiss first," she said, and leaned down to kiss him on his lips. She lingered there, extending their intimacy.

Whoa! Paul thought as she pulled back. There was more in that kiss than *good morning*.

He was wearing a grin as big as the rising sun when he finally took the cup from her hand.

"You're in a very good mood." Paul smiled.

"Yep," she nodded, sitting down. She took a sip of coffee and smiled back.

"Well, this will put you in an even better mood," Paul said. "I just got a text from Bob Mendoza. A bi-partisan group in Congress is introducing legislation tomorrow to ensure families are kept together at the border. It looks like our prayers may be working."

"That's wonderful! I'm happy beyond belief to hear that."

"We will have to celebrate." Paul said, becoming more enthused.

"Yes, we will." She hesitated a couple of moments. "Thank God we can." Jennie sounded distracted. Suddenly she looked straight at him. "Now if our dear leader will stop claiming his remarks were misinterpreted. I'm so tired of that. Politics! Nothing but a bunch of bull," she snapped, making a face like she'd swallowed a lemon.

Wow! Paul thought. *She's still fired up over the false prophet speech.* He gave her a few moments to calm down before he said anything else. Finally, Paul felt safe to take the plunge.

"We have a big day ahead. You've got everything lined out for the wedding, I'm sure?"

Jennie began twisting and turning in her seat before she curtly answered, "Why yes."

How could that question offend her?

"How's Marian holding up?"

"Laughing and crying at the same time."

"That's not surprising. It's a huge day for her. And Henry and Elsie standing up with the bride and groom makes it extra special."

Jennie didn't say anything back, only nodded. She still couldn't seem to get her nest made, crossing first one leg, then the other.

Something had obviously gone off kilter. He decided to switch rows.

"I need to meet with Jim today about new camps. People are still coming. And, of course, I have the morning ministerial roundtable at 8:30."

"Paul Lockhart! I'm going to take this cup and whack you right on your scar! That's enough!"

He smiled, thinking he recognized their old banter.

"Ouch. Glad it's Styrofoam," he teased.

"Did I not just kiss you like I'm madly in love?"

"Well yes, I—"

"You need to brush your teeth, by the way. And could you not see that I was happy beyond anything imaginable?"

"I noticed, yes, and I'll brush. I promise."

"Did you notice I couldn't sit still because I was about to burst wide open with news?"

"I—" A light flashed. Paul dropped his cup as he shot to his feet. "You're—" He reached for her hands.

"Yes! Yes! Yes! I'm pregnant!"

For the next several minutes, as they squeezed one another tight, they proved Marian Cole was not the only person in Brownsville who could laugh and cry at the same time.

✝✝✝

"Amen," Preacher Paul said, his voice barely audible as he concluded the evening's silent prayer. It took him a moment to push to his feet. He was tired to the bone. It had been a long, emotional day. He brushed his hands across his knees, sending puffs of warm dust free. The noises of the others rising to their feet mingled and grew, reminding him of how the wind sounded coming across the cornfield back home, a low moaning that gathered strength as it rolled closer and became a force that rattled the leaves and caused him to widen his stance. No leaves rattled now. The air was still. Glancing toward the river, he saw only dust and water.

He ran his tongue over his lips. They were so cracked he wondered if he could still speak. Clarence stepped up to hear the choice for a closing song. The preacher began, the words themselves sounding as cracked and dry as his lips.

"Shall, we—"

Clarence took up the hymn, his deep bass booming across Riverbank.

"—gather at the river."

In an instant, everyone was singing the next line, slowly, solemnly. The preacher sensed nothing was coming from within him, yet he moved his lips, mouthing the words.

"The beautiful, the beautiful river."

The sound itself had a presence. Paul imagined it lifting him above the dust.

"Gather with the saints at the river."

Then he heard the wind come rolling across the Rio Grande, carrying a lyrical wave of voices lifted in praise. He braced himself, felt the music wash over him, enter his heart, his soul.

How beautiful, Sarah, the words sound in Spanish.

Acknowledgements

Without Bobbie Falin and Noel Barton, fellow members of Skywriters, this work would still be empty pages. They reviewed the manuscript in its entirety and were always there to help me, often at the expense of setting their own projects aside. Kimberly Bartley, another Skywriter, encouraged me early on that this was a story worth pursuing.

Reverend Casey Mathias and Reverend Megan Huston provided Biblical and religious understanding, as well as valuable insight into their profession.

Dr. Cathy Severns' account of a mission trip to the southern border painted vivid pictures of challenges faced by would-be immigrants and those who seek to aid them.

Richard Storey and Marilyn Turner reviewed the manuscript in its entirety. Their comments and corrections were a great help.

Diane Stiffey, paramedic (ret.), guided me through medical field treatment concerns and actions.

Stephanie Drawhorn, surgical tech, helped me understand the life-saving procedures and great pressures routinely faced by members of surgery teams.

Jim Van Fleet traveled most of the Trek route with me. His insight into what the journey on foot would entail was invaluable.

My sincere thanks to each of these talented, patient, and generous friends.

To Mike Parker, Wordcrafts Press publisher, a word of appreciation for making it possible for authors to have their stories told.

Now a message to the real-life model for *Serena*. Seeing you on TV at the center in Texas, crying your eyes out after you had been separated from your mother, set this story in motion. I hope you have been reunited with her. Though I do not know your name,

I still pray that you are forever blessed with happiness and love. Vaya con Dios.

Gerry Harlan Brown

About the Author

Gerry Harlan Brown has lived most of his life in the Bowling Green, Kentucky area. Stints at a factory, a farm, and painting houses have been mixed in with periods as a railroader, a volunteer community crisis counselor, and a professional fire chief. Along the way he acquired an Associate of Arts degree and completed multiple courses in leadership at the University of Virginia and the National Fire Academy.

He credits his twenty-nine years in the fire service for providing the greatest influence on his writing style. For it was by encountering real people from all walks of life, at their best and bravest to their most devastated and petty, which gave him the opportunity to wrestle monsters, included—as ludicrous as it may seem—squirrels, white and otherwise.

Many of the life lessons Gerry learned along the way have been published in firefighting journals.

Canelands is his third novel.

Made in United States
Orlando, FL
07 July 2024

48701195R10250